PRESCOTT PIONEERS BOOK 3

A LIFE RESTORED

Karen Baney

desert life
media

Prescott Pioneers Book 3: A Life Restored
By Karen Baney

Publisher:
Desert Life Media, LLC
Gilbert, AZ 85295

www.karenbaney.com

Printed in the United States of America
ISBN- 978-0-9835486-5-2

To my Lord, Jesus Christ,
the only one who can
restore broken lives.

———

Though you have made me see troubles,
many and bitter,
you will restore my life again;
from the depths of the earth
you will again bring me up.
Psalm 71:20

CHAPTER I

Wickenburg, Arizona Territory

August 19, 1865

The stagecoach bounced over the rough terrain. Caroline Larson tried not to slide into the man sitting next to her on the hard, bare wood seat. The least they could have done was put some upholstering on the thing. Then she would not be jostled so much from the side against the window to the poor young man next to her.

Another jolt of the Celerity stagecoach shoved her into his side once again.

"Sorry," she murmured, glancing at the young man.

"No harm, Miss." A smirk played on his lips causing the jagged scar on his right cheek to wrinkle unattractively. She wondered how he got the scar. The hint of laughter in his voice indicated he was enjoying this.

Caroline stifled a snort of disgust as she looked out the opening with a small canvas cover secured to the top of the window frame. The dust billowing up from the front wheels obscured much of the view, filtering into the interior of the stage. The small town—if one could call it that—of Wickenburg faded behind them. The only good thing about facing the rear of the stage was that she did not have to endure a face full of dust with each breath.

The stage jerked violently, propelling the man across from her forward, landing awkwardly in her lap. She turned her shocked green eyes towards him, narrowing them slightly until the red of embarrassment tinged his cheeks. He offered profuse apologies as he tried to return to his designated seat.

She should have listened to Millie. She and her father had acted as chaperones, escorting Caroline west. Unfortunately, their trip ended in Wickenburg. Millie and her father assured her they would take her the rest of the way to Prescott by mid-September. But she had come this far and did not want to wait another month or more before being reunited with her brother Adam and her best friend Julia.

As the stage crossed over a huge bump, sending Caroline airborne for a few seconds, her mind returned to her present circumstance. Despite Millie's concern, she boarded the stage this morning headed for Prescott. Things were just fine. She could handle the inquisitive looks of these men.

Abruptly, the stage skidded to a halt, propelling Caroline into the arms of the man across from her. Her almost apology died on the tip of her tongue.

"I wouldn't do that if I were you."

Rifle fire echoed in her ears. Her head snapped towards the window. The driver fell from his perch on the front of the stage. As she jerked forward, the young man with scar clasped his hand down on her arm. She turned her eyes toward him. He lifted a finger to his lips and shook his head. He pushed her back against the seat, out the window.

"What'd ya do that fer?" another voice sounded.

"I told him not to reach for his gun."

Caroline froze. The stage was being robbed!

"Y'all come out slow like," the first man shouted.

"Miss," the man with the scar whispered. "Let me go first to make sure it's safe for you."

A lump formed in her throat. She watched as he exited the stage. Maybe she had been too quick to judge him earlier.

"How many more of you are in there?" the first robber's

voice asked.

"Just four more," the man with the scar answered.

That was not true. There were four more men. And her. What was he doing?

"Come out nice and slow."

The rest of the men did as instructed. Caroline hesitated in the shadows, wondering if the scar-faced man—now she wished she would have asked his name—was trying to protect her. Tapping her finger against her temple rapidly, she tried to figure a way out of this situation. Scanning the landscape offered no solutions. Nothing but vast open desert presented itself. There was no place to hide.

For the first time in her eighteen years, Caroline had no solution. No plan.

"Bart!" the first robber yelled. "Check out the stage. Make sure no one else is lurking around."

She heard the distinct sound of a man dismounting a horse. Moments later, shuffling feet sounded just outside of the stage-coach door. Flattening herself into the shadows as much as possible, Caroline wished she had not worn her bright yellow dress this morning. Her dark green would serve much better to hide her now.

"Looksee here," Bart said with a broken-toothed smile. "Come here missy."

He leaned in and caught hold of her foot.

"Unhand me," she said before realizing she had destroyed any hope of hiding her presence from Bart's boss.

As Bart tugged harder on her ankle, she slid off the seat, landing with a thud on the floor of the stage. Kicking his face with her other foot, she freed herself long enough to make a somewhat graceful exit. Bart's beefy arms clamped around her shoulders as soon as her feet hit the ground. He shuffled her to the line of passengers.

Bart flung her toward the scarred man who helped her earlier. The force was so hard she lost her balance and landed at his feet with a whimper. When he kneeled to help her up, the robber cocked his pistol, stopping him in mid-crouch. All she could see was the scar on the passenger's face as she tried to control her breathing. It wasn't as noticeable now as it had been before. For some reason, she found that comforting.

———

The air rushed from Robert Garrett's lungs. In all his life he had never been this lucky. There was no mistaking those flashing green eyes. The young woman Bart just pulled from the stage was Caroline Larson.

As his lackey, Bart, pushed her forward, she fell at one of the passengers' feet. Robert cocked his gun, leveling it at the passenger.

"I think she can stand on her own," he said, covering his momentary shock.

When the passenger made no further move to help her, Robert pointed his gun at Caroline. His sinister smile hid behind the red bandana covering his face. She straightened with that defiant look she always had etched haughtily on her face. He would relish wiping that expression away later. He had to finish business first.

He spoke with an exaggerated accent to further disguise his identity, not that Caroline would recognize his true identity if she saw his full face. "Now, I want y'all to empty your pockets of all yer valuables and place 'em in the bag Bart has. We don't want no trouble, so just do as yer told. Otherwise, I might decide to empty my pistol into this little gal."

Robert plotted his next move, while Bart went down the line taking all the valuables from each of the passengers, including Caroline Larson. He hated her blasted brother, Adam, almost as much as he hated Will Colter. Almost. *Patience. You'll have your revenge soon enough.*

A slow plan was always much better than a hurried one. In fact, robbing this stage had been a bit hurried—it's how he ended up doing it himself, instead of hiring it out. It was a dangerous move to get his hands dirty. After this, he would distance himself from the execution of his plans. Too risky. But if he hadn't been here, he wouldn't have seen Caroline and the ideas taking shape in his head would be a missed opportunity.

First things first. He had to finish this job then rendezvous with his other men. He would have his associate pay off Bart before taking the stage horses to La Paz to sell. He would instruct his associate to return to the stagecoach, where he would leave Caroline alive, and have his associate fetch her and take her to the small shack on the outskirts of his property. He'd let the men have fun with her, as long as they kept her alive. He needed her if he was going to ransom her for money.

Oh, Adam Larson wouldn't have anywhere near enough funds to rescue her. That would be part of the fun. And it would be what would force Will Colter to get involved.

The best part was that no one would have any idea he was involved in any of this. He would clean up, shave, and change into his fine clothes after his meeting with his associate. Then he would head back into Wickenburg and spend the night at the hotel before heading out to Prescott tomorrow as the respectable Robert Garrett.

Inwardly, the swell of anticipation for the next phase of his revenge sent giddy shivers up and down his spine. He would come back despite all that Colter and Larson took from him and he would do it while destroying them.

———

When Bart stopped in front of her, Caroline realized she would need to part with her items as well. Slowly she unfastened the broach her mother gave her and let it slip into the bag. Then she emptied her reticule, thankful she had taken the time to discretely hide half of her money elsewhere on her person this morning.

Once the man had a full bag, he began dumping luggage from the back of the stage, littering things everywhere. He picked through her trunk, strewing her clothing on the dusty ground. Finding nothing of worth there, he went to the next trunk. After several minutes ticked by, he announced he was finished with his search.

Then the boss man dismounted his horse. He came straight towards her. With a small bandana in his hands, he shoved her over to one side of the stage.

"What are you doing?" the scarred man asked, making a move towards the robber.

The robber turned and shot him.

Caroline gasped as the man's body fell limp in a pool of blood. As his face relaxed, the scar became almost invisible. A tear trickled down her cheek.

"Any more questions?" the robber asked. When no one moved, he added, "Good."

He turned her back towards him, pushing her face into the side of the coach. She tried to struggle but stopped when he pressed the barrel of his pistol against her neck. When she stilled, he yanked her hands behind her back and tied them together with the bandana. Then he shoved her to the ground.

"Stay," he commanded. "And don't give me no trouble."

Her heart pounded loudly in her ears as she watched helplessly. He unhitched the team of four horses from the stagecoach. He barked another command to Bart, who then led the remaining four men to the other side of the stage.

At the first rifle shot, Caroline jumped. Looking through the undercarriage, she saw two of the men who sat across from her lying in a heap on the ground. Blood soaked their clothing, and the odd angle of their bodies suggested they died from the same shot. Two more rapid rapports of a pistol were followed by the harsh thud of another man hitting the ground.

Tears streamed down her face as she heard the pleas of the last man. The echo of a rifle cut off his cries. Glancing over to the other side of the coach, she saw his body land on the others.

Quickly, she looked away. Fear squeezed her heart. She would be next.

Raising her knees to her chest, she buried her face in the folds of her skirt, as well as she could with her hands still tied behind her back. *Lord, help. I shouldn't have lied to Papa. But I need you. I don't want to die.*

The sound of men mounting their horses brought her eyes up.

"Boss, ain't ya fergetting something?" Bart asked.

The robber turned dark eyes on her. "Naw. I ain't about to kill a woman. Let her be."

"We just gonna leave her?"

"Yeah. Desert will kill her soon 'nough."

Those were the last words she heard before the robber's loud "Yaw" forced the unhitched stage horses into motion between him and Bart.

Caroline stared after their dust cloud for what seemed like hours, still stunned that she had come out of the ordeal unscathed.

When she was certain they were gone, she stood, arms still tied behind her back. Looking around, she found a rough metal edge to the harness system on the front of the stage. Kneeling awkwardly, she rubbed the bandana against the metal until her hands were free.

Flexing her fingers in front of her, she stopped short at the blood on them. Reaching down to her petticoat, she ripped off a strip and wrapped her cut left hand.

Her stomach revolted at the thought of what she must do next. Taking a few deep breaths, she walked toward the scar-faced man. Crouching down beside him, she searched for any sign of life. There was none. She didn't even get to thank him. She wiped her eyes on the sleeve of her dress.

Caroline proceeded to the other side of the stagecoach. Three of the men's bodies were piled one on top of the other. She wasn't strong enough to move the first to check on the other two, though she could see no evidence that any survived.

The last man lay prostrate nearby. As she approached, she thought she heard him groan. When she kneeled next to him, his body shook violently. She managed to turn him over just as the last spark of life slipped from his eyes.

Jumping to her feet, she staggered to the other side of the wagon. Sinking to her knees, she let the tears fall down her face. Her stomach roiled at all she witnessed. Crawling on her hands and knees she moved only a few feet before she lost the contents of her stomach.

Wiping the back of her hand across her mouth, she despaired. Was she going to die before ever reaching Prescott?

Then the guilt settled in. If only she had stayed in Texas and married Nathan Finley. She wouldn't be in this fine mess.

CHAPTER 2

Larson Ranch, North Texas

April 1, 1865

(Four months earlier)

Jesse Shoemaker turned toward her. This was it. Caroline was pretty sure he was going to kiss her. Part one of her plans might just work out after all.

"You are so pretty," Jesse said, Adam's apple bobbing with nervousness. His dark nutmeg eyes searched hers as his earlier laughter faded into a more serious expression.

Caroline let her gaze fall demurely for a moment, confident in the effect this would have on Jesse. Then she licked her lips, before lifting her eyes back to his. She had to wait only a second before his lips covered hers.

At first his kiss seemed shy, reserved. She thought perhaps she was the first girl he kissed, until he deepened the kiss a few minutes later.

Heat flushed her cheeks when he pulled away—not from his kiss but from her complete embarrassment. There were no sparks. Nothing. Not even a slight flutter of her heart when he kissed her.

What was wrong with her?

He mistook her expression. "I'm sorry. I... uh... don't know what came over me."

Quickly Caroline recovered from her extreme disappointment. Pasting as sincere of a smile as she could muster, she flashed it towards him. It worked. Jesse seemed relieved.

"I hope you're not angry with me," he said as he offered her his arm again.

"Not at all." Not at him—at herself. Why couldn't she manage even a small bit of romantic feeling for Jesse Shoemaker? He was handsome enough. A bit taller than she liked but he had a wonderful smile and a good heart. He was a decent young man, and she ought to be grateful that he had shown interest in her, but she was deeply disappointed. Maybe things would work out better with Nathan Finley.

As he led her back inside the house, she quickly made some excuse to part from his company. Spotting her younger sister, Missy, refilling a dessert tray, she managed to convince Jesse she would return to his side after she finished helping her.

Missy smiled coyly. "Did he kiss you?"

Caroline ducked her head, regretting that she chose to share her plan with Missy. "Yes."

"And was it nice?"

"I don't want to talk about it."

Moving towards the stove, Caroline ground more coffee and started another pot, thankfully her back was turned towards her sister.

"Honestly, Caroline, the way you are acting I would think you dislike Jesse."

Spinning to face her sister, she said, "I like him well enough. It's just that... I don't feel about him the way Mama feels about Papa. There's no..." She stopped trying to explain it. She barely understood it herself and she doubted whether her fifteen-year-old sister had any idea about romance or boys. If she did, Papa would be livid. Of course, if he knew what Caroline was doing, he would be even angrier.

"So, no to Jesse. What about Nathan? Has he kissed you yet?" Missy's wild red curls bounced with her excitement.

She glared through narrowed eyes. She was tired of trying to figure out which one would be the better husband. She had to see which one could set off the fireworks of her heart. So, she devised a plan to spend the first half of tonight's party with Jesse and then the second half with Nathan. The only reason she confided in Missy at all was because she missed her best friend, Julia. This is exactly the sort of thing Julia would have helped her orchestrate.

"I could help distract Jesse," Missy offered.

"That won't be necessary."

"There you are," Nathan Finley said, standing in the doorway of the kitchen.

Surprised to see him, she smiled, bringing her head up slowly as her eyes connected with his pale blue ones. The slow smile that stretched across his lips let her know the look had the intended effect.

"I've been looking for you all night," Nathan said as she came to his side. "Would you care to take a walk?"

Caroline nodded, placing her hand on the crook of his offered arm.

She could do worse than Nathan Finley. His father owned the mercantile in town, which seemed to be thriving, despite the tough times the cattle ranchers faced in the area. The War Between the States financially hurt her father's ranch, as well as many others in the area. For some time, the Union had blockaded their main route to market. The last few years they had to find other markets. Unfortunately, those markets proved more treacherous. That, along with the falling price of Texas longhorns, meant less profit for men like her father.

Jesse's family's ranch was hurting worse than Larson Ranch. Yes, maybe Nathan would be the better choice.

Nathan's work was stable. She always thought him the more handsome of the two, with his blue eyes and sandy brown hair. He wasn't too tall—only a few inches taller than her, instead of the nearly foot difference between her and Jesse.

As Nathan led her onto the front porch, he said, "I've missed you, Caroline. It's been far too long since you've visited the store."

A little flutter rose in her chest. What a sweet thing to say, even if she had just been in less than two weeks ago.

"I've been trying to find you all evening." He turned toward her.

"Oh, I thought you must have just arrived, as I haven't seen you until now."

A smile stretched across his lips. "So, you were looking for me then?"

Looking away shyly, she said, "Yes."

When she looked back at him, he had that look—the one that made her feel warm inside. He lowered his head, stopping just inches from her lips.

"May I kiss you?"

Her breath caught, but she managed a soft "yes" just before he covered her lips. A small flutter twitched in her stomach as he kissed her. Nothing big. Not like she hoped. But it was something.

When he pulled back, she smiled at him. He reached for her hands, taking them in his.

"Caroline, I..." Nathan cleared his throat. "I've come to care a great deal for you. And I think you care for me, too."

She nodded to him to continue.

"I would like to ask your father for permission to court you."

Oh, she had not quite expected that. Not yet. She barely knew him. She wasn't ready. Well, maybe she would have been if there had been some great spark in his kiss instead of the small little flutter.

A noise from the doorway of the house caught their attention before she could respond.

"Get your hands off her!" Jesse Shoemaker yelled, moving closer to Nathan.

Nathan dropped his hold on her hands before facing Jesse, confusion written on his features.

"This is a private conversation, Jesse."

Caroline took a step back, away from the two young men.

"She's my girl," Jesse said as jealousy dripped from his dark eyes.

"Hardly," Nathan replied. "As you can see, she is with me."

Jesse started to lunge toward Nathan who quickly side-stepped him, moving off the porch. As Jesse recovered, he followed Nathan, swinging when he was within range. Nathan ducked.

"Caroline!"

Both Jesse and Nathan turned to look at the owner of the voice. Caroline didn't need to look to know it was her older brother Georgie who called out.

"What is going on?" Georgie asked her as he motioned his sweetheart back inside.

"Ah, um." How could she explain the situation without making Nathan angry or further crushing Jesse. A fine mess she got herself into this time.

Nathan spoke first. "We were talking when he," hooking his thumb over his shoulder in Jesse's direction, "interrupted."

"He was kissing Caroline," Jesse said.

Nathan's face flushed, but he did not deny it.

Caroline's stomach plummeted. She really had not thought through what would happen if Jesse saw that.

Georgie turned to her. "Is this true?"

She nodded, too afraid to speak.

Turning Jesse's direction, Georgie asked, "And what difference does that make to you?"

"She loves me, not him. I kissed her earlier."

The shock on Nathan's face stabbed her in the chest. His lips parted as if he was going to speak, then shut in a firm hard line. He must have read the truth on her face. For all her scheming, she was never very good at lying.

"Caroline—"

"Georgie, please don't tell Papa," she whined, shifting her view towards the front door.

Her father's tall form filled the doorway.

"Tell me what?" he asked through gritted teeth. His gaze

moved to her, then Jesse, then Nathan, then back to her. A scowl of disappointment settled on his brow line. "Wait for me in the kitchen."

Glancing back over her shoulder, the expressions on Nathan and Jesse's faces were no better. Hurt. Anger. Disappointment.

When her feet refused to move, Papa's voice commanded in a whisper, "Now."

Rushing inside, Caroline felt heat flooding her cheeks. She hurried past their guests and into the kitchen to await her fate. Missy followed on her heels.

"What happened?"

"Just go," Caroline said. When she did not move, she added, "Papa is coming to talk to me."

That sent Missy scurrying from the room.

Pulling out a chair from the table, Caroline sat, holding her head in her hands.

She could deal with Papa's anger. Only, that was not what she saw in his face. The disappointment would be hard to bear.

She idolized her father, and she had always felt loved. Her younger sisters sometimes teased her that she was Papa's favorite. She secretly thought she was too. She had always been able to talk him into anything or talk her way out of trouble with him.

But tonight…

What could she even say to defend herself? That she wanted to find love like he and Mama had? That she was bored since Julia left? That she really wanted to leave Texas?

While true, none of those things would take away the look now etched in her mind.

What was she doing anyway? If she found her life so boring, how would becoming a rancher's wife or a storekeeper's wife help? It might take away the loneliness of losing her best friend. But neither of those options seemed very adventurous. It was unlikely that either Jesse or Nathan would ever want to move west.

And she did.

The realization brought her head up. That's what she had wanted to do, for some time now. She wanted to move to Prescott. She wanted to live near Julia and Adam.

Late last summer, she lost her best friend and her brother one night. Julia showed up on her doorstep, terribly abused by her older brother. She had to flee—immediately—to her other brother in the Arizona Territory. Adam was the one to take her there.

Even though Adam had already planned to leave so he could work at Will Colter's ranch, Caroline had not expected to lose her best friend, too.

To think, it had been her idea for the two to travel west as brother and sister. It was a great plan—one that succeeded in saving Julia's life, as she learned from letters since their arrival.

It was just so hard. The three of them grew up together. Caroline felt closer to Julia than to her younger sisters. Adam, only two years older than her and Julia, often played with them when the Colters and Larsons got together. The three had been good friends growing up.

But now she was left behind and she did not want to be.

The noise from their guests quieted down and still her papa had not come to talk to her. She was just about to get up, when both Mama and Papa appeared in the kitchen.

Papa started pacing across the length of the small room, while Mama took a seat across from Caroline.

It was Mama who spoke first. "Your father tells me that two different young men have shown an interest in you."

Caroline's eyes darted up to Papa's face. He looked extremely displeased. She nodded.

"And that you allowed both of them to kiss you."

Her eyes snapped back to her mama. Though her expression was softer, it bespoke of disappointment as well.

"Do you like either of these boys?" Papa asked, stopping to stand behind Mama.

Swallowing hard, Caroline tried to stall. She liked them well enough—but not enough to court or marry them.

"Answer me."

"No."

Papa's hands shot up in the air in frustration. "Haven't I

raised you better than that?"

He started pacing again.

"George, calm down."

He stopped with a clear view of Mama. "Maggie, our daughter is toying with these men. Our *daughter*. How can I calm down?"

"Are you toying with them?" Mama's green eyes locked with hers.

"No. I was going to tell Jesse that I wasn't interested before the end of the night. And Nathan—"

"He was going to ask me for permission to court you. When were you going to tell him?"

"I wasn't sure I didn't want him to court me until just a little while ago."

"You need to tell him that after church tomorrow," Papa said. "Caroline, when a boy kisses you—he's serious. It's a dangerous game you're playing. Leading them to think you care when you don't. I raised you better than that."

"I never led them to believe I loved them," she defended, knowing how hollow the words sounded.

"From what I witnessed out there this evening you did. Both of those young men were fully convinced that they captured your heart. I'll not have any daughter of mine acting in such a way!"

Mama turned to him. "Don't raise your voice. This is about Caroline, not about you."

What did Mama mean?

"She is acting like *her*."

Mama shot Papa a look that silenced him, before saying, "Honey, tell us why you did this?"

Instead of answering, Caroline shot back her own question. "Who am I acting like?"

Mama sighed. "Your papa was in love with a woman once. He wanted to marry her, but she had several beaus and picked someone else instead."

"Maggie!" Papa's face paled.

"George, sit down. You brought it up. I think it's only fair that Caroline understands why you're reacting the way you are." As papa took a seat next to her, Mama repeated her earlier question, "Now, tell us what this is all about."

Still stunned to learn that Mama was not Papa's first love, Caroline looked down at her fingernails. Softly, she started, "I just want to find someone that I can love like you love Papa. Guess I have pretty high expectations, growing up watching the two of you."

Mama smiled. "I can understand that. But why let both kiss you—especially if you were not interested in them?"

"I didn't know how to tell if I was in love. I thought maybe if I kissed them both, I would be able to tell. Only I found out that I'm not in love. Not with either of them."

The room went silent for several minutes. Caroline looked up at her papa. His features had softened, though he looked like he still had a few words for her. Mama seemed to be weighing what she said.

"Love is not something to take lightly," Mama said. "Even though you don't love either of those two boys, I understand that they have grown to love you. It's a painful situation they are in. When you love someone and they don't return that love—it hurts." The catch to her voice spoke of experience, making Caroline feel even worse for her actions.

"There are other ways to find out if you are in love without letting those boys kiss you," Papa said. "You just spend some time getting to know them. Talk to them. Over time, you would know."

"But how do you know if you're in love?"

Mama looked at Papa. "You just do. You think about him when he's not there. You look forward to the next time you'll see him."

Caroline didn't know if she really believed that was all there was to it. She never felt that way about any man. How would she know when she did?

CHAPTER 3

Sunday afternoon had been hard. After church, Papa drove her to Finley's mercantile and waited outside while Caroline talked to Nathan. She apologized for making him think that she felt more than she did. The hurt in his eyes was difficult to see, but she forced herself to look at him as her penance. She told him she would not accept his offer of courtship. He asked if she would reconsider, apparently more forgiving than she would have been. Before turning to leave, she reaffirmed that she was not ready for courting.

The next stop was Jesse Shoemaker's ranch. When she first arrived, his mother escorted her to the parlor with disdain written on her face. Jesse entered the small room and crossed his arms. He would not look at her. She supposed she deserved it. As she apologized, she caught his Adam's apple bobbing up and down as he struggled for control. Then she told him she would not seek a further relationship with him. It was not until then that he looked at her. When he did, tears welled in his eyes. Without a word, he turned on his heel, leaving her standing there.

As Caroline slunk back out to the wagon, she blinked back her own tears. She had not meant to hurt either of these men.

"I'm proud of you, Linny," Papa said, as he helped her back into the wagon, calling her by the nickname he so rarely used these days.

She nodded, not trusting herself to speak. Her shame overwhelmed her.

The ride back to the ranch passed in silence.

When they arrived home, Caroline retrieved a book from her room and a blanket. Then she sought refuge under the big oak tree. After reading the same page for the fourth time, she set the book aside.

What a painful lesson she learned last night. Her plan hurt a lot of people. So did her selfishness. No wonder Papa was so upset. She singlehandedly dashed the hopes of two young men. She caused the Shoemakers to hate her. She caused her parents great disappointment.

Her hope of finding love was no closer to being fulfilled than it was last night. Maybe it was even further away now.

Shifting her position, she laid flat on her stomach and rested her head on her crossed arms with her face turned to the side. The lowly position fit her lowly mood.

"Julia, what would you say to me if you were here?" she whispered. Would her friend have stopped her from this foolishness before she left a trail of destruction?

Perhaps. No matter what, though, she would be here to comfort her in the wake of it.

Sighing, Caroline rolled over on her back. Staring up at the blue sky partially obscured by the leafy branches of the tree, she wondered what was next in her life. With no possibilities for marriage, should she get a job in town? Was it time for her to move out?

Adam was nineteen when he left. At eighteen, she was certainly old enough to be on her own.

Arizona.

The wild territory called her again. If she moved there, she would not be completely on her own. Adam would be there to help take care of her if she needed him. Julia was there. Maybe she could live with Julia at Colter Ranch.

Excitement lit a small spark then began smoldering into a bright flame. This is what she wanted. She wanted to move to the Arizona Territory. She wanted to live close to her best friend and her brother.

Sitting upright, she crossed her arms, raising one to tap a finger against her temple. How would she ever convince Papa to let her go? He would insist she have an escort, if she was even able to get him to agree to the move.

How would she get an escort?

Slowly the idea took shape. Tomorrow she would ride into town and place an ad in the newspaper in Santa Fe. She would advertise that she was looking for a chaperone to take her to the Arizona Territory. She was pretty sure she could get Papa to allow Georgie escort her to Santa Fe. Then her chaperone could take her the rest of the way.

Jumping up from her retreat under the tree, she grabbed her book and blanket and rushed into the house to compose her advertisement.

The next morning, after breakfast, Caroline offered to take their extra eggs into Finley's mercantile so Missy, Bethie, and Helen did not have to stop on the way to school. Despite Mama's surprised look, she agreed to her suggestion.

Pulling the buggy to a stop in front of Finley's, she took a deep breath. Certainly, Nathan would not be expecting her. He might not be pleased to see her. But she needed his help to place the advertisement.

Hand hovering over the knob, she grasped it as determination stilled her nerves. The little bell above the door tinkled, drawing Nathan's blue eyes up from the register he studied. The smile faded from his lips before he finished speaking. "How may I help you?"

Caroline squared her shoulders and approached the counter. Setting the basket of eggs down, she retrieved the small piece of paper from her reticule, unfolding it.

"I would like to place this," she said, sliding the piece of paper across the counter, "in the newspaper in Santa Fe."

A brief frown flitted across his forehead as he read the message. Then his jaw went slack—she presumed in disbelief.

Terse words flew from his mouth. "How long have you been

planning this?"

"Since yesterday afternoon."

Some of the harshness left his features. "Does your father know about this?"

She hesitated.

"Caroline—"

"Look, will you place the advertisement or not?"

"What if I won't?" At her scowl he continued, "Is this about Saturday night? Because if it is, I want you to know that I don't want you to move west. I want you to stay here." His voice softened as he reached for her hand. "I'm still hoping you'll reconsider."

Swiftly, she pulled her hand from his, pretending to smooth some wrinkles from her skirt.

"If you won't help me, then please be quick about settling the account for the eggs, so I can make my way to the telegraph office." She hoped he would not call her bluff. She did not have the kind of money to send this by telegraph.

"I'll see that this gets placed as soon as possible," he said stiffly, before turning to count the eggs. When he finished, he counted out several coins from his register minus the cost of the advertisement.

"Thank you." She smiled coyly, before turning to leave.

She thought she heard a curt "good day" muttered under his breath before the door shut behind her.

———

Just over two weeks later, Missy waved an envelope in front of Caroline's face when she returned home from school.

"Nathan stopped by to give me this for you before school let out. Guess he's still in love with you," Missy's sassy comment annoyed her.

She reached for the envelope and hurried into the solitude of her room, knowing the letter would not be from him.

Dear Miss Larson,

My father and I would be pleased to act as your chaperone on your journey west, though we were not clear on your destination. We will be leaving for the mining town of Wickenburg around the tenth of May. We are going to start a Presbyterian church there for the lost souls working the famed Vulture Mine.

While father's work will keep him busy, if your destination is easily reachable by stagecoach from Wickenburg, then sometime within a month or two of our arrival, we will be able to escort you to your final destination. If need be, you will be welcome to stay with us until other arrangements can be made to see you safely there.

Please write back with your answer soon, so we can prepare for your arrival.

Sincerely,
Millicent Pritchett

Caroline blinked in disbelief. Miss Pritchett and her father seemed quite eager to work with whatever arrangements she needed. She had no idea if Prescott was within stage travel to Wickenburg. No matter, once she arrived, she would find a way to get to Prescott.

Now all she had to do was convince Papa that this was the right move for her.

Following supper that night, she broached the subject.

"Papa, I was thinking. Adam must be getting lonely for the family by now."

Papa looked up from his book. "Didn't we just send off another letter?"

"Yes, but don't you think he would be happy if one of us lived nearby?"

Mama's red hair bounced, nearly tumbling from its pins when her head snapped up.

"Caroline, what are you suggesting?" Papa asked, concern edging his voice.

"I miss him terribly. Julia, too. Things aren't exactly working out well for me here. I just thought maybe I could move to Prescott. I could help at Colter Ranch. Or I could get a job in town. Adam would be close by, and I would be able to visit with Julia often."

With lips stretched in a thin line, Papa placed his book on the small table next to the oil lamp. He looked over to Mama and to the girls. Georgie stood and motioned for the girls to follow him out to the stables.

"Are you that lonely?" Mama was the first to break the silence.

The truth of her words settled over Caroline. She truly was. "Yes."

"It's a long and dangerous journey," Papa said, surprising her by not refusing her request outright. "You will need an escort."

"I have one." Both of her parents shook their heads in disbelief. "Mr. Pritchett is a pastor, and his daughter will be traveling with him. Who better to act as a chaperone?"

"I don't know this Pritchett."

"They are in Santa Fe," Caroline said. "Georgie could go with me to Santa Fe. He could meet the Pritchetts and if he feels at all concerned about leaving me in their care, I would return home with him."

Rubbing his hand across his face, Papa sighed. "Seems you've already got this all figured out."

Caroline smiled.

"Let your mother and me pray on this for a few days."

Jumping up from her chair, Caroline squealed and hugged him. "Thank you, Papa."

"Whoa, I haven't said yes."

"I know," she said, giving him a wink as she returned to her seat. "Yes" usually came next. She was certain it would this time.

CHAPTER 4

Wickenburg, Arizona Territory

August 11, 1865

As the wagon topped a hill, Caroline nearly choked. The town of Wickenburg was positively primitive. In the river valley below, hundreds of tents lined the banks of the river. A handful of permanent buildings stood set back some from the river. Why the whole place, including tents, was smaller than her hometown in Texas.

After spending the last few months on the trail with her chaperones, Reverend Pritchett and his daughter, Millie, she thought she would be relieved to have their journey come to an end. Instead, she found herself dreading how long she might have to stay here before continuing to Prescott.

Finally, nearing the edge of the permanent buildings, Reverend Pritchett pulled the wagon to a stop. "Think this will do as good as any place."

Disembarking from the wagon, both Millie and Caroline looked around at the small cluster of buildings—not large enough to be considered a town with only two saloons, a mercantile, a hotel, and a stage station.

Keeping her voice low so only Millie could hear, Caroline asked, "How much did your father learn about the town before deciding to move?"

"Shhh."

Most of the population in town appeared to be Mexican. Now that she thought about it, most of the miners down by the river were Mexican, too. Probably not the most receptive group for a Protestant church. Then again, Reverend Pritchett might be used to that coming from Santa Fe.

The sun lowered in the sky as Reverend Pritchett set up their tents. "Ladies, these will have to do for a while. At least we won't have to pack up each night."

Caroline nodded, disappointed that their accommodations would not improve anytime soon. Of course, she didn't plan on being here much longer—especially with a stage station in town. Surely the stage traveled to Prescott.

As she and Millie prepared supper over the fire, she started to notice the whistles and shouts from the miners making their way from the river to the saloons across the street.

One bolder young man came toward her speaking in rapid Spanish. Getting too close for her comfort, she took a step back. The man pressed forward, reaching for the sleeve of her dress.

A rifle cocked next to her, stopping the man from further action.

Millie pressed the gun into the man's chest when he failed to back away. She spoke quite forcefully in Spanish. The man hesitated only a second before turning and running down the street.

"What did you say to him?" Caroline asked as her heart pounded in her chest.

"I told him, if he wanted to meet Jesus early, I could help arrange it."

Reverend Pritchett's deep laughter felt contrary to her harried nerves. "That's Millicent for you." He eased the hammer of his pistol back into place and returned it to his holster. "She'll spread the gospel with a rifle if need be."

Taking a deep breath, Caroline watched as Millie transformed from intimidating rifle-wielding woman to her former mousy self. As her anxiety settled, relief replaced it. She was with two very capable chaperones, both of which would come to her

26

defense when needed. Maybe she should stall her plans to leave for Prescott until they could travel with her.

———

After a few days in this wretched town, Caroline's patience fled. Each evening as the miners made their way to the saloons, Millie stood with rifle propped on her hip and Reverend Pritchett kept his pistol handy. The insults spoken in Spanish, though unintelligible to her, grew old. She had to get out of this place.

Finally, on Monday she decided she needed to move forward with her plans. While Reverend Pritchett went to the riverbank to save the miners' lost souls, she carefully slipped from the tents while Millie was preoccupied with laundry.

Caroline headed straight for the stage office. When she stepped into the street, she failed to notice a rider approaching fast.

"Watch out, lady!" a man's voice shouted, as he pulled up hard on his horse.

Dust stirred and pelted her face. Angry, Caroline shouted back, "Watch out yourself! Who rides at such speed in town?"

The man dismounted and moved within inches of her. She could smell the perspiration soaked into his gray shirt. He narrowed his shaded blue eyes. "Express riders."

"What?"

"Express riders ride that fast in town. That okay with you?" The sarcasm coating his words let her know that he didn't really care if it was or not.

Propping her hands on her hips, she tilted her head up slightly to make eye contact. He was only an inch or two taller than her.

"Certainly not. There's no call for such reckless behavior in a civilized town."

"Civilized. Ha!" The man turned his back as he snorted. Retrieving his saddle bags, he laughed. "You must be loony. Downright touched. Look around lady."

He stretched his arm wide, turning back in her direction. "This is some of the most uncivilized country in the whole territory."

"Humph."

Touching his hand to the edge of his felt hat, he said, "Now, if you'll excuse me, I've got some mail to deliver."

Without waiting for her response, he turned on his heel and walked towards the mercantile.

"I never," she said, indignant at that man's behavior. The town might not be the most civilized—well, neither was that express rider.

Brushing the dust from her skirt, she walked past the mercantile, chin jutted high. She stopped at the stage station, pasting a smile on her face. Once through the door, she was greeted by another woman.

"May I help you?"

"Yes. I was wondering when the next stage departs for Prescott."

"Not until Saturday."

Caroline's shoulders slumped. She was hoping to get out of this town sooner. If she had to wait five more days, she would. It wasn't as if she could just rent a horse and ride out by herself.

"How long is the stage journey from here to Prescott?"

"Two days," the woman said. Her face brightened as someone entered behind Caroline. "Thomas, welcome."

"Mrs. Ritter."

Caroline turned at the familiar voice. It was the express rider.

"Supper will be ready in an hour."

"Thank you," Thomas replied. His voice flattened. "Miss."

Then he brushed past her down the hall.

Trying to control her rising temper, she bit the inside of her cheek. That man was positively infuriating.

"Now, where were we?" Mrs. Ritter muttered. "Ah, yes. The stage to Prescott. It makes one stop for a few hours at a station before climbing the mountain. It doesn't really stop overnight. Only for meals and a brief respite to change out horses."

Was this woman serious? A two-day stage ride without stopping? Sighing, she reminded herself this was the only way to get to Prescott sooner.

"Do I need to make a reservation?"

"No need, Miss. We take whoever shows up when the stage is ready to leave. Be here by seven."

Caroline thanked Mrs. Ritter for the information before returning to camp.

———

Saturday morning dawned. Caroline readied for her day while Millie sat outside the tent reading her morning devotion. Stuffing the last of her things in her carpet bag, she lifted the edge of the tent and shoved her trunk outside. She cringed as the leather scraped noisily across the gravelly ground.

"Caroline." Millie called her name.

She darted under the tent flap with carpet bag in hand. Grabbing a handle of the trunk she lifted one side, dragging it along behind her.

When she had taken no more than a few steps, Millie stopped her.

"What are you doing?"

"I'm leaving on the stage to Prescott."

"Please rethink this. Father and I will take you in September, when the temperature cools."

The heaviness of the trunk dug into her palm, so she started moving forward again. "I can't wait any longer."

After a few more minutes of Millie trying to convince her to stay, they said their goodbyes. Caroline promised to write, as did Millie. One more hug, then Millie returned to her camp.

Dragging the heavy trunk behind her, she finally made it to the stage station with only a few minutes to spare. She purchased her ticket from the money Papa gave her before she left Texas. A large, broad-shouldered man lifted her trunk to the top of the stack on the back of the stage.

One of the other waiting passengers offered his hand, help-ing her into the stagecoach, before taking the seat next to her. With a loud *yaw* the stage lurched into motion.

She was on her way to Prescott, she thought, as a smile stretched across her face.

CHAPTER 5

La Paz

August 19, 1865

Flashing green eyes. Silky blonde hair.

Thomas Anderson snorted as he rolled out of bed, annoyed that he could not get that woman's face out of his memory. It had been five days since he nearly ran the sassy blonde over as he pulled into Wickenburg. Yet, her face etched into his mind, and he didn't like it one bit.

Shaking out his jeans, he dressed for the day as the smell of frying bacon wafted down the hall. His mouth watered as he opened the door just as Mrs. Denton hollered down the hall that breakfast was served.

Taking a seat at the table, he bowed his head and closed his eyes, knowing Mrs. Denton would slap his hand if he started shoveling food in his mouth before Mr. Denton said grace. Even though he didn't believe in God, he respected their practice.

Well, maybe he did believe in God. Some. Nothing else explained the bizarre past few years.

At Mr. Denton's "Amen," Thomas shrugged off the thought and focused on his food instead. Following breakfast, he thanked the Dentons for their hospitality, saddled his horse, and made his way into La Paz. After a brief visit with the postmaster, he started on his return route to Prescott with saddlebags stuffed full of mail.

The initial part of the trip from La Paz to Desert Wells crossed the flat desert before winding around the edge of a mountain range. Regardless of the terrain, the three-day journey alone always gave him plenty of time to think. Maybe even too much time.

God, or Providence as his old army buddy used to say, seemed to have some interest in him these days. He gave into the idea that God was the only reasonable explanation for how he ended up in the Arizona Territory.

The road to Arizona started over two years ago, almost to the day when he tried to rob a bank with his friends in his hometown of Cincinnati, Ohio. The robbery attempt was a culmination of numerous rebellious choices he made with his life. He handled his father's death poorly at the age of fourteen. When his older brother, Drew, left Ohio a few short months later to pursue medical training, Thomas lived with his Uncle Peter—a disinterested man who seemed mostly annoyed that he was suddenly saddled with a teenage boy.

So, with more freedom than he knew what to do with, Thomas joined up with some other malcontents in his hometown. The three started drinking and gambling, staying out late—mostly confining their rebellion to rowdy behavior. For six years they managed to keep from breaking any laws.

Then one of them had the bright idea that they could make more money by stealing it from the bank across the street from his brother's clinic. Thomas, drunk and senseless, agreed to the plan. None of them had been prepared for the bank manager's quick thinking. Things went wrong. The bank manager had a gun in the safe and turned it on one of them. Shots were fired. Thomas and his friends ran, leaving the bank manager in a pool of blood.

When he first fled, he thought they had killed the bank manager. Later he found out the man survived thanks to his brother's medical skills. Within a few days, he and his friends were caught and jailed.

Then the strange events in his life started. Because of what he'd done, Drew and his wife, Hannah, were forced to leave town. No one wanted to go to a doctor whose brother was a criminal. Just prior to their departure, Drew visited him in jail and told him they were headed to La Paz in the Arizona Territory.

Days and weeks in the jail did little to soften Thomas's heart. He carried a great deal of anger over losing his mother at a young age, then losing his father. He hated the world and everyone in it.

The day came when he received his sentence. The judge, having been a friend of his father's, decided the Union Army could use another body more than the jail could. The judge sent him to his son's Ohio regiment. Shortly afterward, he was transferred to an Indiana Regiment.

His regiment participated in the Red River Campaign in Louisiana. It was during that campaign that his life took another inexplicable twist. A dispatch rider fell from his horse after being shot by the Confederates. His dying words to Thomas instructed him to take the copper message tube and ride down the line. Being a strong rider, he mounted the horse without thinking of the consequences.

Even though he should have been court-martialed for deserting his post, he wasn't. Instead, he received a new position as a dispatch courier. His new duties took him all over the western theater of the War Between the States, though most of the time he stayed in Tennessee.

The next twist of fate—or Providence, or whatever it was—came following his severe injury in the battle of Franklin. As he learned later, the major general he worked for discovered Thomas's tainted past. Deciding he could no longer trust him, he sent Thomas west and ultimately to the Arizona Territory.

Once in the Arizona Territory, he served at Fort Whipple near Prescott for only a few months. He made several trips across vast desert wilderness couriering military mail between Fort Whipple and Fort Wingate in New Mexico. When the war ended, due to the strange terms of his enlistment he mustered out and settled in Prescott.

His first hope had been to find Drew and Hannah. When he got the job with the La Paz Express, riding mail between Prescott and La Paz, he felt confident he would find them soon. Only he didn't find them. They never settled in La Paz.

Instead, they changed their plans. It was Drew's intent to settle in Prescott. Unfortunately, Drew died in a tragic accident just a few weeks out. Hannah, being left on her own, did her best to get by. She had worked for Betty Lancaster, the boardinghouse owner, where Thomas stayed when he was in Prescott. After she met a local rancher, Will Colter, she married him and moved to his ranch.

When Thomas finally learned of Hannah's whereabouts, he visited Colter Ranch. His unexpected presence nearly caused Hannah to go into labor. A few weeks passed. Then he received word that she wished to see him. She told him she forgave him for his part in the tragedy of her life—perhaps the most bizarre thing that ever happened to him.

He certainly did not deserve her forgiveness. Truthfully, he still felt awkward these few months later when he was around her. She welcomed him into her new family and asked him to be an uncle to her son, even though they shared no blood ties.

Now Thomas spent his days riding for the La Paz Express in the Arizona Territory.

Shaking his head, he pulled back on the reins, bringing his lathered horse to a stop. After a brief greeting to the station's hand, he settled the mail bags on a new mount and took off at a fast pace again.

He still couldn't believe his life. None of it made sense.

The only real reason he even thought to attribute these strange events to God was because of a conversation he had with his friend Paul Lancaster, the son of the boardinghouse owner in Prescott.

"Sounds to me like God brought you here for a reason," Paul said, after Thomas finished telling him the story a few weeks ago. "Maybe even for several reasons."

"Like what?"

"I think one reason was so you could start over. Let the mistakes of your past go."

Thomas remembered growing silence at that point. He had to admit that other than Hannah and Will and Paul, no one knew about his past. And it didn't seem to matter to them, at least not anymore.

"Who knows? Maybe we can't even guess what other reasons He might have."

No, he certainly couldn't understand it.

———

The next evening, Thomas arrived in Wickenburg at Ritter's station. Mrs. Ritter greeted him with her usual warm smile.

"Supper will be ready in a few minutes. Go on and wash up."

He hesitated, thinking again of the blonde-haired, green-eyed woman he met in this town almost seven days ago. He wondered if she boarded the stage yesterday morning or not. Deciding not to ask, he headed out back. As he splashed cool water over his face and neck, he figured she must have, as intent as she seemed when he overheard her conversation with Mrs. Ritter.

Following supper, he played a game of poker with Mr. Ritter. For once, they had no other guests. As usual, he won, having been an excellent player when he used to gamble in Ohio. With Mr. Ritter's exclamation of thanks that the game was not for money, Thomas headed to bed.

The first hour he stared at the ceiling, wishing some of the thoughts of the past few days would leave him alone. He still blamed himself for Drew's death. After all, if he hadn't robbed that bank, the townsfolk of Cincinnati would not have turned against him, and he would have never left.

Turning on his side, he wished he could change things. He wished Drew and Hannah were still happily married, living in the clinic in Ohio. He wished the nephew he bounced on his knee was really Drew's son. He wished he would have learned the lessons of the past two years without it requiring Drew's death.

A lone tear slid down his cheek. Hannah forgave him after all. Maybe one day he would forgive himself, too.

———

A sleepless night gave way to morning as the smells of breakfast pulled Thomas awake. Rubbing his eyes, he sat up, resting his elbows on his knees. Already, the sun seemed too high in the sky.

He dressed for the day in his clothes from the day before. In this heat, he smelled less than pleasant but he had to travel light. Perhaps on the next run he would bring at least one change of shirt despite the sparse room for personal items in his saddle bags. Running a hand over his chin, he decided to skip shaving today. He felt like he was already behind schedule, and he hadn't left yet.

After gobbling down the breakfast, he thanked Mrs. Ritter before walking out the back door to the stables. Typically, Mr. Ritter readied his horse before breakfast. Today, it seemed he wasn't the only person who ran behind.

Once the chestnut-colored mare was ready, Thomas slung his saddle bags and the mail bags over the horse's rump. Mounting the horse, he walked it down to the post office to check for any last-minute mail. None waited, so he urged the horse out of town at a gallop.

Sometimes he hated riding horses so hard. Changing horses every fifteen miles, while it enabled him to cover the distance between La Paz and Prescott in three days, seemed to wear out the horses over time. He noticed the last time he rode this chestnut mare she fought against the hard pace. Thankfully, whatever her ailment had been, she performed well today.

About five miles out of town, Thomas spotted something odd on the horizon. His instincts told him to watch his back. Whatever loomed in the middle of the road ahead, he needed to approach with caution.

On his very first run several months ago, one of the other Express employees explained the tactics bandits and Indians used to surprise riders. One of their tactics was to block the road with a wagon or stagecoach—make it appear to be distressed. When the rider slows as he approaches, the bandits would fire upon the unsuspecting man, stealing the mail or whatever goods he carried, often leaving him for dead.

Pulling to a stop some distance from the obstruction, Thomas checked his pistol and rifle. Both were loaded. He studied the scene ahead of him, though he was still too far away to make out the details. Some sort of carriage or wagon looked like it had been abandoned in the middle of the road.

A pile of something lay next to it. Squinting, he tried to get a better look. The white and brown colors made it difficult to tell for certain, but he thought those might be men. If they were, they were either injured, dead, or waiting for him to ride by before they made their move.

Scanning the brush on both sides of the road, he bit back a sigh. There was no cover. The bushes were scattered and too low to the ground. What he wouldn't give for the dense Tennessee woods.

There was only one way past the obstacle. He had no choice. He had to ride by it.

Perhaps his best bet would be to ride at a gallop. Then he would clear the danger before the bandits had a chance to act.

Digging his heels into the mare's sides, he pushed her for her fastest speed.

Then the thought struck him. What if someone really was in distress? What if he was the only person to pass this way for days? Should he slow down?

No. It had to be a setup.

As he neared, the stagecoach took on a more solid form. No horses. The bodies on this side also became clearer, as did the flies hovering over them.

Slowing the horse's pace some, he considered the scene. If this was the Saturday stage and today was Monday, it had been here unnoticed for two days. If there were any survivors, they would be in rough shape without water in this horrid heat.

Just as he passed the stage, a heavy object struck him hard in the chest. Grabbing it with one hand, he released the reins and went for his pistol. Turning toward the flash of yellow to his right, he pulled back on the hammer of his pistol and aimed.

Then he stopped and frowned.

"What did you do that for?" he hollered at the green-eyed beauty as he slowly he released the hammer.

"You weren't going to stop!"

"You don't know that."

"You were riding at a gallop just a moment ago. I had to do something to get your attention."

"Well, you've got it," he said, dismounting the mare, keeping one wary eye on the blonde woman. Funny how she seemed even sassier than when he first met her in Wickenburg last week.

"Can I have my Bible back?"

"What?"

"My Bible," she said, wiggling her fingers.

Looking down at the object in his hand, he realized she had thrown her Bible at him—it was the heavy thing that slammed into his chest. Thrusting it towards her open hand, he held back a smirk. This was the first time someone had literally thrown the Good Book at him.

Clutching the book to her chest, she let out a large gasp. "You!"

He had worse greetings from a woman before, though this one might just be the most dramatic if he counted the pelting with scripture.

CHAPTER 6

"You!" Caroline shrieked, nearly stumbling over her carpet bag as she took a step backwards from her rescuer, holding her Bible.

"Miss." Came the curt response.

"You're the… the… The express rider."

"Mouthy and observant."

Confused. Flustered. Caroline could hardly believe *this* was God's answer to her prayers for help. The express rider?

When she first met him last week, she assumed she would never see him again. Good thing too. He rubbed her the wrong way then, just as he was doing now with that cocky grin twitching at the corners of his mouth.

"This is not funny."

The grin faded. "Never said it was, Miss."

He looked past her toward the stagecoach. His blue eyes seemed to take in every detail of the scene before him in only a matter of seconds.

"Care to tell me what's going on here?"

A sigh escaped her lips. She needed his help. She ran out of water yesterday afternoon, despite her best efforts to ration it. She hadn't had food in more than a day. Her lips were parched. Her cheeks stung from sitting in the sun too long. He was the first person to come along since the stage robbery. If she didn't get over her irritation with him and win him over fast, there was no telling when the next person might come along.

She couldn't bear being left with the dead men and howling coyotes for one more night.

For a moment she felt dizzy. As she swayed, he moved closer, though he didn't touch her. When she recovered, he asked again what happened.

"We were robbed within miles of leaving Wickenburg on Satur-day morning."

He turned toward his horse and retrieved a canteen. Holding it out to her, he said, "Just a few sips."

The urge to guzzle the canteen dry almost won over his firm instruction. Savoring the water, she complied.

"After they robbed us, they took the horses. Then they shot—" Her voice cracked. "—all the men. They were too heavy for me to move, so I..."

For the first time since meeting him, she caught a slight look of compassion. He dug around in his saddle bags and pulled out a piece of beef jerky.

"Hungry?"

Caroline took the offered food, nibbling slowly. His gaze felt intense as he studied her.

"Anyone else been by since Saturday?"

Her temper flared again. "Do you really think I'd stay here and sun myself all day if there had been?"

His eyes narrowed, as if assessing the truth of her statement.

"Oh, for goodness's sake! You don't think I had something to do with this, do you?"

Crossing his arms, he stared at her for another few seconds. "I suppose not."

As she swallowed the last of the jerky, she waited for him to say more.

"Come on," he said, walking back to his horse.

"Wait. Aren't you going to bury those men?"

"No."

Taken aback, she failed to keep the edge from her voice. "Have you no decency?"

He turned and faced her now, his nose so close to hers she felt the warmth of his breath when he spoke. "Look, lady, I've got plenty of decency. The ground is incredibly hard out here. Could take me the better part of a day to dig graves for that many men. You're already starving and thirsty. We're still ten miles or so to the next station. That'd be the closest place to get you some water and grub. With two of us on this horse, it's gonna take us several hours to get there."

Caroline wanted to argue. It just didn't seem right not to bury those poor men.

"If it's alright with you, I'd like to get to the next station before nightfall. Can't do that if I'm spending the next few hours caring for the dead. Seems to me it makes more sense to care for the living."

"Very well," she replied, seeing the sense in what he said, no matter how wrong it felt morally. Stooping down, she grabbed her carpet bag.

"Leave it."

"I most certainly will not! This is all I have left to my name."

Throwing his arms up in the air, he let out an exasperated groan. "The horse is going to have a time of it carrying both of us and the mail. There isn't room for your bag."

"I'm taking it."

"You are not."

"I am."

He stared her down for a few seconds, then turned and mounted his horse, moving away from her.

"What are you doing?"

"You either stay here with your bag, or you leave it and come with me."

Stubborn man! He was clearly not going to compromise. He was going to force her to leave behind the only other change of clothing she could manage to squeeze into the bag. She would have only this dirty, sweaty, torn dress to her name if he got his way.

"Wait!"

He stopped the horse.

"I'll leave the bag. But I need to take this," she said, holding up the Bible Grandma Larson bought for her when she turned fourteen. It meant too much to her to leave it behind. "It's not negotiable."

"Fine."

Dismounting his horse, he took the book from her hand and stuffed it in his saddle bag. Then he mounted the horse and pulled her up behind him.

"Hold on," he said as he started the horse forward at a walk again.

"To what?"

"Unless you see something else to hang on to, my waist will have to do."

Heat flushed her face as she slowly leaned forward and loosely placed her arms around his waist. She'd never been this close to a man before—unless she counted kissing Nathan or Jesse. For some reason, neither of them struck her as men now that she was sitting on top of a horse with this one. They certainly never smelled as bad.

"Forget to bathe?" she asked under her breath.

"I could ask the same question."

———

Not more than a mile after he rescued this woman, Thomas felt her start to slip off the back of the horse as her hold around his waist slackened.

"Miss!"

A delayed reply confirmed that she dozed off.

"Get down."

"Why?"

Did this woman have to question everything he said?

"We're going to trade places."

She slid off the back, amazingly without further protest. He dismounted then lifted her to the horse before he mounted behind her.

As he slid his arms on both sides of her to hold the reins, his pulse quickened. He had enjoyed her arms around his waist but now found himself enjoying this more. Stop it, he warned himself. He couldn't afford to get mixed up with this feisty woman, no matter how attractive she was.

Over the next incredibly slow mile, he waited for her to fall asleep again. Her head dropped quickly to one side, then snapped to attention again. This routine repeated several times before she leaned back into his chest and rested her head against him. A light floral fragrance registered as he took a sharp breath in surprise. He couldn't believe she pressed against him.

Another mile passed. He tried to control his reaction to her nearness. He was losing. He liked the way she felt against his chest and in his arms. A quick image of him kissing her passed through his mind. He tried to shake it off.

As she slept, she seemed much more amiable than when she argued with him. Her blonde hair brushed against his face as a slight breeze blew by. It had been a long time since he had been with a woman. This one stirred him deeply.

Swallowing hard, Thomas decided he had to move. Pulling back on the reins, he stopped the horse. The young woman stirred.

"Are we there?" she asked, her voice groggy and soft.

"No. Just thought I'd walk for a while. Make it easier on the horse for a spell." And easier on himself.

Mounting up, he nudged his horse forward without a backward glance. His pulse didn't return to normal until they'd nearly reached the next station.

As he pulled the horse to a stop in front of the station, he looked around. The horse that should have been ready and waiting was not. After helping the woman down from the mare, he headed toward the door of the small shack. Just as he reached up to knock, the station hand opened the door.

"Shoulda been here hours ago," the station hand said. As he stepped out into the late afternoon sun, he squinted. A grin lit his face when he noticed Thomas's traveling partner.

"Who's the lady?"

"Ah…" Thomas hesitated, realizing he never asked her name.

"Miss Caroline Larson," she introduced herself.

His stomach plummeted to his boots. Larson.

"Any relation to the horse trainer, Larson?" The station hand asked.

"Adam? He's my brother."

Of course, Thomas thought. Wouldn't that just be his luck? Larson and Colter provided most of the horses for the Express line. She just happened to be Larson's sister.

As Caroline talked about the events leading her to the station, he considered his options. Up until a minute ago, he had half a mind to leave her here until the next stage came through. Now, seeing the station hand's interest in her and given her connection to Adam Larson, he could hardly do that.

No, he would have to take her into Prescott himself.

"Saddle up two mounts," Thomas instructed the station hand.

"Ya ain't planning on pressing on, are ya?"

"Sure am."

"But ya only got another hour or so of daylight left. Seems a bit foolish to me."

Thomas grunted. "Don't recall asking your opinion."

The station hand stormed off to the stables cursing under his breath. He didn't care. He'd already lost too much time as it was. He had to get Caroline and the mail to Prescott tomorrow if possible. At least then he'd only be one day late and would still have two days to rest before his next run. Hopefully Miss Larson had grit.

"We leave as soon as the horses are ready." Tossing her the canteen, he added, "Fill it up. I'll see if I can find another one."

"But where are we going to stay for the night?"

"Wherever we find ourselves at twilight."

She swallowed hard and looked out towards the grassy valley, fear rounding her eyes.

Thomas left her by the well to fill the canteen, not interested in pursuing the conversation further. He had a job to do.

Heading into the stables, he spoke briefly with the still grumbling station hand. He was able to borrow another canteen and get some food stuffs from the man.

A few minutes later, a very nervous-looking Caroline sat atop her horse. He mounted his horse and set the pace at a trot, knowing he couldn't expect a faster pace with only one more station between here and Prescott. He doubted if she would be able to handle such a fast pace anyway.

After about a mile, Caroline started chattering.

"This isn't exactly how I planned things," she confessed.

"Don't suppose so."

"When I left Texas, it was so I could move to Prescott. My best friend, Julia Colter, moved there to live on her brother's ranch. Adam went with her."

Thomas grunted, not pleased with the news that Julia Colter was her best friend. He had so many connections with this annoying woman—all which chewed at his conscience to make sure he delivered her to Colter Ranch safely. He didn't want that responsibility. He just wanted to do his job and deliver the mail.

"I miss her. Julia, that is. We grew up together. Everywhere she went, I went. We used to talk about everything."

When her voice faded to silence, he counted himself lucky. Too bad it only lasted a minute.

"If she was still in Texas, I think she would have kept me out of trouble." She sighed. "That whole business with Nathan and Jesse—that would never have happened."

Thomas didn't want to know. In fact, as the sun lowered in the sky, what he wanted most was for her to shut her trap. He needed to listen for unusual sounds. He needed to make certain they weren't being followed.

Unfortunately, she continued talking away—not seeming to mind that he said nothing.

Finally, he couldn't take it anymore. "Shut your mouth. I think someone's following us."

Other than a sharp intake of air, Caroline didn't make another sound.

As the sun faded behind the mountains, he pulled his horse to a stop and dismounted.

"What are you doing?" she asked.

"Setting up camp for the night."

"We're going to stay here?"

"Yup."

Thomas began removing his bedroll from the horse. At least he had a blanket to lie on. Rolling his eyes, he admitted the right thing to do would be to offer it to Caroline.

"Should I look for some firewood?" she asked.

"No."

"Are you going to then?"

"No."

Pulling out some food from his bags, he handed her a chunk of bread and some jerky.

"How are we going to have a fire?"

Taking a big bite out of his piece of bread, Thomas replied, with mouth full, "We aren't."

"Why not?"

"Too dangerous. It would give away our position to any Indians that might be following us."

When he looked in her direction, he saw her shaking like a leaf. She started to sway, dropping her food to the ground.

CHAPTER 7

Caroline felt the blood drain from her face. Losing hold of the food in her hands, she hugged her arms around her, praying the dizziness would abate. Instead, her body shook uncontrollably as her mind raced.

Camping in the valley provided no cover. If someone were following them, as Thomas suggested, they would be an easy target. Stories of savage Indian attacks filled her mind. Fear took root.

"Hey," Thomas said, placing his hands on her arms.

Air refused to fill her lungs properly. All she could see was images of men and women brutally attacked.

The vision of the pile of dead men from the stagecoach took control of her imagination. Those poor men, their lives ended in a second. When they left Wickenburg in the morning, they had no idea it would be the last morning they would see the sun rise. She almost suffered the same fate.

The stress of the last few days came out as burning tears.

An anguished sob broke from her lips against her will. Thomas drew her towards him. She unconsciously wrapped her arms around his waist, burying her head against his chest. She needed the strength he offered.

For several minutes, she sobbed uncontrollably. How had she escaped the stage robbery as the lone survivor? How had she escaped dehydration and a slow death in the desert? Why her? Why not those poor men?

Had she escaped death twice in as many days, only to be killed in her sleep by violent Indians?

Her breath caught in her throat. *Please, God, I don't want to die.*

Maybe all this was retribution for her lies to her parents. She should have told them the truth—that she didn't have someone to accompany her the whole way to Prescott.

But Millie said she and her father would have taken her—only if she had waited. Suddenly the few months' wait Millie suggested seemed to make sense only she had not taken her friend's advice. Instead, she plowed ahead, like she always did in her brazen way with no thought of the consequences of her actions.

Had she learned nothing from the situation with Nathan and Jesse? There she hurt not only herself and her family, but each of them and their families.

In her present case, she hurt not only herself, but Millie—she was probably worried sick wondering if Caroline made it to Prescott safely. If she died in this valley tonight, Julia and Adam, and probably all Colter Ranch would be hurt.

Then there was the express rider. She ruined his schedule. Hopefully she didn't cost him his job.

Guilt and remorse piled on top of grief. Caroline continued to cry for several more minutes, hoping relief would fill her soul.

———

Thomas swallowed hard. The feel of this woman against his chest sent his senses spiraling out of control. As he rubbed his hands up and down her back to comfort her, he savored the feel of her cotton dress under his fingers. Her body pressed against his. Her arms clutched tight around his waist. The longer she cried in his embrace the more his blood boiled.

Letting out a slow breath, he tried to calm his racing heart and his fierce physical reaction to her closeness. This was Larson's sister. He could not afford to do anything foolish.

When her crying subsided, she looked up at him. Even in the fading light, he could see the terror in her eyes. How he wanted to chase it away.

As he studied her face, he took in the long blonde eyelashes framing her frightened eyes. Her skin looked so smooth, like silk. Her pink lips were full and inviting.

Without thinking, he lowered his mouth to hers, answering the beckoning call her sweet lips. Fire coursed through his veins as he savored the feel of her body crushed against his. His hands itched to memorize her back, but he held them around her waist instead.

Then she kissed him back, shyly at first then growing with intensity. A deep hunger and longing awakened his soul. Her kisses teased that longing into passionate desire. He deepened the kiss, exploring her back with his hands, continuing to press her close.

She mesmerized him and he wanted to make love to her.

Instantly he dropped his hold and stepped back—the thought scaring him senselessly. This was not just any woman. This was Adam Larson's sister.

Breathing heavily, Thomas left her standing there as he headed toward his horse. He never had such an immediate and consuming reaction to a woman before. His heart was still beating violently. He didn't dare look at her to see her reaction to his sudden retreat. Yes, he was retreating from her, just as much as he had from the rebels he encountered in the war. He would have to proceed very cautiously with this woman, for she seemed to hold some sort of power over his common sense.

As he began unbuckling the saddle, he berated himself for his actions. Maybe swearing off saloon girls hadn't been such a good idea after all—not if it left him in such knots that he would nearly take advantage of a decent woman in a desperate situation. The only reason he gave up the girls at the saloon was because he was trying to be a better man. He and Paul talked about it many times. Paul constantly told him that the momentary pleasure wasn't worth the pain it caused. Though Thomas hadn't been entirely convinced that there was anything wrong with the pleasure, he considered Paul a decent, honorable man—someone to emulate—the kind of man like his brother.

He thought if he could be more like Paul, more like Drew, then maybe he wouldn't cause such unbearable pain for himself and those he loved. Maybe he could somehow atone for Drew's death.

All it made perfect sense until a certain blonde-haired, green-eyed woman entered his life and turned it upside down.

As the heat slowly dissipated from his veins, he threw the saddle down. It would act as a barrier between them as they slept on the hard ground tonight. If he could fall asleep, knowing only two saddles separated them.

He tossed his only blanket towards her general direction. He barely glanced long enough to make sure she caught it.

"You'll sleep there," he said as he pointed to the far side of the saddles. "I'll be over here."

She didn't make a sound.

"I'm going to… Um, I'll be back in a minute," he said, needing a break from her intense stare and the emotions it stirred. Hopefully, she would lie down and fall asleep before he returned.

———

Caroline stood there numbly watching Thomas unsaddle the horses. He had kissed her in a way that made her feel like a woman—no longer a schoolgirl—and she liked every second of it. She should be furious. Instead, she felt heady and dizzy in a different way from earlier.

Oh my. If Nathan had kissed her like that… She never would have left Texas. She would have married him, had his children, and eagerly grown old with him.

Only, Nathan hadn't kissed her like that. No, it was the express rider. The man who did everything the opposite way she would have. The man who rescued her.

That must be what it was. She wasn't thinking clearly. She had been through far too much in the last few days. Somehow, she responded to his kiss out of some need to feel safe. Maybe it was just because he had rescued her that she felt that way.

Shaking out the blanket, she watched his back as he walked off. In the deepening shadows, she noted his muscular form. He was only an inch or two taller than her—rather short for a man. But she didn't mind when he was kissing her.

Such ardor. She waved her hand in front of her face to fan herself.

She hoped she could trust him not to do anything untoward. Despite their differences, he seemed like an honorable man.

Until he kissed her.

Heat flushed her cheeks. She wasn't sure she would be able to sleep with the memory of his kiss and the sparks it lit in her soul repeating again in her mind.

As she lowered herself to the ground, she thought about the kisses she experienced with Jesse and Nathan. Those attempts paled in comparison. Those had been her silly naive notion of what romance and love was like.

Love. She couldn't possibly love Thomas. She'd only known him for a short time. She knew absolutely nothing about him. Not where he came from. Not who he was. Nothing, save for the fact that he irked her the first day they met and that he saved her the next time.

But there was no denying the strong feelings she had just experienced. Was it possible there might be something between the fireworks and love?

She just couldn't consider that kind of love. It seemed too… Frightening. Intense. Confusing.

A soft rustle of the tall grass sounded behind her.

"I'm back," Thomas said, as he lay down on the other side of the saddles.

"Good night," she whispered.

Only silence answered.

Releasing a quiet, yet heavy sigh, Caroline tried to fall asleep.

———

The walk helped Thomas calm down some. At least the fire left him. Rolling onto his side so his back faced the saddles, he stared at the valley before him, though the darkness limited his sight.

Call it attraction or lust—whatever it was, he had to keep control. He could not possibly be a better man—a man worthy of respect—if he treated a woman the way he just treated Caroline. If he had been in town, he certainly never would have kissed her. If others had been around, he would not have kissed her.

Yet here he had.

Add that to his list of poor choices: robbery, gambling, drinking, and now this.

What is wrong with me? Why do I keep failing?

Others succeeded at making good choices. Certainly, he could too. He would just have to try harder to be a good man. Keep his mind clear. Think before acting. Yes, he could do it.

Caroline's soft breathing reminded him he was not alone. He thought of that kiss and his desire for her. Maybe he just wasn't strong enough to be a good man. Not everyone succeeded at such a noble goal.

Anything is possible with God.

Paul's words struck him like a punch to the face. Perhaps there was some truth even if he couldn't remember the context of them.

Why would God care?

I brought you here.

Great. Now his thoughts were starting to sound like God. That wasn't possible. God didn't bring him here. A stupid mistake set off a chain reaction that led him to this place. Nothing more. Right?

Shrugging his confusion aside, Thomas closed his eyes hoping sleep would come soon. He would just do the best he could. Someday, he would be a man Drew could be proud of.

CHAPTER 8

Wickenburg

August 21, 1865

Robert Garrett smiled as he shoved the saloon girl to the floor. Wealth in the West afforded many privileges: a plush bed, an ornate room, and someone to share it with. It cost him a fair sum, but he didn't care. He was still in high spirits from the success of the stage robbery and the secret cargo he retrieved from it—worth far more than the horses or the small trinkets from the passengers.

"Get out!" he said, kicking the hung-over saloon girl in the side. She groaned and scurried to the door.

This was going to be a good day, he thought, as he dressed in his fine black striped suit. By now, his associate should have sold the horses from the stage robbery and have headed out to retrieve Caroline Larson.

He marveled again at his good fortune. The West had been much better for him than the South. He laughed out loud. Perhaps he should thank Will Colter for his role in forcing him to leave his home.

No. He hated the man too much.

Besides, he really owed a great deal of his current success to that poor sap—the real Robert Garrett. Trusting fool.

When he headed west from Santa Fe, he ended up traveling

with the man whose identity he stole. Over weeks of travel, he encouraged the real Robert to talk. And talk he did. He talked in that perfect northern accent all about the ranch he was building north of Wickenburg. He talked about how he saved money for years—had it right there with him—to start his new life in the West.

He listened to the naïve man, imitating his accent as a game—at least that's what he led Robert to believe. Just outside of Tucson, he made his move. He killed Robert Garrett in a remote place in the desert. Then he took everything. The money. His horse. His deed. His accent. His identity.

Once the new Robert Garrett arrived at the ranch, he was further pleased to learn that none of the ranch hands had ever met the real Garrett. He hired them all by mail or messenger. Regardless, the new Robert did not take any chances. He fired all the men and replaced them with men more in line with his approach to business.

His associate was the first to be hired, though he kept him from his other men. After all, having a hired gun blatantly on staff was a good way to ruin his image of being a reputable rancher and draw the attention of the authorities—not that there were any.

As a legitimate businessman, he sold cattle to the booming gold town of La Paz. They always seemed in need. The town purchased most of its cattle from California and had it shipped up the Colorado River. He undercut the price enough to ensure several contracts, but not so much that he couldn't make an exorbitant profit.

His other dealings included cattle rustling, with a different twist. Seemed most of the rustlers in the territory preferred rebranding the cattle. Robert's method was to leave the brands intact and provide very authentic looking bills of sale—easy enough with the help of his attorney, Zach Drake, in Prescott.

Something he learned a long time ago was to spread out his business dealings over a large geographic area. It was unlikely that anyone in La Paz would make the weeklong stage journey to

Prescott to verify his paperwork. It meant he had to travel more often, but his ranch was centrally located for most of his dealings.

The other lesson, one he almost forgot recently, was to keep his distance from the less than ethical means of business, such as the stage robbery. However, he did an excellent job with the rustling. He used his associate to hire a gang of Mexican rustlers. Then he used local connections to find unhappy cowboys willing to sell out their bosses for extra cash. He always made those connections through a proxy and never directly. None of those inside cowboys had any idea who Robert Garrett was or how he might be involved. All they cared about was getting paid for information on where herds would be and when the best time was to cut a few from the herd.

He was brilliant and cunning. There was no way he was ever going to get caught.

Whistling to himself, he made his way downstairs carrying his carpet bag. Once outside, he squinted against the bright afternoon sun. Guess he slept later than he thought.

An individual caught his eye. He followed the strange looking fellow around back to the alley way. It was his associate, a man of many disguises.

"She's gone."

Heat rushed to his face. "What do you mean she's gone?"

"She's not where we expected her to be."

"Then someone must have come to her aid. Go back and head north towards Prescott. Find her," Robert growled, very displeased by this unwelcome news.

The strange looking man left.

Robert secured his carpet bag to his horse and headed toward the mercantile. A small crowd gathered outside. He slowed his pace, taking his time to secure his horse so he could listen to the conversation.

"The stage was robbed. A man coming from Prescott said he saw what was left."

Ah, the handiwork of his associate. He was always good at getting the rumors started.

"Was there a young woman there?" A man dressed like a preacher asked.

"Naw. He only said he found the dead bodies of the men. Too old to care for them, so he asked me and my son to go take care of it. Said it looked like they'd been there for a few days."

"But no young woman?"

Robert grew concerned by the preacher's interest in Caroline. Just who was she to him?

"Your daughter?" he asked.

"No. My charge. My daughter and I were to escort her to Prescott, but she ran off."

Robert looked thoughtful for a moment. Perhaps having the preacher ride along with him would be a good idea. He would be able to make sure the man did not come across Caroline before his associate did.

"I'm leaving this afternoon for Prescott. It'll mean camping under the stars for a few nights along the way, but you are welcome to join me."

"Thank you, thank you," the preacher said, looking immensely relieved. "By the way, I am Reverend Pritchett."

"Garrett. Robert Garrett," he said, extending his hand. "Can you be ready to leave within the hour?"

"Yes. I'll make arrangements for my daughter's care, grab a few things, and meet you back here."

Robert nodded his agreement as Reverend Pritchett hurried down the street. After purchasing a few things in the mercantile, he headed back to the hotel for a meal. When he finished, he found Reverend Pritchett waiting for him.

Within an hour of traveling, they came upon the man and his son caring for the dead.

"Perhaps we should stop and help?" Reverend Pritchett suggested.

Robert cringed inwardly before considering the idea. If he stopped with the reverend to lend aid, no one would suspect he had been involved in the crime. He reined in his horse and dismounted. Then he moved items around in his carpet bag until he found a bandana he could tie around his mouth and nose to keep the putrid smell from affecting his stomach.

Next time, he would make sure his associate cleaned things up if he happened to be traveling the same direction.

CHAPTER 9

Colter Ranch

August 21, 1865

I'm getting too old, Ben Shepherd thought, rounding to the right side of his black mare, Sheila. Placing his right foot in the stirrup, he grunted as he heaved himself on the back of his faithful horse.

Over a month ago he switched how he mounted his horse, the first sign that he wasn't as young as he used to be. The frequent pain and stiffness in his left knee was getting worse, though the ointment Mrs. Colter—Hannah—gave him seemed to help some, even if he took a good amount of ribbing from the young cowboys living in the bunkhouse. The pain started last fall after the cattle drive to California and got progressively worse since. Arthritis is what Hannah said she thought it was.

So, it seemed to be easier to mount his horse when he kept his left leg straight, even though it meant pushing off the ground with it. For now, he was managing.

"Hup," he mumbled, and Sheila moved forward towards the smoke house.

Daniel Raulings, better known as Snake, heaved the last crate into the wagon. He nodded a greeting before taking his place on the wagon. The two men headed south on the road to Prescott with their now bi-weekly delivery of Colter beef.

Will Colter sure had done a good job building up his reputation and his business in the short year and a half he'd been here. Ben smiled as pride rose in his chest. Eddie would be just as proud of his son, if he were still alive to witness it. In his absence, Ben was more than happy to fill in, especially since Will was more like a son and less like a boss to him.

As foreman of the Star C back in Texas, Ben watched Will grow from an awkward young lad into a fine young man. Twenty-five years ago, when he first started working as a cowboy on the Star C, he found some healing in watching Eddie interact with his two sons, Reuben and Will. Soon Eddie's family became his own, taking the place of the great loss, he suffered—one that kept him up many nights, breaking his heart for many years. Within a year, he became the foreman and cemented his friendship with Eddie. No wonder he felt so close to his friend's son.

After Eddie died, Ben couldn't think of doing anything but following Will west to the Arizona Territory. Reuben was a mean, hateful man and there was no way he was going to work for him. So, he didn't hesitate for even a breath when Will asked him to accompany him, and he never looked back.

That wasn't true. He did look back—just not to the Star C.

He'd been looking back to Mississippi for years to those beautiful nutmeg brown eyes that first stole his heart. *Sheila, darling, I still miss you. Even after all this time.* For four blissful years his life had been perfect at her side working on the tenement farm in Mississippi.

He was poor. Had come from a dirt-poor family. His pa had been a subsistence farmer when he wasn't drinking. Inwardly, Ben scoffed at the word "subsistence." They barely managed to eke out enough food to feed the large family of twelve and then it was through the efforts of his two brothers and him. Too bad Pa couldn't father more boys than girls.

The best thing he ever did was move out and start working on a tenement farm on one of the area's largest plantations. He had to lie about his age to get the job. He was only seventeen. But with his muscled arms built up from years of farming, and his tall stature, he easily passed for a twenty-year-old. The first few months he worked hard in the fields and struggled to find the energy to cook for himself at the end of the day. Just when he was about to go back home to fetch one of his sisters to come keep house for him, he met Sheila.

Her pa owned the neighboring tenement farm. One day, she stopped by with a pie—a luxurious gift to be sure, given the amount of flour and sugar it took to make—and was appalled at his filthy dwelling. She stayed in the afternoon cleaning up the place. Then the next afternoon, she came back. Clean clothes hung on the line, his only other outfit, and a plate of warm food sat ready on the table when he came in from the field. She flashed him a beautiful smile igniting her nutmeg eyes before she left with barely a word.

It's that smile that stole his heart. When she returned the next day with another meal, she stayed for a few minutes to talk to him. He thanked her for her kindness and offered to pay her in food to replace what she used from her own to prepare the meal for him. She refused, saying the good Lord provided.

Days turned into weeks. Soon, she invited him to eat with her family—her, her pa, and her three younger sisters. So, each evening after a hard day in the fields, Ben made the trek to her home with a light step and broad smile. After only three months of getting to know her, he proposed. She accepted and they were married in a quiet little ceremony with only her family in attendance. His family refused to come.

Shortly after their second anniversary, Sheila gave birth to his son, Elijah. He had his mother's dark hair and nutmeg eyes. Ben instantly loved him.

He enjoyed two more years with his blessed family, eagerly anticipating the birth of his second child.

One evening, after the sun had already set, the plantation owner called him up to the big house. He had something to discuss. Though Sheila begged him to wait until morning, Ben went. It was the master after all. He couldn't keep the man waiting.

If only he had listened to her. Maybe…

It was no use going down that road again. He'd traveled it far too often. He was forty-seven now—their life together a distant memory. One he needed to bury next to her grave. One that he could never quite bring himself to let go of.

He patted his horse, Sheila, on the neck. If she only knew how deeply he loved her namesake. No one knew. Not a living soul knew of his secret life before the Star C. Eddie pried enough information from him to gather that he'd had a family once. He stayed tight-lipped about it with the ever-revolving group of cowboys on the ranch. Only Eddie knew most of his story, and he was gone, too.

No matter. Ben had as much of a family as he could hope for here on Colter Ranch. Will and Hannah were like children to him and their sweet baby James, born just a few months ago, was like a grandson—though looking at him now at this age brought old memories forward.

Julia Colter, Will's younger sister, moved here. She seemed to finally be settling down, learning to accept the love of her beau, Adam Larson. Secretly, Ben hoped when those two finally got married, that she'd let him walk her down the aisle, filling in for Eddie. It would bring him such joy, and he could picture Eddie smiling down from heaven.

Snake started mumbling to himself. The young man always seemed to have something to say, and he sure didn't seem to care if anyone listened or not. He was just content to jabber on and on about nothing.

But all his jabbering jolted Ben's mind back to attention—leastwise it did for a moment. Scanning the tall pine trees lining the road, he searched for any sign of Apaches. He listened for any unusual sounds, like the eerie silence of all wildlife stilling as they sometimes did when the hostiles entered the forest. Today, there seemed to be nothing to worry about. Birds sang their sweet melodies, bringing some light back to his heart.

Then it faded, replaced by the image of a woman who captured his attention over the last year. Snorting, Ben reminded himself he was too old to fall in love. Men his age—well, they just didn't romance a woman or seek out companionship. He'd been a bachelor for twenty-five years, living in a bunkhouse full of young men. He didn't need a woman. Wouldn't know what to do with one if he had her.

Yet, Betty Lancaster's bright smile entered his mind. He couldn't deny that he was looking forward to a visit and one of her delicious meals. That woman could cook better than his mama. Her heart was pure gold, and she seemed to adopt every young person in town. That was a lot of people, considering she had a few years on him.

Still, his heart picked up pace as he thought about her now. She wasn't particularly pretty, but she wasn't homely either. Her girth was a testament to her cooking skills. Her buoyant personality made up for her lack of outward beauty, making her far more appealing to him than he really wanted to admit.

He flirted with her shamelessly last month when she'd been out on the ranch. He couldn't deny that. He was completely befuddled as to why. Shoot, a few times over the last year he even came close to kissing her. Like a man his age had any call courting a woman. There was just something about Betty that got under his skin and made him curious to learn more about her.

He enjoyed watching her with little James. She treated him like he was really her grandson. Ben understood how she felt. Didn't matter that James didn't share his blood. He loved that child as if he did.

He didn't know why he started to think about Betty more lately. Sometimes he wasn't too sure if he was talking to Sheila in his mind anymore or if it was Betty he was talking to. That scared him. It was getting harder to remember what Sheila's voice sounded like. Instead, when he was working through a problem in his mind, sometimes he could have sworn it was Betty's voice answering him. Maybe he was just going loony.

As Snake pulled the wagon to a stop behind the mess hall at Fort Whipple on the western side of town, Ben dismounted his horse to the left. Though it meant bending his knee some, he nearly landed on his hind end the one time he tried to dismount to the right, his left leg giving out. So, it was right side to mount and left side to dismount. If anyone noticed his strange consistent practice, they never mentioned it.

"Morning' Maria," he greeted the Mexican woman in charge of the fort's kitchen with his slow drawl. "Usual spot?"

"Si," came her reply.

Grabbing a crate from the back of the wagon, he followed Snake into the pantry and set the crate on a shelf. Then he picked up two of the empty crates from their last trip before getting another full crate. A few more trips and the fort was resupplied with dried beef goods.

Sending Snake on to town, Ben met with the supply officer for payment.

"Heard there's been some trouble with rustlers down south of here," the officer said as he unlocked his desk drawer. "Seen anything out your way?"

"Nope. But I'll keep an eye out."

The officer handed over the contracted amount and asked when they might be bringing by some steers. Seems they were running low on the fresher variety of beef. After finalizing the arrangements, Ben headed to town.

Snake just finished unloading supplies for the two restaurants and pointed the wagon toward the hotel. A few minutes later, they had Juniper House restocked. Then they went on to Hardy's store, the general mercantile that also stocked various grocery items.

Just as dinner time rolled around, they arrived at Lancaster's Boardinghouse. Knowing the midday meal was a busy time for Betty, Ben suggested they eat dinner first.

As he entered the long dining hall, a swell of noisy chatter pierced his ears. Taking a seat at one of the three tables, he waited for Yu, the young Chinese woman who worked for Betty, to bring him coffee.

"Ah, Mis-tah Shep-ahd," she smiled, trying his name in her broken English. "Bet-tee be glad to see you."

"Thank you, Yu." He smiled in return.

"I go get ha."

A few minutes later, Betty ambled over with two heaping plates of food. Biscuits with chipped beef and gravy. His stomach growled as she set the plates before him and Snake.

"Snake," she greeted. Then reaching out for Ben's hand she gave a squeeze and a very warm smile. "Ben."

"Betty." He smiled back, surprised at her intimate gesture.

"I hope you don't have to hurry back to the ranch," she said, chocolate brown eyes pleading. "I'd very much like a chance to visit."

"You're our last stop for the day. Suppose we can stay for a bit," he replied with a wink.

Pink tickled her cheeks. "Good. Cause I want to hear everything about baby James."

Clutching a hand to his chest, he said, "And here I thought ya were beginning to like me. Now I find I'm just a messenger bringing news of yer adopted grandson."

"Yes, well, anyone bringing me news of baby James might get a treat—in the form of blackberry pie. So, I'm sure it will be worth it."

"Mmm. I can taste it already."

Waving her hand in the air, she turned to serve her other customers.

"I think she's sweet on you," Snake said between large bites of biscuits and gravy.

Shifting uncomfortably in his seat, Ben stuffed a biscuit in his mouth. It was one thing for him and Betty to tease each other. He just didn't like anyone else jumping to conclusions.

Of course he liked Betty. Everyone did. She liked him—well, she liked everyone. That didn't mean she was sweet on him like Snake suggested.

Quit lyin'. Ya know she don't squeeze just any body's hand when she serves 'em dinner.

Ben shoved more food in his mouth to stifle a sigh. Maybe he was lonelier than he wanted to admit. Twenty-five years was a long time.

Living with a bunch of sixteen- to twenty-year-olds was, well, getting old. Most of them horsed around all the time. They needed steady guidance. Half of Will's men were green, though they didn't see themselves that way. Two or three years hardly counted as experience. They still had a lot of learning to do about ranching and about life.

While his evenings weren't quiet—there was always a few of the men in a tizzy over one thing or another—he longed for the quiet. He was tired of acting as a father to the boys. Tired of breaking up fights. Tired of reminding them to bathe every now and then. He wished he could have his own place. But then that might be a bit quieter than he could handle. Maybe it would be better if he had someone to share it with.

Naw. That would require opening parts of himself that were better off tucked away.

Why couldn't he just be content with life as it always was? Just keep plugging on one day at a time.

As the dining hall crowd started to thin out, Snake rose. "Think I'll catch me a game or two of cards."

"Meet ya over at Hardy's store in 'bout an hour. He should have our supplies ready by then. We'll load up and be home just in time for supper."

"Sounds good," Snake agreed, leaving Ben as the lone diner in the room.

Betty appeared in the doorway of the kitchen with two plates in hand. One had a piece of pie on it. The other looked to be her meal. As she slid the pie in front of him, warmth flooded his body. She had a way of disarming all his defenses without even trying.

"Now," she said taking a seat directly across from him, "tell me all about baby James."

He allowed the brief stab of pain in his heart, over the loss of his own Elijah, before he recovered and began regaling her with the latest tales of baby James.

CHAPTER 10

Betty listened intently as Ben began describing her grandson's latest mannerisms and noises, despite having caught his brief frown. No, frown wasn't the right word for it. Seemed like Benjamin Shepherd might be hiding some pain. Well, eventually she would get to the bottom of that. Just not today.

As she finished her last bite of food, she said, "Thank you, Ben. I can't tell you how much I appreciate hearing what little James is up to. I so miss being around my grandchildren."

"How many do you have?"

"Oh, let's see. Catherine, my oldest girl, has two boys and one girl. Nancy has three girls and one boy. And Frank, I think his wife just delivered their third boy." An unexpected moment of sadness brought tears to the corners of her eyes.

Ben reached for her hand and gave it a squeeze. "Must be hard being away from 'em."

Allowing a half-smile to grace her lips, she retrieved her handkerchief from her shirt sleeve. Seems she would cry at the drop of a pin these days. "It is hard. They are all back in Missouri. I had no idea I would miss them all so much."

Pushing away his empty plate, he asked with a wink, "Not that I'm complaining for one minute, but how come ya moved west?"

Betty was surprised she never mentioned it before now. They had talked often over the last year and somehow her reasons for moving must have never come up.

"When Paul talked about moving to the Arizona Territory in search of gold, I tried to talk him out of it. Seems the idea only took deeper root the more I argued against it.

"He's such a good son and has done more than he had to—keeping the farm going after Henry died. He sacrificed so much for me and his sisters and brother. I just couldn't stand being at odds with him on this issue. So I took it to the Lord.

"At first, I just prayed that He would change Paul's mind and make him happy with his life in Missouri. I even tried to take things into my own hands by pushing a young lady or two his way.

"Nothing changed his mind. In fact, he started talking about how I should come with him. I thought he was crazy. I mean whatever would I do with myself in the wilderness? He just looked at me with those blue eyes, so much like Henry's, and he smiled. He said, 'Start a boardinghouse.'"

Ben's smile turned into a deep chuckle. "So that's what ya did."

"Yes. Though it wasn't as easy as all that. I fought for a while. I asked the Lord why he would want me to move west. He told me that I had more children to care for. I never did understand what He meant—until Hannah's first husband died. Then I realized Hannah was one of my children. 'Course she wasn't by birth. But she was one of my spiritual children. And I believe the Lord wanted me to be here for her.

"Then I met Will. And I thought, 'Here's a nice cowboy, maybe a bit lonely. I bet he could use a spiritual mama too.' So, I decided he must be one of those children the Lord had in mind for me to care for.

"And then Julia came. I think she needed a mama the most. Then there's Thomas."

She paused, as it dawned on her he should have been back already from his last run. She made a mental note to talk to Paul later.

"He's hurting over his brother's death. Guess maybe Paul has been better for him than I have."

Ben nodded his head. "Ya been good for all of them—including Thomas."

Though his words were sincere, Betty sensed he was struggling with something. He was too old for her to be his spiritual mother. Perhaps in his case the Lord was just calling her to be his friend.

"Anyway. So here I am. Some of it was for Paul, too. He's always been there for me. I thought it was time for me to sacrifice something for him."

"Surely he didn't ask ya to leave yer children and grandchildren?"

"No. He didn't. But the Lord did. I suppose it was for the best. Seems Catherine's husband was concerned they would have to take me in when Paul left. He's a nice boy, but he felt I would interfere too much with how he wanted to raise his children. He was probably right. I wouldn't have been happy with his controlling discipline. Without love, his form of punishment seemed too harsh to me."

The silence stretched for a minute before a smile stretched across Ben's bearded face. "Yer quite a woman, Betty Lancaster."

Heat graced her cheeks. "Now, I worry about Paul. I just want to see him settle down. Find a good woman and enjoy some happiness for a change."

Taking her hand, he gave a gentle squeeze. "I'm sure it will happen in time."

The clock on the wall chimed twice, riveting Ben's gaze.

He stood to his feet. "I best get on outta here. Should've already met Snake at Hardy's and been halfway home."

Reaching out to stop him, Betty said, "I hope you'll at least bring in my beef before you go."

Red flushed his cheeks above his brown and gray beard.

"Sorry. I'll get the crates now."

Turning on his heel, he rushed out the front door. Within seconds he had two crates of Colter beef stacked one on top of the other in his arms.

"Don't hurt yourself." She mothered him, concerned he was carrying too much.

As she hurried to unload the crates, he said, "I almost forgot to tell ya. Hannah sends her love. She told me to let ya know they're planning on coming in for church on Sunday. Said James is old enough that it'll be okay."

Taking the last item from the crate, she smiled at him, her joy overflowing. "Oh, tell her to stay for dinner with us after. I so want to catch up with her."

Ben nodded. Then touching his fingers to the edge of his hat, he said, "Ma'am."

"Benjamin," she called after him. "Shall we set a place for you at Sunday dinner, too?"

She didn't miss the slight fear in his eyes before his face fell into a shadow.

"Ah... sure... I'd like that." He recovered before jumping up into the wagon, leaving his horse tied in front of the dining hall for now.

Betty waved after him as he maneuvered the wagon down the street in front of Hardy's store. An annoyed Snake paced back and forth on the boardwalk. Hopefully, Abraham Conrad had their order ready so Ben and Snake could load it and head home.

Turning back into the dining hall, she headed into the kitchen. Looked like Liang and Yu already took care of all the dinner dishes. So, Betty stepped out the back door from the kitchen into the grassy area where the laundry hung drying in the sun. She touched the edge of a sheet. It felt almost dry.

Returning to the kitchen, she set several irons on the stovetop to heat. Grinding some coffee, she dumped the grounds into the coffee pot and filled it with water. Then she propped open the back door with a large rock.

The big puffy white clouds in the sky made the August afternoon warmer than she liked. Though it didn't look like rain was coming, the humidity was up judging by the way her shirt clung to her back. Ironing those sheets would be quite a chore this afternoon.

Once the coffee finished brewing, she poured herself a cup and took a seat at the small table in the kitchen, reflecting on her afternoon with Ben Shepherd.

As far as she knew, he'd never been married, though she admitted to never asking the question. Something in the way he carried himself made her think that. And something in his expression when he was talking about James contradicted it. That look. It was almost as if he knew the pain of losing a child.

Draining the last of her coffee, Betty stood and retrieved the first of several sheets from the line. Laying it out on the table, she grabbed an iron. As she pushed the heavy metal across the fabric, she hummed one of her favorite hymns, watching the wrinkles in the fabric smooth.

Lord, I don't know what that man is carrying around in his heart. But he looks sad to me. I ask that you push into his heart and heal his brokenness. If you have a mind to use me in the process, so be it. Thank you for your grace and mercy.

Her prayers moved on from Ben Shepherd to her son Paul. Some time ago, perhaps after Henry passed, she took the verse literally when it said to turn her worries into petitions. As she ironed these sheets, or made the beds in the bunkhouses, or prepared supper, her conversation with the Lord continued.

She asked Him to bring Paul a woman; a wife meant just for him. She had been asking for years—he was thirty-four now, but she would keep on asking. When the good Lord decides to answer, she would pray for her son's wife by name, just as she did for Catherine, Nancy, and Frank.

Sweet Hannah Colter came to her mind. So, she asked the Lord for his protection over Hannah and her family. She asked Him to keep the union between Hannah and Will strong, helping them overcome any obstacles in their way.

Then her prayers turned toward Julia Colter and Adam Larson. Such a sweet couple. They were so in love, but Julia still was recovering from the painful events that led her here. Betty prayed that the Lord would continue his healing in the young woman's heart and that He would direct her and Adam when they should marry.

So caught up in her prayers, Betty failed to hear Paul enter the kitchen. She was startled when he spoke.

"Need some help, Ma?"

"Back already?"

"I saw you rubbing your hand this morning. Figured you could use some help."

She tried to hide it from him. But her hand had been rather stiff lately. She found the best way to get in motion was to rub it for a few minutes before starting breakfast.

Taking the last of the ironed sheets, she handed the stack to Paul. As they walked towards the Mother Lode, one of the bunkhouses, she asked, "How was the mining today?"

Balancing the stack of sheets in one brawny arm, he held the door open with the other. "Not much from panning. I think I'm going to have to build some sifters and start working the ground."

Pulling the first sheet from the stack, she shook it out and made the lowest bed on the bunk while Paul continued.

"Have you heard anything from Thomas?"

"No. He should have been back by now."

"Maybe he was delayed leaving out of Wickenburg."

"Hmm. I'll make up his bunk anyway—in case he gets in later this evening."

"Heard Ben was in town today. How was your visit?"

Thankfully, her head ducked under the bunk as she reached across to tuck in the sheet. Her son would not be able to see the pink on her cheeks.

"What makes you think we had a visit?"

"Ma-aa," he said stretching the word for two or three syllables. "Everyone sees how you two look at each other. Neither one of you is fooling anyone. 'Cept maybe yourselves."

As she finished making the lower bunk she stretched to her full height rubbing her low back. "It was fine."

"Just fine?"

"Well, he might come to church on Sunday with Hannah

and Will."

Round blue eyes stared at her in surprise. "Really?"

"Mm, hmm."

Taking the next sheet in the stack, she made up the next bunk.

"Guess I didn't figure him for the church going type."

"Well, maybe you figured him wrong," she shot back, a little too quickly. Though Betty admitted she often wondered where Ben Shepherd's heart lay. She was just too scared to ask if she was wrong.

When she rubbed her back a second time, Paul took the next sheet from her hand. "I'll finish this. Why don't you go start supper?"

"I can do it," she argued, though she was glad to let him see to the chore. "You shouldn't have to do women's work."

"And you should never have had to do men's work. But you did anyway. Blame yourself, Ma. You raised a thoughtful son." He shot her a big grin before shooing her from the bunkhouse.

"Yes, I did," she said softly, shooting praise from her heart to heaven for her son.

CHAPTER II

Caroline startled at the feel of a body next to her. Her eyes flew open. A hand clamped down over her mouth. She sucked in a sharp breath through her nose. Fear latched onto her heart.

"Shh."

Thomas's breath warmed her ear. Her panic doubled as his hand remained tightly over her mouth. She felt him press up behind her as she lay on the ground. The saddles separating them last night were gone. His arms were strong and his grip firm. Any previous trust she had in him dimmed as her mind raced with the possibilities of what was to come next.

He whispered, "Look towards the western horizon."

Slowly she craned her head. The sky behind her barely lit with early dawn light. On the western horizon, dust kicked up. Cattle. A lot of cattle.

"Rustlers."

Confused, she waited for Thomas to continue, his hand still firmly covering her lips. The smell of dust and horse engrained on his hand filled her lungs with each breath.

"If it's who I think it is, we need to take cover. These are dangerous men—not the kind we want to meet so far from help."

Her eyes widened in terror. She nodded her head to show her willingness to do whatever he asked.

"There's a small cluster of trees to the northeast of us. We must move quickly, but very quietly."

She nodded again.

"I have the horses saddled, but I think it would be safer to walk them. If I remove my hand, do I have your promise that you won't utter a word?"

Bobbing her head up and down, she waited for him to release her.

"Follow me."

His arms loosened their hold. Then he jumped to his feet noiselessly with such grace that made her wonder if he often found himself in dangerous situations. He held out his hand to help her up before grabbing the blanket from her. He motioned for her to carry it.

Handing the reins to her, he took his rifle from its sheath. Then he started to lead his horse towards the trees. She obediently followed behind, heart thundering in her chest. Sweat beaded on her forehead and palms. Her breath came in short shallow bursts. Why, oh why had she not listened to Millie?

A few times he pointed towards the ground, helping her navigate a small obstacle or two. The distance to the trees seemed to take hours to reach. It could not have been more than ten minutes.

Once they arrived, Thomas leaned his rifle up against a tree. He took the two horses and tied them where they would be hidden from the rustlers' view. Then he motioned for her to come to the tree he stood behind. She did.

He pulled her to him and her heart pounded out a furious beat. She stared at his lips as he lowered his head. At the last second he steered his lips towards her ear, dashing her hopes of a repeat of last night's kiss.

"Stay here."

Then he turned away. She grabbed his arm.

"Where are you going?"

He quickly pressed a finger to his lips, requesting silence. He pointed towards a tree near the edge of the open plains. Then he walked to it with his rifle in hand. Once he arrived at the tree, he crouched down, barely visible from her vantage point.

She let out a shaky breath and sunk to the ground behind the cover of the tree.

The sun moved higher, casting a glow on the tall grass covering the valley floor. The mountains to the north glowed with touches of gold where the sun teased the highest points. Deep purple blue shadows filled the crevices. To the west, the dust of the stolen cattle appeared to move farther away.

Caroline's breathing evened out as more time passed. She waited, wondering how long before they would press on.

Warmth dusted her cheeks as she remembered his kiss from last night. The softness of his lips against hers. The way he craved her closeness and drank in her response. A new awakening unfolded in her heart like the blooming petals of a rose. She could never kiss a man now without comparing it to Thomas's fiery kiss.

Once they arrived in Prescott, would she see him again? Should she? She knew so very little about him. Where had he come from? His accent sounded like he was from the North, but it was nothing so obvious like the man she once met from Boston. Thomas's speech seemed somewhat refined—like he was educated and intelligent. He was completely calm in the face of danger. His eyes had taken on coolness. His posture projected confidence as he led her to their present hiding spot.

For some reason beyond her understanding, she felt drawn to him. She hoped she would see more of him once they arrived in Prescott.

A hand touched her shoulder. She shrieked, clutching a hand to her chest. As she jumped to her feet, she realized Thomas was back. She hadn't heard him.

"I think it's safe to move on," he said, slinging his rifle over his shoulder. "There's only one station left between here and Prescott. At the base of the mountain. I'd like to get us back to Prescott tonight, but that'll depend on how much ground we cover this morning. Already lost more time than I would have liked."

Caroline swallowed, suddenly feeling very tired of this slow journey, longing for it to be over. He helped her onto her horse before mounting his own. Then he set the pace towards the mountains at a slow trot.

The sun heated her back to an uncomfortable degree. Sweat trickled down her spine. Her stinging cheeks rebelled against the sun's intensity. She reached for her canteen and took a few sips even though she longed to drink her fill. She had no way of knowing how long it would be before they found more water. She noted Thomas rarely sipped from his canteen and it concerned her.

As perspiration coated her forehead, she began to feel ill. At first dizzy, then nauseated. She needed to stop. Just for a few minutes until it passed.

She pushed her horse a little faster to catch up with him.

"Can we stop?"

"I'd rather not," he answered without looking at her.

"I'm stopping."

"Suit yourself." Thomas made no move to slow his horse.

Caroline let out a long sigh as she reined in her horse. As she slid off the animal, her foot caught in the stirrup. Instead of the graceful dismount she planned, she landed in a heap on her backside as the air left her lungs in a *whoosh*.

The commotion must have captured his attention, because he turned and rode back to where she sat on the ground. A frown crunched his eyebrows together. With an exasperated sigh, he dismounted his horse and walked towards her.

Hauling her to her feet, he said, "Be quick about your business." Then he turned his back.

The nausea intensified and she stood there with her hand pressed against her forehead. Closing her eyes, she waited for the dizziness to cease.

"What are you waiting for?"

Eyes still closed, she felt his hands grip her arms just as her knees began to buckle.

Instantly, his tone softened. "Caroline. Look at me."

She slowly opened her eyes, still not feeling herself. He raised her bandaged hand. The one she cut on the stagecoach hitch. The one she forgot to clean and re-bandage last night.

"What is this?"

"It's nothing."

Cocking his head to one side, he raised an eyebrow. "Nothing, huh?"

He began unwrapping the filthy bandage from her hand. She looked away. Afraid of what it might look like. As the bandage slipped from her hand, she heard his gasp. Tears stung her eyes.

"How… How bad is it?" she asked.

Clearing his throat, Thomas said, "It isn't great but I've seen far worse."

Glancing down, Caroline chanced looking at her hand. The skin around the deep cut was puffy, swollen, and very red. The festering pus she expected was not there. Blood oozed slowly from the wound. Not nearly as bad as she feared.

He kneeled and started to lift the hem of her skirt.

"What are you doing?" She swatted at him.

"Cutting a strip of fabric for a bandage."

"Unhand my dress!"

"Fine." He stood abruptly.

Grabbing the knife from his hand, she swirled her finger, motioning for him to turn around.

Kneeling, she cut another length from her shrinking petticoat. When she finished, she tapped him on the shoulder and handed his knife back. She started to wrap her bad hand.

"Wait."

Not thinking it was such a good idea to leave the wound exposed, she ignored his command. He whipped the bandage from her hand and stalked off toward his horse. After rooting around in his saddle bags for a minute, he returned with a small vile.

"Why do you have to be so difficult?" he grumbled as he took her hand. Squeezing a few drops of iodine from the vile onto the cut, he smiled at her sharp intake of breath. "Might sting a bit."

"A bit!"

Caroline narrowed her eyes. Swiping the bandage from him, she started to wrap the wound again.

"Here, let me do that."

"Not a chance." She smacked away his extended hand.

The frown returned to his face, before he stomped off to his horse. "Stubborn woman."

"I heard that."

When she finished wrapping her injured hand, she carefully mounted her horse—without his assistance this time. As pain seared through her hand, she realized it was a mistake. Biting her tongue, she successfully suppressed a whimper.

Not waiting for him, she kicked her horse into a trot.

———

Infuriating. No other word seemed to describe the way Miss Caroline Larson affected him. Thomas mounted his horse and took off after the annoying, stubborn woman.

This morning when he woke to the unmistakable sound of the rustlers, he almost forgot he had her to think about. He'd been in this sort of situation before. Many times during the war he woke to find his position compromised. Or the times he'd been followed as a dispatch rider. He always seemed to escape the most challenging of situations. But he'd never had to do it with a woman depending on him before.

It was a strange sensation when that realization hit him. His throat constricted. He feared what would have happened to her if they had been caught. The worst that he would have faced was death. She, on the other hand... He could only imagine what fate she would have suffered before death.

The thought stirred a new protectiveness in him. He felt the heavy burden of responsibility. He had to get her to Prescott unharmed. He had to reunite her with Adam. Any other outcome... Well, Adam would never forgive him.

He wasn't really equipped for this hero thing. He felt entirely inadequate. The moment he saw her stir this morning; he was afraid she would give away their position. The only thing he thought about was keeping her silent.

Until he laid down next to her and drew her into his arms. Then the only thing he could think about was how perfect she felt there. Well, that and what it might be like to kiss her again.

Perhaps confusing was another word he would add to the list that described Caroline. That's how he felt when he was around her.

Pushing thoughts of her aside for the moment, Thomas scanned the horizon. If he figured correctly, it was almost noon. The rustlers and the stop to change her bandages set them even further behind. There was no way they would reach the next station early enough to change out the horses and head into Prescott tonight. The best choice would be to stay put at the station. Spend the night. Then head out first thing in the morning.

So much for time off between runs. Tomorrow would be Wednesday. His last day off before he would have to head out on his next run to La Paz. He came to depend on those few days to rest up and recharge for the next grueling trip.

Not this time. He would be fortunate if he got Caroline settled safely before he had to leave again.

Lifting his felt hat from his head, he ran his fingers through his damp hair. Drew did that a lot, too. Only he tended to do it more out of nervousness than frustration like Thomas did. Setting his hat firmly back on his head, he let out a long sigh.

Two more hours passed before they arrived at Perry Quinn's station. Station was a bit of a glorified term for the place. Perry had a barn to stable several horses for the La Paz Express in addition to his own ranch horses. His small cabin sat only a few yards from his cowboys' bunkhouse. The place seemed deserted.

Thomas reined in his horse in front of the small cabin. He dismounted and tied his horse to the hitching post before helping Caroline down. Then he secured her horse.

Walking toward the cabin, he realized he barely knew Perry Quinn. Most of the time he stopped at this station only long enough to fill up his canteen and toss the mail bags onto a fresh mount. He didn't even know if there was a Mrs. Quinn or not.

Reaching his hand up, he rapped a hearty knock on the door.

When there was no answer, Thomas opened the door. He motioned Caroline inside.

"Wait here."

"Won't the owner be upset that we've entered his house un-invited?" she asked, her eyes rounded with concern.

He bit back a frustrated sigh. "You're in the West now. Men in these parts expect visitors to make themselves at home. That's how we all survive."

Her face revealed her hesitancy. He held a chair out for her, and she finally sat at the table.

"Perry Quinn runs this place. He and his men are decent. If you come across any of them before I do, just explain why we're here. I'll be back."

As he started to leave, her voice caught his attention again. "Where are you going?"

"To find Perry."

He pulled the door shut behind him, effectively ending the conversation. She seemed set on questioning everything he did. It was getting old.

Untying his horse, he mounted it and rode out toward a herd of grazing cattle. He found Perry rather quickly.

"Was concerned when you didn't show up yesterday," Perry said. "Especially since the stage hasn't shown up yet."

"The stage won't be coming. The lone survivor is with me."

"Is he okay?"

"She's fine."

Perry's eyes rounded. "You sure *she* ain't been… hurt?"

"Positive. She's been with me for the last two days. She's at your cabin now. Name is Caroline Larson."

Yanking back on his horse's reins, Perry turned to look him in the eye. "Larson. She related to—"

"Adam Larson. Yes. He's her brother."

"Best go get her settled then."

CHAPTER 12

Caroline looked around the small cabin. A bed stood against the wall in the far corner opposite the table. A trunk rested at the foot of the bed. A dresser lined the wall next to the bed. A comfy chair watched the empty fireplace. The cabin had a few feminine touches. Curtains. Neatly organized pantry shelves. A few pretty things scattered on various surfaces. She wondered where Mrs. Quinn might be. She certainly made the small space feel cozy.

A brief knock sounded before a man entered the cabin, followed by Thomas. The man stopped abruptly.

"You forgot to mention she was young. And lovely."

Thomas appeared suddenly nervous, turning his hat around in his hands. "Ah… Perry Quinn, meet Miss Caroline Larson."

"A pleasure," Perry said, reaching to take her hand. He placed a kiss on top.

The way Thomas described him, she expected Perry to be older—much older. Why couldn't he be more than twenty-five years old! So tall, too. A good foot taller than Thomas and her. Something about him reminded her of Will Colter. Maybe it was his height.

"Mr. Quinn." She smiled.

"None of that now. Perry will be just fine."

"Perry then. Is your wife around? I would very much like to meet her."

Sadness settled around his eyes before he quickly looked

away. "She… um… She passed almost a year ago."

Caroline bit the inside of her cheek, annoyed that her mouth got her in trouble again. "I'm sorry for your loss."

Perry cleared his throat and changed the subject. "You look like you might enjoy a chance to freshen up."

He walked towards the trunk. "My wife's things," he said, opening the lid. "Please have a look and see if you might be able to use them."

"Oh, I couldn't."

Thomas shifted uncomfortably. "Perry, that's a very gracious offer. I'm sure Caroline appreciates it, especially since most of her things were lost in the robbery."

Perry's eyebrows shot up, hiding under the shadow of his hat. He recovered from his surprise quickly and turned to her. "Well, in that case, I'd be very honored if you helped yourself to everything in the trunk. I'm sure a fresh change of clothes would be welcomed."

"Are you certain?" Caroline hesitated, feeling rather uncomfortable taking his wife's things.

"No sense in them just sitting here when you could use 'em."

"Thank you."

A curt nod answered. "I'll fetch you some water to freshen up."

In a minute, he was back with a pail of water. He showed her where he kept some soap. Then he escorted Thomas from the cabin.

"Tell me exactly what happened with that stage." Caroline heard Perry's muffled voice as the door latched shut. She couldn't hear Thomas's response.

Carefully, she pulled each of the dresses and undergarments from the trunk at her feet, still feeling rather awkward about taking these things. She held the first dress up to her body, holding the edges by her side. Mrs. Quinn's waist and bust must have been a bit fuller than hers. With a makeshift belt the dress should suffice until she found time to take it in later.

The next items were a few undergarments. Clearly not the

number she was wearing. Perhaps she would feel less warm on the ride to Prescott with fewer layers.

She picked up an apron and almost tossed it aside. Looking at the long ties, she decided she could cut them from the apron to use as a cinch around her waist. Digging around in the trunk she found a pair of scissors and set about the task.

Once she had the clothing laid out, she checked the latch on the door. For her own peace of mind, she slid a chair in front of the door. At least that way if anyone attempted to enter, she would have some warning. Then she stripped down.

Caroline would have preferred a nice long bath with hot water rather than a quick scrub from a pail. This was better than nothing.

As soon as she finished washing up, she donned one of Mrs. Quinn's undergarments. Thankfully it had long ties, and she was able to tighten it enough so it would stay in place. Then she donned the simple gray calico dress. As she suspected, the bust and waist were somewhat roomier than what she needed. She took the old apron tie and knotted it around her waist. That took care of the waist. The bust still felt too loose.

Going back to the trunk, she discovered a broach. She gathered some of the excess fabric on the neckline and folded it over. Then she secured it into place with the broach. Pleased with the results, she picked up her yellow-now-dirt-brown dress and petticoats. She cut off a few strips the petticoats for bandages. Turning the dress over in her hands, she didn't think it was salvageable. But she would try once she got to Prescott.

Picking up one other dress from Mrs. Quinn's things, she stuffed it in a sack with her ruined yellow dress. She put the remaining items back in the trunk and closed the lid. She would tie the sack to the back of her horse tomorrow because it now contained all the clothing she owned.

Glancing around the room, she tidied the place before removing the chair from in front of the door. She lifted the bucket of filthy water and carried it outside, dumping it on what appeared to be a garden. Then she set the bucket back inside.

She took the brush she found in the trunk and began the long process of trying to brush out the tangles from her hair. She wished she could have washed the dust and grime from it. At least the brush helped smooth it out enough so that she could fashion it into a chignon.

Once she felt normal again, she tried to determine what to do with herself. When would the men return? Perhaps not until supper time, which was a good hour or two away.

Walking back outside, she stood in the shade of the porch. She heard the men's voices in the barn. They discussed something for another minute or two before the voices quieted. Caroline headed in that direction.

Quietly, she slipped into the barn and listened for any hint of where they might be. A soft splash sounded further back. She followed the noise. When she was close enough to see, she let out a little gasp.

Thomas stood, with his back turned, shirt off. Even the top of his long johns hung over the waist of his pants. His back was marked with a few round dents of marred flesh. Scars from the war? Other than that, his back looked perfect to her. Muscled. Strong. She stared at him, unable to move her gaze.

When he started to turn, she jolted from her trance. He saw her and quickly grabbed his shirt, clutching it close to cover part of his chest. A wry smile played at the corner of his lips. She hadn't noticed how blue his eyes looked before—like little drops of the deep Arizona sky captured in tiny orbs—now glistening with a hint of laughter.

"What are you doing here?" he asked, his voice very controlled and just above a whisper.

"I... um..."

What was she doing there again?

He circled his finger using the same gesture she used earlier in the day, requesting that she turn around. Heat singed her cheeks, and she quickly turned her back to him.

"I wasn't sure if you were planning to press on to Prescott tonight," she said, her voice quivering from her nerves.

The sound of water splashing was the only noise that answered. She waited.

"You can turn around now," he said.

She did. His sandy hair formed long wet clumps across his forehead. He ran his hands through his wet hair several times before leaving it. His shirt covered his chest now, though the memory of his back would stay with her for some time.

Feeling self-conscious, she crossed her arms over her chest.

His gaze traveled the length of her body, resting on her green eyes. What seemed like minutes passed. Caroline's patience grew thin.

"What are your plans?"

A strange expression crossed his features before disappearing. He hesitated.

"It's too late to try to head up the mountain. We would lose daylight before making it up. We won't reach Prescott tonight no matter how hard we try."

"Don't you usually ride the rest of the way in one afternoon?" She challenged him.

He narrowed his eyes slightly. "Yes. But that's by myself on a trail I know well. You'll be much too slow."

"You don't know that."

"And you don't know what we'll find on that trail. It's too risky."

She expelled a long, drawn-out sigh, ending with her shoulders slumping. She was tired. She just wanted to be there already, safe with her brother and friends.

"Look," he started as he came closer. He reached out and placed his hand on her shoulder. Warmth spread from his touch.

"I promise I'll get you there tomorrow before night fall. Probably even in time for supper. Maybe even by noon. It's just not safe to head up that mountain at night. I would only attempt it if our lives were in danger."

Caroline blinked back the tears. Frustration chaffed on her nerves. She should have listened to Millie.

"I'll talk to Perry, and we'll work out arrangements to stay here tonight. No more surprise wake up calls, okay."

Swallowing back the lump in her throat, she nodded. He squeezed her shoulder then removed his hand.

"Good."

He stood in front of her, making no move to leave. When she looked up into those gorgeous blue eyes, her breath stopped. His gaze darted across the features of her face, leaving a burning trail behind. He lifted his hand and almost touched her cheek before he dropped it suddenly to his side.

Stepping back, he said, "You look nice."

Caroline couldn't help the laugh that fell from her lips. "Ha! You get kicked in the head or something?" She couldn't imagine anyone looking frumpier than she did now in clothes that were too big for her.

A grin lit his face. "If you feel up to it, you might head on up to the house and see about fixing up some grub. Perry mentioned the boys usually take turns. I'm sure you can cook, and it might be a nice way to thank him for your new outfit."

I'm sure you can cook. The voice in her head was mocking. Of course she could cook. Narrowing her eyes at him, she stared him down. He held her gaze.

"Humph." She turned on her heel and marched out of the barn back up to the house. She'd show that Thomas just how good of a cook she was.

———

Thomas breathed a huge sigh of relief when Caroline stormed off. He could hardly stand to be alone with her without his blood pumping fiercely in his chest. She did look lovely in that gray dress, even if it swam on her. The gray caused the green in her eyes to stand out. And it drove him insane.

Grabbing the pail of water he used to clean up, he headed outside of the barn to dump it. Perry had ridden back to his cattle after securing Thomas's promise that they wouldn't try to press on this afternoon. He wanted to and Perry talked him out of it, using the same arguments he just parroted back to Caroline.

The only reason he considered trying to make it up that mountain was because he wanted a day to rest before heading back out again. He was tired. Weary. He'd thought that the slower pace would be less stressful for him, but watching out for Caroline seemed the opposite. On the positive side, he hadn't had time to think about his life and the way he really messed it up.

Instead, every waking thought shifted to Caroline. Who was she? How was he going to get her to her new home safely?

He wondered if one of those men on the stage was her escort. Strange to let a woman travel alone with a man. He could attest how difficult that was.

Running his hands through his hair, Thomas moved to a spot in the sun, hoping his hair would dry faster. He had such thick hair. It was getting too long, brushing against his shirt collar which irritated him. He was going to get it cut in Prescott, but now he'd have to wait until he made it back to La Paz.

When the supper bell rang, he looked up. Caroline stood on ringing the thing. She looked like she belonged there. Then she waved at him before darting back inside. His pulse jolted.

Perry's men rode in with the cattle, rounding them into the corral. His herd was much smaller than Will Colter's. Looked like only a few hundred head and about three men besides Perry. As they cared for their horses, Thomas ambled up to the cabin.

"Smells good," he said as he opened the door. "Guess you do know how to cook."

Caroline spun around with her hand on her hip. "Of course I do. Grew up on a ranch feeding a bunch of hungry mouths. I'm the oldest girl so Mama enlisted my help early on."

He held up his hands in defense. "I was just teasing."

The words seemed to disarm her. "Oh. Have a seat."

He stood, not wanting to sit before she did. Wasn't that proper etiquette? Hanging back by the door he watched her place the large portions of food on the table.

Perry and his men entered. "Miss Larson, this is Hank, Jack, and George. Boys, this is Miss Larson."

Caroline's eyes grew wistful as the last man was introduced. Her voice came out soft as she said, "George is my papa's name."

"Pleased to meet you," she added in a more normal tone.

"Ma'am," they said in unison, each reaching for their hats.

Perry stood and held out a chair for Caroline. Thomas mentally kicked himself for not thinking of it as everyone else took their seats.

Stomach growling, Thomas reached for the dish of potatoes in front of him. When Perry suggested they pray, he swiftly brought his hand back to his lap. Heat rose to his cheeks.

Perry's prayer was short, yet something about it suggested he was very comfortable talking to God. Reminded him of Paul.

The sound of dishes being passed roused Thomas from his thoughts. He reached for the fried potatoes, this time dropping a spoonful of them onto his plate.

"Thank you for cooking for us, Caroline," Perry said, squeezing her hand. Thomas tensed at the gesture. "It's been a long time since we've had a meal like this."

Caroline glanced at Thomas before responding, "It's the least I could do to thank you for your generosity."

"What brings you to the Arizona Territory?" Perry asked.

"My best friend, Julia Colter, is here. And my brother Adam works at Colter Ranch. I miss them both. The three of us are close."

Thomas almost snorted. He figured she had no idea how close Adam and Julia were these days. There was talk of a wedding soon. Caroline probably didn't even know.

"Colter. Would that be Will Colter?"

At her nod, Perry continued, "Met him and Adam once a couple months back in Prescott. I was picking up a few more horses from them for the stage line. He's got a pretty big ranch up there from what I hear. More than a dozen men working for him."

"Makes our outfit look pretty small," Jack commented.

"Got to start somewhere," George countered.

The conversation continued. Thomas focused on his food

while he listened. When Perry asked about her journey so far, he started paying attention.

"I traveled to Wickenburg with my friend, Millie, and her father."

Thomas couldn't help himself. "And why didn't they escort you the rest of the way to Prescott?"

Her cheeks flamed and her gaze dropped to her food. She fidgeted with her fork for a second before answering. "Reverend Pritchett was busy preaching to the miners. I..." Her voice softened. "I was eager to see my brother. I figured I'd be safe on the stage. There were plenty of other passengers."

Silence settled over the room.

Tears pooled in the corners of her eyes and Thomas wished he could take his provocative question back. Her voice cracked when she said, "I didn't think... Those poor men."

She jumped up from the table and ran outside.

Perry scowled at him for a second. Then he stood and followed her.

"Nice going, Anderson," Hank spat out.

Thomas pushed his plate away, the food turning to rocks in his stomach. He excused himself from the table. As he stepped out onto the porch, he caught Perry's scowl over the top of Caroline's head. He held her tightly to his chest, rubbing his hand on her back in comforting circles. He whispered calming words to her as her body shook with sobs.

Thomas's anger burned.

He hurried off the porch. "I'll sleep in the barn," he shot over his shoulder.

Once in the barn, he paced back and forth, not sure why he suddenly felt jealous of Perry. Seeing her in his arms did something to him. He wanted to comfort her, like he had last night. Only it was his words that drove her into Perry's arms.

Looked like his record was intact. Score another mistake for Thomas. Maybe he just didn't have it within him to be the kind of man Drew was.

CHAPTER 13

"I'm sorry," Caroline said, pulling back from Perry's comfort-ing arms. She walked toward the porch rail turning her back on him. She dabbed her eyes with the sleeve of her dress.

"Millie was right. So is Thomas. I should have waited until the Pritchetts could bring me the rest of the way. Maybe those men wouldn't have died."

"That wasn't your fault." Perry's voice was soft as he moved to stand next to her.

"One of the men—I didn't know any of their names—he came to my defense when the robbers tried to tie me up. The leader shot him for it." The flood gates opened again, sending long rivers of tears down her face. She hugged her arms around her torso. Her voice sounded hoarse to her own ears. "He was helping *me*. If he hadn't—"

"He still would have ended up dead, but with less honor. You said they killed all the men anyway. That was clearly their inten-tion from the beginning."

Caroline pursed her lips. Perhaps he was right.

"I know it's hard, but you need to stop blaming yourself. Thank the Lord that he spared your life."

He did, didn't He? God spared her life. Why? Why *her* and not those men?

Swallowing back the flood of questions, she silently stared out towards the barn. The sun had already climbed down behind the mountain, leaving the bluish-purple shades of twilight behind. The scratch of wood chairs against the floor from inside the cabin signaled Perry's men were finished with their meal. Moments later, the three cowboys exited the cabin with hushed well wishes to her.

Rousing from her burdened thoughts, Caroline turned toward the cabin. "I suppose I should clean up in there."

Perry followed behind. "I can take care of it. Why don't you sit and relax?"

The last thing she wanted to do was sit idle. Her jumbled heart would take over and drive her insane reliving the last few days' events.

"Please, you've done so much. Let me help," she said as she started stacking the dishes in the wash basin.

"Very well then. You wash and I'll—"

Perry stopped abruptly when he turned to help clear the table. His glistening eyes settled on the broach at Caroline's neck. She subconsciously raised her fingers to touch the piece of jewelry.

"It was Lydia's mother's."

"Oh, I'm sorry. I didn't think." She started to unpin it, intending to return it to him.

"No, no. You can wear it. Borrow it for now."

Caroline weighed his words carefully. He obviously struggled with the offer. "I'll take good care of it and send it back with Thomas when he returns."

A brief frown flitted across Perry's eyes. "I'll be in Prescott in a month or so. I'll just pick it up from you then. If you would be agreeable to a visit from a friend?"

Her lips stretched into a soft smile. "I'd like that."

Clearing his throat, Perry said, "I'll go fetch some water for the dishes."

He hurriedly made his exit.

Sighing, she retrieved the rest of the dishes from the table. It would take a little while to heat some water when Perry returned.

Looking around the small room, she tried to imagine what

Lydia Quinn must have been like. It was a strange train of thought, but one that kept her mind from churning over her troubles. She walked closer to the dresser near the bed. No photographs. She wondered if Lydia was tall or short. Judging by the length of the dress Caroline wore, Lydia was even shorter than her. The broach—a family heirloom, much like the one Caroline just lost on the stage—must have been important to her. She saw that in the way Perry talked about it.

She should leave it here, where it belonged. There had to be some other temporary way to fix the looseness of the dress without taking the treasured jewelry from its home. Crossing her arms over her chest, she tapped a finger rapidly against her forehead. *Think, Caroline.*

The door creaked open, and Perry filled the reservoir on the stove to heat the water.

"I was thinking," he said, "that I'll sleep out in the bunkhouse. I've an extra bunk there. Then you would have the privacy of the cabin."

Caroline turned to face him. Did this man have no end to his compassion?

"Thank you."

Once the water heated, they completed the dishes with casual chit-chat about his ranch. Then Perry excused himself.

Lifting the lid of the trunk, Caroline found a night dress, something she forgot to pull out earlier, and readied for bed. After she turned the oil lamp down, she stared at the ceiling of the unfamiliar room. Her mind taunted her.

Images of the men on the stagecoach danced before her eyes. The friendly smiles of some when she first boarded. The smirk on the scarred man's face when she bumped into him because of the jostling of the stagecoach. What color were his eyes? The image of him being shot, his body slumping to the ground. The sounds of more shots. The pile of dead bodies they left behind.

The dark eyes of the man who ordered their deaths.

Lord, forgive us for not caring for those men. Please let me forget.

———

Thomas woke with a start. He took a deep breath to calm his pounding heart so he could listen for what woke him. Hearing nothing, he moved from the hay he slept on in the stable, trying to make as little noise as possible. He grabbed his pistol from his gun belt that he left slung over a rail in the stable.

He walked to the barn door and slowly nudged it open. He scanned the area near the cabin, but he saw nothing. After looking towards the bunkhouse, he waited several more minutes.

As a dispatch rider in the war, his premonitions had saved his life many times. Just because he could not see the trouble with his eyes, he believed there was someone out there.

Then, the glint of a gun reflecting the moonlight caught his eye. A figure stood on the porch of the cabin, trying to get the door open.

Without thinking twice, Thomas fired his pistol into the air. Within seconds the figure scurried off the front porch and rounded the corner of the cabin away from him. Thomas cautiously moved to where he last saw the man.

"Thomas?" Caroline's frightened voice came from inside the cabin.

He didn't answer, not wanting to give away his position. He rounded the side of the cabin just in time to see the figure jump on his horse and gallop away.

The sound of a gun cocking behind him brought him up short.

"Turn around."

"It's me, Thomas."

Perry let out a sigh of relief. "What's going on?"

"Saw someone trying to get in the house. But he rode off."

"Boys," Perry said, "look around the property. See if you find anyone else. Thomas, you go make sure Caroline is alright."

Thomas knocked on the door. No answer.

"Caroline, it's me. Thomas."

The scraping of a chair against the wooden floor answered.

Then the door flew open.

"Are you okay?" he asked.

"I'm fine," she answered, tentatively.

Her long golden locks traveled down her back to her waist. She had a blanket wrapped tightly around her, all the way to her chin. Again, Thomas felt the strong compulsion to kiss her. He moved forward to pull her into his arms.

"Are you alright?" Perry asked as he brushed past Thomas.

Caroline threw herself into Perry's arms and rested her head against his chest for the second time today. Thomas fisted his hand at his side, annoyed that Perry pushed him aside so quickly. He wanted to be the one to comfort her.

"We heard someone sneaking around the house," Perry said. Thomas bit back a sharp retort. "The boys said he's gone now. Do you want me to stay close?"

"Please."

"Stay here. I'll go get a blanket and rest on the porch. That way if he returns, he'll have to go through me first."

"Thank you, Perry."

Thomas grunted before heading back to the barn.

Thank you, Perry. Caroline's sweet voice echoed again in his ears as the image of her golden hair cascading down her back played with his mind. He couldn't believe Perry took credit for keeping her safe. If Thomas had not warned them, they probably would have woken to an empty cabin in the morning, wondering what happened to Caroline.

As he lay back down in the hay, he tried to get his jealousy under control. He should be on that porch protecting her, not Perry. He should have gotten the praise for keeping her safe.

———

The next morning, Thomas woke with the sound of the cock crowing. Standing he brushed loose bits of hay from his pants. He hadn't slept well after the late-night interruption. And he hadn't slept well for days. It was wearing thin. He was exhausted and more than ready to be back in Prescott.

Plopping his felt hat on top of his head, he walked towards the cabin. The smell of bacon frying drew him forward at a quicker pace. Laughter from inside the cabin had the opposite effect.

Slowly he opened the door. Caroline laughed, wiping away tears from the corners of her eyes. Perry stood nearby with a broad grin on his face. Thomas bit back a sardonic comment. He didn't like what he saw.

"Oh, Thomas," Perry greeted once he realized he had company. "What time were you thinking of heading out?"

Caroline turned back towards the stove without greeting. She pushed around food in the skillet on top of the small iron stove.

"Soon as breakfast is done, I'd like to get Caroline to town as soon as possible."

She snorted. "I'll bet."

"You could always travel on without her. She's welcome to stay here until we make the trip in or until her kin could come escort her."

Caroline smiled at Perry's suggestion and Thomas's stomach rolled over. There was no way he was going to leave her here with four young unmarried men. He was about to say so when she spoke.

"Perry, that's a very kind offer. And I appreciate it."

"But?"

"But I'm eager to go home."

Perry glanced away, his smile fading. "I understand. I sure have enjoyed having you here."

"Please, visit when you're in town."

He took Caroline's hand and gave it a squeeze. "I look forward to it."

Thomas clenched his teeth together so tightly he thought his jaw might pop. No wonder he fell for her. She played him just like she was playing Perry now. Acting all sweet and charming and helpless.

It stung.

At least he'd realized what she was really like before too much damage was done.

The cowboys joined them for breakfast. Thomas kept to himself, concentrating on eating instead of the way Caroline and Perry seemed to be getting along so well. When the meal finished and Perry started helping her with her bandage, Thomas excused himself under the guise of saddling their horses.

Grunting, he hefted the first saddle onto the horse he rode yesterday. What was wrong with him? Why did it bother him so much that she smiled and spoke softly with Perry? He had no claim on her. His chest had just been the lucky target of her good aim with her Bible. He just happened to come along to rescue her.

Cinching the straps tight on the saddle, he fought against his frustration. The way Perry was acting wasn't much better. The man had a wife. Granted, she was six feet under and more than a year ago. But still. He was acting like a schoolboy all sucked into Caroline's dangerous web. He ought to know better.

And suggesting she stay there! Where did he get off with such a suggestion? Why give Perry a few more days with her and she'd probably willingly ride into Wickenburg to fetch that preacher so she could get hitched.

With both horses saddled, canteens filled, and saddle bags packed, Thomas led the horses to the cabin.

"Be safe," Perry said to Caroline as he gave her a kiss on the forehead.

"She will be," Thomas grunted.

Caroline scowled at him but took her time saying goodbye to Perry. It galled him.

"Let's go."

Another scowl shot over her shoulder in his direction before Perry helped her mount. "Thank you again, Perry, for your generosity."

Thomas started his horse off towards the mountain without a word. The soft trot of her horse behind him confirmed she was following.

"What's gotten into you?" she challenged him once they were out of earshot of Perry Quinn's ranch.

"Me? I could ask you the same question."

"What are you talking about?"

"Really, Caroline? You don't think I'm that kind of a fool, do you?"

She pulled her horse in front of him and stopped, causing his horse to come to a standstill. One hand landed on her hip as her eyebrows formed a sharp V.

"What is wrong with you?"

Thomas swallowed. Was she oblivious to how she was acting with Perry?

"Threw yourself at him enough, didn't you? No wonder he invited you to stay. He thought you might be interested him."

"I did not throw myself at him. I was just being friendly."

"Ha! About as friendly as you were when you kissed me, you hussy!"

The words were out, hanging like thick black smoke between them, choking out reason and respect.

"How dare you! I think your memory fails you. You kissed me!"

For some ridiculous foolish reason, he wanted to do so again. Now. Turn her fire of anger into the fire of desire. For him.

Instead, he stayed firmly seated on his horse.

Her anger faded some. Then her face softened. Her voice sounded incredulous as she said, "You're jealous. You're jealous of the attention Perry showed me."

"Hardly," Thomas spit out the lie. He maneuvered his horse around hers then kicked it into a trot. Her laughter rung in his ears before the sound of a trotting horse followed behind him.

———

Unbelievable, Caroline thought. Thomas Anderson was jealous.

Oh. Her laughing died. That must mean he's interested in her. Why else would he be jealous?

A sound behind her caught her attention. She had already caught up to Thomas, so she twisted in her saddle to investigate what she heard. Off in the distance, a man was riding a black horse. Something about the rider seemed familiar to her, but she couldn't place it. The familiarity left a hush of fear settling around her, only she couldn't figure out why she was reacting that way.

Surely many riders traveled this trail between Wickenburg and Prescott. There didn't seem to be too many roads in the territory from what she witnessed so far. It would make sense that they would be somewhat well-traveled.

Yet, how come she'd not seen a soul in the first day and a half while she was stranded after the stage robbery. Now someone was behind them.

Her palms grew moist, and her heart plunged to the ground. Hadn't Thomas said he thought someone was following them?

Thomas turned in his saddle to look at her as they arrived at the base of the mountain. A frown formed between his brows as he leaned to see farther behind her.

"How long have we been followed?" he asked.

"I... I don't know."

"You should have told me."

Caroline shrugged, hoping he wouldn't pick a fight with her right now.

"The mountain trail is steep and very narrow at some points, though wagons do travel on it. I want you to ride in front. There's really only one way up, so I'm not worried about you losing the trail. Set whatever pace you and your horse are comfortable with. And be careful."

Caroline nodded and started up the sloped mountain side trail. At first the trail casually climbed, but before long they were in some steep switchbacks. She looked down at the side of the mountain and swallowed hard. They gained a great deal of elevation in the matter of minutes.

When the trail leveled out, she stopped for a moment to

steady her nerves. The spot was wide enough that Thomas came up next to her.

"Doing okay?"

"Yeah."

He turned and looked back down the trail. She followed his gaze. The rider was gaining on them, though not too quickly.

"Who is he?" she asked.

"Doesn't look familiar to me. But it's not unusual to see other riders on the trail."

When he turned to face her again, she caught his look of concern before he hid it. "Let's keep going."

She nudged her mare into motion again. The trail steepened suddenly after that point. Caroline had to lean forward to keep her balance at the odd upward slope. She thought it must be frightful in a wagon, if it was even possible.

After hours on the trail, the harsh angles softened and the trail appeared relatively flat again, though sloping slightly upward.

"We're almost there," Thomas announced.

Forgetting all her fears about the rider following them, Caroline smiled. Soon she would be reunited with her friend and her brother. Soon this journey would come to an end.

CHAPTER 14

Prescott

August 23, 1865

"Thomas is back," Paul announced as he scooped up another round of filled plates to serve their hungry diners.

"Praise you, Lord!" Betty breathed in relief.

She had been so worried about Thomas Anderson when he didn't return from his express run on Monday. She sent many prayers heavenward that he would be safe and that whatever caused his delay would be resolved quickly. She even asked the Lord not to take him yet. He wasn't ready—hadn't given his heart over—and she couldn't stand the thought of the nice young man spending eternity in hell.

As she bustled into the dining hall, she quickly spotted Thomas. Engulfing him in a huge embrace, she said, "So glad you're back. Been beating down heaven's gate for you."

She stepped back from the embrace and patted her hand on his scruffy cheek, like she would with her son. *Thank you, Lord.*

"You don't look worse for the wear," she said. "What kept you so long?"

A young blonde woman standing next to Thomas cleared her throat.

Thomas answered, "Betty, I'd like you to meet Miss Caroline Larson. Miss Larson is what has kept me so long."

She didn't miss his rogue grin, and she figured he was deliberately teasing her. Then the name registered. "Caroline Larson. Any relation to Adam?"

"He's my older brother."

Swallowing the girl in her arms, she said, "Welcome to Prescott, dear!"

As Caroline pulled back, she smiled brightly. "Glad to be here. Safely."

"Sit, sit. Paul will bring you some dinner."

Both Thomas and Caroline sat down at the closest table. My, what a cute couple they would make. *Stop it, Betty. No match making. You've got more important things to see to now.*

"Tell me what happened," she said as she took a seat.

"It was a normal run up until I got a few miles outside of Wickenburg. All a sudden Miss Larson throws the Good Book at me."

"You weren't going to stop," Caroline moaned.

"I was going to. Anyway, turns out Caroline was on the stage headed to Prescott when they were robbed. All the men were killed. She was the only survivor."

Betty's breath caught in her throat. "Poor dear. How long were you on your own?"

"Almost two days before Thomas came along."

Thomas related the story of the last few days in between bites of food, with a few interruptions from Caroline. Seemed like the two of them had become rather close in a short amount of time. At least that's the impression they left.

Jed and Hawk, two of the cowboys from Colter Ranch entered the dining hall, followed by a man dressed as a preacher.

"Betty," Jed started. "Do you know if Thomas is... Oh, you're here." He turned to Thomas. "This is Reverend Pritchett. We met him on the road back from Fort Whipple where we delivered a few head of cattle. He wants to know if you've seen a young woman on the trail."

Thomas grinned. "You mean her?"

"Reverend Pritchett," Caroline greeted, drawing the clergyman's attention.

"Oh, praise the Lord. You did arrive safely. I was so worried when I heard the stage was robbed."

Betty followed his gaze to Caroline's hand.

"You're injured. Goodness. We better get you to a doctor."

Betty chimed in. "Doc Armstrong's clinic is across the street."

Reverend Pritchett held out his hand for Caroline and then escorted her from the building.

"Do you think you could take Caroline back with you?" Thomas asked Jed.

"You want us to take a pretty girl back with us?" Hawk asked before Jed could answer. "Pretty sure we could figure somethin' out."

"Hawk will give up his horse. He could stand a good walk," Jed shot back, grinning from ear to ear.

"Or we could just hire a carriage. Make sure she's comfortable."

Betty smiled at the young boys' antics. Both were probably close in age to Caroline. Right now, they were acting a bit foolish. Neither would stand a chance of winning over Caroline—not with the way she looked at Thomas as Reverend Pritchett escorted her from the dining hall.

Ah, young love, she thought. She remembered that look. It was the same one she used on Henry when she first fell in love. Could hardly pry her eyes off him.

Jed and Hawk dove into their meals.

Betty stood, feeling a bit guilty for having stayed in the dining hall too long. "Thomas, I've had your bunk ready since Monday. Why don't you go on and get settled."

———

"I'm glad you're safe," Reverend Pritchett said as soon as they left the confines of the dining hall. "But what were you thinking to run off like that?"

"I was impatient," Caroline said, admitting fault. "If I had known it could be so dangerous, I never would have done it."

"When we heard that the stage was robbed, I feared the worst."

Caroline nodded, hoping he would let it go.

Reverend Pritchett pushed open the door to the clinic. Chaos greeted them. A small boy ran around in circles as his frantic mother called out his name, imploring him to be still as she cradled a crying infant close to her chest. A man sat in a corner chair glaring at the noisy child as he rubbed his temples with one hand. His other sat limp in his lap. The woman next to him fidgeted with a handkerchief nervously, turning it round in her hand.

"Will you be alright?" Reverend Pritchett asked. "I will see about renting a carriage to take you the rest of the way."

She nodded and took the last available seat in the cramped parlor.

The doctor soon escorted a young man from the exam rooms to the parlor. Looking around at his waiting patients, Caroline saw him bite back a quick sigh before he greeted the woman with the colicky infant and high-strung son.

Turning towards her, he asked, "What brings you here today?"

"A cut on my hand. Betty suggested you take a look at it."

"Will you be fine for a few minutes?" the doctor asked, concern shadowing his face.

She nodded.

At her reassurance, he led the woman and infant and her son back to the exam room.

Leaning her head back against the wall, Caroline closed her eyes and let out a long breath. She was positively exhausted from the last few days. She just wanted to get to Colter Ranch and collapse into bed for a few hours rest.

"Miss. Miss." The gentle masculine voice pulled her from her foggy daze.

Then she shot upright, looking around the now empty parlor. Heat warmed her cheeks as she realized she must have fallen asleep.

The doctor helped her up from the chair and introduced himself as Dr. Hank Armstrong, though most called him Dr. Hank. She introduced herself as he led her back to an examination room.

"I apologize for the wait. Seems like I either have no patients or several all at once." His light laugh set her at ease.

"Let's see that hand."

She held out her bandaged hand and let him unwrap it.

"What'd you cut it on?" he asked as he studied the wound.

"The stagecoach harness."

His eyes found hers. "It wasn't rusty, was it?"

Stories of the terror of lockjaw fought for attention in her mind. She pushed them aside and closed her eyes, trying to visualize the harness. Unconsciously, she brought her other hand up and began tapping her index finger against her temple rapidly. Images of the murder of the other passengers came first. She concentrated harder.

Opening her eyes, she answered, "I don't think so." She looked away as tears threatened.

"How long ago did you cut your hand?"

"Um, three or four days, I think."

"No fever or chills."

She thought for a moment. "I've been rather warm, but I've also been in the sun. No chills, though."

"I see. Is your skin sore at all from the sun exposure?"

"A bit."

Moving to the counter, he began mixing together a few things while he gave his diagnosis. "I think your hand will be fine. Given how old the wound is, I think you are safe from lockjaw. Just put this salve on it and keep it bandaged for a few more days."

Turning to face her, he applied some of the salve on the wound and bandaged it.

"Where are you staying?"

"Colter Ranch. At least I will be soon."

A smile split Dr. Hank's face. "That's wonderful news. I'll write up some notes for Mrs. Colter and she'll have you back to normal in a few days."

Once her hand was bandaged, he turned back to his counter. He scribbled some things down on a sheet of paper and folded it before mixing up another concoction.

"Use this," he said, handing her the second mixture, "to help with the sun exposure on your face. And give this to Mrs. Colter."

Caroline smiled, wondering how this man seemed to know Will's wife so well. She remembered from one of Adam's letters that Will had married and that his wife was a gifted healer. Perhaps she had worked with the doctor on occasion.

When Dr. Hank led her back to the parlor, Reverend Pritchett stood.

"Feeling okay, Miss Larson?"

"Right as rain," she replied before thanking the doctor.

As the reverend led her out of the clinic, he said, "I would like for you to talk to the sheriff about the stagecoach robbery. Give him as much information as you can to make sure these renegades are caught."

Caroline nodded, despite the knot that formed in her stomach. She just wanted to put the whole thing behind her.

As they neared the sheriff's office, her gaze snagged on a man dismounting a black horse in front of the saloon. Something seemed very familiar about him, but she couldn't place it. She thought he might be the same man on the trail to Prescott.

The meeting with the sheriff tested her nerves. It was so difficult to bring forward the images of that horrible day. She did her best to describe the two men who robbed the stage and murdered those men. Even though Reverend Pritchett told her the men had been given a proper burial, she still felt guilty for having left them there.

CHAPTER 15

By the time Reverend Pritchett led her from the sheriff's office, she was more than ready to go. He had a carriage waiting for her. A grinning Hawk waved and smiled at her from his horse. Jed smiled and tipped his hat. Reverend Pritchett took a seat next to her and they were on their way to Colter Ranch—at last.

Hawk chatted about the ranch, but Caroline paid little attention as she took in the surrounding landscape. Adam's descriptions in his letters failed to do the scenic beauty justice—especially when they topped a hill overlooking the ranch. Whitish gray granite mountains jutted up from the valley opposite the hill the wagon traveled down. A blue lake shimmered at the base.

"Adam and Julia are getting married. Everyone is really excited about it."

Hawk's announcement jolted her attention away from the beautiful scene. All the enjoyment of God's creation faded in an instant as she tried to fathom the idea of her brother and her best friend getting married.

The knot in her stomach tightened as the shock started to wear off. Things were not going at all as she planned. She was supposed to leave the boredom of Texas and head off to great adventures with the two people she was closest to in the world. Instead, without her presence the two had somehow formed a deep bond—one that excluded her.

Caroline's mood threatened to sink into despair as she

thought of all that had gone wrong. Lying to her parents. The stagecoach robbery. The death of those men. The bizarre rescue. The kiss from Thomas. Nearly being caught by rustlers. Perry Quinn.

Now this. Julia and Adam were looking forward to a happy life without her.

Would they even be excited to see her now or would she just get in the way?

Her excitement about seeing them again turned into trepidation as Reverend Pritchett stopped the carriage in front of the cabin. She had missed the rest of the trip down to the valley floor and failed to get acquainted with her new home.

Jed dismounted his horse and knocked on the door of the cabin as Hawk helped her down.

"We have visitors," Jed announced before returning to take care of his horse.

A woman a few years older than her stepped from the cabin, balancing a baby on one hip. As she stepped into the sunlight, her blonde hair lit with fiery touches of red. She introduced herself as Hannah Colter before offering Caroline an affectionate smile.

"Adam will be so excited to see you." Turning towards Reverend Pritchett she said, "Thank you for bringing her safely to us. Would you care to stay for supper?"

"I'm afraid I must return to town this evening so I can head back to Wickenburg first thing in the morning."

Caroline thanked Reverend Pritchett for coming all this way. She asked him to send her love to Millie before he pulled the carriage away from the ranch house headed back up the road to Prescott.

Looking around, Caroline wondered where Adam and Julia were. She didn't have long to wait for the answer.

"Adam and Julia are over in the corral working with the horses," Hannah said as she led the way.

A squeal of delight echoed across the valley floor. "Caroline!"

As she looked to the sound of her friend's voice, she barely caught sight of her before Julia squeezed her tight. Caroline wrapped her arms around her friend and instantly felt at home, most of her earlier fears melting away.

"You're here! I can't believe you're here!" Julia exclaimed excitedly, her brown curls bouncing as she jumped up and down. "What? How?" She stammered for a few seconds before shouting at Adam.

"Your sister is here!"

Adam led the horse he was training around the corral and stopped once he came into her view.

"Linny?" The nickname came out as his eyebrows shot up in surprise.

"Adam," she said, her excitement returning.

He removed the training bridle from the horse and let it run around the corral. Climbing over the railing, he landed just in front of her, pulling her into a hearty hug. "It's so good to see you. What are you doing here?"

As he stepped back from the embrace, he slid his arm around Julia's waist. Caroline swallowed a moment of fear, turning her attention towards his question instead of his loving hold on her best friend.

"I decided it was time for a change. I missed you both terribly," she confessed.

"I have a million questions," Julia said, her eyes lighting with exuberance.

Hannah's soft voice interrupted. "I'm sure you're tired from the long journey, Caroline. Perhaps we should let you freshen up and rest a bit before supper. Then you can tell us everything."

Julia nodded in agreement. "Come. You can share my room, for now." She glanced over at Adam who smiled back.

As Julia took her hand, she led Caroline back to the cabin.

For now. The words hinted again at what Hawk mentioned earlier. The way Adam looked at Julia. Caroline tried not to sigh. Nothing was like she dreamed.

"This is my room," Julia said as she ushered Caroline into a small room off of the kitchen area. "Looks like the boys have already brought in your things. I can't believe this is all you brought."

Caroline smiled wanly, not wanting to get into all the details of her oversized dress or her undersized wardrobe. A yawn escaped her lips before she could cover it.

The excitement on Julia's face dimmed. "Hannah was right. We should let you nap before supper. You've got an hour or so."

Julia moved towards the door, then stopped. "I'm so glad you're here. I've missed you so much." With one last hug, she left Caroline alone in the room.

Sitting down on the edge of the bed, Caroline leaned down to unfasten her boots. She wiggled her toes, glad to be free from the cramped boots. She unpinned her hair before falling back on the bed.

Disappointment tugged at her heart. Nothing was what she thought it would be.

———

"My first question," Adam started, "is how did you ever get Pa to agree to letting you move out here?"

Caroline scooped a spoonful of fried potatoes onto her plate. For once she considered her words before answering. "I told him you were probably lonely and needed your little sister to keep an eye on you."

She laughed but didn't really feel it. In the few short minutes since supper started, she clearly understood her brother was anything but lonely. Somehow, in the year since he left home he had very obviously fallen in love with Julia. She tried to convince herself she was happy for them. She was. Sort of.

"I'll bet," Adam replied. "I do know Pa well enough to know he didn't let you come here on your own. How come we didn't get to meet your chaperone?"

His fishing made her uncomfortable. She wasn't ready to tell him and the large group of people at the table, some of which were strangers, that she had snuck away.

"Seems like I'm doing all the talking. What about you, Adam? How have you been?" She quickly stuffed a bite of food into her mouth to keep from having to say more.

"Well," he paused, glancing at Julia. "I'm doing well."

"Might as well tell her," Ben said. "Think Hawk already spilled the beans on yer secret anyway."

"I… um… Julia and I are getting married."

Caroline wanted to act shocked. Her impulse was to respond in a dramatic way. But she was too tired.

"How long have you two had feelings for each other?" she asked the question she didn't really want the answer to. It was too strange to think of them as a couple.

Julia spoke up. "It's hard to say exactly when. I think something just changed for us on the trip west. It took me quite a while to see it, but I think Adam knew long before I did."

"He did," Will interjected.

Red mottled Adam's face. Ben and Hannah laughed.

"They're right," Adam said. "I think I fell in love with Julia the night we left Texas. If not then, it would have been somewhere along the way." He turned to face Julia, the love dripping from his round green eyes. He reached for her hand and held it.

Still looking at his future wife, his words were intended for Caroline. "Julia certainly tested my patience at times. But she eventually came around. I can hardly wait for her to become my wife."

As silence fell over the table, a sight Caroline never expected to see greeted her eyes. Julia leaned close to Adam and placed a soft kiss on his cheek. When she sat upright again, her eyes looked just as serene and as full of love as Adam's did.

Caroline choked on the potatoes. Unable to swallow properly, she burst out in a coughing fit. Ben patted her on the back as everyone stared at her. Eventually the offending piece of food found its rightful place. She reached for her water; eyes lowered in humiliation. Gulping down some water started to soothe the lingering tickle in her throat.

"You, okay?" Adam asked, concern creasing his brow.

"Fine." She managed the word before taking a sip of water.

"Anyway," Julia said, "the wedding is in just a few weeks. Oh Caroline! I'm so glad you're here. Will you stand for me at the wedding?" At her nod, she continued, "It will be so perfect, now that you're here."

Caroline certainly didn't feel like it would be perfect. *Stop being so selfish. Just be happy for them.*

The rest of the meal passed as Adam and Julia caught her up on all the goings on of the last year. Following supper, Adam and Julia went for a walk, leaving her behind. Hannah insisted she didn't need help with the dishes and suggested Caroline rest.

An awkward half hour of silence passed as Caroline tried to figure out what to do with herself until Julia returned.

"Adam wished you pleasant dreams," Julia said breathlessly as she entered the cabin and plopped down on the couch next to Caroline. "He retired to the bunkhouse."

She nodded. Then she yawned.

"Come, let's retire to our room," Julia suggested.

Once they were ready for bed, they both climbed in.

"It's just like when we were little girls," Julia said. Turning on her side, she propped up her head on her hand. "I've missed you so much. I'm so glad you're here. It's been pretty strange not having you to talk to all this time."

Caroline shoved aside her disappointment about things not being as she hoped. She was relieved to see Julia felt the same as she did.

"I've missed you, too."

A moment of silence honored their sincerity.

Caroline giggled. "I kissed Jesse Shoemaker and Nathan Finley."

Julia's eyes rounded in surprise. "You did not!"

Nodding, she added, "On the same night, too."

Julia shook her head. "Still getting into trouble?"

"More than you know."

Then Caroline launched into the story of how she ended up in Wickenburg. She told of how she left her chaperones and caught the stage. She cried when she relayed the events of the robbery and murders. She laughed when she told of how Thomas rescued her. She told Julia everything. Everything except how Thomas kissed her and how she would never forget it.

As the hour grew late, their whispered giggles and tears subsided. Silence reigned. Caroline's eyes grew droopy, her heart content that she had been reunited with her best friend.

CHAPTER 16

Prescott

August 23, 1865

Traveling with a preacher for two days was a terrible idea—at least that is what Robert Garrett learned on his trip to Prescott. After spending much longer than he wished cleaning up the stage robbery, the preacher tried repeatedly to engage him in conversation. He held back a shout of joy when they arrived in Prescott this afternoon and the preacher parted from his company.

Tying his horse in front of the saloon, Robert walked away from the establishment and towards Zach Drake's office. Judging by the large number of cattle he spotted headed south, he needed to hurry up and get his paperwork in order and sent off with his associate.

"Robert," Zach greeted him when he entered the attorney's office. He offered Robert a seat and closed the door. "Purchase more cattle recently?"

"Yes," he said. His associate arrived shortly before he did and handed him a slip of paper which included counts of the cattle from each ranch. Robert slid the piece of paper across the table to Zach.

"Hmm. It will take me some time to draw up the necessary paperwork." Scanning the list he added, "Not sure if I have a signature for Perry Quinn."

Zach unlocked his desk drawer and opened a file folder, then flipped through it. "Ah, here it is."

"What about Colter?"

"Had that one for a while now. His is one of the easier signatures to duplicate."

Robert smiled. What great fortune to find a corrupt attorney who also dabbled in forgery.

"I have something else I could use your help with," Robert said.

Zach nodded to him to continue.

"I'm looking for someone who might be able to make a connection for an associate of mine. He's looking to meet someone from Will Colter's ranch that might be interested in making additional income."

"Ah. Trent Montgomery is the man to see. He owns the saloon on the end of Montezuma Street."

"Is he trustworthy?"

Zach laughed. "As much as any criminal can be."

"Understood."

"I do know that most of Colter's men are above board. The few that might be of interest to your friend tend to frequent the saloon on Saturday evenings, though I heard they made a delivery out at the fort today. Might even catch them in town tonight."

Robert thanked Zach for the information and decided to pick up the paperwork tomorrow morning.

Heading back toward Trent Montgomery's saloon, he kept an eye out for his associate. He had one more assignment for him before he left in the morning. Despite the early hour—it wasn't even supper time yet—Robert entered the saloon. He spotted his associate dressed as an old miner, paying for his drink in gold dust. Perhaps he could get the man to teach him a thing or two about disguises. If he hadn't known in advance what to look for, he never would have recognized him.

Robert did not acknowledge him. Instead, he made his way to the bar and ordered whiskey. The stuff in the West was not as good as what he got back home, but it did its job. A lovely little gal walked towards him, her ample bosom barely restrained by her clothing.

"In the mood for some fun?" she asked.

"A little pleasure in the afternoon might be nice," he answered, gulping down his whiskey. He pushed back from the bar and followed her up the stairs.

She led him to a room in the back that could not be seen from the stairs. Then she opened the door and motioned for him to enter. The room was not empty, nor had he expected it to be. His associate sat on a chair in the corner.

"Leave us," Robert said. "But come back in fifteen minutes. He's not my type."

The saloon girl nodded.

"Paperwork will be ready in the morning."

His associate nodded.

"While you're here, see what you can find out about Colter's men. Rumor is that some of them are in town today. I need you to get one of them to work for us. Trent Montgomery might be of assistance."

"How much you willing to pay?"

"You know the rules. Try to get him for as little as possible. Just enough to make him turn on that uppity rancher."

"I'll find out who they are. Then give 'em a spell to get nice and drunk before talking to 'em. Always seem to be freer with their thoughts that way."

A knock sounded at the door.

"Good. Sounds like I'll have plenty of time for the little lady before joining you back downstairs."

His associate nodded and left as the saloon girl entered the room. Yes, a little pleasure in the afternoon was exactly what he was looking for.

———

Robert felt much more relaxed as he returned to the bar. He took a seat next to his associate but did not acknowledge him. He ordered whiskey and began sipping it as his associate engaged the bartender in conversation.

"Looking for Trent Montgomery."

"And you are?"

"Pete Vance," his associate said. That was a new name—one he hadn't heard him use before. Good. It was probably better that way.

"Why you looking for Montgomery?"

"Just looking for information that he might know."

"Well, you're gawking at him."

Robert shifted in his seat, pretending not to hear the conversation.

"Know any of Colter's men?" Pete asked.

"Only a couple of them come here. Happen to have two of them here tonight."

"Might ya be willing to introduce me?"

"That one there," Montgomery said, pointing towards a man seated at a poker table, "is Owens. His buddy, Whitten, is the ratty looking one sitting across from him."

Pete nodded and started to stand. He turned back toward Montgomery. "If I was looking to find one a bit unhappy with Colter, who might I talk to?"

"Owens. Guess there's some bad blood between him and the horse trainer out at the ranch."

Pete pulled out some extra coins, more than enough to pay for his drink, and tossed them on the counter. "Thanks for your help."

Montgomery greedily swiped the coins from the counter and pocketed them.

Robert tossed him a coin for his whiskey and asked about a poker game. Montgomery directed him to the same table that Pete headed towards. Two of the men that had been playing vacated the table.

"Can I join you gentlemen?" Robert asked as he reached for one of the empty chairs.

"If ya like losing yer money to a couple of cowboys, be our

guest," Whitten said.

Robert took a seat, noting that Pete had already joined the game. Besides him, Pete, Owens, and Whitten, only one other man played the game.

As the first round was dealt, Pete asked, "Where you boys work?"

Owens snorted and looked at his card.

Whitten replied, "Colter Ranch."

"Is that the man who supplies beef for the fort?"

"The same."

Bets were placed and the game began. Pete continued to pump the two Colter cowboys for information. He was good. Every question seemed like the most natural thing that anyone might talk about during a friendly game of poker. Robert was very pleased.

Just when Robert thought Owens might stay tight lipped the entire night, he started venting his frustrations.

"Can't stand working for that high and mighty Colter. Won't never let us get out for any entertainment. Works us too hard. An' he sits there in that fancy house with his pretty wife and makes a fortune while the rest of us can't even enjoy our earnings," Owens said, flinging his losing hand of cards across the table.

Owens continued, "Ain't the only one either. That trainer. He's something else. Gets treated like family."

"Maybe if he weren't marrying the boss's sister, it'd be different," Whitten added.

"Naw. He's been treated better'n us from the start."

Owens went on for some time talking about how much he hated Colter, Larson, and his family. Robert smiled inwardly. Again, he was the beneficiary of good timing and good luck. He had no doubts that Owens would be more than willing to carry out his plans.

Later that evening, his associate stopped by his room at the Juniper House, no longer looking like Pete Vance.

"He's in."

The simple message was all Robert wanted to hear. Now he had someone on the inside at Colter Ranch. His plan was coming together perfectly. He still had another week or so in town to finish securing contacts at the other area ranches.

Soon he would begin taking larger numbers of cattle from these foolish ranchers. He would know exactly when and where to strike—well not him. The rustlers working for him.

Slowly he would take back what Colter stole from him. And the best part was, in a week or so, he would ride into that ranch as a respectable businessman, looking to purchase some horses. It would give him the perfect opportunity to see with his own eyes the best way to make Colter pay. Perhaps it would involve harming his wife. Or perhaps something even better would present itself.

Colter cost him everything. His ranch. His home. His wife. His children. Oh, he wasn't too upset about being free from the entanglements of family. In some ways that made his life much simpler. But losing his wealth had been a significant blow—one that almost cost him the only thing more precious to him than money—his life.

He survived. He was rebuilding. Soon enough he would have his revenge.

A brief moment of frustration sprung forward. His associate failed to grab Caroline Larson. He had been too late and now she was here in Prescott, probably already on her way to Colter Ranch. He missed that opportunity. He hated missing opportunities. If his associate had not been so successful in many other ventures already, he probably would have terminated his dealings with him.

Larson might have escaped his wrath for now. Somehow, someway, he would find a way to take his revenge on both Colter and Larson. Neither would avoid paying for all they took from him. He never wanted anything so bad before. And he always got what he wanted.

CHAPTER 17

Following supper at the boardinghouse, Thomas walked the short distance to one of the saloons across the street. He was still tied up in knots over Caroline Larson and the events of the past few days. He hoped a few drinks would relax him enough so that he could get plenty of sleep tonight, especially since he had to start his next mail run tomorrow.

As he took a seat at the highly polished wooden bar, he nodded to the bartender. Within seconds a full mug of beer slid down to his waiting hand.

Was it really just ten days ago that he sat in this same spot, sipping the same drink, thinking what a mess he had made of this life?

Now his mind was filled with memories of Caroline holding tightly against his chest as he kissed her sweet lips. The desire ignited by that kiss would not die. Not even when he thought about how she argued with him at every chance.

He grunted and took a long swig of his beer.

"Frustrated?" Paul asked as he took a seat next to him.

Thomas answered with another grunt.

"Thought I might find you here."

Guilt pierced his armor ever so slowly. So much for being a better man. He'd never go looking for Paul in a place like this. Yet here his friend sat next to him, knowing this is where he'd be.

"What'll ya have?" the bartender asked Paul.

"I'm fine."

"If you're gonna be warming that stool, then you'll be having a drink."

"Whatever he's having then," Paul answered before turning his attention back to Thomas. "How you doing?"

"Not well."

"Figured."

Thomas sighed and took another swig of his beer. The bartender slid a full one down to Paul. Paul ignored it.

"Kinda surprised you ordered something," Thomas said.

Paul slid it towards Thomas. "Don't plan on drinking it."

Thomas frowned, suddenly irritated at his friend's unbelievable self-control. "And why not? How come you never drink?"

Paul looked away. "It leads to too much trouble and pain."

Leaning his head back, he drained his beer and slid the empty mug away. He fingered the handle of the full mug Paul gave him.

"What's got you so out of sorts?" Paul asked.

"Caroline." The name sped from his mouth without hesitation.

Raising an eyebrow in question, Paul asked, "The girl you rescued? What's she got to do with anything?"

"She's cast some sort of spell over me," Thomas replied dryly before taking a sip of his beer. Then he told Paul about everything—the trip, the kiss, her flirting with Perry Quinn. His insatiable and unreasonable desire for her.

When he finished, Paul remained quiet for several minutes as Thomas continued to nurse his beer.

"Do you know how to respect a woman?" Paul asked.

The question hit him as hard as if Paul had swung one of his beefy arms at him. Did he know how to respect a woman? A woman he fancied?

When he failed to answer, Paul continued, "You respect a woman that you desire by not acting on it—by not dwelling on it. If you truly want to treat her properly, you have to get to know her. Can't do that if all you are thinking about is the pleasure of bedding her."

Thomas swallowed hard, convicted of his disrespectful thoughts and still shocked by Paul's frankness.

"Caroline is not the type of woman you would find here. If she is anything at all like her brother, she has strong beliefs and morals. She's not the type of woman who would get involved with a man like you."

The words stung.

A man like him. He was a wretched man. A bank robber. A gambler. A drunk. A man seeking to fulfill his own selfish desires with no regard for the damage it would cause to others. He could never hope to be a good man like Drew.

"You can."

Had he uttered the words aloud?

"You just can't hope to be a good man on your own. See that's the problem with you, friend. You try to do it all on your own, with your own power. But you just aren't strong enough."

Thomas shifted to look Paul in the eye, his anger getting the better of him. "And you are?"

Sympathy settled on Paul's face. "No, I'm not. Not on my own."

Confused, Thomas asked, "What are you talking about?"

A heavy sigh lifted then dropped Paul's broad shoulders. "The reason I understand you so well is because I was once where you are now. I was trying to live up to my pa's reputation. Only I had a temper, a penchant for women, and an uncontrolled lust for whiskey. It took me to the darkest place in my life."

Paul's eyes glazed with deep regret.

"I was about your age when I destroyed my life."

What was he talking about? This was Paul. He was one of the most upstanding, decent men that he knew. What could he have ever done that was so wrong?

"After my pa died, I became his instant replacement. I had to run the farm. I had to help raise my brother and sisters. I had to comfort my ma. It was too much pressure for a seventeen-year-old to bear.

"As I watched my sister grow up and move on, I became resentful and angry. Why couldn't I have what she had? Why did I have the responsibility of taking care of Ma and the others?

"That resentfulness and anger drove me to the saloon. I soon discovered how wonderful whiskey was. It helped me forget the heavy responsibilities that waited for me at home. It helped me feel invincible. It helped me have the courage to be with the girls upstairs. The whiskey fed the lust and soon the lust took over.

"At first, I just spent Saturday nights at the saloon. Then it became two nights, then three, then more."

Paul cleared his throat.

"No matter what I did, I couldn't hide from the fact that I had turned into the worst kind of man—a man so far removed from the honorable man my father was. By the time I wanted to change, I felt helpless to do so. I needed more. More women. More whiskey.

"Then, one night I came home from the saloon early, before the rest of the family turned in. When I got back home, Nancy's beau was kissing her on the porch. He wasn't being forceful or anything, at least that's what I learned later. I was out of my mind with rage. I grabbed him and started pounding his face. I was about the same size as I am now, and he was this thin speck of a man.

"I don't know how long I hit him. I just kept going and going. Nancy was screaming at me. Ma came rushing out. Frank tried to stop me but ended up with my fist in his face. I kept going—until Ma came out of the house with a rifle in her hand.

"'You stop that now, or so help me, I will shoot you,' she said. Then she cocked the gun. I looked into her eyes and saw she was dead serious. I stopped."

Paul turned toward Thomas, the ache of his crime weighing heavily.

"I nearly killed him. I spent some time in jail for what I did, making my Ma's tough life even harder. The time I spent in jail, I just kept thinking how I let my pa down and how I wanted to be good like him.

"I tried to be good on my own and I kept failing. The call

the whiskey and women whispered in my ear, tempting. I'd have a few good days then before I knew it, I was right back where I started.

"Finally, my Ma had a serious conversation with me. She told me that if I didn't change, she would rather run the farm by herself, hard as it would be, than to have me there. I told her I was trying.

"You know what she said to me, Thomas?"

Thomas shook his head, still shocked by Paul's story.

"She told me I wasn't really trying 'cause if I was, I'd be on my knees admitting my weakness and asking the Lord to change me.

"So, that night, that's exactly what I did. With the house all quiet, I got down on my knees beside my bed. I just started talking to God. I told him about the mess I'd made of my life. I told him what I did to Nancy's beau and how she wouldn't look at me when I entered a room. I told him how I wanted to stop drinking and stop chasing women and stop trudging my pa's name through the mire. I told him I tried to change, and I just couldn't do it.

"For hours I prayed. Then, at the end of it, I had this peace that came into my heart. I was different—new."

Paul slapped his hand down on Thomas's shoulder and gave him a little shake.

"I ain't good now. I still, in the deepest parts of my heart, want to go back to that way of life. But whenever I start feeling that pull, I turn my thoughts to God. I ask him for strength 'cause I'm too weak. I ask him for help. I ask him to keep my heart pure. I don't ever try to do it on my own anymore. It just doesn't work."

Paul released his grip on Thomas's shoulder then leaned forward propping his elbows on the bar.

Thomas sat in stunned silence still trying to make sense of Paul's story. The Paul he knew was decent and honorable. He was a strong man, not just physically but in character. How could he call himself weak?

Slamming his fist down on the table, Paul said, "Just don't wait for your life to be destroyed before you get it, Thomas. You can't be like Drew without Him."

The words cut through his heart as anger boiled. What right did Paul have to speak to him that way?

"Get out."

Sad lines formed around Paul's eyes as he stood. He opened his mouth as if to say more but closed it instead. Turning his back on Thomas, he walked out the doors of the saloon leaving a hurt and confused man behind.

Draining his beer, Thomas slammed the empty glass down on the bar so hard it shattered. He shook his hand at his side to brush away any loose fragments.

He didn't need God. God took his mother away from him. In Thomas's experience, God wasn't too helpful, nor kind.

Another beer disappeared quickly, followed by another, until the pain and regret of his failures numbed.

Caroline's golden blonde hair and flashing green eyes floated across his blurred vision, quickly followed by Paul's words. *She's not the type of woman to get involved with a man like you. A man like you.*

Thomas pushed himself away from the bar and stumbled toward the stairs. They were all wrong. All of them. Paul. Caroline. Inside he was a good man. He just had too much guilt hanging around his neck. And he needed to forget it for one night.

Lifting his foot, he climbed the first stair. Then the next. Then the next. Until he found himself in front of the door to one of the soiled dove's rooms. He reached for the handle, hoping to find relief for his tormented mind.

———

"Dear, it's well past time for you to get up," Betty's voice invaded Thomas's dream.

Rolling over, he groaned. As he sat up, his head started pounding.

"Come on. You don't have much time. I saved you a plate of breakfast, but you best start moving or you're gonna miss leaving on time."

His run! That's what she was talking about. He had to ride out today.

He quickly dropped his feet to the floor. Betty hurried from the bunkhouse, leaving him to dress in peace. As he finished buttoning his shirt, he glanced out the window. It had to be after ten in the morning. He was already late.

Moving to the wash basin, he splashed some water on his face and grabbed what he would need for his ride. He ran to straight for the back door of the dining hall.

"Here," Betty said, thrusting a biscuit toward him.

He held it with his mouth as he took the wrapped cheese and jerky, she handed him next. He stuffed those in his saddle bags as he ran off toward the livery, throbbing the whole way. Thankfully, Craig already had a horse saddled. He threw his saddle bags over the horse's rump and tied them down. Then he led the horse to Juniper House, the hotel where he picked up the mail. Once he retrieved the mail, he secured it on the horse and mounted. His heart beat out a frantic rhythm as he kicked the horse to a gallop.

Thomas tried to calm his nerves as he tried to recall the previous evening. He must have drunk more than he thought.

Pieces of his conversation with Paul came back to him. He wasn't good enough for Caroline. He couldn't be a decent and honorable man on his own.

He groaned, as he remembered standing before the soiled dove's room. He almost lived up to everything Paul had said about him. Almost.

With the one smidgen of self-control he had left, he had used it to carry his feet back down those stairs without going through with his original intent. Instead, he ordered several more drinks, letting the beer dull his mind. He vaguely remembered someone helping him stumble back to the boardinghouse.

It was probably Paul.

The pounding of the horse's hooves matched the beat

drumming in his head, making the first part of the ride miserable. Thankfully, he reached the head of the steep mountain trail quickly. This leg of the ride required that his horse walk—a much slower pace than any other part of the ride—giving him time to think.

He was a horrible friend. All the advice Paul was trying to give him, and he practically threw it back in his face. What a story, too. He could hardly fathom Paul ever being anything like him.

Thomas concentrated for a moment on the difficult switchbacks, guiding the horse with his reins. Once he passed the worst part of the steep descent, he breathed a sigh of relief.

Then he remembered his first stop would be Perry Quinn's station. He wasn't ready to see him again so soon. He would undoubtedly ask about Caroline and he would have to stare into those lovesick eyes and tell him that she was well when all he wanted to do was upstage him in some way.

He pulled his horse to a stop for a moment and looked out over the valley. It was stupid, given that he was already behind schedule. But he just needed a minute to collect himself.

His life was a mess.

Don't wait for your life to be completely destroyed before you get it.

He was getting pretty close to that. Not too much more he could do wrong, except maybe kill a man—which he would never do intentionally. He'd already done so many things wrong. Paul had pretty much told him that he'd continue to keep doing things wrong without God.

But his mother had died because she thought God was calling her to care for those sick people. He grew up without her because of God. What could he possibly do to help Thomas?

I can change your heart.

He sat up straighter in his saddle and looked around. The words were so clear he thought for certain that a man had spoken them. Seeing no one, he settled into the saddle and kicked his horse back into motion, trying to push the words from his mind.

He could do this on his own. He just had to try a little harder is all. When he got to La Paz he wouldn't drink more than one beer. When he got back to Prescott the next week, he would avoid the saloon altogether. For his time off, he'd go out to Colter Ranch. Spend some time bouncing his nephew on his knee.

Caroline would be there.

That was just fine with him. He would find a way to resist her teasing smile and lovely lips. He would do what Paul suggested—he'd get to know her, and he'd force himself to stop thinking lustfully towards her. He could do it. He would do it. And he didn't need God's interference.

CHAPTER 18

Colter Ranch

August 26, 1865

Ben wished he hadn't promised Betty he would go to church tomorrow. He wasn't looking forward to it. Last time he set foot on church property was to bury Eddie. Other than attending Christmas services with the Colters, he hadn't been to church since the Sunday before Sheila and Elijah were ripped from him.

Now he promised Betty he would be there tomorrow.

"So, cowboys ain't your thing?"

Owens' voice reached Ben's ears before he rounded the corner to return Sheila to the stables. He caught sight of the slimy cowboy standing a bit too close to Julia.

"If you like stable boys so much, I might be persuaded to change professions."

Ben tensed. He didn't like Owens' tone nor how he reached up to touch Julia's face. He moved forward to intervene, but Julia saved him from the trouble. She brought her knee up quickly, hitting her mark. Owens doubled over in pain.

"Don't touch me again. Or next time, I might find a weapon that does even more damage."

Ben stifled a laugh. The situation was serious, but the look on sweet Julia's face would make any man think twice about crossing her again. As Owens moved past him, he grabbed the young man by the neck and hauled him off to the side of the barn, leaving his horse unattended.

"I catch ya doin' somethin' like that again and it'll be the last thing ya do on this ranch."

Owens bit his lip and narrowed his eyes as he tried to stand up straight.

Ben shoved him hard against the barn wall. He brought his sturdy forearm up to rest on Owens' neck. "Ya understand me?"

Owens nodded.

Staring down the younger man, Ben loosened his hold. "Same goes for any women on this ranch. Ya better be respectin' them more'n yer mama or yer whiskey."

As Ben took a step back, he pushed Owens away from the wall. "Git on outta here."

Owens hurried away toward the bunkhouse.

Ben sighed, trying to get his pulse to slow. It burned him the way Owens treated just about everyone. He wasn't too sure he wouldn't put a bullet in that cowboy if he tried something like that again.

"Ya did good," he said to Julia as he entered the barn again.

"I can hold my own."

Ben grunted.

"You forget. I grew up on a ranch. I know how to handle a tough situation." The smile on her face faded and she looked away.

She had handled every situation that came her way—except the one. The one time Will wasn't there to protect her. Ben hadn't been there either. What Reuben, her oldest brother, had done to her—wasn't right.

Adam called her from the corral.

"Don't say anything to him," Julia pleaded. "He'll just worry."

"It's his right to worry about ya. Specially if yer gonna be his wife soon."

"I just don't want him to get hurt. You know Owens could beat him."

"Yah. Just be careful."

"I will," she shot over her shoulder as she hurried from the barn.

Ben removed his saddle from Sheila and began brushing her down in the silence that settled over the barn. His thoughts returned to what tomorrow held.

Going to church was going to be hard. He left his faith behind when he lost Sheila and Elijah. Since then, he hadn't talked to God or about Him. Didn't have nothing to say.

But what if God had something to say to him tomorrow?

He'd ignore it. Just like during all those Christmas services. He didn't have to let down his guard. He didn't have to give in.

Then why was he so scared?

————

Sunday dinner was not going according to Betty's plan. She had been excited when the Colters showed up with Ben in tow. Though, now sitting at the table across from Ben's scowling face, she couldn't help but think this had been a huge mistake.

He greeted her warmly before services. But after—the scowl had already taken up residence and hadn't budged. Something in that message had him downright angry.

Lord, help him work through it. Whatever it is, you know it. He knows it.

Baby James squirmed in her arms, looking for something only his mama could provide, so she handed him off to Hannah who stood and sought privacy in the kitchen. Betty considered joining her when Ben spoke.

"Tell me this, Reverend Page, what gives you the right to preach about grief?"

Betty sucked in a gulp of air sharply. Somehow, judging by the tone of his voice, he took what Reverend Page said about grief the wrong way. She wracked her brain trying to think of what he said could have caused Ben to take offense. All she could recall was that Reverend Page said that Christians aren't to mourn like others mourn because we have hope in Christ's resurrection. What could possibly be offensive about that?

Reverend Page gently laid his fork beside his plate. In a very calm voice, he answered, "I have experienced my share of grief. I assure you this morning's message was as much for myself as it was for you."

"Fer me? What got ya thinkin' that?"

Betty bit her tongue. Why was Ben taking this so personally when Reverend Page had really been speaking to all of them?

"I think by your reaction, perhaps it was meant for you," Reverend Page replied, taken aback by Ben's anger. "To answer your first question, the most recent grief my wife and I have experienced was the miscarriage of our first child. I assure you there is no greater grief than the loss of a child."

Narrowing his eyes, Ben pressed his lips into a thin line. Then he parted them as if to speak, though no sound came forth. Instead, he stood abruptly, hurrying to the front door.

Betty stood and chased after him.

"Ben, wait," she said, catching him just before he mounted his horse. "Reverend Page meant no offense. Nor did he mean to minimize your grief."

Without looking her in the eye, he shrugged away her hand from his arm. "I ain't rejoicing in my loss. Never have. Won't start now," came the response through gritted teeth.

"Reverend Page isn't asking you to."

"Isn't he?" Fiery gray eyes turned on her. Pain creased the corners of his eyes. The firm set of his lips bore a stubbornness—outright refusal—to let go of his grief.

For once, she felt utterly at a loss for words. She wanted to touch him, to squeeze his hand or wrap him in a warm embrace. Something that would help ease his obvious burden. But with her hesitation, he found a way out.

Mounting his horse, somewhat awkwardly for such an experienced horseman, he glanced down at her. "Don't ask me to come to church again, Betty, if this is the sort of thing Page is going to preach. I don't need a young pup telling me how to grieve."

With a *yaw* and a kick in his horse's side, Ben Shepherd galloped down the road, leaving her staring at his fading back.

"Lord," she prayed in a soft, yet audible voice, "I don't know what that man has experienced to cause him to latch on to his pain so tightly. But I do know that you can take even the most stubborn of men and turn their hearts towards you. So, that's what I'm asking you to do for Benjamin. He needs you more than he knows."

CHAPTER 19

Colter Ranch

September 1, 1865

Her first week at Colter Ranch was ending. Nothing was as Caroline expected. She thought when she left Texas that she would arrive at Colter Ranch, and everything would be the same. She and Julia would still be close, like they had been for so many years. She thought that she and Adam would still be close, too.

As she washed the breakfast dishes by Rosa's side, her shoulders sagged. She was on the outside. Adam and Julia would be getting married in a few weeks. They would be husband and wife. They would live happily ever after. And Caroline would be the odd person out.

She already felt it. The two of them spent most of the day working with horses together, while Caroline tried to make herself useful to Hannah in the house. Then they sat across from each other at supper, often conversing in hushed tones while other conversations went on around them. She felt like she learned more about Hannah since arriving than she had about Julia or Adam.

Three weeks. That's all she had left to figure out what to do with herself. Will's new house would not be quite ready by the time Adam and Julia married. So the Colters and Larsons would share the cabin until the larger, more modern house was finished.

There was no room for her. She couldn't stay in Julia's room anymore, because Adam would be there. While Hannah tried to make room for her in the living room, Caroline didn't feel comfortable sleeping in the open room with no privacy for who-knows-how-long.

Lifting the wash basin from its place, she carried it outside and dumped it on Hannah's garden before returning it inside. The day was pleasant, so she stepped back outside to the front porch. Taking a seat in the rocking chair, she tapped her finger against her temple, trying to reason through her current dilemma.

Should she try to move into Rosa's tiny shack until the big house was ready? Or should she move to town and get a job—live on her own?

Everyone kept trying to convince her that she was welcome at Colter Ranch for as long as she wished to stay. Yet, she could not deny that there was no place for her here. She didn't belong.

She wanted to talk it over with Julia, but her friend was so wrapped up in her upcoming wedding that she didn't seem to have the attention span to help Caroline think things through.

Really, moving into town made the most sense. She was eighteen—plenty old enough to be on her own, not living off of the charity of the Colters or her brother. She could find work at one of the stores in town.

A rider coming down the lane drew her attention. Something about him looked very familiar. As he pulled the horse to a stop in front of the corral, she recognized Thomas. What was he doing here? Had he come all this way to see her?

As soon as the thought flitted into her mind, her hopes soared. Maybe he had been thinking about her as much as she had about him.

"Morning," she greeted as he neared the front door.

His face remained expressionless as he greeted her in return—not the reaction she hoped for. "Is Hannah around?"

She found it odd that he was looking for Hannah. "She's inside with baby James."

His face lit up. "Is he awake?"

That was the look she hoped he would have for her, not Hannah's child. His reaction perplexed her. Just why would he care about the infant?

Annoyed, she shrugged in response. He left her standing there as he entered the house.

Curiosity moved her feet from the porch into the house. She just *had* to know what this was all about.

"Thomas!" Hannah greeted him with a kiss to the cheek. "Back from your run?"

"Yes."

"Uneventful, I hope."

He sighed heavily, glancing Caroline's direction. "For once." Then he exaggeratedly rolled his eyes, keeping a straight face for a few seconds before breaking into a grin. He was teasing her.

"Can I see my nephew?" he asked.

Nephew? Caroline's stomach tightened. How was he related to the Colters?

"He's just up from a nap. Let me get him." Hannah replied before entering her bedroom.

"Nephew?" Caroline couldn't resist asking the question.

Thomas ignored her. Instead, he held out his arms to receive baby James eagerly. As he cooed and fussed over him, Caroline frowned. None of this scene made any sense to her.

"How is he your nephew?" She tried again.

Hannah answered him. "My first husband, Drew, was Thomas's brother. He is my brother-in-law. Even though James is Will's son, we welcomed Thomas into the family as our child's uncle."

Caroline's jaw dropped for a few seconds before she caught the un-ladylike behavior. "You're related to *him?*" She pointed from Hannah to Thomas.

"In a manner of speaking, yes."

Thomas, her rescuer, was related to Will's wife. A gentle throbbing pulsated at her temple. She reached up to rub the headache away. She had no idea what to say.

Her silence went unnoticed as Thomas continued to make

silly faces at James. Each action caused eyes full of wonder to pop open wider and an angelic smile to form on the baby's face. It was clear that Thomas truly loved this nephew of sorts.

Caroline shook off her daze and moved to the kitchen area to begin fixing the picnic lunch planned in an hour or so. She cooked up the scheme of a picnic to spend more time with Adam and Julia. She figured if the three of them rode out to a scenic place, she might be able to learn more about what happened over the last year. It was her way to reconnect with them both. Hopefully they would stop ogling over each other long enough to realize she was there.

Setting out a basket, she began wrapping cheese, jerky, bread, and other goodies. Then she placed each item in the basket. Looking up, her gaze connected with Thomas's. He had been watching her carefully and now he looked away suddenly, cheeks blazing with red. Her stomach fluttered and she felt her cheeks heat as quickly as his.

The memory of their shared kiss warmed her face even more. Maybe he had been thinking about her after all.

Focusing on her task, she added the last of the items to her basket.

Julia and Adam burst through the door.

"Ready?" Julia asked.

Caroline nodded.

When Adam noticed Thomas, both he and Julia greeted him.

"Are you here for the day?" Adam asked Thomas as he handed the baby back to Hannah.

"Sure."

"Care to join us for a picnic?"

Caroline narrowed her eyes as her face heated again. This was supposed to be *her* time with Adam and Julia. What was he doing inviting Thomas?

Then Thomas turned to look at her. "Love to," he answered with a wry grin on his lips.

He seemed to enjoy making her uncomfortable.

———

Thomas noticed Caroline's displeased look when her brother invited him to the picnic. It was reason enough for him to say yes. The look that followed his answer was even better. For some reason, he enjoyed goading her. And she fell for it so easily. A smirk spread across his face.

He followed Adam and Julia outside to the corral, with a quiet Caroline lagging behind. He took the blanket Adam handed him and tied it to the back of his saddle. Both Adam and Julia mounted their horses, before Adam took the picnic basket from Caroline.

When Caroline tried to mount her horse unsuccessfully, Adam teased her. "Always the last one ready."

As the heat rose to her cheeks, Thomas took pity on her. He moved next to the horse, cupping his hands together to give her a boost. Though she accepted his help, she said nothing. He mounted his horse and followed behind the others.

Adam led them to a clearing on the mountain that flanked the western edge of Colter Ranch. "Julia and I found this spot last week. I think you will agree the view is lovely."

Caroline's foul mood seemed to lift a bit. "It's perfect."

She slid down off her horse, far less gracefully than Julia. Adam and Thomas dismounted. Untying the blanket from his saddle, Thomas shook it out.

"Where do you want this?" he asked, thrusting it in Caroline's direction.

She took the offered blanket and spread it out on the flattest area of the clearing before taking a seat. Julia took the picnic basket from Adam and sat down, spreading out the food. Adam sat next to Julia, leaving a spot open next to Caroline for Thomas, so he took it.

"So," Adam started, "I hear you are my sister's rescuer." The light in his eyes hinted at amusement.

"Just happened along at the right time."

"Well, I'm grateful you did," Adam said. He turned toward

Caroline. "Though I'm still not quite sure how she managed to get Pa to agree to such a foolish journey."

Julia laughed. "Caroline could get a bull to think it's a horse."

Thomas smiled.

Caroline frowned.

"She always manages to find the cleverest ways of getting others to do what she wants," Adam said. "Especially men."

"What are you talking about?" Caroline's green eyes flashed dangerously towards her brother.

"Come on. I'll bet before you left Texas you got at least one kiss from Jesse Shoemaker."

Thomas watched as Caroline's jaw slackened and as she stammered. "What? How did you—"

"It was so obvious he was smitten with you. Him and another dozen boys." Nudging Thomas with his elbow, Adam added, "I just don't get what they see in her. She always seemed like a handful to me."

Thomas was tempted to agree with the later statement, though he understood well what any man would see in her. She did have a sly way of getting what she wanted—that much he'd seen already. She was beautiful. When she didn't act contrary, she could be downright sweet.

Her expression was anything but sweet at the moment.

"Just what are you saying?" she asked, crossing her arms over her chest.

"Nothing, really. I'm just teasing you."

Julia interjected, "He's just playing, Caroline. Don't take him so seriously."

As Caroline uncrossed her arms, Thomas wondered if she would let it drop so quickly. He could tell the words hurt, even if that wasn't the intent. It made him wonder just how much truth there was behind the teasing—if she really managed to toy with men so easily. She certainly had with Perry.

"Perry sends his greetings," Thomas said. "He was happy to hear you made it to your new home safely."

Caroline sent a strained smile his way.

Adam rolled his eyes. "Another beau already. You've been here, what, a week?"

"Perry is not a beau. He's a widower."

Thomas stifled a snort. He's a widower alright. One that seems to have forgotten everything about his late wife. One who peppered him with a dozen questions about Caroline as he changed out his horse, both on the trip to La Paz and on the return trip. Yeah, not a beau.

"He was a very gracious host when we stayed at his ranch overnight. He even gave me several things to replace my lost wardrobe, out of Christian charity. Nothing more."

Thomas raised an eyebrow then caught himself. He could not disagree more with her assessment.

"That was very kind of him," Julia agreed.

Silence fell over the group as tension still sizzled from Caroline.

Thomas noted the gray dress she wore today was one of the ones from Perry, only it seemed she found time to tailor it to her curves. The gray color made the green of her eyes that much more noticeable. She looked stunning in the work dress. He could only imagine what those poor boys in Texas struggled with when she wore something fancier. Well, maybe he could imagine.

He found himself staring at her lips. When she cleared her throat and offered a brief scowl, he knew he had been caught.

"So, Thomas, strange that you would happen to know Will's wife," Caroline said with a challenge.

"She was married to my brother before he passed on," Thomas answered, looking off into the valley below.

Caroline's voice softened. "I'm so sorry."

"It's nice to have found her and to have some family nearby."

Julia asked, "How did you end up in the Arizona Territory?"

Thomas recounted the story—at least the most innocuous parts of it. He said nothing about the bank robbery or his jail time. Only that he enlisted to fight for the North.

"It's so perfect that you would go from dispatch riding to

working for the La Paz Express," Caroline said, smiling. "Isn't God amazing?"

"If you believe in that sort of thing."

Her smile faded and he wished he would have just agreed with her. He hadn't wanted to leave the impression that he believed in God when he didn't.

"Well, whether you see it doesn't change the fact that He has a hand in your life."

He glared at her. Of course they were on the opposite sides of this issue. Why not? They had been on pretty much everything else.

Julia changed the topic to her wedding. Caroline seemed less enthused about the picnic and any topic of conversation for the remainder of the outing. He wondered if she was mad at him for his comment or if she had grown weary of the wedding details. He certainly had.

After a leisurely hour, the four packed up and headed back to the ranch.

Once at the ranch, Caroline and Thomas volunteered to take care of the horses while Adam and Julia headed to the house with the picnic basket and blanket.

Thomas rushed through caring for his horse and Adam's. By the time he had finished, Caroline had just started on Julia's horse.

"Need some help?" he asked as she struggled to lift Julia's saddle from the horse.

Caroline stepped back and motioned for him to take the saddle. Then she grabbed the brush from where it balanced on the edge of the stable gate while he removed the rest of the horse's gear.

Thomas couldn't help but ask the question that had been on his mind since Adam brought it up at the picnic.

"So, you like to toy with men?" he asked in a teasing tone.

Caroline stopped mid-brushstroke. Propping one hand on her hip she turned to face him, as he removed the bridle from the horse. "No!"

"Hmm. Your brother makes it sound like you left a trail of

broken hearts back in Texas."

When her cheeks flushed, he knew it was true.

"Then, of course, there's Perry. The man couldn't hardly stop talking about you each time I stopped at his station."

"Oh," she whispered.

"I can see why," Thomas continued. Though his brain warned him to tread carefully, he ignored it. "The way you flirted shamelessly with him, he probably thinks you're madly in love with him."

She lifted the brush to continue caring for the horse. Without looking at him, she responded, rather calmly, "I did not flirt with him. I was just friendly. That's it. I thought we already covered this."

He laughed, slapping his leg from the hilarity of her statement.

"You do know what flirting is, right?"

She flashed him an angry glance while she kept on brushing.

"It's those coy looks you give a man that tangle with his feelings."

She turned to face him, tilting her head down while moving her eyes up to connect with his. "Whatever do you mean?"

She was doing it now and it drove him crazy.

"Please tell me you realize you just did it."

She shook her head.

Really? Is she that naïve?

Stepping closer, he pulled her to him.

"That look," he whispered. "To a man, that is an invitation."

She swallowed and asked softly, "An invitation to what?"

He moved his lips to inches from hers. "This."

Then he lowered his lips to hers, savoring her sweetness. When she didn't hesitate to kiss him back, his senses exploded. He quickly ended the kiss, taking a large step back from her. His breath was ragged, as was hers.

Fool. In trying to teach her a lesson, he learned one himself. She was dangerous, stirring his desire even more this time than the last. He couldn't trust himself around her. Perhaps this was the exact thing Adam understood too well—that Caroline had a natural ability to turn a man inside out.

He looked into her eyes and was surprised by what he saw there. Innocence. Embarrassment. Desire.

Lifting his hat from his head, he ran his fingers through his hair. Maybe she really was that naïve.

As her face reddened more, she turned back towards the horse.

"I suppose you've made your point," she said, the hurt obvious from her tone.

Instantly, he regretted his actions. "I'm sorry—"

"Caroline!" Julia's panicked voice preceded her into the stable. "Caroline!"

"Back here!"

Julia appeared in front of the stable gate. She was shaking and her face had drained of all color.

"He's here."

Caroline moved toward her friend. "Who is here?"

"It's… It's Reuben."

Thomas frowned in confusion. Who was Reuben?

CHAPTER 20

Caroline held back her gasp, hoping not to frighten Julia further. She had to calm her friend down.

"Julia, there's no way Reuben could be here. He's dead."

"I swear it is him. He looks different. But… but the way he dismounted his horse… That's just how Reuben did."

She pushed past Thomas, still very upset with him for his little stunt. Kissing her only to prove a point. The nerve. She put it from her mind, resolving to deal with him later. She ushered Julia outside.

As they neared the stable entrance, Julia slowed her pace, digging her heels in. "I don't want to see him again. Not after what he did to me."

A sob tore from Julia's throat and her shaking increased.

"Talk to me. Tell me who you think looks like Reuben."

"A man… He rode into the ranch… Talking to Adam and Will now." Her voice broke heavily with several sobs, making it difficult for Caroline to understand more.

"Thomas," she said over her shoulder. "Can you please go see who arrived?"

He grunted, not seeming too pleased about her request. But he walked towards the ranch house.

Caroline tried to comfort Julia, whispering soft words in her ear as she rocked her back and forth. If it really was Reuben, then she could understand Julia's fears. He had hurt her in the worst way possible. She had been there for Julia the night of his horrific deed, arranging for Julia to flee with Adam. She couldn't stand seeing her relive this.

But Reuben was dead. True, no one had ever found a body. That wouldn't be the first time someone encountered Hiram Norton's men and mysteriously disappeared without a trace. A few times the unfortunate soul would be found, or rather his remains, months later in some remote place.

Caroline remembered overhearing a conversation Mary Colter, Reuben's wife, had with another woman at the mercantile. Mary said that Hiram and his men showed up to collect on a debt Reuben owed. Last she had seen him, he was in his office. When she came in from hanging the laundry, Reuben was gone. Instead, Hiram waited at Reuben's desk with an offer for Mary. Caroline hadn't heard anything further that day. It was later that the rumor circulated that Reuben had been killed.

Something in her gut told her he was gone. It was unfathomable to think of him leaving his wife and children behind, much less the Star C in which he took so much pride.

Nevertheless, Julia held on to her tightly, very distraught over the unexpected visitor.

Thomas approached from the ranch house. "His name is Robert Garrett. Says he's from Indiana. Has a good Midwestern accent too."

"There," Caroline said to Julia. "That proves it can't be Reuben. Why he could no more hide his Texas heritage than you or I can."

Julia pulled away from her embrace. Hesitantly, she asked, "Are you certain?"

"He said he's got a ranch down near Wickenburg," Thomas said. "He heard of Will's reputation for providing quality horses, so he made the trip to see about purchasing a few. Neither Will or Adam seemed to recognize him."

Caroline waited to see what Julia's reaction would be. Slowly she stood a little straighter. Folding her arms across her waist, she said, "I guess you must think me touched."

"Not at all." Caroline reassured her. "If he did something that reminded you of Reuben—well, it's no wonder that you would react that way."

Will, Adam, and Robert Garrett emerged from the ranch house, walking towards the stables.

"Let's take a walk around the lake," Caroline suggested, steer-ing Julia that direction.

As they walked past the men, Julia stopped, following Robert with her eyes for several minutes.

"I think I'd like to go lay down," Julia said, before darting in-to the house.

She sighed. For the first time in weeks, she lifted a prayer heavenward, asking God to be with Julia.

"Who's Reuben?"

She jumped at Thomas's voice, sounding behind her. In her haste to help Julia, she hadn't noticed him following her.

"Her brother. The oldest of the Colter children."

Thomas nodded, not pressing for more details.

"Shouldn't you be heading back soon?"

"Naw. Hannah invited me to stay for supper and even of-fered up the extra bunk in the bunkhouse for the night. I thought it might be nice to spend the time here."

She walked to one of the rockers on the front porch and sat. The temperature seemed more pleasant in the shade, especially with a hint of coolness on the breeze. Thomas sat in the other rocker. She wished he'd go bother someone else.

Her anger started to rise. Even though she hadn't fully un-derstood what he was saying about her flirting and looking at men a certain way—that didn't give him the right to kiss her. His quick apology made her wonder if it had meant anything at all to him. She liked it as much as she had his first kiss. She wasn't really sure if she was mad at him or just mad at herself for enjoying it so much.

She let out a long slow breath, trying to dissolve her anger. Maybe she was naïve in the ways of men. She knew how to get her way with Papa. But beaus? Well, if she was really honest with herself, there was a lot of truth in what both Adam and Thomas had said. She did tend to get her way.

Perhaps Thomas's warning was well-meant. After all, she had no idea how deeply men seemed to react to her. She was shocked when Nathan showed an interest in her even after her embarrassing scheme.

Then there was Perry. From what Thomas said, Perry seemed smitten. She hadn't tried to win his affections. She didn't want him to think of her as anything more than a friend.

The broach. She still had his wife's broach. She would have to see him again. Maybe when he next came to Prescott, she would be able to tell if what Thomas said was true. She could fix this—tell him how much she appreciated his kindness when she was in need but make it clear that she held no romantic feelings for him.

She only thought of one man that way.

"Look," Thomas said, disturbing the quiet, "I'm really sorry for saying all those things earlier. I didn't mean to hurt you."

At least he didn't apologize for the kiss.

"What you said is true," she confessed. "I'm just a silly girl, ignorant in how my behavior affects others."

He angled his chair to see her better.

"You are far from a silly girl."

Caroline crossed her arms and looked away. She certainly felt like a silly girl.

"Maybe a bit naïve. But you are an amazing, beautiful woman."

She turned to look at him, doubting his sincerity. His expression was quite serious.

Thomas fidgeted with the arm of the rocker. He suddenly seemed very nervous. He cleared his throat twice. Then he parted his lips as if he was about to say something else before locking them tightly shut.

An awkward silence settled over them.

Caroline pushed her rocker into motion, relaxing her posture. She and Thomas always seemed at odds with each other.

Yet, she felt drawn to him.

"Seems to me," she started, "that you and I got off to a bad start from the first time we met in Wickenburg. Perhaps we should agree to start over?"

The right side of Thomas's mouth turned up in a half-smile. "I'd like that."

"Me too."

Baby James cried from inside the house, providing the escape she hoped for. "If you'll excuse me, I'm going to see how I can help Hannah."

At his nod, she turned and went inside the house.

She found Hannah changing the baby's diaper in her room. She waited until Hannah entered the main room again before asking about whether they should begin supper preparations. Hannah laid the baby in a bassinette near the kitchen then outlined the planned meal. Caroline grabbed several potatoes and began peeling.

Her face flushed and she smiled, thrilled that Thomas called her beautiful.

"What's the dreamy look for?" Hannah teased.

The heat on her face grew more intense. "Thomas kissed me," she expelled the words with a rush of air.

A frown crinkled Hannah's forehead. "How much do you know about Thomas? Or even why Drew and I left Cincinnati?"

Caroline sighed. "I know Thomas was in the war. That he rode dispatches for an important major general. I know that he rescued me when I was stranded in the desert." Her voice faded as she tried to think of something more.

"Rescuing you was probably one of the best moments in his life. One of the few selfless acts to his credit." A hint of bitterness sounded in Hannah's voice.

"It sounds as if you don't care for him much. Seems rather odd to invite him to stay for the evening, if that is the case."

Hannah turned back to the food items she set out and busied her hands. Sighing heavily, she said, "It has long been my prayer that he would act more responsibly and spend his time and energy pursuing good things. While he's changed some since leaving Ohio, I can still see the draw and pull of his old pursuits."

Caroline continued peeling the potato, confused by Hannah's cryptic words.

"Unlike you, I have known him rather well for a number of years. I've seen the best of him, and the worst of him. I know just what kind of heartache he's capable of inflicting."

"Why are you telling me all this?"

Hannah turned to face her. "Because, that dreamy look you just had—letting him kiss you—" She shook her head. "It's far more likely to end in your broken heart than the dream in your mind's eye."

Tapping her foot unconsciously, Caroline bit back a sharp retort. It sounded to her like Hannah didn't really care for Thomas, which made no sense considering she let him treat her son like his nephew and she let him visit her home often and sit at her dinner table.

"So, you don't think he is a good man?"

Hannah turned back to the meal preparations. "I think he is a man who desires to be good but doesn't quite know how to get there yet. He's torn between living up to the expectations he thinks Drew had and living for pleasure and for whatever he thinks freedom is.

"It was very difficult when he lived with Drew and I back in Ohio. There was no peace in our house when he was there. And his actions ultimately led to us leaving."

"Do you hate him for it?" Caroline asked with an edge to her voice.

"No. I have forgiven him for many wrongs. And I see the man he is trying to be. I just don't think it is wise for any woman to give her heart to a man who is searching for something he can't even define."

Caroline rinsed the peeled potatoes and began cutting them into smaller chunks. Though she barely knew Hannah, she felt like she could trust her judgment. She seemed to be a wise and fair woman.

Yet, the memory of Thomas's kisses was not easily erased. He made her feel like a woman, and she liked it.

"How old is he?"

Hannah paused, thinking. "Twenty-two."

Only four years older than her. That was a reasonable age difference.

She dropped the potatoes into a pot of boiling water on the stove.

He was a handsome man. Sandy brown hair. Blue eyes. He didn't laugh often, but sometimes she thought she saw a hint of it in his eyes, especially when he was being contrary. Though he was barely taller than her, she didn't mind. His arms felt strong when he pulled her to him. She felt safe there, even if she had been upset by his reason for his kiss.

Will entered the ranch house. "I've invited Robert Garrett to join us for supper. He should still have enough daylight to make it back to Prescott if he leaves right after."

Hannah stretched up on her tippy toes to place a kiss on his cheek before chasing him from her kitchen. As he left, Rosa entered.

Caroline suddenly felt the small kitchen area became too crowded. She wiped her hands on a towel and excused herself, feeling awkward again. She just didn't know what to do with herself. It seemed there was more than enough help at Colter Ranch to see to all the cooking and cleaning.

Stepping outside, she took a deep breath, letting the light fragrance of pine and juniper ease some of her tension. She moved toward the lake, deciding a walk would suit her mood just fine. As she reached the nearest shore, she heard her name being called.

"Care for some company?" Thomas asked.

She nodded and he fell into step beside her.

"I don't fit in here," she confessed, preferring to talk out her problems.

"Didn't you grow up on a ranch? I would think this would be second nature."

Gazing out at the shimmering blue water, she squinted against the harsh reflection of the late afternoon sun.

"True, I grew up on the ranch. But Will seems to have more than enough help. He doesn't need another woman under foot. Besides, when Julia and Adam get married in a few weeks, I'm not going to have a place to stay. I just don't know what I'm going to do with myself."

"You could always move in with Betty Lancaster. Maybe she could use some help at the boardinghouse."

"I guess. I had been thinking about trying to get a job in town. I mean, I'd still be close enough to visit Julia and Adam often. And I wouldn't be nearly so bored if I had a job."

They were almost around the lake when the supper bell rang. She quickened her pace so as not to keep the Colters waiting. Thomas easily matched her stride.

When they arrived at the house, she paused, catching her breath before entering the room. Will, Hannah, Julia, Adam, and Robert Garrett were already seated.

"Sorry," she apologized under her breath.

Will quickly introduced her and Thomas to Robert Garrett. Something seemed familiar about him—though nothing like Reuben. No, it was something else—like she had met him before, here in the Arizona Territory.

She took her seat across from Thomas and bowed her head as Will said grace.

When she looked up, she noticed Julia's pale face. She stared at her plate of food, avoiding any eye contact with Robert.

Caroline studied him as the conversation floated around her. He looked older than Will. He had dark brown eyes and light, almost blonde, hair. His posture was rigid like someone more refined. His skin was tanned from much time in the sun. His voice was deep and flowed with a definite Northern accent. There was no doubt in Caroline's mind that he was from the North.

Yet, his tone sounded familiar to her.

She shook her head slightly, not able to determine how or where she had met him.

The meal ended rather quickly and Robert thanked the Colters for their hospitality before he left, indicating he would send some men to retrieve the horses he purchased within the month.

Thomas also took his leave, heading to the bunkhouse, probably eager for the company of other men.

She stifled her sigh as Julia stood and made some excuse to walk with Adam. They were so enamored with each other. She supposed that was what love was like.

Things really had worked out much, much differently than she expected when she left Texas. Maybe she wouldn't feel so out of sorts once she settled on where she would live and what she would do.

———

Robert smiled to himself as he headed back to town. The trip to Colter Ranch had been extremely productive. First, he learned that no one recognized his real identity. Caroline had not seemed to recognize him from the stagecoach robbery either. That was good.

He purchased the horses he needed for his ranch, ironically with the money he made from the sale of the stagecoach horses—horses that had been trained by Larson.

Another key piece of information he picked up tonight was the Thomas Anderson connection. The express rider was the one who rescued Caroline—the one she seemed to be smitten with. He also had some sort of connection to Will's wife, though Robert didn't completely understand what it was. He would keep an eye on Anderson. See if things went anywhere with Caroline. Who knows, he might be able to provide some leverage for inflicting pain on Caroline or Adam—perhaps even the Colters.

Best of all, he learned that Colter had a son. There was no better way to destroy a man's life than to strike at his son. It would require extreme patience on his part, but the plan forming in his mind would eventually yield the most painful blow to Colter.

CHAPTER 21

Colter Ranch

September 17, 1865

Ben Shepherd climbed into his bunk as the rest of the men settled down for the night after a long day working the cattle. It was quieter than normal, with a good number of the men gone to drive part of the herd to California. For the first time in twenty-five years, Ben was not on that drive. Instead, he stayed behind at Will's request while Warren Cahill acted as trail boss.

He felt strange on the morning the boys pulled out with one thousand head. Usually, it was his job to make sure they kept out of trouble on the drive. Now, that part of his job seemed to be parceled out to the younger Cahill. Will hadn't really explained his reasoning for the change. He just asked Ben to stay, leaving no room for arguments.

He shouldn't be too surprised. Will knew about the stiffness in his leg. Even gave him a funny look or two as Ben tried to awkwardly mount his horse. *Face it, Ben. Ya ain't getting any younger. Boss knows it.*

Young or not, he worked twice as hard today since they only kept a few men at the ranch to manage the two thousand head left. With the contracts Will secured in town and at the fort, there was a good chance they would all stay at the ranch next year. He hadn't worked that hard in a long time and he was weary.

Rolling onto his side, Ben closed his heavy eyes and drifted off to sleep.

———

"Benjamin," Sheila greeted him with a kiss on his cheek as he stepped into the small one room shack after a long day plowing the field in the sweltering heat. "Supper is almost ready."

He nodded, taking his seat at the head of the table. A gurgling cry came from the bed in the corner. Ben stood and scooped his son, Elijah, into his arms, a smile unconsciously gracing his lips.

"He's been fussy all day," Sheila said. "Think he's coming down with something."

Ben bounced his son up and down on his knee trying to comfort him. That familiar sense of overwhelming love flooded his heart—the same way it did every time he held Elijah in his arms. As his son quieted, he returned him to the bassinette so he could eat the meal his wife prepared.

As he looked at the simple bland fare before him, he felt a pang of guilt. As a poor tenement farmer, he couldn't afford better food. He was lucky to be able to provide enough for two meals a day, not providing any better than his father had even though he worked twice as hard and with immeasurably more integrity.

When Sheila took her seat across from him, he bowed his head. "Thank you, Lord for this food before us and for the strength it provides. Amen."

After the meal was finished, Ben started to stand. Sheila stopped him. "I have something special for you."

A smile lit his face as she set a small cake in front of him.

"What's this for?"

"To celebrate."

He searched his mind for a minute. It wasn't his birthday. Nor was it hers. They already celebrated their fourth anniversary a few months ago. The memory of that celebration widened his smile and warmed his heart.

"I have some news," she said, partially answering his question. "Elijah is going to have a brother or sister soon."

Ben shook his head trying to understand what she was telling him. Then it settled into his heart. He was going to be a father again.

Abundant love filled his soul. He stood and moved to where his wife sat, pulling her to her feet. Pressing his lips against hers, he kissed her deeply as he held her tight. Her lips eagerly drank in his caresses for several minutes until she leaned back in his embrace, gazing into his eyes with abiding love.

"Another child," he whispered in disbelief. "When?"

"I'm about three months along now, so in another six months."

He held her close for a minute, joy filling his heart. She finally broke the embrace.

"Eat your cake, Benjamin," she said, lightly pushing him towards his seat with a playful smile lighting her face.

Before he got the first bite to his mouth a knock sounded at the door. Laying the fork down, he squeezed Sheila's shoulder before seeing who was there.

It was one of the house slaves from the plantation house.

"Massah be callin' for ya," he said.

"Tell him I'll see him first thing in the morning," Ben replied.

"He say you come now."

The oddity of the request concerned Ben. Usually, the plantation owner conducted his affairs with the tenement farmers in the morning. Strange that he would request Ben's presence tonight, with little notice.

When he turned to look at Sheila, her nutmeg brown eyes widened in fear. "Don't go."

He understood where that fear came from. A few weeks ago, they had been visited in the middle of the night. Ben had heard nothing, but it was obvious by the state of things in the house that someone had broken in. Since then, he took extra precautions at night—securing the house, not leaving Sheila and Elijah alone.

But the master gave him little choice tonight.

"I'll be back soon," he promised, before following the slave up to the big house.

The meeting was bizarre. First, it was held in the library and not the master's study. Ben had never been in this room before. Then, as the master conversed, he seemed nervous and chatty, not really discussing anything of significance related to the crops or to Ben's farm. It made no sense. He didn't appear to be getting to the urgent matter—whatever it was—anytime quickly. After an hour, Ben tried to excuse himself, but the master kept him there.

Until one of the house servants burst through the door.

"Fire!"

Ben bolted to his feet as the hair rose on the back of his neck. Something seemed wrong. The strange meeting with the master. Now a fire.

As he scrambled out the front door, he scanned the horizon. Smoke floated thick on the breeze. Fire blazed in the night sky. Shouts came from the slave quarters as men and women rushed to find the source of the fire.

He spotted it. Just to the right of a large tree. His stomach lurched as he realized he was staring at his own house. Heart pounding loudly in his ears, he took off running towards home.

"Sheila!" he screamed breathlessly as he got closer.

The small shack that had been his home burned with a fierce heat. The walls and roof were on fire. Angry red flames licked thirstily for more fuel.

His feet beat out a frantic rhythm.

"Sheila!"

As he neared, he scanned the area. Panic constricted his throat. She was not outside. Nor was his son.

"Sheila! Elijah!" his shouts sounded above the deafening flames.

Arriving at the door, he saw it was bolted tightly shut—from the outside. Panic turned to rage. He charged the door with his broad shoulder. It barely moved. Again, he knocked on the door, blinded with fear. His wife and child were inside. He had to free them.

Blood trickled down his shoulder from a cut. Still, he tried one more time. The door came loose. Sheila lay on the floor, not moving. His son clutched closely to her chest.

He stepped a foot over the threshold as the loud splintering of the roof echoed in his ears. Then he watched, stunned, when it collapsed onto his family. The force of the impact knocked him back on the ground.

When he looked up, several men stood around him with large sticks in their hands. One held a torch.

"Should never have married a darkie. Ain't right, mixing white blood with hers."

A sharp blow struck him in the head and everything went black.

———

Ben woke, drenched in sweat. It had been years since he dreamed about the night he lost everything. The night Sheila died. The night his heart died.

His chest heaved as he tried to take a steady breath.

Rolling off his bunk, he stood and quietly left the stifling bunkhouse. Standing on the porch, he looked out into the darkness of night.

Oh, how he missed her. Her soft ebony skin. Her tightly curled coarse black hair. Her dark nutmeg eyes. Her bright white teeth framed with dark plump lips as she smiled at him. Her alluring hips. Her gentle touch. Her sweet spirit.

Tears formed rivers down the side of his face. She had been gone so long. He couldn't remember what it was like to hold her in his arms. He couldn't remember the feeling of her body next to his at night. Her face was growing elusive, her voice distant. The memories faded—almost nothing was left.

"I don't want to let ya go," he whispered to the night. "I love you. Still."

His son would have been twenty-six today. His unborn child would be just two years younger.

Ben pounded his fist down on the porch railing as the utter loneliness ripped through his heart. He held back the angry wail threatening to explode from his mouth.

It hurt so much.

Gripping the railing, he bowed his head. If he had never married her, she would not have died. It was his fault. He knew better than marrying her. He was white. She was not. That should have meant she was off limits.

As many times as he tried to reason with his heart, it just wouldn't listen. He loved her. He loved Sheila for who she was. Funny, happy, loving, kind. She had a calming effect on him. He always felt at ease and secure around her. She helped heal the wounds inflicted by his drunken father, both emotional and physical. She was his life.

Then she was gone.

———

Wake up, Betty.

The familiar voice stirred her from a deep sleep. It wasn't the first time the Lord had woken her in the middle of the night. She knew what the call meant.

Sliding from her bed, she kneeled. Clasping her hands together, she rested her forehead on them. *Who is it, Lord? Who needs my prayers?*

Ben Shepherd.

For a brief second, Betty thought she heard wrong. She thought perhaps one of her children or grandchildren in Missouri needed covered in prayer tonight.

But Ben Shepherd?

Lord, Jesus. I don't understand, but here I am. Put your covering of grace and mercy on Benjamin. You know his heart, his hurt. You know what he needs at this late hour. Send your angels to protect him and comfort him. Fill him with your peace and love.

On and on she prayed for Ben Shepherd until her head began to droop. Then she crawled into bed and fell back to sleep, warmed with confidence that God heard her cries.

———

Ben didn't know how long he kneeled on the bunkhouse porch—only that the stiffness in his leg sent shooting pain up to his thigh.

He wasn't exactly sure what just happened. He'd been railing against God, mired deeply in his grief one minute. Then the next, a strange peace fell over him.

He began talking to God, pouring out all his pain. Telling Him how much he missed his wife and children. How he wanted them back. How he was so sorry that his love for her caused her death.

Something changed in his heart. He wasn't the same. He wasn't drowning with grief anymore.

Twenty-five years of not speaking to God were washed away as if they never happened. He remembered the faith Sheila shared with him. He remembered how it had once been his own—his lifeblood. He reached out and embraced the loving Father that was so incredibly different from his earthly one.

Then he wept. He wept tears of relief, tears of joy.

An image of Sheila bouncing two little boys, one on each hip, filled his vision. The light around her glowed brightly. Her smile was even bigger than he remembered.

Let me go, Benjamin. It's time.

And he did.

———

She was in love. Betty sighed. At the age of fifty-two, her husband long gone, all thought of loving another man pushed aside, and here she was as giddy as a schoolgirl waiting for Benjamin Shepherd to arrive.

A smile stretched across her face as she dished up another plate full of dinner for her hungry boarders and other diners seeking a hearty midday meal. Paul had noticed her behavior more than a month ago. He even told her that she had feelings for Ben. He was right.

Two nights ago, her midnight vigil for Ben hadn't really ended though she fell asleep. When she rose yesterday morning, he consumed many of her prayers all the way through the present morning.

Then, just before serving dinner, she felt a calm peace. Reassuring. Gentle. Something happened to Ben Shepherd, and she was pretty sure it involved an encounter with God. That realization broke open the lock she kept on her heart. If Ben was truly walking with the Lord, as she knew in her heart that he was, there was no reason to hold back. No reason at all.

"Got a few more, Ma," Paul announced as he picked up four plates, skillfully balancing them in his arms before walking back into the dining hall.

Well, maybe there was one reason to hold back. Her son. What would happen to Paul and how would he manage this boardinghouse if she left?

Whoa there. There's a long distance to cover between opening my heart to Ben and becoming his wife. Heat flamed her cheeks as she grew embarrassed by her rash thoughts.

"Betty," Ben said, coming up behind her.

Her heart fluttered. The glow in his gray eyes drew her in. Something definitely changed in Ben Shepherd.

"Have a seat, Benjamin," she said. "I'll bring you some dinner."

In two blinks of her eyes, she was back.

A long sigh escaped his lips. He took her hand in his.

"Missed ya," he said before brushing his lips across the back of her hand.

Betty's heart picked up speed when his gray eyes searched hers. For a brief second, she thought he might kiss her. But he didn't. He led her to the kitchen, away from the few lingering diners. She poured two cups of coffee and set them on the table.

"Got so much to tell ya."

He motioned for her to sit then he took the seat across from her.

"I… I'm not sure where to begin." His gaze dropped to the table, one hand firmly gripping a coffee mug as if it would give him the courage he needed to speak.

She wanted to suggest he start with whatever happened two nights ago. But she knew better than to push the Lord's timing. She just wanted to know. More than anything.

"I never apologized to ya for my abrupt departure from yer dinner table a while back. I'm truly sorry. I know how much ya love having friends and family around a table and I know I caused some trouble that day."

She could hardly believe what he was saying. Why he had to be talking about the Sunday he came to church and left in the middle of dinner. It's the only time she'd seen him angry. Or was it afraid?

That had been almost a month ago.

Reaching for his hand, she curled her fingers around his. His eyes looked up from the coffee mug and connected with hers. She smiled.

"All has been forgiven, Benjamin."

"I know I ain't said much about my life," Ben said. "But I'd like to tell ya more."

"I'd like that."

"Might take me some time."

She laughed. "We've got plenty of it."

He smiled, but it faded too quickly. His gaze fell back to the barely sipped coffee again.

"I was married. Long time ago."

Of all the things he could have confessed to her! She just never thought, not even for a second, that he had been married once. As she recovered from her shock, she kept her lips sealed in an encouraging smile.

He glanced up then his eyes darted away again. "She died."

His voice cracked and tears reddened his eyes. "Along with my son and unborn child."

Lord, send your comforting love to this poor man who has lost so much.

He swiped at the tear that rolled down his face. "My son, Elijah, would have been twenty-six a few days ago."

"I'm so sorry, Ben."

She stood and pulled him to his feet. Then she wrapped her arms around him. He eagerly accepted her embrace, burying his head on her shoulder. Other than the slight tremor of his shoulders, he made no sound.

Minutes ticked by as she held him. Finally, he lifted his head and looked into her eyes. His were red and tear-streaked. A shy smile turned up the corners of his mouth as he took a step back.

"Don't know why I just told ya that." He pinched the bridge of his nose then pulled his hat down lower to shade his eyes.

A small laugh escaped his lips. "Guess I'd tell ya just about anything, Betty Lancaster. Better keep my secrets guarded."

Though he was teasing, she wanted to allay his fears. "Your secrets are safe with me. I am honored you told me."

"Ain't told anyone besides Eddie, Will's pa."

She wanted to ask more. What was his wife like? How long had they been married? How old was his son when he died? How did it happen?

Yet, his posture stiffened. The nervous way he fidgeted with the coffee mug after he hastily sat down again told her he was retreating. But she did have one answer. It was on his son's birthday that she woke up to pray for him. The Lord was doing some mighty work on him.

"Anyway," he was saying, "I wanted to let ya know I'll be coming for Sunday dinner... If ya might have me."

Hope soared within her chest. Joy barely restrained itself in her smile.

"I'd be delighted to set an extra plate. And to save you a seat at service?"

"Appreciate it. 'Course I'll see ya at the wedding first."

She smiled. She was looking forward to time with him on Saturday, but now she had even more to look forward to.

CHAPTER 22

Colter Ranch

September 23, 1865

"Eddie, ya'd be so proud of Julia," Ben whispered as he led Sheila from her stall. "She asked me—can ya believe it—to stand up fer her in yer place. Wish ya were here, but I'm right proud to be doin' it."

Ben hurried through brushing down his black horse before he saddled her. Leading her outside, he tied her reins to the top rung of the corral. Then he went back inside to prepare a horse for the wagon. He and Will had to get the women on their way to Prescott before the boys would let Adam out of the bunkhouse. Funny how sentimental cowboys could be when one of their own was getting married.

After hitching the horse to the wagon, he climbed up on the seat and drove the wagon a short distance from the barn to the ranch house. Setting the brake, he climbed down, trying not to muss his suit. A smile teased the corners of his mouth. Wouldn't Betty be surprised to see him all gussied up.

"Is Adam out there?" Julia's excited voice sounded from the other side of the door as he approached.

"Naw, little Jewel. Covington, Jed, and Hawk won't let him near a door or a window."

Julia opened the door and let Ben in.

"Can you help us get all these things in the wagon?" Hannah asked him.

"Yes ma'am," he answered trying to keep the awe from his voice. He knew the womenfolk had been baking and cooking up a storm but never expected the huge spread on the table. Why wasn't there hardly an inch of the tabletop showing. He wondered if one wagon was going to be enough.

"Wait," Hannah stopped him as he reached for a few of the food items. "Maybe we should put Caroline's things in first."

Caroline ran back to the room she shared with Julia and returned with a carpet bag. Ben took it from her; his brow wrinkled in confusion.

"I'm moving to town," Caroline said. "You think Betty will let me stay with her for now?"

"I'm sure she'll let ya stay long as ya need."

Her shoulders lifted then sagged as she let out a huge breath. "Good."

He took her carpet bag and headed outside, placing it towards the front of the wagon. Guess it made sense, her moving to town. He'd feel a bit awkward living in a small cabin with two married couples. Though, Will told him the big house would be ready in a few more weeks. He shrugged. Not really any of his business either way. Long as Adam was fine with it, him being her nearest kin, then no one else had much to say.

Will neared the wagon with an armload of food which he deposited in the wagon. Ben followed him back inside to retrieve more items. In no time they had the wagon full of food, leaving some space for Caroline to ride in the back.

"Ready?" Will asked his wife and sister.

Julia let out a little laugh. "I'm as ready as any girl can be on her wedding day."

Ben noticed the slight sheen in Will's eyes as he pulled his sister close for a hug. When he seemed to hold on longer than Julia wanted, she pushed him away.

"It's not like I'm moving away. I'll be back in a few days," she said.

"We'd better get going," Hannah said.

Will escorted her to the wagon and lifted her onto the seat. Then Julia handed baby James up to her before climbing up onto the wagon. Ben helped Caroline get settled in the back. Then Ben and Will mounted their horses and led the way to town.

Since Julia insisted on getting there before noon, Ben and Will would have some time on their hands before the afternoon wedding. His preference would be to spend that time with Betty. But she would be much too busy serving up dinner for her boarders and with any last-minute preparations for the wedding.

Maybe he would stop by the barber shop for a cut and shave.

———

Caroline lifted her face to the warm sun, enjoying the gentle breeze tickling her cheeks. Julia would have a perfect day for her wedding in the town square. Though she wondered at first why Julia wanted to have the wedding in town instead of at the ranch, she understood after she told her about the number of friends she made during her time working at the Juniper House. Both the hotel manager and owner, along with many of the staff, planned to be in attendance.

She lifted her hand to her lips to stifle a giggle. If anyone had asked her two years ago which one of them would be married first, she would have said herself. Strange how God has a way of changing the most obvious of plans.

Look at her. A year ago, she never dreamed she would be in the Arizona Territory with her brother and her best friend. She would not have thought she would have met a man who caused her heart to race every time she saw him.

She hadn't asked if Thomas would be there today or not. From what Hannah told her, his schedule for the Express only allowed him one weekend a month in Prescott. His other stays were midweek. She didn't think that either Julia or Adam were close enough to him to make sure the wedding fell on his weekend in town.

Regardless, she hoped he was there. None of Hannah's warnings kept her from thinking of him. She wasn't sure how much she trusted Hannah's opinion of him. After all, she had said that she and her first husband left Ohio to get away from him. That sounded like she didn't care for him as much as she might try to convince others she did.

Caroline sighed. Though the day was about Adam and Julia, if Thomas was there, she would try to spend more time with him. His kisses left no doubt that there was something between them. He even seemed more agreeable after she suggested they start over.

Julia pulled the wagon to a stop in front of Lancaster's boardinghouse. She hopped down before Will or Ben dismounted, reaching up for her nephew. Will helped Hannah down while Ben assisted Caroline from the back.

Brushing the dust from her skirt, she looked up when she felt eyes staring at her. Was her skirt accidentally caught on the wagon or something?

"Need some help?" Thomas's voice sounded behind her.

She glanced down, noting there was nothing wrong with her attire. When her gaze connected with his, he smiled then pointed towards the items in the wagon.

"Oh. Sure."

"Hannah, dear!" Betty's voice announced her presence near the wagon.

"Betty," Hannah said. Anything further was cut off by a huge embrace.

"Let me see that grandson of mine." She fussed over the baby then turned her fussing toward Julia in the form of another big hug. "Are you excited, dear?"

"Very."

"Caroline, dear," Betty greeted, headed her way. She barely blinked before being crushed against Betty's bosom. "Hannah tells me you are looking for a place to stay."

When had she mentioned that? "Ah, yes. On Monday I'll start looking for a job."

"You are more than welcome to stay with me as long as necessary. Paul will move out to one of the open bunks."

Thomas stopped next to her, grinning. "You're moving to town?"

She swallowed and nodded, her stomach fluttering in response to his happy reaction.

He didn't stay still for long. With arms full of wedding feast food, he hurried inside. Paul, Will, and Ben helped with the rest of the goodies.

Caroline reached over the side of the wagon to grab her carpet bag. Betty led her to the private rooms near the kitchen in the back.

"You can just toss your things over there on that chair for now. I'll fix up Paul's bed for you later." Turning to Julia and Hannah, Betty asked, "So what are the plans? Are we styling hair? Or would you like some dinner before the primping begins?"

Baby James fussed in Hannah's arms. "Looks like one of us is hungry."

"You go ahead and nurse James, dear. Ladies, come with me." She led the way to the kitchen.

"I'm not sure how much I can eat right now," Julia said as Betty placed a huge helping of food in front of her.

Caroline was about to suggest they could share when Betty placed an equally large plate in front of her.

"Just eat your fill, dear. Don't want you swooning from hunger in the middle of your wedding."

Julia's eyes widened before she lifted the first bite to her mouth in an exaggerated fashion. Caroline giggled.

"Where's your man?" Betty asked.

Caroline nearly choked until she realized the question was directed at Julia.

"He'll be along later."

———

Thomas allowed his heart to soar as he set the last crate of food on one of the dining hall tables. Caroline was moving to town today. After the wedding and the feast, she would not be returning to Colter Ranch. She would stay here.

It had been three weeks since the picnic with her, Adam, and Julia. Three weeks since he kissed her—the second time—and he could not get her out of his mind. He thought about her when he was on the trail. She said she wanted to start over. So did he.

He wanted to talk to her, to spend time with her, without being irritable or goading her on. He wanted to learn more about the mysterious Caroline Larson.

Now she would be here in town. The weeks when he was in town on Mondays and Tuesdays, he could see her in the evenings. The weeks where he was here for Fridays, Saturdays, and Sundays, he could see her in the evening and plan an outing with her. Hopefully he would be able to control his attraction and get to know her as Paul suggested.

He was trying so hard to be a better man. He hadn't been to the saloon in over a month. Well, there was one night in La Paz. But he had not gotten drunk or done anything others would think shameful.

It was more difficult to avoid the saloon in La Paz than it had been here. In Prescott, he had Paul keeping tabs on him. He had even taken to helping Paul or other townsfolk on his days off. But in La Paz he had too much idle time on his hands. Other than sleeping in the morning after he arrived, he found the two days off to be much too long. On this last trip, Mr. Denton suggested the steam ships coming into the dock might need some help unloading and delivering supplies. Thomas decided he would investigate it on his next trip.

"Hey Thomas!" Paul's call interrupted his thoughts. "Can you give me a hand outside setting up benches for the wedding?"

"Sure."

He lifted the other end of the first bench Paul grabbed and the two carried it out to the designated area. In a few minutes they had all the benches moved from the dining hall.

"Craig Roundtree said he had a few makeshift benches we

could borrow for the day. Ma thinks half the town will be here."

Thomas could understand that. He had lived here long enough to know both Julia and Adam were well loved.

After a few trips across the street to the livery, Paul and Thomas had everything set up.

———

Betty smiled at the three women seated at her kitchen table. They were the closest she had to daughters in this wild territory. Homesickness for her own girls threatened to bring tears to her eyes. She was missing so much of her flesh and blood grandchildren's lives.

I am where you called me to be. Thank you, Lord.

Hannah stood, handing the baby to her. "Will you hold him while I help Julia with her hair?"

"Of course, dear."

Hannah led Julia back into Betty's private room. Betty and Caroline followed. As Hannah began working Julia's hair, the four women chatted.

"How did you know you were in love with my brother?" Caroline asked.

Pink graced Julia's cheeks. "It was more of a gradual realization for me, I guess. It's so different when you've known someone all your life. I knew he was steady, dependable, and honest. I didn't have to learn about his character or who he was. I think perhaps when he gave me the horse figurine for my birthday, I really started to see him differently. I missed him when I was working at the hotel, and I couldn't talk to him whenever I wanted."

"I'm not sure I'll ever be able to tell," Caroline mumbled.

"Dear, you'll know. It will be something special. A man will capture your attention. You won't be able to think of any other besides him."

Caroline began brushing out her hair. "Is it possible to fall in love and barely know him?"

Hannah glanced up from the ringlet she was pinning into place on Julia's head. A brief frown shaded her eyes before disappearing. Betty knew there was something behind the look, so she weighed her words carefully.

"I think it is possible to be attracted to a man and barely know anything about him. I don't know about love though. I think love is more settled. It grows as you learn more about him and his character."

Caroline tapped her finger rapidly against her temple.

"Uh oh," Julia let out a groan. "I know that." She waved her finger in the air towards Caroline's tapping finger. "Are you sweet on someone?"

Caroline quickly lowered her hand to her lap. Red dusted her cheeks. "Maybe."

Hannah spoke up. "You need to put him from your mind."

"Who?" Julia asked.

Then it dawned on Betty. Only one person would cause Hannah's sternness. It had to be Thomas.

"Think about what I told you." Hannah directed her eyes towards Caroline.

"That is your opinion. Perhaps I hold a different one."

"What are you talking about?" Julia asked.

Caroline's defensive posture softened. "Never mind, Julia. It's your wedding day. We should be talking about you."

Betty made a mental note to talk to Caroline more about the subject in the coming days while she stayed with her. If she truly held feelings for Thomas—it would be wise to caution her. He needed more time to get his heart in order.

"Have you and Adam talked about children?" Caroline asked.

Julia stammered, "Ah… Sort of… We'd like children. We would welcome them whenever they come."

"Are you nervous about tonight?"

"Caroline!"

"I was just asking. I'm sure Hannah or Betty could set aside any fears you might have."

"What would you know of it?"

"Mama talked to me about what to expect before I left Texas. She said she didn't want me in a situation where there might not be other women around to ease my fears."

Betty smiled as she swayed back and forth, lulling James to sleep. Caroline was a little more on the brazen side.

"I… Hannah and I… We talked."

A curt nod was Caroline's response.

When both Julia and Caroline were ready, Betty handed James back to Hannah. She left the three women to check on all the preparations. She couldn't stand the thought of something not being ready for the big event.

As she stepped out the back door, she nearly collided with a gentleman.

"Oh, excuse me."

"Betty."

"Ben!" She gasped. My, he looked handsome in his dark gray suit and clean-shaven face. Without the gray flecks of his former beard, he looked younger. *Be still my heart.*

A grin brightened his face. "Been a long time since I left a woman stricken mute."

She glanced down at her food splattered apron while reaching a hand to her hair. She must look a sight.

Then he did the last thing she expected. He moved close and lightly brushed his lips across hers. It was just a brief kiss. But the intimate gesture spoke of a promise.

"Ya look pretty," he said.

"Now I know you can't be Benjamin Shepherd. He wouldn't tell such a lie."

He chuckled. "Might look a bit prettier if ya stopped nosing around out here and got rid of that apron. Yer son got everything under control."

Betty hesitated. Paul was a good man, but organizing things—well, that wasn't his gift.

"Shoo, sweet woman."

"Fine. But if anything is out of place, I'm holding you responsible, Benjamin."

"I love ya, too," he hollered behind her.

Heat rushed to her face. Had he really just declared his love? Must be the wedding. Turned normal people into foolish romantics.

———

Ben chuckled as Betty returned inside, not quite sure what came over him to say such a thing. He meant it, though. He did love Betty Lancaster. Probably hadn't picked the best time to say it.

Adam paced back and forth near the area where the ceremony was set to begin in another fifteen minutes or so. He looked more excited than nervous. Ben knew he had waited a long time for this day—much longer than little Jewel, as he knew his heart long before she knew hers.

"Might go calm him down a bit," Ben suggested as he walked past Will.

Will nodded and headed that way.

Reverend Page moved toward the front and spoke briefly with Adam and Matt Covington. Ben wondered how Adam decided on Covington to stand with him versus Jed or Hawk. The four were all close friends. Must have been tough to pick one.

Soon Will took a seat near the front. Hannah joined him with the baby.

Covington circled around to the back of the crowd as Caroline appeared from the kitchen doorway.

Ben wiped his sweaty palms on his pants. *For ya, Eddie. I'm doing this for ya.*

"Ready?" Julia whispered in his ear.

"Yer beautiful, little Jewel. I know yer ma and pa be looking down from heaven proud as can be."

She sniffed. "Stop before you make me cry."

Then he led his little Jewel down the aisle and gave her away to her new husband. Other than marrying Sheila and seeing the birth of his son, this was the best moment of his life.

A small tear slid down his cheek and Julia glanced at him as Reverend Page announced the couple as Mr. and Mrs. Adam Larson. She smiled at him—that big, bold Julia smile.

I love ya, little Jewel. Lord, bless her and Adam with a long life full of joy.

CHAPTER 23

Caroline woke up the next morning when Betty closed the door between her private room and the kitchen. Groaning, she rolled over on her side, not willing to get up yet.

Julia and Adam's wedding seemed like such a blur, each part moving too fast for her to keep up. She proudly stood next to her friend. She hugged Julia in the line for food, telling her how happy she was to finally be her sister. Then Adam swept Julia away for a few dances before they left the crowd for the hotel.

Thomas appeared at her side and danced with her most of the night, until Ben declared it was time for everyone to retire.

She closed her eyes again, remembering what it felt like dancing with Thomas. His hand on her waist. Her skirt brushed against his legs as it swayed in the momentum of the dance. The way he looked at her.

At one point he ushered her away to the empty, dark dining hall. He told her how beautiful she looked. Then he kissed her with the same fiery intensity of his very first kiss. It awakened a craving in her that felt like it could never be satisfied. He went on kissing her for a long time, until some sound in the kitchen announced they were no longer alone. He quietly led her out the front of the dining hall and wished her pleasant dreams.

She raised her fingers to her lips and sighed. Her mama's voice tried to warn her to be careful, but she pushed it aside as she threw the covers back from her bed. As she stood, she stretched tight muscles.

If she was going to be staying with Betty, the least she could do was rise and help her prepare breakfast for the hungry boarders before church. After washing up, she dressed and fixed her hair quickly, then joined Betty in the kitchen.

The two women almost completed preparing the meal by the time Liang and Yu arrived to help serve. Caroline grabbed several mugs and the coffee pot and entered the dining hall.

"Caroline," Thomas greeted, letting his fingers brush against hers as she handed him a mug of coffee.

Warmth rose to her face as she wished him a good morning. When she turned back towards the kitchen Betty stood in the doorway.

"Come dear. Let's sit for a while. Liang and Yu can manage things for now."

Betty filled two mugs of coffee and led Caroline into the private room to two cushioned chairs. Caroline was suddenly nervous, feeling like she was in trouble.

"Dear, I'm a little concerned," Betty started. Then she took a long drink of her coffee.

The pause made her more uncomfortable. "About?"

"I saw you with Thomas last night. I saw the way he looked at you and the way you looked at him." Betty slowly took another sip. "He's not like the sweet boys you knew back in Texas, dear. He's lived a rough life and chosen very poorly at times."

"People can change."

Betty gave a slight nod. "Yes, they can. But it takes time." She paused again, draining the rest of her coffee. "Dear, I know you care for him. That is very clear. And I suppose he cares for you, given the amount of time he spent with you in the dining hall last night."

Caroline's face burned. She didn't think they had been caught.

"I'm not trying to tell you what you should or should not do, dear. Goodness knows I'm in no position to question another's actions. I will ask you this: Do you know where his heart stands with the Lord?"

She held her hand up, keeping Caroline from answering. "I'm not asking you to give me an answer. Just spend some time and think about it. I know from what Julia has told me that you are a God-fearing woman. Guard your heart, dear, and choose your actions wisely."

Caroline fought with the anger that sprung to the surface. She loved Thomas. What was so wrong with spending time with him? Kissing wasn't a sin.

Betty stood and sighed heavily. "I only say these things, dear, because I care about both you and Thomas. Please sit for a while and finish your coffee. The Pengs and I can manage caring for the board-ers."

As Betty closed the door, she shot to her feet and paced back and forth. She could answer Betty's question this second. No, she did not know where Thomas stood with the Lord. And no, she wasn't sure she would act any differently knowing the answer.

Dropping back into the chair, she sighed. She rested her head in her hands. She was so confused. She knew what she should do. But she didn't want to stop seeing Thomas. He made her feel beautiful and womanly. He made her feel with such intensity. She even hoped that this might lead to marriage.

But if he did not believe she did, she could not marry him. She knew what the Bible said. Her parents taught her well. *Do not be unequally yoked.*

How did she get herself in this situation? Her heart was already entangled, snared, trapped. Again, she rushed into something without considering the consequences. Perhaps, she could forget what she felt.

She could not.

Maybe she just needed to pray that Thomas would come around. Yes, that is what she would do.

———

Thomas waited until the singing had been going on for a

while before he took a seat at the back of the dining hall. Only the reverend and his wife could see him enter. Everyone else, including Caroline, faced forward singing loudly. With several rows of people he didn't recognize between him and Caroline, he was sure he would go unnoticed.

He didn't want anyone to see him here. He wasn't even sure why he came or what he hoped would happen. Even though he attended church at his father's request after his mother passed, Thomas never paid attention. Once his father was gone, he stopped going. Drew never tried to force him, and Uncle Peter certainly did not care.

After leaving Caroline last night, he ran into Paul. That's why he was here. Paul said nothing to him—he didn't have to. The disappointment on his face was enough to start the guilt forming in his heart. He knew better than to sneak off with Caroline, even if he had no intention of taking it any farther than just kissing her.

When he saw Paul's face, he remembered what he said—that a girl like Caroline would never let herself get involved with a man like him. He never asked Paul what he meant. He didn't need to. Thomas knew what he was. He was a bank robber, a gambler, a drinker. His actions cost his brother his life, so maybe he should add a murderer to that list. Not one of those things would a decent Christian girl seek after. If she knew the truth she would have nothing to do with him. And that would break his heart.

Perhaps that was why he was here. She would want a man like the one he was pretending to be—a man like Drew or Paul.

Paul was right. He could not be like them without some help. His actions every time he was around Caroline were proof of that.

So, if going to church made such a difference for Drew and Paul, could it possibly make a difference for a scoundrel such as him?

When the music ended, Reverend Page stood and began reading, "'But when this priest'—he's talking about Jesus—'had offered for all time one sacrifice for sins, he sat down at the right hand of God… This is the covenant I will make with them after that time, says the Lord. I will put my laws in their hearts, and I will write them on their minds.' Then he adds: 'Their sins and lawless acts I will remember no more. And where these have been forgiven, there is no longer any sacrifice for sin.'"

Thomas's heart jolted. *Their sins and lawless acts I will remember no more.* Was that even possible? How could anyone forget what he had done? He couldn't.

Hannah did.

No, she hadn't forgotten. She had forgiven him. That's what she said. She forgave him. She never promised to forget.

Thomas's palms grew sweaty. He shifted in his seat. The bench he was sitting on sagged under the weight of the bulky man who sat down next to him blocking him in. He glanced and immediately recognized Paul.

"Forgiveness from our family and our friends can be flawed. Sometimes it's hard for us to forget," the reverend was saying. "But forgiveness from God is perfect. He tells us that he will not remember our lawless acts anymore. There is no long list of mistakes, no reminder of our failures. Instead, there is grace—lawless acts wiped clean.

"This forgiveness is not without action on our part. We must accept the sacrifice Jesus made for us. We must ask for his forgiveness to receive it.

"But oh, when we do! It is given freely. Our sin is remembered no more."

Thomas swallowed hard. It was a tempting thing—to reach out and grab onto what Reverend Page described.

Only Thomas could not do it. He remembered all too well God's part in the man he had become. If only He had seen fit to let a hurting broken boy grow up in his mother's love. Perhaps then he would not have any lawless acts in need of being forgotten.

As soon as Reverend Page bowed his head to pray, Thomas swiftly climbed over the back of the bench and ran out the door, clutching tightly to his hurt and pain.

———

After a day of churning emotions, Caroline welcomed Monday. At least she would be too busy looking for a job to think about her conversation with Betty and her subsequent discomfort in the church service or her disappointment that Thomas was not in attendance.

No, today she had to focus on why she moved into town.

Following breakfast, she walked down the street to Hardy's mercantile. Betty mentioned this morning that she thought Abraham Conrad was looking for some help. With her encouragement, Caroline decided it was as good of a place to start as any.

A little bell rang a light sound overhead as she entered the store. A man looked up from the counter and two other men in the store glanced in her direction. She straightened her back and approached the counter with a smile.

"Abraham Conrad?"

"Yes," the short middle-aged man behind the counter said as he pushed his spectacles up on his nose.

"I'm Miss Caroline Larson. Betty Lancaster said you might be looking for some help."

"Ah, yes. I'm looking for someone to help stock shelves, help customers, and keep the place clean. Do you know how to cipher?" he asked with a smile.

"Yes. I received high marks in school for ciphering."

"Good. Would you need a place to stay as well? I've got a room available above the store."

She thought for a minute. While she could probably stay with Betty indefinitely, she would like the privacy of her own place. "Yes, I would."

"When can you start?"

"Um, today?"

Abraham chuckled. "That'd be fine. Step around the counter and I'll show you how to help this gentleman."

Caroline did as instructed and smiled at the customer. She paid careful attention to how Abraham marked what the man owed in his register. The second customer in the store finished moments later and she watched the process again.

Once both customers left, Abraham showed her around the mercantile and the storeroom in the back. He showed her where the cleaning supplies were kept and had her start dusting down the shelves she could easily reach.

The bell announced that another customer entered the store. She turned from the shelf she was dusting to greet him.

"Good morning—oh, Adam and Julia!"

"Caroline? What are you doing here?" Adam asked.

"Working." She shrugged her shoulders and smiled.

"You certainly didn't waste any time."

After some brief chitchat, she helped them secure their purchases and Abraham helped her with the account. She gave them both a hug before they headed out the door.

"Don't be a stranger," Julia said. "Please come visit us at the ranch soon."

"I will," she answered, not sure when or how she would next head out.

"Friends?" Abraham asked curiously once they left.

"My brother and my best friend, who are now husband and wife." She sighed. Things really were turning out much differently than she expected.

Early in the afternoon, Abraham let her leave to get some lunch. She headed over to Betty's, entering through the back door.

"Oh, there you are dear. Did you speak to Abraham?"

"Yes, he offered me the job and the room above the store."

"Dear, you are more than welcome to stay here for as long as you like," Betty said, concern wrinkling her brow.

"That is very kind of you, but I'm sure Paul would like to have his place back now."

"If you're certain…"

"I am. Thank you so much for your hospitality." She gave

Betty a hug. It would be nice knowing she was nearby.

She turned and went into the private room, quickly gathering her things. Carpet bag in hand, she returned to Hardy's store. Abraham led her up the stairs on the outside of the building to a nondescript door at the top. He slid a lever and opened the door.

"Might be a little dusty. Hasn't been occupied yet. Since I don't take to the stairs very well, I had Mr. Hardy add a small room at the back of the store for me. All the wood you'll need for cooking or heat is stacked under the stairs. I have a young lad that comes by a couple times a week to keep up our supply."

Turning to leave the small room, he said, "Take as much time as you need to get settled, then come back down."

She nodded and closed the door behind him.

There wasn't much to the small room. A bed sat in one corner, the stove in another, and a small table with a chair stood near the door. There was a rocking chair near the corner opposite the stove. A small dresser stood next to the bed. Within two steps, she stood at the foot of the bed—a very small room indeed. But it would be plenty of space for her.

After folding her dresses neatly in the dresser, she circled the room. At the end of the day, she would borrow the duster and cleaning supplies from downstairs. She would get the place cleaned in no time.

A smile stretched across her lips. She was sure she would like being independent.

———

The bell above the door chimed. Caroline tossed a greeting over her shoulder as she finished arranging a few bolts of cloth.

"Caroline?" the familiar male voice drew her full attention.

"Perry! How are you?" she asked, turning to face him. He reached out and squeezed her hand.

"Very good. And you? Are you working here now?" His gaze was intense as he looked down into her eyes.

She suddenly remembered what Thomas said—that Perry

was smitten with her or something like that. She withdrew her hand from his and fidgeted nervously with the fabrics on the shelf.

"I'm well. I've been working here for almost two weeks now. Can I help you find anything?"

"May I leave this with you?" he said, extending his hand holding a piece of paper. "I have a few other errands to run."

"Certainly." She took the paper and glanced over it to make sure she could read his writing. That was one lesson she learned rather quickly, though not quick enough for one of her customers with terrible handwriting. Poor man ended up with something very different than the tooth powder he'd been looking for.

Perry thanked her and left the store.

Caroline started to pull items on the list from the shelves when she remembered that she still had his wife's broach. She called Abraham to keep an eye on things while she went upstairs to retrieve it. In the time since she had visited Perry's ranch, she sewed a nice little pouch for the broach to keep it safe. Tucking it inside her reticule, she hurried back down the stairs.

Just before entering the store, a figure on a horse in front of the newspaper office caught her eye. Her breath left in a rush. Something about the way the man sat in his saddle reminded her of the "boss" of the stagecoach robbery. When she heard him speaking without seeing his face, she was certain it was him.

Quickly ducking into the store, she watched him from the front window, heart pounding fiercely within her chest. If it was him and he saw her, would she be safe?

Then he turned and she shot a hand to her mouth to stifle her scream. It was Robert Garrett!

That couldn't be. Mr. Garrett seemed like such a nice man when he visited Colter Ranch. Yet, there had been something about him that reminded Julia of Reuben. Though she didn't see the resemblance, perhaps he was hiding something, and Julia had sensed it.

Her fear paralyzed her, and she stood watching as he approached the store. Just before he entered, she ran to the counter and grabbed Perry's list before darting into the storeroom. Surely something he needed would be back here and she wouldn't have to face Robert Garrett.

She listened as Abraham greeted him. She hid in the storeroom, closing her eyes and listening to the sound of Robert's voice. It sent shivers down her spine. He had to be the same man.

Slowly she sank to the floor, bringing her knees up to her chest. She hugged them tightly, fear refusing to leave. What would she do? Who could she tell?

The clink of the bell announced another customer. She stood and peeked through the curtain. Perry was back and she hadn't completed his list yet. He stood engaged in a conversation with Robert Garrett.

Squaring her shoulders, she swallowed her fear and joined Abraham behind the counter.

"Caroline," Perry said, turning her direction, "Have you met Robert Garrett? He's a rancher a day's ride south of my place."

She nodded.

"I had the pleasure," Perry said, "of meeting Caroline when she needed to recuperate from her journey after the stage she rode in was robbed."

She felt all the blood drain from her face when Robert Garrett's eyes darkened as he looked her way. The expression stayed on his face for only a second, but it doubled her fear that he was who she thought.

Perry continued, oblivious to the silent exchange. "Have you heard anything down your way, Garrett? Guess it happened not too far from your place."

Robert cleared his throat and answered hastily, "No. It was a pleasure seeing you again Quinn, but I must be on my way."

Perry offered a farewell then turned to face Caroline. He sucked in a sharp breath. "Are you alright? You look rather pale."

"I'm... fine." She managed, before taking a seat on a stool they kept behind the counter.

"Caroline," Abraham said, "why don't you go rest for a bit. I'll see to the rest of Perry's order."

She nodded and stood. Perry escorted her up the stairs to the door of her room.

"I hope you feel better quickly." He traced a finger along her cheek. "Perhaps the next time I'm in town you will be able to join me for supper."

Her fear trapped her words in her throat. She nodded in response before opening the door.

"Goodbye, Caroline."

"Wait!" she said, remembering his wife's broach in her reticule. She pulled it out and handed it to him.

His eyebrows wrinkled in confusion. "What's this?"

"Something very important to you."

He untied the strings of the little pouch and pulled out the broach. Instantly, his eyes reddened with unshed tears. He cleared his throat several times.

"Thank you."

He leaned forward to place a light kiss on her lips, but she turned her head to the side at the last second, so his lips brushed her cheek instead. Thomas was right. Perry Quinn did care for her.

"Goodbye," she said, hurrying through her door. She closed it then leaned against it, the throbbing in her head draining her energy. As if Perry's obvious feelings for her weren't bad enough, she still had to tell someone that she suspected Robert Garrett was involved with the stage robbery. But first, she needed to lie down.

CHAPTER 24

Colter Ranch

October 11, 1865

"Boss," Pedro said to Will in his heavy accent. "Many cattle are gone."

Ben lifted his coffee mug to his lips taking a sip. Despite the seriousness of Pedro's news, he wanted to be on his way to town as soon as possible.

"I noticed something's off, too," Cahill said. "Didn't do a head count, but something seemed outta place between the start of the day yesterday and the evening."

"Rustlers?" Ben asked.

"Maybe," Cahill said.

Will frowned. "You think it could be some of the same men you ran into on the way to California?"

"Good chance," Cahill replied.

Ben rubbed a hand across his beard. Too many things were on his mind today. Had he noticed anything unusual? He thought about it for a bit. After the boys got back from the drive to California, he had been spending less time with the herd and more time taking Colter beef to their customers in town.

But he did remember something odd.

"Might be nothin'," he said. "When the boys were gone, I noticed we had a few strays far off. Saw a rider near 'em and figured it to be one of our boys rounding 'em up. Can't recall if I saw 'em make it back to the herd."

"Who was riding out in that area?" Will asked.

"Think it might have been Owens."

After a long stretch of silence, Will said, "Don't say anything to any of the cowboys. Let's keep our suspicions between the four of us. Pedro, try to get the night crew to keep the herd a little closer to the ranch. Cahill, keep an eye on Owens and Whitten during the day. Make sure there's nothing funny going on there."

"Ya thinkin' inside job?" Ben asked.

"Might be. Best to be careful. Owens, Whitten, and maybe Bates would be the ones I trust the least. Ben, keep an ear open when you're in town. See if you hear any rumors about rustlers."

Ben nodded as Will stood, ending the meeting. He picked up the basket he set on the table and eagerly headed out the door. Taking a deep breath, he let the concerns of rustlers fall to the back of his mind. He had more important things to worry about.

He smiled as he dropped the basket and blanket into the wagon behind the seat. He was pleased with himself for thinking of such a great surprise for Betty. She never took time off from running that boardinghouse. Well, today he would make sure she did.

She wouldn't have anything to worry about either. After services on Sunday, Ben pulled Paul aside and shared his plan. Paul reassured him that he would make sure everything was taken care of at the boardinghouse. He'd get the Pengs to plan supper and he would stay in from his claim to help with whatever needed done.

Ben really liked Paul. He seemed to be a great son, always watching out for his ma, in such a way she didn't even realize it. It was obvious Betty adored her son, too. What grit she had in following him out here, not knowing how harsh the wilderness might be.

Lightness settled over his stomach. He really cared for Betty. He just had a few things to tell her before he could ask her to be his wife—that is if she wanted to after hearing what he had to say. No, he wouldn't ask her today. Wouldn't be fair. She'd need some time to absorb the stories about the worst part of him.

He sighed as he climbed into the wagon. Releasing the brake, he set the horse in motion up the hill with Owens riding next to him.

Owens. That kid was starting to be more than a handful. He bucked Ben's orders whenever he could. He stirred up a bunch of trouble with Adam before the wedding. Thankfully, now that Adam moved into the house there was a little more peace. But it seemed Owens was looking for his next victim to antagonize and he was deciding between Jed and Hawk. Might just be that he was involved in the missing cattle.

Then there was the alcohol. Ben found more than one bottle of liquor hidden in his bunk. Seemed no matter how many bottles he found and emptied, Owens always had more stashed all over the property. Of course, it didn't help that Whitten and Snake liked to partake often enough. Ben was pretty sure they helped Owens hide it.

He was sure Owens was the culprit. But what he couldn't figure out was where he got all the money for that much alcohol. A bottle here and there, well that was normal for any cowboy. But it was like Owens had cases of the stuff hidden.

Maybe he'd talk to Will about letting the boys off into town on Saturday nights. Most of them would probably want to go, but he and the ones that stayed back should be enough to take care of the cattle. That would mean he would be dead tired for Sunday services. But if it kept the liquor off the ranch, it might be worth it.

Ben wasn't just dedicated to keeping out the liquor because of his loyalty to Will. No, he had his own demons he was fighting, and he was trying to keep the youngest cowboys from getting sucked into that trap. Jed and Hawk were far too willing to please others. Adam had been a great influence, but if the boys kept getting teased by the older ones, he didn't think they'd stay clear of trouble much longer. How would they fare if he moved out?

Even though he wanted his own place, he would wait until

Betty agreed to marry him before asking Will. He was pretty sure Will would let him build a cabin regardless. He just wasn't sure he was ready to hand over the boys to Warren Cahill quite yet. It's not that Cahill wasn't a good man—he was. It was just that he was much closer in age to the other boys, at least the older ones. Ben wasn't sure if they would listen to him.

He rubbed his stiff neck with one hand, keeping control of the horse and wagon with the other. Seems the boys did alright with Cahill on the last drive. Maybe he was just being silly.

Or afraid.

It had been a long time since he wasn't living in a bunkhouse full of men. If he was honest with himself, he was a bit scared at the idea of making such a major change in his life after all these years.

He loved Betty. He knew it. He even prayed about it. Didn't make it any less frightening to open his heart again.

———

Betty sighed.

"Aren't you going out to your claim today?" She asked her son as he filled the wash tub with water and started shaving some soap into it. When she tried to take it from his hands, he blocked her with a broad shoulder.

"I got it, Ma. And no, I'm not going out today. Thought I'd give you a hand here. Maybe even tackle laundry without you."

Now she was getting annoyed. "You shouldn't be doing this."

"You shouldn't be working yourself so hard seven days a week. You need to take it easier."

What was he up to?

She heard a wagon pull to a stop in front of the boardinghouse, though since they were in the back, she could not see who it was.

"I believe that's for you."

"What are you talking about Paul?"

"Ma, just go look," he replied with an edge of irritation in his tone.

Slowly she turned, giving in to her son's request. As she rounded the corner to the front, she let out a little gasp. "Ben!"

Her pace quickened, as her pulse did, and she rushed to greet him.

"Is my schedule off? I didn't think you were due to deliver more beef until next week."

He leaned toward her and kissed her cheek.

"Naw, yer tracking it right. Thought I'd surprise ya with a picnic lunch."

Heat tickled the round flesh of her cheeks. She smiled, getting excited about the idea of an afternoon off. Paul must have been in on it.

"Can ya take some time away?"

"Absolutely. Let me just go—"

"They'll be fine. I'm sure Paul has everything under control."

He took her hand, not letting her argue, and he helped her up to the wagon. Then he walked around to the other side and took a seat next to her.

"Thought it might be nice to sit down by the creek. Brought an extra blanket in case yer cold."

The fluttery sensation, she remembered from the early days of her romance with Henry, returned only this time it had everything to do with the man at her side. For once she had nothing to say.

So, she reached over and patted his hand instead, truly moved that he arranged something so special for her.

"Don't worry," he said, "I didn't make the grub. Hannah took care of that fer me."

Betty laughed. "I wasn't worried, Benjamin."

In just a few minutes, he pulled the wagon up in a clearing near Granite Creek. After helping her down, he reached into the wagon and retrieved two blankets and a basket. He shook out one blanket and laid it on the ground. Then he set the other blanket and the basket there. He helped her sit down before awkwardly making his way to the ground next to her.

"Guess it's getting harder to sit on the ground." He laughed the awkwardness off.

She knew what he was saying. It seemed things just didn't move as limberly as they once had.

Though it was early October, the air was not too cold yet, so she felt comfortable without the other blanket.

"Thought we might talk a bit before eatin', less yer hungry now?"

"I'm fine."

In the next seconds of silence, the creek gurgled cheerily by. The sound of miners sifting the dirt upstream faintly floated on the air. The crisp scent of juniper filled her lungs. When was the last time she just sat?

"How are things at the boardinghouse?"

Betty giggled. "Busy as always. Paul has started some plans to build a house with rooms for boarders. Now that the sawmill is churning out boards daily, he's eager to see us in some nicer rooms. Actually, I think he's tired of getting booted out of our rooms every time I take in a woman boarder. He says this way, any women needing a place will know they have it and it's safe. He plans to keep most of the men boarding in the bunkhouses."

"Ya looking for a nicer place?"

"I'm content with what I have. Like I said, I think it has more to do with Paul than me."

The silence returned. Instead of it being awkward, it was peaceful. She really enjoyed just being with him and she never felt the need to fill all their time together with conversation. So, she sat comfortably, content to let him lead the conversation. She sensed he had something on his mind.

"Betty, I… I want to tell ya about my past. I know it ain't who I am now, but I care a great deal for ya and want ya to know it."

She smiled encouragingly and gave his hand a squeeze before returning her hand to her lap.

"I told ya some about Sheila, right?"

At her nod, he continued. "She was my life. I was young then, not even in my twenties when I met her. She took care of her pa and sisters on the tenement farm next to mine. I was struggling to live alone. It was hard enough to farm each day. I just didn't have much energy to cook and clean up things at the end of the day.

"She took pity on me and began bringing by food or doing my laundry. Before long, she invited me to eat with her pa and sisters.

"I knew even then that I shoulda said no. Too many folks woulda had a problem with that much. But my heart—well it ignored what made sense. I fell in love with her."

"I don't understand," Betty said.

"She, her pa, and her sisters were freed darkies. In the south, in Mississippi, that weren't much better'n a slave. Folks there don't like to see white blood mixed with their kind.

"Thing was, I knew all that. I knew if I married her, it would mean trouble fer me, fer her, fer our children. Oh, and we both wanted children. Lots of 'em. But I married her anyway."

He looked off to the distance, swallowing hard. Betty's heart hurt for him. She could see this was painful.

"It's my fault she died. They killed her just 'cause she married me."

As he told her the horrible story of the night his family was killed by fire, Betty's hand rose to her throat and her prayers rose heavenward. She listened intently, feeling his pain.

"After I got hit on the head, I blacked out. It was late into the night that I woke. Only, I wasn't on the farm anymore. I was in town in a back alley, outside a tavern.

"Somehow, I staggered to my feet and entered the place. I found some money in my pocket, more'n I remembered having, and I sat down and drank. I stayed in that place for days, not barely movin' from that stool. Drink after drink after drink. I couldn't bear to be without the whiskey. I couldn't remember.

"Don't know how many days I was there a'fore my sister found me. She somehow dragged me outta the place and got me back to her home. She'd married and she convinced her husband to let me stay.

"I didn't make it easy. I just sat there day after day on the floor. I kept drinking myself senseless.

"Finally, her man got fed up with me and kicked me out. Told me I needed to start living, cause no matter how much I wanted to be dead, I weren't."

Tears streamed down his face.

"So, I found a saloon. And I drank some more.

"Days blended into weeks, then into months. Don't know how long I was there. Just know that I eventually ran outta money."

He paused, rubbing his hand nervously on the leg of his pants. He looked into her eyes then quickly away before he continued.

"Some dreaming fool from Texas came into the saloon one day. Said he'd been looking for hard workers to come take a chance on his brand-new ranch. His eyes glowed with excitement and life. He was about the same age as me. It was something about them blue eyes that got my attention.

"He sat down next to me and told me I didn't have to be broken no more. I could start a new life on his ranch. Said he was looking for someone honest that he could trust.

"Then Eddie Colter did what only a fool would do. He took the drink from my hand and said I had enough. It was time to leave the drink and leave the pain. He helped me stagger out to his wagon.

"We left for Texas that night—a crazy fool rancher and a drunken broken-hearted farmer. After a day of travel without the liquor, I got real sick. He helped me. Sometimes he'd say something about me needing to stay away from the drink. Other times, he'd read scripture or prayed over me."

He turned and reached for her hands. "Betty, I ain't had a drink since Eddie pulled me from the pit. He saved me."

Ben released one hand to wipe away the tears on his face then he took her hand again. "I'm telling ya all this 'cause I want ya to know what kind of man I was. I care too much fer ya not to tell ya everything about me—all the good and all the bad."

Betty's breath caught in her throat. Her heart fluttered and danced within her chest. She saw the look of love in his eyes and knew he was offering her a precious gift—his heart—in the only way he knew how.

"I love you, too, Benjamin."

His eyes went wide, and he straightened his back. "Ya do?"

"I do."

He leaned closer stopping inches from her face. "I ain't kissed no one ever but my wife."

"And do you want to kiss me now?"

"Yes."

She waited a second. Then another. Was he waiting for her permission? "Are you going to tease me all day, Benjamin, or are you going to kiss—"

Then he kissed her, sweetly on the lips. The kiss wasn't very long, but it told her so much about the man that captured her heart. Regardless of his past, he was good, honest, and very much worthy of her love.

He pulled back from the kiss and laid a hand on her cheek. "I love ya, Betty Lancaster."

She smiled, heart full.

"Now, let's eat," he said with that grin that turned her heart upside down.

The rest of the picnic was much more lighthearted. Betty shared the news from the latest letters she received from her children in Missouri. They laughed together at the stories of her grandchildren.

He shared the latest news from the ranch. Hannah was pregnant again, at least he thought she was by the way she was feeling sick in the mornings. Will was putting the finishing touches on their new house, planning to move his wife and son into it by the end of the month. Adam and Julia seemed incredibly happy together, though ready to have the place to themselves.

Betty was so enjoying her time with Ben that she completely

lost track of time. Suddenly she noticed the sun was rather low in the sky.

"Oh dear!"

"What is it?"

"Supper! I completely forgot about getting back to start supper."

Ben smiled at her. "There's no need to rush. Paul has everything under control."

Regardless of Ben's repeated reassurances, she felt terrible for neglecting her duties for so long. She started to pack up the basket, so he helped. In a few minutes he had everything loaded in the wagon, including her, and delivered her back to the boardinghouse as the first boarders arrived for their evening meal.

"I best be heading back," he said. "I had a good time with ya today. See ya on Sunday?"

Betty was eager to get to work, but she gave him just another minute of her time. "I had a wonderful time, Benjamin. I'll see you soon."

Then she hurried off to the kitchen, ready to jump in to help finish the preparations and feed her boarders. Taking a deep breath, she wondered to herself, just where things might be going with Benjamin Shepherd? Would she be leaving the boardinghouse in Paul's care permanently?

CHAPTER 25

Prescott

November 15, 1865

"Thanks for all your help, Thomas," Paul said as he shook his hand. "Couldn't have finished this without you."

His friend turned his gaze towards the two-story house. It had been a lot of hard work. He helped Paul every spare moment he had in Prescott over the past month or so. The days off in La Paz ended up being the only down time Thomas had in over a month. But he had been happy to do it.

He even worked through Sunday services when he was in town on the weekend, despite Paul's protests. There was no way he was going back to that church. He had been a mess since the last time he attended. Thoughts of forgiveness and redemption warred with anger over his mother's death. He couldn't reconcile the two and he had no desire to stir things up again.

Thomas stretched his arms, hoping to relieve some of the tightness in his back. It was good to see the newest boarding-house building completed and before any snow arrived. When Paul shared his dream with Thomas, the two decided they could get it done before snowfall. With the help of a few boarders, they had.

The only downside to all his hard work was that he hadn't seen Caroline in over a month. At night when he finally had a moment to think, or when he was in La Paz far from her, he would ache missing her so badly. Her smile. Those wild green eyes. Oh, how many times had the memory of her kisses gotten him through the night?

He rushed into the bunkhouse and grabbed a bucket. If he hurried, he might be able to clean up and run over to the store and ask her to dine with him. If not tonight, then he would have to wait until his next stop in Prescott, for he had to leave on his next run tomorrow.

Retrieving a bucket full of water from the town well, he hurried back to the bunkhouse as fast as he could. He stripped out of his dirty sweaty clothes. Then he scrubbed as quickly as he could, hoping the cold water would still wash away the stench of a hard day's labor. He splashed water on his hair then ran his fingers through it. Grabbing a towel, he dried off before dressing.

Thankfully he had purchased a third outfit. Otherwise, he might not have enough clean clothes for tomorrow's ride. As it was, he would have the clothes he now wore. Betty hadn't been able to wash his other clothes after his last ride yet.

Slapping his hat down on his head, he ran from the bunkhouse, noting the line out the door for supper at the dining hall. He dashed across the street to Hardy's store. Pausing by the door, he tried to catch his breath. He looked through the window and saw Caroline helping a customer. She looked lovely in her pale green dress.

As he pushed open the door, his heart rate spiked at the sight of her. A little bell chimed overhead.

She looked up and smiled at him. "I'll be with you in a minute, Thomas."

He nodded as she turned her attention back to her customer. He walked around the store waiting for her to finish. The young woman Caroline was helping seemed to be rather needy as the minutes ticked by slowly.

Finally, the young woman left, and he approached the counter.

Caroline stuck her lower lip out and crossed her arms. Lowering her head, she looked up with her eyes. His heart jumped to his throat.

"I haven't seen you in ages."

He cringed. She was upset. He should have found a way to stop by sooner.

"I've been helping Paul with the boardinghouse."

She smiled and touched his arm. "I'm just teasing you. I know you've been busy."

He let out a slow breath. "I was wondering if you would like to have supper with me at Osborn's restaurant tonight."

"I'm just finishing up here."

Abraham appeared from the back room. "You go on. I'll close up."

She raised an eyebrow in question but dropped it back in place with Abraham's nod.

"Guess I'm free now," she said, moving to his side. She looped her hand around the crook of his arm before he even offered it, the action sending tingles up his arm.

Maybe it was a good thing he hadn't seen her for a while—with the way she drove him mad.

Thomas led the way down the street towards Osborn's.

"How have you been?" he asked.

"Fine." She grew quiet. "How much do you know about Robert Garrett?"

He stopped and looked at her. "That's an odd question."

"I think... He was in town a while back and he reminded me of... He reminded me of one of the stagecoach robbers. Seems Perry Quinn knew him. They had a rather long conversation in the store. I got the impression that Perry thought well of him. I'm just wondering what you think."

Thomas tried to keep a lid on his jealousy at the mention of Perry Quinn's name. He shouldn't be surprised Perry would see Caroline when he was in town, given that she worked at one of the three mercantiles in town.

He searched his mind for anything he had learned about Garrett in the months since his visit to Colter Ranch.

"I caught a glimpse of him in Wickenburg a few rides ago. He was headed into the saloon."

"Anything else?"

Thomas placed her hand back in the crook of his arm and continued walking to the restaurant. "Can't think of anything else. He doesn't impress me as a man that would have to rob a stagecoach for money."

"They took the horses, too, you know."

"Right. Probably sold them somewhere south of the border."

She sighed. "I told the sheriff my suspicion and he said he'd check it out. I just got the feeling he didn't really believe me."

They arrived at the entrance of the restaurant and the owner sat them at a table for two near the back of the restaurant. The candle flickering on the table cast a warm glow on Caroline's face. She was so beautiful.

To distract his train of thought, he asked, "Have you been out to the ranch recently?"

"No. Not since I left. I'm hoping to get out for Thanksgiving, but Abraham said it's too dangerous to travel alone."

"Perhaps I could take you out on the Friday after Thanksgiving? I will be finishing a run on Thanksgiving day."

Her eyes lit up. "That would be wonderful. Ben should be in town this week. I'll ask him to tell Hannah we'll be delayed a day. Maybe she will wait and celebrate when we can join them."

He smiled, appreciating her thoughtfulness. "That would be great."

Mr. Osborn arrived and took their orders.

Once he left, Caroline asked, "Do you believe in God?"

Thomas nearly choked on his water. The question came so bluntly and unexpectedly. Old grievances with God churned in his stomach. He was afraid to answer her question truthfully.

"I believe there is a God."

Her crestfallen face shouted her disappointment.

He hastened to explain. "I believe God exists. And I believe he has his own methods of controlling certain things. I just can't believe that he cares about us. If he did why would there be so much evil and pain in the world?"

Caroline looked down at her hands in her lap. "It's not like he causes the pain." Her voice was a soft whisper. "We do most of the pain-causing." She looked up and locked gazes with him. "It is our choices and decision—the bad ones—that cause most of our pain."

His anger simmered just below the surface. "And just what choice or decision did I make that caused my mother to die?"

Her eyes widened in shock. She cleared her throat. "Okay, there's some pain that doesn't result from our choices. But then we can choose how we deal with the pain."

"Have you ever had anyone close to you die?" he asked, not even trying to hide the accusation in his voice.

"No."

"Then consider yourself fortunate."

An uncomfortable silence settled over the table. Thomas kicked himself for being so sensitive about her question. It was the first time he had spent time with her in so long. He didn't want to ruin it by arguing about God.

After the food arrived, Caroline bowed her head, further irritating him. He noisily started eating. A few seconds passed and she looked up. She began eating her meal, though he could tell she was unhappy.

"I'm sorry," he said, reaching across the table to touch her hand. "I didn't mean to ruin our supper."

"It's fine."

Her posture and dedication to consuming the meal told him it wasn't fine. But he was afraid if he said anything more about God, he'd upset her further. So, he turned his attention towards the meal, despite the tense silence.

"I'm sorry about your mother," she said at length. "How old were you when she passed?"

"Five."

"Julia lost her mother when she was young. I know it is a hard thing to deal with."

Thomas nodded, hoping she would drop the conversation

soon. He didn't want to talk about it.

Caroline sighed, pushing her plate away from her. "It will be nice to visit the ranch again. I really miss Julia and Adam. It's lonely here."

He chuckled. "You impress me as a woman who handles living on her own quite well."

She smiled and he rejoiced that their earlier tension seemed to vanish.

"I suppose I do well enough."

As the meal concluded, he rose and escorted her back to the mercantile. Stopping at the foot of the stairs, he turned toward her.

"I've missed you so much, Caroline."

She fidgeted nervously with her heavy shawl and looked away. Something had changed. Had she fallen for someone else? Or had he stayed away too long?

He pulled her close and she stiffened. "What is it?"

"Thomas, please don't."

"Don't what?"

"Don't kiss me."

The words hit him like a splash of frigid water to the face. "I know you care for me," he stated boldly. Why was she acting so strange? Before supper she seemed eager to see him, glad that he was there. Now she was trying to distance herself.

"I do care for you." She looked away. "But I shouldn't."

Thomas's throat narrowed. Had someone told her about his past?

"Why not?"

She looked at him now, sorrowful eyes pleading. "I can't let myself care for you. Not if you don't share my beliefs."

She shrugged away from his hold and ran up the stairs, leaving him stunned at the bottom. She was rejecting him because he didn't believe in God.

He coughed, feeling the real physical pain of rejection almost as if she had impaled him with a sword. Why would she do this? Why cut his heart out so coldly?

Paul's words echoed in his mind. *She'll never give her heart to someone like you.*

Oh, the pain! If only he had listened to his friend. If only he hadn't let her get into his heart. Discouraged, disillusioned, Thomas headed for the one place that could always numb the pain. His friend whiskey called him from the saloon. This time he answered.

———

Caroline slammed her door shut and threw herself on her bed. Sobs shook her body. She should have asked him that question long ago. Not now. Not after she already loved him.

How foolish she was!

This was so much worse than what she did to Jesse and Nathan. So, much worse. She saw the raw pain in his eyes. She trampled his heart. And his wasn't the only one bleeding.

It hurt. It burned.

She hated herself. She hated what she had become.

She was the worst kind of woman—one who carelessly tossed away a man's love.

Only it wasn't careless. This was wise.

Oh, she wanted to be with him. She wanted to marry him. But wouldn't they always be on opposite sides because at the core they did not value the same things?

Tears soaked the arm of her dress. Her head throbbed as her heart bled. This was the most horrible feeling. The fullness of her wretchedness now exposed.

Lord, forgive me. Help Thomas to forgive me.

———

The day after Thanksgiving, Caroline wondered if Thomas would still take her out to Colter Ranch. She would not blame him if he didn't—not after how she hurt him.

She must have wounded him terribly. She heard the rumors from some nosy men as they shopped in the mercantile. One of them said they saw Thomas leave the saloon too drunk to walk back to the boardinghouse. She did not know if he tended to drink or not. She assumed not, as she hadn't heard anything before now.

Regardless, the men had been talking about the night she rejected him. She shared some responsibility for that.

So, given all that, she readied herself for a busy day at the mercantile assuming she would not see or hear from him.

As she opened the front door, a man caught her arm. "Are you ready?"

She whirled to face Thomas. "Ah… Yes."

"I couldn't get a wagon, so a saddled horse will have to do." His voice sounded flat. His face was unreadable.

"I didn't expect you to still take me."

Thomas snorted. "I said I would. Now let's go."

He moved to his horse and mounted it, letting her struggle with mounting her own. She finally managed it. He kicked his horse into motion, and she followed behind wordlessly. The stiffness of his back indicated that he would not be much of a chatty traveling companion for the day.

She sighed.

The trip seemed twice as long in the silence, so she was grateful when they finally arrived at the ranch. He didn't offer to help her down, so she clumsily slid off the side of the horse, nearly losing her balance once she hit the ground. Funny, he had enough common courtesy to bring her here, but not enough to help her with her horse.

Adam gave her a hug then took her horse to the stables.

"Caroline, I've missed you," Julia squeezed her tight.

She stepped back from her friend's embrace, noting the warm glow on her face. "Looks like marriage agrees with you."

"I hope you find the perfect man someday," Julia said. "It is so wonderful to be married to someone you love so much."

Her stomach dropped, but she managed to keep the smile on her face. She doubted she would love anyone as much as she loved Thomas.

Julia grabbed Caroline's hand and led her into the new ranch house. The building was a cute two-story plank board structure. Julia chatted on and on about all the great things about the house. The kitchen was separated from the dining area, which was separated from the large living area by a wall. Each room seemed cozy.

"Will built four rooms upstairs. Can you believe it? Four rooms? He told Hannah he plans on filling them to the rafters with children."

Caroline smiled, not really feeling up to laughing at what she knew was a joke.

"It's so nice to have our own space," Julia was saying. "Though, we still take meals together as a family up here. But if I ever want to cook—not that I really would—I can."

She laughed at that. Julia never was one who wanted to spend much time in the kitchen.

Adam came in followed by Thomas. She avoided his gaze as Adam wrapped her in a bear hug.

"Out of sorts today, Linny?"

"I guess."

"Missing Pa and Ma and the girls?"

She hadn't really been until Adam mentioned it, but it would be a good disguise for the true source of her low spirits. "Yes. This is the first time I've been away from them for Thanksgiving."

"It helps having the Colter family here. And Thomas."

Baby James squirmed in Hannah's arms. Thomas lifted the small child into his arms, swaying back and forth.

He was a good man. He just made some mistakes sometimes. Oh, and he didn't believe in God. Other than that, she could envision him as a good father, holding her child.

Caroline went to give Will and Hannah greetings, hoping to remove that thought from her mind. She needed to let go of Thomas, not picture him in her life in new ways.

In a few minutes, everything was set out on the table. Everyone took their seats as Ben hurried in. "Sorry I'm late."

Once he was seated, Will led them in a prayer. It was a very nice prayer, matching the theme of the day well. He thanked the Lord for his family and friends, for their health, and for His provision. Then he surprised everyone by praying for those in the family that were sorrowful for the day, that God would lift their spirits and direct them in His path.

As everyone echoed his "amen," Caroline looked around the table. Who could Will have been talking about? Her? Thomas? Someone else? Everyone seemed happy to her. Even Thomas seemed happy as he engaged Hannah in conversation.

At least he did until he glanced at Caroline. She saw the pain in his eyes before he looked away. He must hate her.

It didn't matter. She did what she must. In time both their hearts would heal. He would forget her.

Or maybe he would come to the Lord.

No. She must not hope for that. She just had to let him go.

CHAPTER 26

Prescott

December 14, 1865

Caroline looked up as the bell over the door announced a visitor. A blast of cold air followed the lovely woman in, before she shut the door behind her. From her stylish gown, Caroline knew her customer had to be Margaret McCormick, the wife of Richard McCormick the Secretary of Territory.

"Brrr." Margaret shivered as she made her way to the stove to warm up first.

"Mrs. McCormick?"

"Yes, but you may call me Margaret. And you are?"

"Caroline Larson."

"Pleased to meet you, Caroline. My, it is quite chilly outside."

"Yes, it is. How might I help you, Margaret?"

She rubbed her hands vigorously together for a moment before turning towards Caroline. "My darling husband has permitted me to make some purchases for the Governor's Mansion. Dull place. Have you visited?"

"No. I've heard it is rather large, but I have not had the pleasure of visiting."

"Oh, you simply must come visit me soon. I'm afraid I might go out of my mind rumbling around in that place all winter with no company."

Caroline was surprised. Surely her husband of a few months was plenty of company.

"While Richard and Mr. Fleury are constantly in residence, it is not the same as the good company of a woman friend," Margaret explained, almost as if reading her mind.

Caroline smiled, warming to Margaret quickly.

"Now, about my purchases. The mansion is desperately in need of a woman's touch. There's hardly a thing of beauty in the place. Though, Richard would likely say otherwise."

There was something about the way she glowed every time she mentioned her husband's name that piqued Caroline's interest.

"You love your husband very much, don't you?"

Margaret giggled in a light feminine way, much like what the upper class of the East were trained to do. Caroline had read many a story about such training, but this was her first time meeting a refined wealthy woman face to face.

"I do love Richard very much. Tell me, do you believe in love at first sight?"

She thought of Thomas, though she had resolved not to, and heat flushed her cheeks.

"I can see you do. Well, my Richard and I—we fell in love instantly. I believe with each passing day, our love grows deeper and deeper."

"How long did you know him before you married?"

"Only a few months. I met him on a steamboat bound to New York from San Francisco late this spring. He was such a gentleman and ever so kind. Once we arrived at our destination I found it difficult to part his company. But soon enough he found me again and asked me to be his wife. I couldn't bear the thought of being apart from him again, so we married near my family's home in September."

Margaret's admiration was clear.

"Now, about the mansion. I'm looking for something suitable for window coverings. Something heavy enough to keep out some of this cold air."

Caroline led her to the bolts of fabric, pointing out several that might work. She wondered if she and Thomas would end up as happy as Margaret and Richard. They seemed to be very devoted to one another, and they had known each other for less than six months from the sounds of things.

"Do you and Richard disagree on things?" Caroline ventured.

Margaret giggled again. "Of course. There are some things about which we are on entirely opposites ends. But we do not let those disagreements become an obstacle in our marriage."

"How do you do that?"

"Love, Caroline. Love. If you love a person enough, those differences just don't matter."

Caroline carried the bolt of fabric Margaret selected to the front counter and cut out the amount she requested.

An idea began turning in her brain even as she wished Margaret a good day. What if she loved Thomas enough that it wouldn't matter that he didn't agree with her about God? Surely, if they truly loved each other they could move beyond that.

Excitement began to build. Maybe there was hope for her and Thomas after all.

———

The next day, Thomas entered Hardy's mercantile. He should have expected the place to be busy. It was Saturday. He spotted Caroline helping a lady pick out some lace and trimmings to go with her fabrics.

He moved close to the stove to warm up while she finished with the customer.

"Thomas," she greeted as the lady customer left.

Her eyes lit with excitement, and he started to wonder if she had changed her mind about him. He hoped so. He had been miserable since their supper outing. The more he tried not to think about her, the more he thought about her. She invaded his dreams. He loved her.

It was that love that drove him to seek her out today.

"I thought… Would you like to have supper with me this evening?"

"Yes." She didn't hesitate for even a second. "I would love to."

His heart flipped up and over within his chest. He missed her so much. It would be a grand evening, just having her near.

A few more customers entered, and he excused himself, promising to stop by before they closed at the end of the day. He had a few hours until then, so he headed to the livery to help Craig for a while. Having lost track of time, he ended up rushing to clean up before he had to meet Caroline.

When he arrived back at the mercantile, several young men gathered around the counter opposite Caroline. Her cheeks were flushed and she kept lowering her head in that maddening way. The men responded by leaning closer or saying some comment that caused her to laugh.

Jealousy rose. He hated seeing other men so interested in her.

He pushed his way forward. Gritting his teeth, he asked, "Ready?"

"Thomas! Um… Yes. Let me get my coat."

She disappeared behind the store room curtain and returned, buttoning her coat as she walked. "Where to?"

"A new place." He failed to keep his anger hidden.

"Are you upset with me?"

"No."

"You are."

"Enough!" His voice came out much harsher and louder than he intended. Another couple walking along the street stared as they walked past.

"Why are you upset?"

He stopped and turned to face her, his anger boiling. "I thought you weren't going to flirt with men anymore. Didn't you learn your lesson last time?"

"I wasn't flirting."

"Huh." Thomas grunted.

"I wasn't."

"If you had flirted with them anymore one of them was bound to take you up those stairs and have his way with you. That's how soiled doves act, not decent, respectable women."

Caroline's eyes burned with fury. She reached up to slap his face, but he caught her wrist.

"How dare you!" Tears streamed down her face. She kept shaking her head.

Thomas realized how awful his words were. He started to apologize but she turned and ran back to her room above the store. Groaning he kicked himself. Had he really just equated her to a lady of the night?

What was wrong with him? Why did he destroy every good thing in his life?

Guilt and shame nipped at his feet, pushing him towards the saloon—the only place a scoundrel like him deserved to be.

———

Caroline let the tears burn. How could he say such a hurtful thing? Did he really believe she threw herself at men?

She hated him. He was an awful, mean, spiteful man. She hoped she never saw him again.

Having lost her appetite, she dressed for bed and crawled under the covers. She buried her face and let her broken heart spill out her grief in hot tears. She had been a fool for loving him.

She fell into a fitful sleep.

The next morning, she rose and readied herself for Sunday services and the dinner that followed. She was embarrassed for having given her heart to Thomas. He would be gone on his next run tomorrow morning, so she would only have to avoid him for one day.

She fixed her hair, not really caring how it looked. Then she grabbed a piece of dry toast to appease her growling stomach. She still didn't feel like eating, but she didn't want her stomach rumbling during Reverend Page's sermon either.

Caroline made her way across the street to the boarding-house and took a seat near the back. Julia and Adam greeted her and tried to get her to sit with them. She made a lame excuse of there not being enough room for her.

Throughout the singing and even through the sermon, she was distracted. How could she have been so wrong about Thomas? How could she have given her heart to him?

Her eyes began to burn, but she blinked to try to keep them from spilling over. She couldn't stop loving him if she wanted to.

And she didn't want to.

When the service ended, she feigned illness to get out of Sunday dinner with the Lancasters, Colters, Pages, and Larsons. She couldn't sit there and pretend to be happy. Betty fixed a plate for her to take with her for later if she felt up to it and encouraged her to stop by for supper if she wanted some company.

Hurrying back across the street, she skipped up the stairs and into her small room. Tears streamed down her face before she could even get the door shut. She set the plate of food on the table, took off her coat and flung herself onto the bed.

Her heart was too broken to manage anything but grief. She gave herself over to it.

She woke up again in the late afternoon. Her stomach cried to be fed, so she sat down at the table and picked at the plate of food from Betty in between quiet sobs.

She wanted love to overcome all odds. She wanted her love to win Thomas—for him to love her as much as she loved him—and for their love to conquer this present dispute. But she couldn't see how.

Perhaps time is what they needed. Time to cool down while he was on his next ride. Then maybe the day after Christmas, after he returned to town, he would seek her out and set things right.

Once Caroline finished with her meal, she dressed for bed, even though it was still light out. Burying her face in her pillow, she cried herself to sleep.

Sometime later, she woke to a pounding on her door. It had still been daylight when she retired so she hadn't even set the lamp on her nightstand.

"Caroline."

Thomas. What could he possibly want? Whatever it was, she didn't care. She wanted nothing more to do with him. He could just stand outside and freeze!

The pounding continued. "I know you're in there. Please, Caroline. Let me talk to you."

She stuffed her head under her pillow to muffle the sound.

"I'm sorry. I was wrong."

Still, he knocked on the door.

Throwing the pillow aside, she threw back the covers and found a lamp. She lit it and stood in front of the door.

"Caroline."

She looked at her clock. It was after midnight! What was he doing here?

"Stop it! You'll wake Abraham."

"Caroline, please. I'm sorry. I'm a pitiful, jealous man. I'm sorry. Please let me talk to you."

She stood, hand hovering over the latch. *Don't let him in. Remember what he said.* But he didn't mean it. He came to apologize. *It's too late in the night. Have him come back in the morning.* But he wouldn't go away if she didn't listen.

"Caroline, please forgive me."

She ignored the war within her mind, and she slowly lifted the latch.

———

Thomas swallowed hard when she opened the door and let him in. She looked so beautiful with her long golden hair falling to her waist, part of it over her shoulder, cascading down her front. She was in her night dress—no robe he noted.

The sight of her made him mute. All his words of apology blurred in his lightheaded mind. Maybe he had one drink too many. He hadn't kept close count. But he wasn't drunk. Just a little loose and lightheaded.

Goodness, she was attractive. The night dress did little to calm his racing heart. It hid just enough of her curves to entice his imagination and spark a smoldering ember of passion.

She closed the door behind him. Then she crossed her arms over her chest, further chipping away at his hard-fought self-control.

"Don't you think you've said enough already?"

He allowed the words to pierce his heart. He deserved it.

"I'm so sorry," he said, reaching out to touch her. She backed away. "I was jealous."

"Why?"

Why was he jealous? Because he loved her. He wanted her for himself. He didn't want any man to look at her in the way he did.

"I love you."

His heart rammed his ribs. He was certain she could hear it. His palms grew sweaty. She glared at him. He longed to pull her into his arms and kiss her, showing her how much he loved her.

She took another step back. Then she turned and started pacing.

"You have a funny way of showing it!" Her voice went hoarse as the tears started to flow. "I've never been with a man, yet you accuse me of being... of..." She threw her arms up in the air and let them fall at her side.

He let her anger wash over him. "I know. I was wrong. So very wrong. Please, give me another chance."

She stepped closer to him and poked him in the chest. "You have no right to be jealous."

"I know."

"No... You don't know. I love *you*! Not another man. You!"

"You do?"

She nodded, swiping at her tears impatiently.

He pulled her to him. A big mistake. The thin night dress did little to calm the fire in his veins that ignited instantly. He brought his lips down to hers and drank greedily of her sweetness. His hands roamed over her back as he pressed her closer.

She hooked her arms around his neck and held him tight. She responded to his kiss with such intensity he took a step back to lean against the door, tightening his hold on her.

Hungry desire took over the little bit of sense he had left. The lightheadedness from the alcohol intensified with the intoxicating feel of her body pressing against his. He swept her into his arms and carried her to bed.

A moment of sanity interrupted his passionate kisses as he stopped for a breath. Her green eyes glowed in the light. She pulled his lips down to hers and kissed him with such desire he lost all hope for control.

In the only way he knew how, he showed Caroline how much he loved her.

———

The next morning, Thomas stirred as dawn threw a few rays of light in through the window. The sweet smell of Caroline's hair roused him fully awake. She lay next to him, her head on his bare chest.

What had he done!

Oh, sweet innocent Caroline!

He gently slid her off his chest. Then he slowly, very carefully climbed from her bed. Panic shot through him as he searched for his clothes. He quickly dressed.

Hesitating for a moment, he stood and looked at her sleeping form. Then he bent down and placed a kiss on her cheek. She murmured something then rolled over.

Quietly, he crept across the room to the door, closing it behind him. As he carefully made his way down the stairs, he looked up and down the street to make sure no one saw him. Once at the bottom of the stairs, he rushed across the street. Just a few feet shy of reaching the bunkhouse door, he heard his name.

"Thomas!" Paul grabbed his arm. A dark scowl crossed his

forehead. "What did you do?"

"Nothing."

Paul crossed his arms as his stern gaze bore through Thomas.

"Look, I'll fix it. I'll make everything right when I get back."

"How will you do that?"

"I'll marry her. I'll provide a home for her. I'll do right by her."

Paul shook his head in disbelief. "How could you? She was an innocent young woman—barely even a woman. Were you drunk?"

Thomas brushed past him, wanting to escape from the question. A strong hand came down on his shoulder.

"Were you drinking?"

"What does it matter?" he shot back. "I made a mistake. I'll make it right, I promise."

He shrugged off Paul's hand and darted inside. Finding his bunk, he laid down, overwhelmed by his own failure.

This was the worst mistake of his life. Worse than robbing a bank. Worse than stealing. Oh, he had stolen alright. He stole her trust. He knew better. She trusted him and he led her down a path that would change their lives forever.

He had to leave on his next run to La Paz. But he would be back late on Christmas Day. He would make everything right. He would marry her. He could still fix this. No one would have to know he dishonored her. Her reputation would be safe.

Turning his head into his pillow, he cried. He really messed up this time and it was Caroline who stood the chance of paying the biggest price for it.

CHAPTER 27

Wickenburg

December 25, 1865

Thomas mounted his horse, eager to be on his way home to Prescott. This ride seemed longer than before. His thoughts hounded him constantly about what he had done and what would await his return to Prescott this evening.

He was the worst kind of man for taking advantage of Caroline's trust and of the situation.

To make it right, he would marry her tomorrow, if he could convince Reverend Page to hurry the wedding. He and Caroline were due to head out to Colter Ranch to spend the day with family. Though she might wish to get married in front of her friends and family, he would insist they marry in town before leaving. He was too scared that Will or Hannah would talk her out of it. Then again, Adam might not even permit her to marry him.

No, the best course of action was to marry her in the morning. If Reverend Page refused, then he would ask the judge to perform the ceremony.

This was not how he envisioned marriage. He snorted. He never saw himself getting married. Now he had to—for Caroline's sake. It was the honorable thing to do.

Marriage would not be so bad, he tried to convince himself.

She was beautiful and she stirred his blood like no other. When he staved off his jealousy, he easily recognized that she had a good heart. She cared about others and always offered a friendly and encouraging smile. His only concern was about their tendency to argue. That would get old very quickly.

Perhaps it wouldn't. He would only see her for a few days every seven days or so. His job would have him gone often. Their time together would be limited.

The heaving of his horse's sides reminded him to pay attention to the road. He was just yards from the next station. Once there, he reined in his horse and dismounted.

As he threw the saddle bags over the rump of the waiting mare, the station master commented, "Looks like snow."

Thomas followed the man's raised finger to the sky. Dark gray clouds hung low. In the distance, the top of the mountain to Prescott vanished behind the clouds. For the first time that morning, he noticed the cold wind starting to pick up. If it was this chilly on the valley floor, he could only imagine how frigid it would be going up that mountain.

He quickly mounted his horse and pressed her for top speed. If a nasty snowstorm was rolling in, he would do whatever he could to beat it. He had to get to Caroline today.

As the hours passed and as he continued to change horses, he grew increasingly concerned about whether he would be able to make it to Prescott. The pregnant clouds were ready to birth a chilly snowstorm in a fitful rage.

A mile out from Perry Quinn's ranch, the snow started to fall in heavy blankets, dusting the grassy valley. When he arrived, Perry stood waiting for him, no horse saddled and waiting.

"Thomas," Perry greeted. "Please come inside and warm up."

"Where's my horse?"

Perry let out a heavy sigh. "Don't think you should be pressing on in this weather. It's getting bad down here. That mountain is gonna be dangerous."

Thomas scowled. "I have to make it into Prescott tonight."

"That'd be a fool's errand. The mail is not worth risking your life."

I must get to Caroline. Thomas bit his tongue to keep the words to himself.

"Are you going to saddle me a horse or do I have to do it myself?"

Perry shook his head. As Thomas turned toward the stables, Perry grabbed his arm.

"Please, stay the night with us. It's not safe for you to continue today. Wait out the storm here."

Thomas shook off Perry's hand. "I have to go."

"At least have Christmas dinner with us before you go. Warm up. Go with a full stomach."

He saw through the offer. Perry was trying to use his hospitality to get him to stay. It wouldn't work. Caroline was waiting for him up that mountain. Snowstorm or not, he was going to her as quickly as possible.

"I'm going."

He led his spent horse to the stable and removed his gear. He selected the chestnut mare, one of his favorites, and got her ready for the ride in a matter of minutes. When he led her from the barn, Perry stood in the doorway, arms crossed.

"Step aside," Thomas said, annoyed that Perry seemed so set on delaying him.

"I will not."

Thomas pulled his pistol from his belt. "Step aside."

"You would really shoot me for trying to keep you safe?"

He cocked his gun. Narrowing his eyes, he replied, "Naw. I'd shoot you for standing in the way of me delivering this mail."

Several seconds ticked by. Perry stood steadfast. Finally, Thomas waved the pistol at him, and he moved. Once outside, he uncocked the pistol and holstered it before mounting the mare.

"Don't be foolish!"

He heard Perry's voice over the thundering of his horse's hooves.

He did not look back. Instead, he pressed the horse forward, despite the cold snow swirling around him.

As he reached the base of the mountain, his cheeks stung from the cold. He still had more than an hour or two to go before he would reach town. Maybe longer, since the snow grew heavier and made it nearly impossible to see the trail. Pausing for a moment, he tied his bandana around his nose, cheeks, and mouth, leaving only his eyes exposed to the elements.

With a shiver he pushed the horse forward up the mountain.

About a half hour up the side of the mountain, his horse's hooves started to slip on the trail. She nickered and spooked with each step. He leaned forward, resting his torso on the back of her neck as he whispered soft words in her ear. She calmed some.

Suddenly, her hoof slipped. She lost her footing. She scrambled near the edge. Frightful whinnies broke from her mouth. Thomas pulled back hard. He tried to steer her away from the edge. Her hoof slipped over the side.

As she slid off the trail, her front legs gave out. He flew over the top of her head. He landed on the frozen ground with a hard thud. She fell on top of his left leg. The snapping sound sent waves of nausea over him. The horse rolled from his leg and fell to her death, screaming wildly all the way.

The force of his fall rolled him further down the mountain. His arms flailed. He grabbed for anything that would stop his descent. His chest smacked into a thick pine tree. The air *wooshed* from his lungs. Then he fell no further.

He closed his eyes as the pain ripped through his body. Warmth rushed to his face as the pain overwhelmed him.

He opened his eyes again. He looked at his leg and saw the white bone protruding from his flesh and trousers. Waves of warmth and lightheadedness washed over him. He could not breathe.

His eyes fluttered shut.

Lord, I don't want to die. Don't let me die. I have to make things right for Caroline.

Blackness floated before his eyes and pulled him under.

———

Caroline had been in a wonderful mood all week. Thomas loved her. She loved him. Perhaps Margaret had been right. Love could overcome anything.

Memories of her night with Thomas brought a blush to her cheeks as she stoked the fire in her stove this Christmas morning.

She should not have let him into her room that night. She should have felt some remorse for it, but she didn't. Well, maybe she did some.

As her mind churned through her situation this week, she came to only one conclusion. Thomas would absolutely marry her now.

She smiled. Her heart wanted nothing else. She could hardly wait for him to return tonight. She was certain he would ask her to marry him.

She already knew how the wedding would play out. They would get married at Colter Ranch in front of her friends and family. Adam would probably try to talk her out of it, but she wouldn't listen. He couldn't stop her from marrying Thomas. Besides, she would easily be able to convince Adam that her heart would settle for no one else.

Everyone would celebrate and be happy for them. True love would win. Then she and Thomas would head back to Prescott as husband and wife.

No one would ever know that she gave herself to him before they were married.

They would live happily in the little room above the store.

A flicker of sadness dimmed her joy. He would probably be gone a lot. She had no doubt he would keep his dangerous job riding for the express. She would miss him so much when he was gone. But she would make up for it when he was in town. She would cook his favorite meals and spend as much time with him as possible. Maybe she could ask Abraham for those days off.

If he let her keep her job.

Her heart pounded in her chest. She would be bored senseless if he made her quit working at the store. They wouldn't be able to live here. They would have to build a cabin in town.

What would she do with herself?

And what were his favorite meals? She had no idea. It wasn't something they had talked about.

Her hands grew sweaty. What had they discussed in their times together? What did she really know about him?

She stood from her seat at the table and went to the kitchen to wipe her hands. She put some water on the stove for tea as her stomach started to turn.

Caroline tapped her finger against her temple. Think. What did she know about him?

He was from Ohio. He was handsome. He had a good job. He made her heart dance every time she saw him. Her cheeks flushed again as she remembered the last time she saw him.

Then reality hit hard, knocking her back a step. None of these things were enough to build a marriage on. That's what Mama would tell her.

What had she done!

He didn't even share her beliefs—not that she did a good job of living out those beliefs lately.

She prepared some tea and brought the cup and teapot to the table. Sinking into the chair, she rested her head in her hands.

This was a dreadful mess. Worse than kissing Jesse or Nathan. Worse than anything she had done before.

She was a wretched Christian. How could she even call herself that after what she did?

But she had to marry him, didn't she? It was the only answer to make all this right.

She slowly sipped on her tea, listening to the howling wind outside. The noise sent shivers up her spine, fitting her sullen mood. A tear slid down her cheek and she wiped it away.

She glanced at the clock on her wall. She needed to meet Betty and Paul to head out to the ranch soon.

She checked her pile of wood, not wanting to worry about it when she returned later. It was low. She shrugged her coat on and opened the door.

A foot of snow hid the landing outside her door with little

wisps swirling away on the wind. She grabbed her broom, for lack of anything better, and began brushing the snow off the landing and over the back open railing. Once the landing was clear, she closed her door and worked on each stair one at a time until she made her way to the bottom.

Caroline paused, catching her breath. She looked up and down the streets—empty of everything except snow. She set her broom against the outside wall of the store then she went to get several logs from underneath the stairs. Arms full, she climbed the stairs carefully. At the top of the stairs, she nudged the door open with her foot and piled the wood just inside the door. She made several more trips, wondering how long the snow might fall or how deep it would get. Once she had a good supply upstairs, she retrieved her broom and closed her small room.

Carefully making her way back down the stairs, she crossed the street through a foot or more of snow to Lancaster's. She didn't feel like she would be very good company, but neither did she want to spend Christmas day sulking alone in her room above the store.

"Dear!" Betty exclaimed at the sight of her shaking the snow from her cold booted feet just inside the dining hall. "I'm so glad you ventured out, but I'm sorry we won't be able to go out to Colter Ranch. Paul says he thinks it is going to continue to snow throughout the day."

Caroline greeted Betty with a hug.

"Come sit by the fire, dear. Here's some coffee to warm you up."

She took the offered coffee, mostly so the heat would thaw her cold fingers as she sat near the fireplace. Several boarders sat at the tables around the room. Some played cards while others talked of news from around the territory.

"You look worried, dear." Betty took the seat next to her.

"Thomas should be coming back today."

A heavy sigh lifted Betty's shoulders. "I know. I've been praying for his safety. Hopefully he had the good sense not to try to come up that mountain today."

Caroline nodded. "Maybe he'll wait the storm out at Perry's ranch."

"I hope so, dear."

Even as Betty agreed with her, Caroline could not escape a sudden, unreasonable fear picking at the edges of her heart. Before she could dwell on it too long, Betty started serving up a big Christmas meal.

Following the meal, Betty led everyone in round after round of hymns and Christmas carols. Caroline joined in the singing, though none of the words penetrated her heart. She worried that Thomas might be stuck out in this bad weather. She worried that he might not want to marry her when he returned.

Finally, the sun lowered in the sky.

"Paul, why don't you walk Caroline home?" Betty suggested.

He held her coat for her then waited as she buttoned it up. Grabbing a shovel, he swung it over his shoulder and offered her his other arm.

As soon as they were outside, he said, "Don't worry about him."

"Who?"

"Thomas. He'll be fine."

She raised an eyebrow in confusion, but Paul made no further comment. Once at the store, he cleared the newly piled snow from her stairs and the landing. Then he carried several more armloads of wood up to her room.

"Merry Christmas, Caroline."

"Merry Christmas."

She turned and climbed the stairs. At the top, she glanced down the street towards the direction Thomas would ride in. No wagons lined the streets. No men on horseback. No hoof prints in the two feet of snow. Everyone was huddled safely inside away from the angry, snarling snow.

Still there was no sign of Thomas.

Her heart sank as she sealed herself in her warm room. As she banked the fire in her stove, she shot a prayer heavenward.

Lord, I know I don't deserve to have you listen to my prayers. I've failed miserably. I hurt myself and I hurt you. But if I might ask just this one thing—please keep Thomas safe.

————

A few days later, the snow finally stopped. Caroline had not tried once to leave her cozy room. With the wood both she and Paul piled inside on Christmas day, she had no need to leave. She opened the door earlier this morning and found snow piled almost to her waist. She quickly shut the door, before any toppled inside.

The air stayed very cold. She needed more water but didn't see how she would manage getting out of her room, much less down the stairs and out back to the pump. Even if she did make it to the pump, it would probably be frozen.

Grabbing a pan from the stove, she opened her door and scooped up a pan-full of snow. In a few minutes over the heat of the stove, the snow turned to sweet water, quenching her thirst.

The next few days repeated a similar routine. She was never more thankful that her pantry had been well stocked just prior to the onset of the snowstorm. She fixed meals from items in her pantry and she melted snow from the landing for her water.

Another day passed, now a week and a half after Christmas. Caroline finally braved the chilly temperatures. She cleaned off the landing and the stairs then made her way down to the store.

"Glad to see you survived," Abraham greeted her as she entered. "I was gonna clear off your stairs and check on you in a bit but looks like you saved me the trouble."

"Have you been out at all?"

"Nope. I came into the store a few times and peeked out the front windows. Haven't seen any activity until today. If you're feeling up for it, I'd like to open the store today for folks."

"That would be fine."

In the week that followed, the weather seemed temperamental. The sun came out and blazed for a few days, melting all the snow off in a hurry and warming the ground to a sticky gooey mud. Then, just as Caroline didn't think she could stand to mop the store floor one more time, the weather turned frightfully cold again. Snow began falling in sheets just like the week of Christmas, piling foot after foot on the ground.

Abraham shared his concerns with her one morning when the skies had been clear enough for her to venture down to the mercantile again.

"We're running low on several items. Coffee, sugar, flour, tea. Don't think we're going to get resupplied any time soon, either. Once this snow melts off, it'll be back to the mud. The roads up the mountain will be rough on the freighters. Just hope this all clears up soon."

Caroline did, too. There was still no sign of Thomas going on three weeks after Christmas. If what Abraham said was true, she didn't think he would fare much better on bad, sticky, muddy roads.

She just wanted him home. Soon. So, they could get married before anyone discovered her secret.

CHAPTER 28

Sweat soaked his hairline. He heard voices talking, but he couldn't tell if he was dreaming or if the voices spoke about him in real time.

"Mollie," a male voice said. "What do you have there?"

Cold air hit his face and Thomas thought about complaining but his lips felt as if they had been sewn shut.

"Found 'im busted up like this over th'edge," a woman's voice replied. "He's lucky that his mount done screamed all the way to her bloody death."

"Why did you bring him here?"

"Cause, Perry, my man won't take none too kindly to me showin' up with this here half-dead un. Specially since him and me didn't 'xactly part on the best of terms."

"Yes, but why here?"

Thomas heard the grunt of several men under the strain of a heavy weight. He felt himself float then rest on a soft warm bed. Warmth. At last.

"You the only one in these parts that ever treated me nice. Cain't just drop off a half-dead man with just anybody. I know you. You'll save 'im if ya can."

"That I will."

Thomas didn't hear anything more for some time. Then later another conversation penetrated his weary mind.

"Gotta do it, Perry."

"I can't, Hank. I wouldn't know how."

"You look outside lately? Snow's a blowing something fierce. There's no chance we could get him to Prescott. Not any time soon. And there ain't no doctor in Wickenburg. You gotta set that leg. Then sew him up. It's his only chance."

Silence.

Thomas wanted to plead with Perry to do as Hank said for whoever needed it. The fear in Hank's voice said the poor man didn't have much hope to survive without Perry's help.

"I'll do it. Lord, give me the strength."

A hard tug on Thomas's leg nearly brought him upright. But searing hot pain pushed him under again.

———

Thomas woke with a start. His breath came with sharp stabs to his ribs. He looked around, confused about where he was or how he had gotten there. Something seemed familiar about the cabin.

How did he get here?

Pain shot up his left leg and he took in a rapid breath of air. More pain, this time from his ribs, forced the breath to be shallow. His head started pounding.

He tried to recall what he remembered last. Arguing with Perry about going up the mountain on Christmas day.

The pain intensified and his stomach roiled. His body shook uncontrollably, like he was chilled, yet he felt like his skin was on fire. A groan escaped his lips. Then another.

"You're awake," a male voice said.

Thomas tried to keep his eyes open to see the man, but the pain was too much.

"Drink this."

Liquid touched his lips, and he swallowed. It burned a trail all the way to his stomach. Any clear thoughts grew hazy and soon the pain numbed. Sleep called him again.

———

"Thomas."

He groaned in response.

"Wake up."

His heavy eyes slowly opened. A familiar face hovered over his.

"Perry?"

"Yes."

"What happened?" The fog of sleep began to clear. Thomas felt terrible. His left leg throbbed. His throat was parched. His entire body felt stiff and sore. Pain shot from several places, but it didn't feel as overwhelming as before.

"Here drink this," Perry said, bringing a cup to his lips while he cradled Thomas's head in his arm.

He took several sips then Perry gently laid his head back down on the pillow.

"You had an accident."

"What kind of accident?"

"You fell down the side of the mountain."

He panicked. "When?"

"Almost a month ago."

Thomas struggled to sit upright. He had to get to Caroline. He was supposed to marry her. That much he remembered. "I have to go."

"Lay down."

Perry's grip on his shoulders pushed him back into bed. Thomas tried to struggle but he felt weary and weak.

"Take it easy. Here, drink some more."

A foul liquid touched his tongue leaving a bitter aftertaste.

"I have to go, Perry." His eyelids started to feel heavy. "I promised I would make things right with Caroline."

Anger shaded Perry's reply. "What did you do to her that you have to make right?"

Sleep slurred his words. "I have to mmmarrrry…"

The next time Thomas woke, he felt more alert. There was less pain now. He looked around the room as memories became clearer.

He wronged Caroline. He was on his way to marry her. But he was caught in the snowstorm. His horse… He remembered falling. He remembered the icy cold.

Then he remembered Perry saying he had been here a month.

Thomas closed his eyes again, this time in frustration and not in sleep. What must Caroline think of him?

She probably thinks I ran. A tear slid down his cheek. He had more honor than that. He had to get to her.

He started to sit up when strong arms held him against the bed.

"Stop moving." A scowling Perry leaned over the bed. "You're going to hurt your leg again and it is far from being healed."

"I have to get to Caroline."

"So, you keep saying." Perry's voice sounded cold.

"I have to—"

"Marry her. Yes, I understand. Whether you remember it or not, you recounted the entire reason why you have to marry her."

Perry faced him, anger creasing deep lines in his forehead. "How could you take advantage of such a sweet young woman?"

"I love her."

"Love! That was not love, Thomas. That was a complete lack of respect and self-control. That was lust!"

He swallowed back his defense.

"You have no idea what love is." Perry spat out the words before storming out of the cabin.

Perry was right. Thomas did not have any idea what love was. He never felt it before—not until he met Caroline. But he did love her. No matter how wrong his deed was, it did not change his heart. He loved her completely.

And he had to return to her.

Throwing back the covers, Thomas swung his right leg over the side of the bed. Then he tried to move his left. He couldn't make it move on its own. Looking down, he noted the large wrapping of bandages around it. At first, he thought it might not all be there. But it was. It just wasn't working quite right.

He grabbed his thigh and dragged the sluggish appendage over the side of the bed. As soon as his foot hit the floor, fierce pain shot through his leg forcing all the air from his lungs. Sweat beaded on his forehead. A wave of nausea flowed over him. His vision danced and blurred. He screamed, unable to stop himself.

The door flew open.

"What are you doing!" Perry shouted as he reached down and returned Thomas's left leg to the bed. Next, he lifted the other. Then he helped him lie down.

"You are in no condition to go anywhere."

"Caroline—"

"Enough! You will lie in that bed until I say you can get up or I will get the boys, and we'll tie you to it. Is that understood?"

Thomas nodded.

Perry's anger subsided. "Good. Now drink this."

The fog returned and he slept again.

————

Caroline woke up after a fitful night of sleep. Standing in front of her wash basin, she splashed water on her face. The cold liquid felt good against her hot skin. As she dressed for her day, she considered what she might make for breakfast.

The thought of food sent her stomach lurching. She took several deep breaths, laying one hand over her stomach, hoping it would settle soon. Then she lifted a wrist to her forehead. It seemed warm. Perhaps she was coming down with something.

She took a seat in a chair at the table and waited a moment for the sickly feeling to leave her. A little surprised when it did, she thanked the Lord for it. She decided not to take any chances by eating anything. Instead, she made her way down the stairs to the mercantile.

Abraham greeted her as she entered. She smiled and returned the greeting, still not feeling completely like herself.

"You look a bit pale this morning," Abraham commented as she took her place behind the counter.

"Didn't sleep well last night."

Abraham nodded before he returned his attention to the ledgers.

The bell above the door rang, announcing a customer. Caroline stifled a sigh. Probably someone looking for coffee or sugar or one of the many other goods they ran out of over a month ago.

"Dear!" Betty greeted. "How are you today?"

Caroline stepped around the counter to receive Betty's energetic embrace.

"Well enough. Have you heard anything from Thomas?" she asked, still holding out hope that he would return any day. He had been gone for two months now.

The smile faded from Betty's lips and sympathy clouded the earlier excitement in her eyes.

"I'm sorry, dear. I'm sure he'll be home soon."

Betty reached out and squeezed her hand.

Caroline struggled to hold her tears at bay. She missed Thomas and she wanted him home. Whether he married her or not, she just wanted to know he was safe and well.

"Keep praying for him, dear."

With a heavy sigh, she forced her thoughts away from her sorrow. "What can I help you with this morning?"

"I don't suppose there's any chance you received a shipment yet? The men are getting quite grumpy about the bitter watered-down coffee I've been making by reusing the grounds."

Imagining the taste she had come to despise, Caroline's stomach cramped. She agreed wholeheartedly with Betty's boarders—drying out used coffee grounds and reusing them was only one very small and unpleasant step above going without coffee altogether.

Abraham looked up from his ledgers. "I'm hoping we'll get more supplies in soon. Now that the snow has melted off and the muddy roads are drying out, I think we should see a supply wagon soon."

"Well, when you get more coffee, let me or Paul know. Seems the men can get by without sugar, but coffee—" Betty shook her head.

"That and their tobacco," Abraham said.

Caroline suddenly felt dizzy. She reached for the stool behind the counter to sit for a moment.

"Are you alright, dear?"

"Just a little tired."

Betty gave her a skeptical look but said nothing more about it. "Abraham, Caroline, have a lovely day," she said as she left through the front door as two more customers entered.

"Caroline!"

She looked up at the animated voice of her friend. "Julia!"

The distance closed between them as Caroline rushed forward to give Julia a hug. "I've missed you so."

"What about me?"

Caroline rolled her eyes at Adam's question. "I've missed you, too, big brother."

Adam gave her a quick hug.

"I have a little tea left. Why don't you come upstairs and visit with me for a few minutes?" She looked to Abraham to make sure her suggestion met with his approval. He nodded.

She led the way up to her little room and set some water on the stove to boil as Adam and Julia took a seat at the small table.

"Not a very big space," Adam commented. The frown on his face hinted at his disapproval.

"It's plenty big enough for one."

"How have you been?" Julia asked.

Caroline hesitated. She had been very sullen since Thomas left on his last run and never returned. She had yet to tell Julia about her feelings for him, as the last time she saw Julia was in mid-December, the morning before the last time she saw Thomas. She had been out of sorts then and had avoided the big Sunday dinner.

"Fine."

Julia's eyebrow shot up and Caroline knew that her friend understood her true mood. Hoping to dodge more questions, she gathered some mugs and her teapot. Then she changed the topic.

"How is my brother treating you?"

"Like she's my princess," Adam replied.

"Hardly," Julia shot back. "He refuses to let me ride any of the green horses. He won't let me ride out with the cowboys to the herd. And he won't let me ride alone out of eyesight. How is a girl supposed to enjoy this beautiful land?"

Caroline giggled.

"I think it's a good thing I'm not letting you near the green horses."

Interest piqued, Caroline asked, "Why not?"

Julia's cheeks flamed red.

Adam started to speak, but Julia interrupted him. "It's too early to tell, but I think we might... We may have a little one on the way."

Caroline's cheeks flushed. An unexplained moment of sadness threatened. She managed to chase it away with a forced smile that grew more sincere as she considered what this news meant. "An aunt? Are you telling me I will be an aunt?"

Adam nodded, grinning ear to ear. Julia smiled, then looked at her husband with the most loving and endearing expression Caroline had seen. It even surpassed the way her parents looked at one another.

She wondered if she looked that way when she thought of Thomas.

"That's wonderful news!" she exclaimed, hoping her churning emotions went unnoticed.

Adam came and gave her another quick hug. "Aunt Linny," he said. "I'm going to leave you two while I see to a few errands."

She wished him farewell and repositioned herself, so she sat directly across from Julia.

"Why are you sad?" Julia asked.

The direct question surprised Caroline. She hesitated a moment before answering.

"Thomas. He's been gone for two months... No one has seen him or heard from him since before the first big snowstorm."

"Do you have feelings for him?"

Caroline shifted her gaze from Julia to the window next to the stove.

"You do."

"I love him." Her voice broke with the sorrow she had been holding back. She rested her head in her hands and sobbed.

Julia moved from the other chair to stand next to her, placing her arms around her shoulders. "I'm so sorry he's missing. I know it must hurt."

Caroline nodded as the sobs subsided some.

"Do you know... Does he share your feelings?"

Heat flushed her cheeks as she remembered the last night she saw him. "I think so."

"Then I'm certain he is as eager as you are to be reunited."

A dim light of hope flickered. He would return soon. He had to. She needed him to.

CHAPTER 29

Prescott

February 15, 1866

Robert Garrett bit back a frustrated sigh. He was relieved that the snow finally melted and that the roads were mostly passable. The blizzard, followed by a fast warm up followed by another snowstorm, really set his plans back a few months. He was hoping for more cattle from the rustlers this winter.

As he entered Zach Drake's office, he thought about his big plans. Sometime later this year he would set his ultimate plan into motion. He could hardly wait. But he had to. Moving too quickly would put himself and his plans at risk.

His meeting with Zach was quick as he dropped off the counts of purchased cattle—well, the ones he wanted papers for anyway.

He smiled as he headed toward the saloon. Owens was working out nicely. Prior to the snowstorms he managed to help his rustlers gain about one hundred head, in addition to some two hundred head they stole from Colter's men on the cattle drive to California. Though three hundred might seem like a small sum to a big ranch like Colter's, with over three thousand head at his peak, it was enough to be noticed.

Good. He wanted Colter to notice. He wanted him to lose faith in his men. He wanted to make him worry.

Then, when Colter just started to feel the pain, Robert would initiate the rest of his plan—one that would bring Colter more pain than he could ever imagine.

———

Ben Shepherd awkwardly dismounted his horse, his leg giving him more trouble today than normal. He and Snake escorted Adam and Julia to town today. Or perhaps it was the other way around, since he and Snake were the ones that had to come. Many of their customers waited much too long for their supplies of beef from Colter Ranch.

He smiled as Adam thumped down the stairs from Caroline's little room above the mercantile.

"Too much chatter?" he teased Adam.

"Too much work. I need to catch up with Craig Roundtree about horses for the express. Do you need help before I go?"

"Naw. Snake and me got it."

Adam agreed to meet them at Lancaster's for dinner. Ben nodded, though he hoped his dinner plans might be different and include some quiet time with just him and Betty.

The two months of being snowed in at the ranch gave him plenty of time to miss her and to think. Since he finally let go of Sheila and made things right with God, he found his thoughts turning more towards Betty. The idea of staying alone much longer held no appeal for him. He wanted her in his life and at his side at the ranch.

And that was one of his worries. Would she be able to leave her son and the boardinghouse she worked so hard to make a success?

Well, that's what dinner was for. He hoped to find out just that.

He and Snake unloaded a crate of beef at Hardy's mercantile. Towards the end of last year, they started stocking supplies of jerky. After wishing Abraham well, he and Snake made the rounds at the fort, the hotel, Jackson's boardinghouse, Osborn's restaurant, and finally Lancaster's boardinghouse—just in time to steal Betty away.

He stood in front of the back door of the dining hall kitchen. For a minute he wondered if Betty still cooked in there or if she moved operations up to the nicer, house-like boardinghouse. He followed his nose and opened the back door to the dining hall.

"Benjamin!" Betty exclaimed.

She moved quickly to his side, placing a light kiss on his cheek before he even managed to set the crate of beef down on the counter. Once he did, he wrapped his arms around her and gave her a light kiss on the lips.

"So, ya missed me?"

"Very much. And the boarders have been craving some Colter beef."

Ben smiled. "Glad I ain't disappointing anyone today."

"How is everyone out at the ranch? I've been worried sick not hearing any word for two whole months. Is Hannah well? Will? Adam? Julia? Oh, and Baby James? Will they all be coming for services on Sunday? I hope so. I miss everyone so much."

"Ya talking to yerself or ya want me to answer?" He winked.

She sighed. "Tell me everything I've missed."

"I will, on one condition."

She raised an eyebrow in question.

"Have dinner with me over at Osborn's. Let Paul and the Pengs take care of yer boarders and come with me."

Ben held his breath as Betty hesitated. He watched each argument cross her face before she finally agreed. He let out a long breath and waited while she told Paul where she would be. Then, he offered her his arm and led her down the street to Osborns.

Once they were seated at the table, she repeated her list of questions. "How is Hannah?"

"She's doing better. Was really sick fer a spell."

"So, she is with child?"

"Yah. Said he'll be along in July."

Betty laughed. "He? I'm hoping for a girl. Oh! Another July baby?"

Ben nodded.

"Guess Will wasn't joking about filling up all those rooms in his new house."

He chuckled. "Think he was dead serious. How's yer new house?"

She looked down at the plate of food before her. "It's nice."

"But?"

"But I was just fine where I was. I don't need anything fancy."

Ben took a big bite of the fried chicken on his plate. Tasty.

"How is everyone else?"

"Good. Will hopes they can make it next Sunday. Adam and Julia came in today. He wanted to check on Caroline."

Silence stretched as they both worked on their meals. Ben debated how he might bring up how she would feel about leaving the boardinghouse.

"Ever think of leaving?"

"Leaving?" Betty asked, confusion written on her forehead.

"Leavin' the boardinghouse. Doin' something else."

She laughed nervously. "I don't know. I've been far too busy to think about much else besides running the place."

"If the chance came to leave, would ya take it?" His heart pounded as he waited for her answer.

She glanced away. "I... I suppose it would depend on the opportunity. I'd hate to leave Paul. I mean, this place was my idea. It's not fair to run off, leaving him saddled with the place."

Ben let out a slow breath. "Maybe he wouldn't see it that way."

"I don't know. Sometimes I get the feeling he doesn't like so much responsibility."

"Why ya say that?"

Betty pursed her lips. He was pushing the subject too hard. Her heart was still tied to the place. She'd need some gentle coaxing to be ready to leave. He'd give her time.

"Baby James is jabbering a lot these days," he said, changing the subject.

As the light of her smile brightened her face, he decided he needed to take things slow. Give her time to get used to the idea of a different life than the one she built here. Help her see it might be nicer to share it with him at the ranch.

————

Betty knew she overreacted to Ben's comments about leaving the boardinghouse. She just wasn't ready to let go. Not yet.

He was still pretty new in his return to his faith. She was still new to the idea of marrying again. She had her own share of pain to overcome.

She sighed as she started fixing supper for the boarders. She thought she dealt with the pain of losing Henry, but sometimes it crept up on her unawares. He'd gone to be with Jesus well over fifteen years ago. She thought the grief would be completely gone by now.

It wasn't. Nope.

Sometimes she still missed him so much. He had a gentle spirit and a kind smile, maybe not too terribly different from Benjamin in that regard. Their marriage settled into a good partnership, one involving give and take. He always did his best to provide for her and the children.

A tear slipped from her eye.

"Ma?" Paul's voice was filled with concern. "You alright?"

"Fine, dear. Just thinking about your father." She glanced in his direction.

Pain crinkled his face briefly, before he wiped it away. Sometimes she wished he would allow himself to feel it.

"Benjamin was here today."

"I can see that." He gestured towards the stocked pantry. "And I noticed you weren't around earlier."

She smiled. "Can't sneak anything by you."

He crossed the room and wrapped her in a hug. "No you can't."

"I love you, son."

He released his hold. "Love you, too, Ma."

Then his face split into a big grin. "Better get cooking. Think I hear the first boarders arriving for their grub."

She swatted at his arm, but he moved away before she made contact. He gathered some coffee mugs and the pot and left the room.

Betty wondered what she would do if Ben asked her to marry him. She knew that's what his questions were all about this afternoon. He was trying to gauge her feelings about leaving Paul and the boardinghouse.

In truth, it was Paul she would have the hardest time leaving. The boardinghouse was just something to keep her busy. A way to make a living and love on as many people as she could. But Paul was her only child in Arizona. It would be hard to go, even if it was just out to Colter Ranch. She would miss him dearly.

She started dishing out plates of food. As soon as she had filled several, Paul returned and took them out to the boarders.

He smiled at her when he came back for more.

No, she was not ready to go.

CHAPTER 30

Quinn Ranch

April 1, 1866

Thomas sat up with a start as someone entered the cabin. The familiar man stood in the doorway, his face in shadow. He slowly approached the bed where Thomas spent much of the last three months.

"Hello, Thomas."

A sudden unexplainable fear gripped his heart as the man's face came into full view.

"Drew?" That was impossible. Drew was dead. Hannah said she saw him die with her own eyes.

"You should have called me sooner," Drew said as he lifted the covers from Thomas. Bending over at the waist, he carefully studied his wounded leg. "I could have set your leg properly. Then you might still be able to ride. You're fortunate it did not get infected."

"What do you mean I won't be able to ride?" Thomas's heart thrummed against his chest. Riding was his life. He had to ride.

"Sorry brother. Your leg has healed crooked. It will give you much pain in the months and years ahead. You won't be able to mount a horse for a very long time, if ever. Your days as an express rider are over."

He stared into Drew's blue eyes. Odd, he hadn't taken his

bowler hat off. He was wearing a dark brown suit, much like the one he wore when he came to visit Thomas in jail—was it really over two years ago now? He didn't look a bit different. He was exactly as Thomas remembered him.

"How do you know I'm an express rider? Where have you been?"

"I know many things, Thomas. More than when we spoke last. I know that you will marry very soon."

"How—"

"I'm so disappointed in you. Caroline is a sweet young woman. Very innocent. Very easily influenced. I'm sad that you corrupted her. You haven't changed."

"I've tried to change," he replied, desperate for Drew's approval. "I stopped gambling. I stopped drinking—well most of the time. I even went to church a few times. I did many good things in the war. I have a good job and even some good friends."

"You've stopped gambling?" Drew's voice scoffed. He walked to where Thomas's trousers hung from a peg. He reached into a pocket and pulled out a heavy pouch of gold. "Where do you suppose this came from?"

He swallowed hard. How did Drew know about that?

Closing his eyes, he lowered his head in shame. He had been so confused and angry with himself after he left Caroline. On his last run, while he was in La Paz, he drank heavily. The call the cards and the smug look on one player's face enticed him to sit at the table. He won a sizeable pot that night.

But there was no way for Drew to know this unless he had been following him. If so, why had he kept his presence hidden for so long?

"Where have you been?"

"Answer my question first. Where did this money come from?"

"Gambling."

"Exactly. You haven't changed. You can sit there and re-count the list of good things you've done. But I know how many bad things you've done. I know what you did to Caroline. I know the shame she will face because of you. How can you say that you've changed when you've slid down further than ever before?"

Thomas wanted to argue, but he had the same thought many, many times over the past three months confined to this bed. Taking advantage of Caroline had been worse than robbing that bank back in Cincinnati.

"I see you are beginning to see things my way. So, what are you going to do about it? Just trying to be a good man has gotten you nowhere. How will you change? Do you really want to change?"

"Yes."

"Then do it."

Thomas bit back a curse. "How? I've been trying, but I don't know how."

Drew laughed—an odd sort of laugh, not like Thomas had heard from him before. This whole conversation was bizarre. How could he be speaking with his dead brother? How could Drew know so much—things that no one else knew?

"You sat in church enough times with me and Father to know the answer. Even your good friend Paul told you what you needed. But you are still running anyway. Are you afraid of what will happen if you do what you know you must?"

"You're speaking nonsense!" Thomas yelled, wearying of the cryptic conversation.

"Am I?"

"Yes!"

"So I say, walk by the Spirit, and you will not gratify the desires of the flesh. For the flesh desires what is contrary to the Spirit, and the Spirit what is contrary to the flesh. They conflict with each other, so that you are not to do whatever you want.

"The acts of the flesh are obvious: sexual immorality, impurity and debauchery; … jealousy, … selfish ambition, … envy; drunkenness, … and the like. I warn you, as I did before, that those who live like this will not inherit the kingdom of God."

Thomas recognized the words. They were from a passage in

the Bible that Perry read the other morning.

And this time they pierced him to the core.

He gratified his desires by using Caroline. He was jealous when she spoke to other men. He was envious of Paul and Perry. Being good men just seemed so easy for them. He drank more often than he would admit to anyone.

All these things called to him, pulling him under. He had no strength to fight the desires of his flesh.

But Drew just said that the Spirit desires what is contrary to these things. He wanted to desire what the Spirit desired.

A small flicker of hope lightened his broken heart. Maybe he could change.

Drew continued, "But the fruit of the Spirit is love, joy, peace, forbearance, kindness, goodness, faithfulness, gentleness and self-control. Against such things there is no law. Those who belong to Christ Jesus have crucified the flesh with its passions and desires."

Those who belong to Christ Jesus.

Thomas knew what that meant. Drew belonged, Paul belonged, Perry belonged. All of them were admirable men. All of them displayed peace, love, kindness, self-control. These were the things he wanted.

The answer was clear.

Drew was right. He had been running from what he needed to do—ever since he lost his mother. He held on to bitterness and anger, letting them turn into rebellion, then selfishness. He lost all control and gave into the titillating insatiable desires of his flesh: whiskey, gambling, and lust.

What he had done to Caroline had been selfish.

He closed his eyes as tears squeezed their way through against his will. He needed Jesus to crucify his flesh. He needed Jesus to take his evil heart and make it something pure.

"Thomas! Thomas!" Perry's voice broke through to his contrite heart.

He opened his eyes. Drew was gone. Instead, Perry sat in the chair next to his bed, concern written all over his face.

Thomas looked down at his body. Covers hid his form all the way to his chest. Sweat poured from his brow. His heart thundered heavily.

"You were thrashing in your sleep," Perry said. "Are you alright?"

Thomas took a deep breath to steady himself. "Drew was here."

"Who is Drew?"

"My brother. He was here."

"No one besides me has been here for hours. The men left after breakfast this morning. After you ate, you fell asleep again."

Confusion clouded his mind. It all seemed so real. He really thought he was speaking to Drew.

Yet there were clues. He wore the same clothing as when Thomas saw him last. He hadn't aged at all, but to listen to Hannah's stories, he looked much older toward the end of his life—the stress of the journey westward wearing on him.

It all had been a dream.

But the words Drew spoke were true. His realization that he could never be the kind of man he sought to be without Jesus— that was also true.

Tears singed the corners of his eyes.

Perry leaned forward. "What is it?"

"Nothing. Can you leave me? I just want to be alone."

Perry's eyebrows raised in question. He held his gaze for a few seconds before standing and leaving the cabin.

Thomas closed his eyes again as the sobs tore from his mouth. He was a wretched, awful man. And he wanted to change more than he wanted anything else in his life. He wanted a new life.

"Lord," he whispered, "I can't do this on my own. Drew was right. I always knew what I needed to do. I did pay attention in church. I heard the things Pa's pastor said. I know who you are. I'm tired of running. I'm tired of failing. I'm tired of making a dreadful mess of my life. Can you forgive me?"

Sobs shook his body as he silently let go of the lifetime of bitterness and anger against God and against himself.

Slowly as the minutes passed, his sobs subsided, and a peace settled over his heart. The restlessness and rebellion that drove him all his life started to loosen. The guilt he felt over Drew's death softened. His self-hatred for what he did to Caroline dimmed.

"Lord, I want you to take control of my heart. I want you to crucify the desires of my wicked heart. I want you to replace it with those things Drew said—kindness, gentleness, self-control."

For the first time, Thomas felt a rush of freedom, though still confined to his bed. His heart unburdened. His life restored.

———

When Perry returned to the cabin to start supper, Thomas threw back the covers.

"Will you help me to the table?"

Perry nodded and stood beside the bed as Thomas slid his legs to the edge. Pain shot through his left leg, as it had every time he tried to stand over the past few weeks. He gritted his teeth as he accepted Perry's help to stand. Perry placed Thomas's arm over his shoulder while he hugged Thomas to his side with his arm at Thomas's waist. Slowly, careful not to put much weight on his left leg, Thomas made it to the table. Once seated, he stretched his leg out straight.

Returning his attention to the meal, Perry started peeling potatoes.

"I can do that," Thomas offered. Perry handed over the knife and potatoes, moving on to other preparations.

"You seem in much better spirits."

"I am."

The silence stretched as Perry cut the peeled potatoes into smaller chunks.

"When can you take me home?" Thomas asked.

Perry didn't answer right away. Instead, he dropped the potatoes into a pan with hot lard. He added some salt and stirred before he turned around to face Thomas.

"I think it would be best if you stay for a few more weeks or a month. Start moving around more. Maybe you can help with the horses in the morning and when the boys return in the evening. See how you do before we attempt such a long trip."

He resisted the urge to argue. He was ready to go home—ready to marry Caroline if she would still have him. But he saw the wisdom in Perry's suggestion.

So, he waited.

Over the next week he worked on fashioning a cane out of a sturdy branch Perry brought him. He used it to hobble around the cabin. It was exhausting, but each day he pushed himself more.

The following week he fell into a routine of walking to the stables. Then he would sit and rest for a while before he started caring for the horses. Once the horses were readied and the men off to herd their cattle, Thomas tried picking up other light chores in the barn. By noon, he was worn out and headed back to the cabin for a nap.

After his nap, he stayed in or near the cabin, often times sitting on the porch reading Perry's Bible. He had not told Perry about his transformation, but he thought Perry suspected the truth.

The days rolled by until Thursday morning came and so did reality invade Thomas's shelter. As Perry was leaving to go herd his cattle, he stopped in the doorway.

"Do you think you could ready a horse for the express rider this afternoon?"

Thomas sucked in a quick breath of air, feeling like he had been punched in the gut.

A frown formed on Perry's forehead. "I thought you heard him come through earlier this week."

"When did he start?" He tried not to sound hurt as he asked the question.

"He's been through three or four times now since the beginning of March."

Thomas agreed to see to the express rider's horse, a little perturbed with Perry. Then another thought occurred to him as Perry closed the door behind him. Had Perry let anyone in Prescott know he was alive and recovering? Did Caroline know or had she assumed the worst?

Hurrying—well as much as he could with his bad leg—he made his way to Perry's desk. He shuffled through the drawers until he found some paper and something to write with. He sat down and thought about what he would write.

What could he say to Caroline? That he loved her. That he changed. That he never meant to leave her this long and he would be there just as soon as he could.

Maybe she didn't want to hear from him. Maybe she grew to despise him when she had a chance to fully realize the consequences of their last night together.

Staring at the blank sheet of paper, he finally decided not to write. He would see her soon enough. It would be better to speak his heart in person and not give her room to misinterpret his words on paper. Surely, she would be able to see love in his eyes and hear the sincerity in his words.

Sighing, he stood and checked the clock on the wall. The rider would be here soon enough, and it still took Thomas much too long to walk to the stables and to get a horse ready. He grabbed his cane and began to hobble toward the barn.

CHAPTER 31

Prescott

April 30, 1866

Caroline stifled the tears that threatened to spill over as she heaved into the pit of the outhouse. The awful smell intensified the roiling of her stomach. She retched a second time, though there was nothing left to expel.

She could deny it no longer. Soon everyone would know.

And Thomas was missing or dead or gone. It depended on which rumor she listened to.

One rumor, supposedly started by that lush—Cowboy Mollie—down at the saloon, reported that Thomas might be alive. She found him nearly dead and left him with one of the ranchers down in the valley below the mountain.

Caroline didn't put much faith in this rumor. Mollie had a reputation for being loose with her tongue, her liquor, and with many men who weren't her husband. She wasn't trustworthy.

Another rumor spread that Thomas had run off with some woman. No one could describe this mystery woman. Nor could they provide any more details.

Still more rumors swirled. He was dead. He was seen in Wickenburg recently. He ran because he got some poor girl pregnant.

That last one nagged at Caroline's conscience. It seemed the most likely reason to her, especially since she would be the girl he was running from.

A sob escaped her lips, and she stifled it with her fist.

"Caroline?" Abraham's voice came from the other side of the outhouse door. "Are you alright? One of the customers said she thought you might be ill."

Great. Some of the town busybodies probably already suspected her condition.

"Fine. I'm fine. I'll be in shortly."

A few seconds of silence ticked before the shuffling of Abraham's feet let her know she was alone again. She cracked open the door just to be certain.

Stepping from the outhouse, she hurried to the water pump. She filled a bucket with some water and dipped a cup in. Then she drank of the cool water, letting it settle her stomach, though it could not settle her fears.

Fear. It described her state of mind for months now. She first thought she might be with Thomas's child five weeks after the night she spent with him. Then as each week and month passed, she grew more certain.

Last week, she worked into the night to start letting out some of the fabric at her waistline on her dresses. She plotted ways to hide the little mound that started bulging her belly. It was small and easily hidden now. But soon enough it would not be. Tongues would wag. Her reputation would be tarnished.

Her reputation was the least of her worries. What would she do if Thomas didn't return to marry her as she hoped? She would either have to find a husband who would overlook her mistake—how could she ask that of anyone—or she would have to raise this child alone. Neither option felt right.

She wanted Thomas back. Only every little hope she held on to eventually was torn away.

Dinner after services yesterday acted as a murderer of her hopes. She remembered the conversation all too well.

"I miss Thomas," she confessed during a lull in the conversation. Julia, who sat to her right, squeezed her hand.

"I wouldn't pine over him, if I were you," Hannah said, a frown wrinkling her normally graceful face.

"Why not?"

Hannah started to say something, but Adam interrupted.

"How well do you know him?"

"Well enough."

"Really?"

Exasperated, Caroline replied with an edge to her tone, "I know him well enough to miss him."

Hannah whispered, "I doubt that."

"What is that supposed to mean?"

"Do you know what he did in Cincinnati?"

Caroline shook her head, failing to see what this had to do with anything.

"He was a drunk and a gambler and a—"

"Enough." Will's command caused Hannah to purse her lips.

Julia's jaw slackened. Later she told Caroline she had never seen Will speak to Hannah so firmly and that she had never seen Hannah so angry before.

It didn't matter. What Hannah did manage to say shredded Caroline's hope. She did not really know Thomas. She knew little about his past and little about how he spent his time when he was in La Paz. If what Hannah said was true, she would not be surprised to learn of him drinking or gambling when he was there. Perhaps he even did both when he was in Prescott.

She didn't know.

All she knew was that she carried his child. And she still loved him. If he asked, she would marry him for those reasons alone.

Stirring from her tumultuous thoughts, she headed towards the front of the store. A movement off to her right caught her attention and her gaze quickly followed.

Then her heart threatened to stop. A man stood not more than ten feet from her. Everything about him reminded her of the stage robber named Bart. His height. His demeanor. Worse yet, he was speaking to Robert Garrett, the man who reminded her of the boss of the stage robbery.

Pin pricks danced up and down her arms. Her breathing grew shallow as she moved to the shadow of the walkway in front of the mercantile. She tried to listen to their conversation.

Their voices were much too low, but she gathered from Robert's stiff posture that he was trying to distance himself from the man. Finally, she managed to clearly hear what Robert said.

"You have me confused with someone else."

Then Robert turned her direction. When he saw her his eyes clouded with a frown.

Caroline's legs trembled. It was the same look he gave before he murdered the first man on the day of the stage robbery. Her breathing grew shallow, and she forced her legs to move, taking her inside the mercantile. She was positive those two men were the robbers.

"You look pale," Abraham said, leading her to a chair in the back while nodding to customers along the way. "Are you sure you're not ill?"

"I just... The stage robbers... They are here."

He nodded with understanding. She told him a few weeks ago about the robbery.

"I'll send someone to fetch the sheriff. Just stay in here for now."

A half hour later, the sheriff sat across from her in a similar chair asking her more questions. Seeing the two men stirred new memories of the day with clearer details. She carefully recounted as many as she could to the sheriff.

"I've been checking into Robert Garrett," the sheriff said. "Haven't found a thing. He's well respected down his way. Seems to operate on the up and up. Nobody's got a thing against him."

Caroline nodded.

"But I'll keep an eye on him when he's in town. See if anything is out of the ordinary."

"Thank you, sheriff."

A few days later, after her morning routine of illness, Caroline took her position behind the counter in the mercantile.

"Linny," her brother's familiar voice greeted her as he approached the counter.

"Adam. How's Julia?" She asked, though she had just seen her a few days earlier at Sunday services.

"Sick in the mornings. I guess little ones do that to their mothers."

She half-smiled at his response.

He handed her a list. "I'll be back in an hour. Then I'll take you for dinner before I head back to the ranch. Sound good?"

She nodded.

He frowned. "Are you alright? You seem out of sorts."

"I'm fine." She lied.

His green eyes searched hers. Then he gave her an impromptu hug. "You can tell me all about whatever is troubling you when I return."

She nodded and waved as he left.

Looking down at the list, she scanned it and started gathering the items. Abraham smiled as she entered the aisle where he was helping one of their customers. She smiled back, hoping he wouldn't ask her again today if she was well. Though she had been late every morning this week, he said nothing to her. Instead, he asked her if she felt ill. She denied it, even though she was certain her pale face gave her away. At some point she would have to tell him about her situation. She just hoped he would let her keep her job. Without it, she didn't know how she would be able to support her child.

"You have a strange glow about you," a woman customer said when she rounded the next aisle.

Caroline rushed from the aisle before the woman could say anything further. She knew what glow she was talking about. She remembered how Mama looked when she carried each of the two youngest girls. She noticed the same glow on Hannah and Julia as they both were expecting children in the coming months. Unfortunately, there was no way to hide it.

Looking around the shelves she searched for the items on Adam's list. One of the items was on the shelf above her. Moving closer, she stretched her arm up and stood on her tip toes. As she did so, she caught the hem of her skirt under the toe of her boot, causing the fabric to pull taut over her slightly protruding belly.

"Oh!" the woman customer exclaimed as she moved into the aisle. "You're with child!"

Caroline dropped her arm immediately to her side as her face heated.

"The glow, the sickness. That explains everything," the woman customer went on in a rather loud voice.

Caroline quickly denied it. "I'm not. I've just felt a little under the weather."

"Oh no, child. You most definitely are. All the signs are there."

"I... um..."

Turning on her heel, she headed away from the customer and now stood face to face with the angriest Adam she had ever seen. He grabbed her arm without a word and half-led, half-dragged her from the store, up the stairs, and into her room above the mercantile.

He let go of her arm once the door was closed and began pacing across the floor.

"Is what that woman said true?"

Caroline's gaze darted to the ground. She had never been any good at lying to Adam.

His voice was eerily calm as he asked again, "Is it?"

Tears rose to sheen her eyes. She looked up at him and he stopped pacing. Slowly he sank into one of the chairs by the table. Disappointment shaded his eyes. Disbelief slackened his features.

"Who is the father?"

Her tears flowed freely then. In a low whisper, she replied, "Thomas."

Adam's brows moved together forming a frown.

"How? When?"

Caroline bristled at the invasive questions, even if they did come from her brother. "Before Christmas. It was the last time I saw him—the last time he was in Prescott—before the blizzard."

"Did he force himself on you?"

"No."

Adam shook his head for several minutes, saying nothing.

She took the seat across from him, waiting for him to do something. She envisioned several possibilities. He would take her back to the ranch today, make her quit her job and pack up everything. Or he would yell at her for being foolish.

"What do you plan to do about it?"

She hadn't expected that. "Do?"

"Yes. Will you try to find a husband to care for you and your child? Will you move back to the ranch and allow me to support you? What will you do, Caroline?"

She swallowed. In a soft voice, she said, "I'm hoping Thomas will come back and marry me and we can raise our child together."

Silence thickened as Adam rubbed his hand across his forehead.

"And if he doesn't come back?"

"I… I don't know."

"It's going to be hard. Raising a child, working—if Abraham will allow you to keep your job."

She blinked. He knew her well. He knew she wouldn't want to move back to the ranch. He knew she wouldn't want to snag up the first man that crossed her path.

"I know. But if it is what I must do, then I will do it."

"You don't have to. You can come home. Stay with me and Julia."

"Oh, I'm sure that's exactly what you want. Newly married with a pregnant wife and a pregnant sister in the house. Then when the babies come? Two newborns under your roof?"

"I would do it if I must."

"Well, I hope it won't come to that. I hope Thomas," her voice cracked betraying her true lack of confidence. "I hope he will return soon. Or that Abraham will let me keep my job."

"When will you tell Abraham?"

"Soon. I suppose I will have to after today."

Adam nodded. Then he sighed. Then he drummed his fingers on the table. "I shouldn't give you an option. I should just take you back today."

"But you won't?"

He shook his head. "It's your choice. You made it all the way here without my protection. You've been living on your own for some time now. I'm here if you need me, but I won't tell you what you should do."

"You don't hate me, do you?"

Adam stood and gathered her in his arms. "I don't hate you, Linny. I never could. I'm disappointed. I know you will face pain from the things the townsfolk will say about you. Your child may grow up with whispered rumors. My heart hurts for you and your child. But hate you? No."

"You're a good man."

He released the embrace. "Tell Abraham today. But try to keep it from others as long as you can. I may tell Julia, but other than that, not a soul will hear of it from me."

"Thank you."

He squeezed her hand. "Shall we go and finish up my shopping list?"

She nodded and then preceded him down the stairs and back into the mercantile.

Later, long after Adam left, and just before they closed the store for the day, Caroline told Abraham. She made him swear he would not tell a soul. He agreed. And he did let her keep her job. As long as she wanted it, she could have it. He told her he could not possibly send a woman away to fend for herself if he didn't have to.

She thanked him before returning to the solitude of her room.

Things would be so much easier if Thomas would return. He could marry her, and they would raise the child together. People would talk about the timing of the birth of the child from the wedding, but it wouldn't matter. Her child would grow up with a father and people would eventually forget.

She just needed Thomas to come home.

CHAPTER 32

Quinn Ranch

May 8, 1866

Thomas threw his cane across the corral in frustration. No matter how many times he tried, he still could not get his left foot into the stirrup. Short of overturning a crate and standing on it, there was not even a tiny possibility of him mounting a horse.

It irked him.

For the past few years, he made his living on the back of a horse. He felt at home there. He felt like a man there. Riding was the one positive thing that defined him. He took the opportunity given to him as a dispatch rider during the war and he turned it into a good job afterward.

He had to ride.

Leaning his head against the flank of the horse, he closed his eyes. Perry would tell him to pray.

Lord, I want to ride again. How can I provide for Caroline if I can't ride?

Guilt threatened to extinguish the sliver of hope in his heart that he would one day be able to ride again. No matter how many times he asked God to forgive him for what he did to Caroline, he could not forgive himself. Worse yet, if he couldn't figure out some way to provide for her…

He wasn't trusting God. He was still trying to figure it all out on his own. "Then show me what to do."

The horse snorted at the sound of his voice. He opened his eyes and stepped back. Looking around, he found his cane near the stable entrance to the corral. Slowly he limped to it. Bending down, he picked up his cane from the ground before shuffling back to the horse. Taking the reins, he led her inside and removed the saddle.

He just finished brushing the horse down when Perry returned from an afternoon out with his herd.

"How are you doing today?" Perry asked the same question he had every afternoon for nearly a month.

"Fine."

Thomas hesitated as Perry began unsaddling his mount. He wondered if he should bring up returning to Prescott again. It had been a few weeks since they last spoke of it.

Plowing ahead he said, "When you planning on heading to town again?"

Perry sighed. "Not sure."

Thomas waited a few seconds for his temper to settle. How long was Perry going to put him off?

"I need to get back. I'm well enough to travel in a wagon."

"I know."

"If I could mount a blasted horse, I'd take myself back. Why are you stalling?"

Perry grunted as he brushed down his horse.

Thomas moved closer, trying to get a glimpse of Perry's face. Perry dodged his view.

"What's going on? Why won't you take me back to Prescott?"

Perry didn't acknowledge his questions.

"I have to get back to Caroline." He pleaded his case.

"Ha! I'm sure you do. Do you have any idea what is waiting for you when you return?"

Thomas swallowed. The look in Perry's eye told him he received some news—news that Thomas probably wasn't going to like.

"Did she marry someone else?"

"No!" Perry shouted. "No one would have her."

"Why not? She's wonder—"

"She's pregnant. With your child."

Thomas's heart slammed against his rib cage. Staggering, he took a few steps back to lean against the stable wall, waiting for the words to make sense.

"At least that's the rumor. I've been asking the new express rider to find out whatever he could. Turns out the rumor around town is that she is with child. No one knows who the father is."

Perry turned cold eyes toward him. "But you do."

The air grew thick in the stable. The smell of hay and horse suddenly turned his stomach. He felt trapped. He had to get out of there. Turning on his heel, he quickly headed for the barn door.

Perry chased after him and grabbed his arm. Anger and accusation shrouded his words. "*This* is why I haven't taken you back. Your reaction proves you haven't changed at all. You would run instead of doing what honor dictates."

"I'm not running," Thomas said breathlessly, as if he had been running and running hard. The air refused to fill his lungs properly.

Perry snorted in disgust. "You don't deserve her."

Thomas hung his head low. "No, I don't. But I love her. And I will do what is right."

Silence stretched for several minutes before Perry let out a long breath.

"I'll take you this weekend."

Unfortunately, the joy he thought would come with those words felt vacant considering what Perry just told him. He would return to Prescott and marry Caroline as soon as possible. Hopefully that would ease some of her shame and quiet the rumors.

———

"Whore," a male voice accused as Caroline walked down the

street toward Lancaster's.

Caroline's face heated, but she kept her eyes on the ground in front of her. She'd been called much worse in the past few weeks as rumors circulated about her condition. That nosy woman who first suspected truth wasted no time in making sure the entire town knew.

The name calling started, followed by cold shoulders and snobbish glares—some of them even came from church members.

It was all her due penance for her sin.

As she neared the back door at Lancaster's, she looked up. Betty hung laundry over the line to dry in the warming May sun. She was one of the few who treated her no differently, despite the rumors.

Today, she needed a friend—especially after what that mean Robert Garrett said. Seemed like he was in town an awful lot the past month or two. It was a wonder his ranch survived without him as controlling as he seemed to be.

"Oh, dear! What a pleasant surprise!" Betty's last words were muffled as she engulfed Caroline in a huge hug.

"I was hoping… I could really use a good talk."

"Sure thing, dear. Just let me get these last few things on the line. Why don't you head into the house to the kitchen table?"

"You moved into the house?"

"Yes. Paul really insisted. He said he needed the space off the dining hall kitchen for storage now. I think it has more to do with him wanting to keep me close. He's living there and keeps telling me how much time he spent designing my room. Why, I was just fine with the one I had. But sons—they can be demanding when they put their mind to it."

Caroline smiled, but it quickly faded. Would her child act that way?

"You go on now. I'll be right there."

Caroline walked the short distance to the newest boardinghouse structure—a much more traditional boardinghouse like the ones she remembered from Texas.

She opened the door and stepped into a lovely parlor area. A man in a nice suit looked up from the paper he was reading then quickly looked back down. To her right, there was a small table with a register and to her left was a staircase. She moved through the parlor and into the dining room. It looked big enough to accommodate the boarders who stayed in the house, but not big enough for those in the bunkhouses. Off to the right of the dining room was the kitchen.

Tentatively, she peeked in. The small room had a quaint table in one corner and a brand-new iron stove in the other. Pantry shelves lined one wall above a workspace area. The basin stand was near the stove, but not too close so that the heat of the stove would become overwhelming. What a lovely place Betty had to work.

Spying the coffee pot on the back of the stove, she checked it. Empty. Instead of waiting to be served, she found the coffee beans, ground them with the hand cranked grinder, and set a fresh pot on to brew.

She took a seat in one of the chairs at the table just as Betty bounded into the room.

"Coffee should be almost ready," Caroline offered.

"Thank you, dear. Now tell me, what brings you here—and before the store is closed for the day. Abraham didn't let you go did he?"

"No. He told me to take the rest of the day off after an unruly customer upset me."

"I see."

Betty handed her a cup of steaming coffee and pushed two little containers of creamer and sugar toward her.

Caroline launched into her story as she fixed her coffee. "Robert Garrett came into the store this afternoon."

"He's that rancher that you think was involved in the stage robbery?"

"Yes. Well, he started spouting off all kinds of nonsense. He said that he knew who my baby's father was. How could he know that?"

"I don't know, dear."

"Anyway, he said that he saw Thomas down in Wickenburg. Said he was drinking and bragging about how he dodged having to marry me. He kept going on in great detail about Thomas and the soiled dove hanging on his arm."

Betty frowned.

"You don't think it's true, do you?" Caroline asked.

Betty thought for a moment. "I don't think so. If Mr. Garrett is who you think, he may just be telling you stories to upset you—sort of throw you off. Keep you from being certain he was involved in the robbery."

"Or maybe it's his way of paying me back. Maybe he wishes he would have just killed me then."

Betty patted her hand. "No matter his reason for doing it, I don't believe what he's saying."

"Why? Why don't you believe it?"

"Because, deep in his heart, Thomas is a good man. He has a sense of honor. Others might not see it, but I've always seen it. It's that same sense of duty that his brother had. You know, he's more like Drew than he thinks. He's just been carrying around too much bitterness to see it."

Caroline took a sip of her coffee as she considered Betty's words. When Robert first said all those things to her, she believed them. But now, hearing Betty's thoughts, she wasn't so sure.

"But why has he been gone so long? Why doesn't he come back if he has all this honor?"

"Dear, I think God is keeping him away."

Confusion swirled in her heart. "What do you mean?"

"I think the good Lord has been working on him. Working on him real hard. Chipping away at that bitterness and anger he carries around. Cleaning out his guilt. Thomas blames himself for his brother's death. And there's something more, though I don't know what. I think maybe the Lord is using this time to deal with Thomas on these things."

Her eyes burned as the tears shoved their way forward. She was guilty too. She had done things she should not have, and she carried around too much guilt for it.

"Oh," Betty said. "Do you need me to pray for you, dear?"

The tears ran rivers down her face as she nodded.

"Lord," Betty started as she grabbed both of Caroline's hands in hers. "Caroline needs to know that you forgive her for her mistakes. She needs to know that you still love her. Help her to trust you with Thomas and with her unborn child as she turns her heart back to you. She's heard the call your voice—I can see it in her eyes—gently beckoning her back to you. She loves you even though she's been a little lost for a while. Wrap her in your loving arms and help her to look to you and let go of the shame she is hiding. In Jesus' precious name. Amen."

Silently in her heart, Caroline asked God to forgive her for letting Thomas be with her. She asked him to forgive her for lying to her parents and for not waiting for Millie and her father to escort her to Prescott. She poured out all the lies and plans and mistakes of the last year and laid them at her Father's feet.

Slowly, as she kept her eyes shut, she began to feel something within her heal. Pain and brokenness were replaced with peace—a soft, gentle feeling that she hoped would never leave. When she opened her eyes, Betty smiled at her.

"He loves you, dear. And He will never leave you. Not even when you think all is lost."

Caroline believed Betty. She even felt it deep within her heart.

Suddenly, it didn't matter what the townsfolk said about her. It didn't matter what names they called her or what looks they gave her. It didn't matter if Thomas never returned or if he came back tomorrow.

She wasn't alone anymore. Well, she had never been alone. God had been with her all the way. She saw that now. He had been there when she needed rescued after the stage robbery. He had been there when she yielded to temptation by spending the night with Thomas. He had been there through everything. It was just her own stubbornness that blinded her from seeing he was always there.

Lord, I want to change. I want to be different. I want to always remember you are here and that you love me. I don't want this peace to leave.

She looked into Betty's eyes—the deep glowing eyes of a woman who walked closely with the Lord. *I want to be like her. Always putting others before myself. Always close to You.*

Betty reached out and patted her hand again before standing. "Best get supper started for the house boarders. They'll be looking for something soon."

Caroline smiled.

"Why don't you stay and eat with us?"

"I'd like that."

CHAPTER 33

Prescott

May 12, 1866

For the first time in five months, Thomas set sight on the precious town of Prescott, though not on horseback. Instead, he sat on the wagon seat next to Perry with his good leg bent at the knee and his bad leg stretched out straight, throbbing with each bump and jostle.

Five long months. The town had grown considerably since he left in December. He had changed even more than the town.

He inhaled the fresh pine scented air, letting it fill the depths of his lungs. He missed that ever-present fragrance almost as much as he missed Caroline.

The thought of her caused his gaze to drift to Hardy's mercantile. Richard McCormick, the Secretary of Territory, entered with his wife Margaret. Thomas wondered briefly how they would react to seeing Caroline and if she was able to conceal her secret any longer.

Everything within him screamed at him to jump down from the wagon and run into the mercantile, sweeping her into his arms. But jumping and running were foreign acts now. Walking took plenty of effort. Besides, he needed to see Craig Roundtree first.

As Perry pulled the wagon to a stop in front of the livery,

Thomas slowly climbed down. When his left leg hit the ground, he grunted from the sharp pain that shot through it. It passed soon enough. Reaching over the side of the wagon, he grabbed his cane. Perry came around to his side to face him.

"Thank you for all you have done for me, Perry. I owe you more than I could ever repay."

"Take care of her. Treat her well and you will have done enough to satisfy the debt."

The two men embraced awkwardly for a fraction of a minute. Thomas wished Perry well before he turned to face the livery.

Nothing changed about the livery. It still looked the same. Yet, for some reason, Thomas found himself wanting to take in every detail—almost as if he didn't trust that he would see it again for another five months.

Shaking off his trepidation, he pushed the door open and stepped in.

"I'll be with you in a moment," Craig's voice boomed from elsewhere. When he rounded the corner and came into full view of the entry, he stopped suddenly. "Well, I'll be! Thomas Anderson!"

"Craig."

Craig closed the distance and slapped him hard on the shoulder. "You're alive."

"And still kicking most of the time."

"Tell me what happened. Where you been?"

Thomas shuffled his feet before answering. The long ride made his leg stiffer than it had been in weeks. He slowly paced back and forth to get it loosened up while he told Craig about the accident that nearly took his life.

"Been at Perry Quinn's ranch since."

"Good to have you back and in one piece."

Thomas nodded.

An uncomfortable silence settled between them. Thomas struggled with what exactly he might say, knowing his position with the express had already been filled. Not that it mattered much. He couldn't mount a horse, much less ride it across miles of open desert.

"Look," Craig started. "I didn't know if you were coming back or not. Mr. Vincent was pressuring me to get the line going again. Since he owns the express, I was in a rough spot. Had to hire someone to take over."

"I understand." He did. It just hurt to know that he would never do the job he was made to do ever again.

"If you're planning on staying in the area, Lount and Noyles are always looking for more men down at the sawmill. It's on the bank of Granite Creek, just a few minutes from town."

"Thanks, Craig. Can I tell them you sent me?"

"Sure. Be happy to recommend you."

He turned toward the door.

"Glad to know you're okay," Craig said before wishing him well.

Once outside, Thomas let out a heavy sigh. He really wasn't okay. He was torn up inside. He'd been trying to figure out what he would do once he got here. He had no plan, so he appreciated Craig's suggestion.

As he walked across the street to the boardinghouse, he lifted a brief prayer heavenward, asking God to show him what to do—something he had forgotten until now.

Searching the grounds, he tried to figure out where Betty might be. He walked toward the house he helped Paul build, thinking that might be the best place to start. As he neared the bottom of the stairs of the porch, Paul emerged from the building.

"Thomas!"

Bounding down the stairs, the much taller and beefier Paul swallowed Thomas in an embrace. "You're alive!"

Apparently, everyone must have thought him dead, Thomas thought.

"Yes. Finally, well enough to come home."

Betty dashed out of the house. "What's all this racket—Thomas!"

It was her turn to squeeze him with a hug tighter than any he remembered from his mother. She placed her hands on the side of his face as she stepped back. "Let me look at you." Her gaze swept all over his face, stopping on his eyes.

"I know that look." She pulled him into a gentler embrace. "Welcome to the family."

Thomas stammered as he extracted himself from her arms. "Fa—family?"

"The family of God. I see it in your eyes."

He shook his head, baffled by her astuteness.

Paul took his hand and pumped it up and down in a shake. "That's wonderful. It really is."

"Come," Betty said as she ushered him up the stairs and into the house. "Sit and tell us everything."

He sat at the kitchen table, stretching out his bad leg. He rested his cane against the nearest wall. Then he started telling her and Paul everything that happened—even his strange dream about Drew. Then he told them about the conversation with Craig.

"I feel a little lost now," he admitted. "I need to find a job so I can provide for Caroline."

"Do you plan to marry her?" Paul asked.

"Yes. If she will still have me."

Betty smiled knowingly yet said nothing.

"I could use some help around here for a few days. Maybe even a week," Paul said. "Got a lot of odd jobs that need taking care of. Interested?"

"I suppose. I need to take some time to find something permanent."

"Great."

Betty said, "I'll ready one of the lower bunks in the Mother Lode for you."

"I'd appreciate it."

"When are you going to see Caroline?" she asked.

"Soon as possible."

———

"So the rumors *are* true," Margaret McCormick said as she approached the display Caroline was working on.

Thinking Margaret was referring to her condition, as everyone seemed intent on doing these days, she moved to the side. She lowered her head and her voice. "Yes."

"You do have a shipment of hats from San Francisco!"

Caroline's head snapped up. Margaret wasn't looking at her at all. Instead, she grabbed her husband's hand and pulled him close to the display of hats.

"Just look at these, Richard. Very fashionable."

Caroline stepped away and ran to hide her protruding belly behind the counter before anyone really made a comment about her. Heat flamed her cheeks. She should have known Margaret would not participate in idle gossip. She was much too kind for that.

Being forgiven by God and being forgiven by the townsfolk seemed to be two entirely different matters. As she approached the fifth month of her pregnancy, her body changed. It seemed the little one wanted more room. It was getting more difficult to hide.

"Caroline," Margaret called her name as Richard moved to the other side of the store. "Would you be so kind as to help me?"

She nodded and hurried to Margaret's side.

Margaret spoke softly. "I apologize for my double meaning earlier. It was not my intent to embarrass you. I wanted to see how you are faring. You have become quite dear to me."

"I am faring well enough." She kept her voice low.

"And the father? Will he do the right thing?"

Caroline looked away. "I don't know where he is."

"Ah. But you love him very much."

She nodded, trying to choke back her tears. She loved him. She missed him. She ached for him to return.

"I shall keep you in my prayers."

"Thank you."

Margaret's next statement was said much louder, for all the customers to hear. "Don't you think this hat is just perfect for me?"

Caroline smiled. "It suits you well."

"Then I must have it. Tell me, are you accomplished with a needle?"

She nodded.

"Perhaps, if I left you something extra, you would be able to sew me a matching reticule?"

"I would be delighted to," Caroline answered, knowing full well that Margaret had skill enough of her own.

Lowering her voice again, Margaret said, "Something for you to put away for the future."

A humbled smile stretched across Caroline's lips. Margaret was truly generous, thinking of her needs. She wondered if a matching reticule were even that important to Margaret.

"Are you ready, my dear?" Richard McCormick asked, coming alongside his wife.

"Yes, dear husband."

Slipping her hand into the crook of her husband's arm, Margaret wished Caroline a good day.

She waved farewell. Just as she started to turn, a familiar face appeared in the doorway that the McCormicks just vacated.

She blinked—not certain she wasn't dreaming of those blue eyes and sandy brown hair and that infectious grin that stole her heart long ago.

"Thomas." The name fell from her lips like a soft downy feather.

She broke her eyes from his intense gaze, dropping hers to the cane in his hand. His left leg curved oddly to one side, the damage visible despite being shrouded in trousers. A wound like that must have taken a long time to heal.

Then it dawned on her. None of the rumors were true. He hadn't stayed away because he wanted to. He was not able to return before now.

She looked back up into those perfect blue eyes. They told her what she hoped to hear. He loved her and he came back for her.

———

Thomas's mouth went completely dry at the sight of her. Her rosy cheeks glowed with an alluring iridescence. Her lips were pinker than he remembered. Her flashing green eyes sent his pulse pounding vigorously through his veins.

As her gaze traveled down to his injured leg, he let his travel down to her swollen waistline. It was bigger than he remembered, confirming the rumor Perry heard. She was with child.

His child.

His heart felt overwhelmed with the burden he placed on her. He hobbled as quickly as he could to stand directly in front of her.

"Caroline," he whispered, taking her left hand in his right. "I came as soon as I could. I'm sorry it was too long."

Her eyes darted away from his but not before he noticed the light sheen. "I must tell you—"

"I want to speak to you first. Can you leave for a while? Come take a walk with me."

"I—"

Abraham's voice drowned hers out. "Go."

Thomas offered her his arm and carefully led her out of the mercantile. There were a few wooden benches randomly dotting the brilliant green of the town square. He picked the closest one and helped her sit down before he took a seat next to her. Though he wanted to see her eyes as he spoke, his leg begged him to rest.

"It has hurt me more than I could explain—having been away from you for so long. I know how it must have looked to you, and I am sorry."

"Where have you been?"

"On Perry Quinn's ranch, getting well after a horrible accident. When I last saw you…" He noted the red splotching her cheeks. "I was wrong for what I did, Caroline. All I could think of was returning as quickly as I could to marry you—to make things right.

"I was so eager to return that I acted foolishly. I took off and tried to head up the mountain even though a snowstorm blew in. I just had to get back to you and I wasn't thinking.

"Then, my horse spooked. I couldn't control her and she went over the side of the mountain. I fell a good ways too.

"Perry cared for me better than a brother. He did the best he could to mend my leg. Unfortunately, the snowstorm kept him from getting to a doctor when I needed one the most. By the time I saw a doctor, my leg was already forming into the shape it is now."

Thomas paused, staring at her profile. She looked straight ahead. Then she turned glistening eyes toward him. His heart broke at the pain there.

"I didn't think you were coming back."

"Oh, Caroline. I wanted nothing more."

He shifted sideways, propping his good leg on the bench. Then he took both her hands in his. He wanted to get down on one knee, but that would be far too difficult.

"I know I have nothing to offer you right now—nothing more than my name—but I willingly offer it to you and to our child."

She gasped. "What are you saying?"

"I have no job. I can't ride anymore. But I will find some way to support us. Will you be my wife?"

———

Caroline's tongue felt like dead weight inside her mouth. He was offering her exactly what she hoped. He was offering her marriage. Though it sounded like that was all he offered.

What about love? Did he care for her?

Old fears clawed at her, forcing her to listen. He didn't share the same faith. They would be unequally yoked. But it was his child. He would give her the security of marriage. He would be by her side to raise their child.

"You own my heart. You carry my child. Please, share my

life."

He did love her. Weren't those things enough?

"Tell me, what is holding you back?"

She couldn't understand her own reasoning at this point. She doubted he would understand. If she were wise, she would keep her fears to herself and gleefully accept his offer. But she couldn't. Would it be better to raise her child alone than to be married to someone who didn't believe what she did? It was her mistake that put her in this position. Making a second mistake would not make it right.

"What about faith? We don't share the same faith." She looked down at her hands.

Thomas placed a finger under her chin and lifted her face. "But we do."

She searched his eyes. Could it be true?

"We do," he said again.

"Then, yes. I'll marry you!"

He pulled her to him, lightly sweeping his lips across hers. The sweet touch sent fire burning from her lips to her stomach. She sensed he was holding back.

"I'll speak with Reverend Page tomorrow. Given the circumstances, would you prefer a quick wedding?"

She nodded.

"Next Saturday you and I will start our life together."

One week. Just one week and she would have what she had been begging God for. She would marry Thomas. Everything would work out just fine.

CHAPTER 34

A week later, Caroline stood next to Thomas in front of Reverend Page and a small group of family and friends. As the reverend spoke of the importance of love, she let her mind wander. The only part of this scene that matched what she dreamed of since childhood was that Julia stood by her side. Nothing else turned out the way she expected.

She was in a town in the middle of the vast Arizona wilderness. She glanced at the man who was to become her husband in just a few minutes. She still knew so little about him. But she carried his child.

Her only family present was Adam. He sat in the front, looking none too pleased about the situation. Mama and Papa were hundreds of miles away in Texas. They would be so disappointed in her.

Blinking rapidly, she tried to keep her melancholy thoughts away. This was her wedding day. Despite the odd way it arrived, she loved Thomas. She wanted to be his wife. They would make a fine home together and share a happy life.

A cool breeze tickled the back of her neck. Since there were only a few guests—the Lancasters, Larsons, and Abraham Conrad—Betty offered the grassy area between the dining hall and house for the ceremony. The weather was perfect in the shade.

Reverend Page started the part of the ceremony where she would agree to love and cherish her husband—an easy promise to make. The words came from her mouth, yet she felt as if she were watching the scene unfold as if she was not a part of it. Thomas smiled at her as he spoke his words of commitment.

Then, quicker than she imagined, Reverend Page introduced them as Mr. and Mrs. Thomas Anderson. She smiled and glanced over at Thomas. He wore a smile masked over concern. Perhaps this wasn't what he imagined his wedding day would be like either.

Betty ushered the small gathering into the dining room in the house. She instructed Thomas and Caroline to sit on one side. Julia and Adam sat across from them. Paul sat at the head of the table, Betty at the foot. Abraham Conrad wished them well, returning to the mercantile instead of staying for the meal.

After Paul led them in a beautiful blessing, he asked Thomas, "Any luck finding a more permanent job?"

Thomas nodded. "I start at the sawmill on Monday."

Though she didn't know her husband very well yet, she did pick up on the edge of concern in his voice. Paul must have as well.

"Worried your leg will bother you?"

"Yes. It was hard enough to help you around here last week with some of the repairs to the bunkhouses. I'm not sure how standing most of the day will affect me. Hopefully, I'll adjust quickly."

She reached for his hand under the table and gave it a squeeze. She loved how comfortable he seemed talking to Paul about his fears. Perhaps they were even better friends than she realized.

"Where will you live?" Julia asked.

Caroline answered, "Above the mercantile for now. Abraham said we can stay there until I stop working. We thought it would be best for me to keep my job until the baby comes."

"That's good. Are you finding time to start making things for the baby?"

Caroline sighed. "Not as much as I would like. I'm so tired when I finish at the store at the end of the day that I haven't sewn much."

"Dear, we'll make sure you have everything you need," Betty said. "Sometimes it seems like it is forever before a child arrives, but then it is gone before you know it. I've been working on items for both you and Julia. Oh, and one item for Hannah, even though she should have plenty from James's birth."

"I heard that Mrs. Avery may have some baby things," Paul added. "Maybe she would be willing to loan you a few items?"

"That's a wonderful idea!" Betty exclaimed. "I'll speak to her for you."

Caroline nodded. As the conversation moved on to other topics, some of her sadness returned. She doubted very many brides spoke of similar things on their wedding day.

Once the meal finished, she and Thomas walked to their small room above the mercantile—their home. Paul greeted them at the bottom of the stairs.

"I took all your things up already," he said to Thomas before wishing them both a good evening.

"Shall we?" Thomas asked.

Caroline inched up the stairs next to him as he braced one hand against the outside wall next to the stairs. His other hand clutched his cane with a tight grip. He stepped up with his right leg, then brought his left leg up to the same stair before moving on to the next. It was painful to watch how he struggled. And he would have to do this daily.

At the top he paused to catch his breath. Then he held the door open for her. Once inside, she turned to face him.

The look in his eyes sent her heart fluttering. He closed the door and leaned his cane against the wall. Then he pulled her to him.

"You look amazing, wife."

He lowered his head to her lips and hungrily kissed her sending waves of heat through her body. She wrapped her arms around his neck and pressed close. She returned his kiss with fervor. He broke his lips from hers and began trailing kisses along her neck as he lodged his hand in her hair.

"Help me with these blasted hair pins," he whispered near her ear.

She reached up and unpinned her hair faster than ever before. Once it was free, Thomas ran his hands through her hair. His lips covered hers again as he started shuffling her towards the bed.

———

The next morning, Thomas woke to Caroline's light touch on his bare chest.

"So many scars," she murmured.

"So many brushes with death."

"From the war?"

He rolled onto his side to face her. "Yes."

"You were a Union soldier?"

Thomas frowned. Had he never told her about his time in the war?

"For a while. Then I became a dispatch rider, carrying messages from colonel to colonel. Eventually, I rode for generals."

She pointed toward his scars. "Was it painful?"

"Each one was, yes. Some healed quickly. Some took longer."

Not as long as my invisible scars. Those were still healing.

Her green eyes softened. Then they lit with mischief. "Hungry?"

"Ravenous. I don't recall my wife serving me supper last night."

Pink colored her cheeks. "I don't recall my husband complaining either."

He grinned at their light banter and this new side to Caroline he hadn't seen before.

She rolled her eyes and made a great labored show of leaving the bed. "I suppose I'd best feed you, then."

He watched as she readied herself for the day. As she moved toward the kitchen, he hurriedly slid from the bed, trying to keep his bad leg from her sight in case she happened to turn around.

He managed to hide it from her last night. The long ugly scar on his leg shamed him. For as long as he could, he wanted to shield her from it.

Once he was dressed, he took a seat at the table. Caroline placed a plate of bacon and eggs in front of him. Then she sat across from him and bowed her head. He bowed his head as well, waiting several uncomfortable seconds for her to pray.

"Thomas?"

He opened his eyes and glanced at her. Her head remained bowed, and her eyes closed. She expected him to say grace. Clearing his throat, he tried not to panic. What had his pa always said at mealtimes? He had no idea.

Lamely, he offered up what he hoped was an acceptable prayer. At his "amen," Caroline looked up and smiled at him.

After breakfast, they attended Sunday services, still being held at Lancaster's. Several of the church members congratulated Thomas and Caroline on their wedding. Hannah was one of them, though her offer was couched in warning—that he should take good care of Caroline. Other church members snubbed them, probably because of the circumstance surrounding the rushed wedding.

Thomas shrugged it off as he and Caroline returned to their home.

Taking a seat in one of the rocking chairs, Caroline chatted as she sewed some tiny garment. "Tell me about your life before the war. I know so little about it."

His heart picked up pace at her innocent question. He was not sure how much he wanted to tell her about that life or if she would understand.

"I lived in Cincinnati, Ohio. My mother passed when I was very young. My father owned a mercantile. I went to school like every good lad. There's not much to tell." *Liar.*

"What about your brother? Did you get along?"

Thomas snorted before he could catch himself. "There was a time that we did and a time that we did not."

The silence stretched uncomfortably. When he glanced at

Caroline, he noted her wrinkled brow. Somehow his answers upset her.

Hoping to change that look on her face, he asked, "What about you? Do you get along with your brother?"

That did the trick. She talked for the next half hour about her large family—two older brothers and three younger sisters. She told him how she and Adam and Julia spent a great deal of time together growing up. On and on she went, until it was time to prepare supper.

He didn't mind her long conversation. He enjoyed hearing about her family. They were his family now. And it kept her from asking more about his past.

———

The next morning, Thomas slowly made his way down the stairs, his leg already bothering him. The walk to the sawmill did little to help loosen it up.

As he neared the massive mill, the loud screeching of the metal saw cutting wood pierced his ears. He looked around and spotted George Lount, one of the owners of the mill.

"Let's start you out sweeping up the saw dust," George yelled above the noise. "Dangerous stuff when it gets under foot. Almost like walking on ice."

Thomas nodded as George thrust a broom his direction.

After sweeping half the morning, George had him move to stoking the steam engine fire. At first, Thomas thought the job would be easy. After fifteen minutes, the heat from the fiery beast caused him to perspire so much that his shirt clung to his chest like a wet rag. He took very few steps in this job. Mostly he bent down to load up a shovel full of scrap wood. Then he flung it into the fire compartment. The constant bending and lifting burned his muscles—something that would have felt good had it not also caused a dull throbbing pain in his left leg.

A whistle blew, signaling a break for everyone. Thomas grabbed his cane, and the packed lunch Caroline prepared for him. He found a cool shady spot near the creek. Clumsily, he lowered himself to the ground.

The rushing of the creek water sounded muffled after hours of listening to a roaring fire, the loud hum of the steam engine, and the piercing sounds of the saw. A breeze rustled the leaves of the shaded trees, offering him some relief.

He devoured his meal, wishing there had been more.

Another whistle blew, announcing it was time to resume work. Taking his cane, he braced hard against it to lift himself from the ground. By the time he stood, all the other men were already back to work at the sawmill. His bad leg complained as he shuffled toward the large steam engine.

"You alright?" George shouted over the noise. "Ain't looking too good."

"I'm fine."

"Let me show you the next area. See how these boards come off the saw and how he's pushing them down the line?"

Thomas nodded.

"That's what I want you to do. Whenever you get a bark piece, carry it to the pile over there. Think you can handle it."

No. Thomas nodded anyway. He needed this job.

By the time the end of the day came, he wasn't entirely sure he would be able to walk all the way back to his home, much less manage those stairs. Slowly, with pain shooting up and down his leg, he put one foot in front of the other. In twice as much time as it took him to get there this morning, he made his way home.

He stood at the bottom of the stairs for a few minutes. He smelled awful. Caroline would probably insist he wash up before supper. Spotting the water pump behind the mercantile, he made his way to it. He filled a bucket and splashed a good amount of water on his face and neck. If it wasn't in clear view of the street, he would have removed his shirt. Maybe he would talk to Caroline about setting up something down here where he could wash up properly at the end of a hard day.

He turned back toward the stairs. One at a time he forced himself up them. When he opened the door, delicious aromas greeted him.

"Welcome home." Caroline kissed his cheek.

He flopped into a chair at the table letting his cane slip to the floor with a clatter. Caroline tried to engage him in conversation, but he was too tired to pay much attention. As soon as the meal ended, he fell into bed, despite her protests that it was too early.

In the middle of the night, he woke with a start, his left leg cramping wildly. He cried out. Caroline stirred.

"What's wrong?"

"My leg."

She reached to light a lamp next to the bed, but he grabbed her arm.

"No need... to light..." The pain shortened his words.

"Should I fetch the doctor?"

"No."

"Tell me what to do."

He curled into a ball, rubbing his leg with one hand. In the darkness, Caroline followed his arm to his hand to his leg. Gently, she began rubbing his leg. The intensity of the pain lessened some, but it still hurt.

Thomas moaned.

"Do you want me to make some willow bark tea?"

She didn't wait for his answer. Instead, she slid from the bed and lit a lamp. She put some water on to heat and made the tea for him. Once it was ready she brought it to his side.

"Drink."

He took the offered mug and sipped the awful tea he had become so familiar with. As he drank, she brushed his hair back from his forehead. What had he ever done to deserve such a woman?

When the tea began to dull the pain, he relaxed again and finally fell asleep.

———

The next morning, as he neared the sawmill, he dreaded

what the day would hold. A nagging voice in the back of his mind told him he would not last at this job. Though his heart desired to do well and succeed, physically he could not handle it. His leg hurt him from the moment he woke this morning.

After half a day trying to keep up with the boards fresh from the saw, George Lount pulled him aside.

Thomas looked at the saw dust covered floor as George said, "I been watching you all morning and… It pains me to do this. I know you have a little one on the way. But I just don't think milling is the right work for you."

Thomas's head snapped up and he looked George in the eye. "Are you firing me?"

"Hate to do it, but yes."

Rage burned in his veins as he clenched his jaw shut, lest he say something foolish. Grabbing his cane, he left the mill behind.

How could this be happening to him? He trusted God to help him find something. What would he do now?

Making his way down the street, he stopped and leaned against a post on one of the buildings. The only thing he had ever been good at was riding. Well, that wasn't true. He had been really good at gambling too. Poker was his game of choice. He could read the other players as easily as could be. He just had a natural talent for it.

An idea started growing in his mind. Perhaps he could take some of the money he had left from his winnings in La Paz back in December, and he could use it at the poker tables.

No. He had changed. He wasn't that man any more. He wanted to do honest work.

Sighing, Thomas looked further down the street, the idea sliding to the back of his mind. He could not go home. Caroline would be upset, though she probably wouldn't even know he was there until the mercantile closed for the day. His feet led him in that direction anyway.

A sign in the window of the newspaper office caught his attention. "Help wanted," it said.

Maybe this would be a better job for him. He might even be

able to sit for part of the day.

The heavy smell of ink tickled his nose as he entered the building. The place seemed empty, but a small bell sat on the front counter near the door. Thomas rang the bell. A short man appeared from the back of the building behind a wall.

"Can I help you?" he said. He started to extend his ink covered hands and then thought better of it.

"I see you're looking for help."

"Ah, yes. Any experience with printing presses?"

Thomas shook his head.

"Clerical work?"

Again, he shook his head.

The man looked Thomas over from head to toe, his gaze snagging on the cane in his left hand. "Name's Hand. Tinsdale Hand. I'm willing to start you out on a trial basis if you're willing to learn."

Thomas introduced himself. "I am a fast learner. Just tell me where to start."

Hand explained that his duties would include clerical work at the front desk in addition to selling newspapers. He would help with the printing as well as cleaning up the shop. Hand led him to the back where the printing press was located. Trays of letters sat on a counter.

"Those are all set for this edition," Hand explained. "I'm in the middle of the printing process. I'll show you how to do it. Next edition, I'll show you how to set the letters. That will be one of the biggest parts of your job."

By the end of the afternoon, Thomas's discouragement faded. He thought he picked up the printing process quickly. Hopefully he would pick up the other duties just as quickly. Maybe he was better than gambling and riding.

A smile stretched across his lips as he climbed the stairs to his home. He could do this. He could provide for his wife and his coming child. He didn't have to rely on his past to make a new and better future.

CHAPTER 35

Prescott

May 23, 1866

"He lost his job at the sawmill," Caroline said.

Betty held back a sigh as her heart went out to both Thomas and Caroline.

"But he started at the newspaper this morning."

"That's good, dear," she said, reaching a hand across the table to reassure Caroline with a gentle pat.

"I just wish he would open up more."

She remembered wishing the same thing countless times in her marriage with Henry. Men were just different and most that she met tended not to open up their hearts even to those closest to them. Such news would not be welcomed, so Betty held her tongue.

"He seems so… So down. Like he's lost or something."

"Well, dear, he's had a lot to deal with. He was used to making his living riding for the express and for the Army before that. I'm sure it is difficult to find something else he is good at."

"I know. I think he's still in a lot of pain, too. He's woken up in the middle of the night several times due to cramping or pain in his leg. And he's exhausted when he comes home at night." Caroline picked at the remnants of her lunch. "I just want him to be happy. And I want him to stop dodging my questions about his past."

Though concerned, Betty smiled. She wanted to give Caroline hope in the midst of her newlywed jitters. "He has to find his own way, dear. It may take him awhile to figure it all out. And he's a husband, soon to be a father. That can add a lot of pressure for a man. Give him time."

Sighing heavily, Caroline pushed her plate away and stood. "I'd better head back to the mercantile before Abraham starts to wonder what's keeping me."

"Thank you for coming, dear. I loved having you."

Betty waved farewell to Caroline as she left. She couldn't shake a feeling of concern for the young couple. From their conversation, it didn't sound like Thomas had told his wife anything about his past. While it seemed to be breaking Caroline's heart, Betty thought it might break her heart even more to learn the truth.

Oh, she had seen a definite change in Thomas since he returned from his time at Quinn's ranch. But she worried that the change was tentative at best—especially if he continued to struggle with finding work. So far it looked like things were working out. Betty decided a prayer would be just the thing to help her stop worrying about the couple. *Lord, help that young man to trust you deeply. Help him to find his place.*

She smiled as she looked around the kitchen in the house. She had been quite content in the small room off of the dining hall kitchen, but Paul insisted she move into the house to the room he made especially for her. Her heart nearly burst with love for her son.

All his life, this was how he showed his love. He did things for her. He just happened to appear to carry a load of laundry into the house on a day when she was feeling tired from raising his three siblings alone. He stopped at the mercantile on his way home from picking up his sisters and brother from school because she had mentioned she was almost out of flour. It was those little things that warmed her heart and reminded her of the sensitive man he was underneath the very tough exterior he tried to portray in his late teens and early twenties.

She knew he had been hurting over Henry's death just like she was—like the other children were. But he tried to run from it. That was what got him into so much trouble.

Betty sighed heavily. He wasn't that man anymore. She should remember that when she worried that Thomas would not change. Paul had. It had been slow at first. Sometimes he did well, and sometimes he failed miserably. Thomas's new faith would likely work itself out in a similar way.

A knock at the doorway startled her.

"Ma'am. You want some of the beef in here too?" Snake asked.

"Sure," she said, trying to keep the hesitation from her voice. Ben normally brought her beef.

As if reading her mind, Snake said, "Ben said to tell ya he'd was busy with a bunch of errands in town today and he won't have time to stop by. He said he'd see ya Sunday if not before."

Warmth spread to her cheeks. "Thank you, dear."

"Ma'am." Snake nodded as he set a crate of beef on the table. Then he turned and left.

An edge of sadness wedged in her heart. She had been looking forward to seeing Benjamin today. It seemed they had much more time together with fewer distractions when he delivered beef than they had during Sunday dinner. Their little gathering had grown to include the Colters, the Larsons, the Pages, the Andersons, the Morgans—a family that farmed near Colter Ranch—and even a few of the younger cowboys from Colter ranch. What were their names again? Oh, yes. Jed, Hawk, and Matt. Sweet young lads. She suspected their frequent attendance had something to do with Caroline, though they continued to come to church after she married, so maybe that wasn't the case.

She loved the big meals. It was how she always pictured this stage of her life. Big family dinners. Grandchildren running around. She just wished Paul would settle down and start a family of his own so some of those grandchildren would truly be hers.

After putting away the beef, she left the quiet of her kitchen and headed toward the laundry line. She started pulling down the dry sheets and folded them neatly in a basket.

"Need some help?" Paul asked.

She smiled. "Thank you, son."

He followed her to Gold Rush carrying the basket for her.

"How was your time with Ben?"

"Oh, he wasn't here."

"Thought I saw some of the boys from the ranch."

"Yes. Snake was here. I didn't see who else came with him. I guess Ben was a little busy today." She couldn't keep the disappointment from her voice.

Paul set the basket on one of the lower bunks and handed her the first set of sheets. "I'm sure he must be if he'd forego an afternoon with you," he teased.

Betty shrugged.

"You gonna marry him, Ma?"

"Heavens! Where did that idea come from?"

"I think you two would be great together. He's patient—have to be to put up with you."

"Hey—"

"He's kind. He loves you very much."

Betty tucked the corners of the sheets under the mattress of the lower bunk. Picking up the next set, she moved to the next bunk.

"You don't love him?"

She stopped tucking in the sheet and turned toward her son. "I do love him."

"Then you'll marry him."

It wasn't a question. Her son seemed to understand her heart better than she did. Well, her heart was not what held her back. It was her head.

"What about you, Paul? Would you run the boardinghouse by yourself?"

"I have the Pengs."

"But you'll need more help than that."

"I'll get by. Always have."

She sighed. "If I didn't know better, I would think you *want* me to leave."

Paul hugged her and rested his head on the top of her head. "Never. But I think it's time you put yourself first. You been seeing to the needs of others for so long, you've forgotten that it's okay to do something for yourself. Marrying Ben—well you'd just have to care for him and enjoy life with him."

He stepped from the embrace. A roguish grin spread across his face. "And you'd be close to the Colters and their babies."

"Paul!" She swatted at his arm, but he moved away. "I see what you're saying."

"Just think about it, Ma. You deserve to be happy."

"He has to ask first."

The extra twinkle in Paul's eye made her suspicious. Something was going on and she thought her son might be in on it.

———

Just hope she's not too disappointed, Ben thought. If it wasn't for his little plan, he never would have given up his dinner with Betty. He missed her, despite seeing her every Sunday. It just wasn't the same as their quiet meals together when he was in town during the week.

He hoped to change that all very soon.

"Here's some fabric that should work very nicely for curtains," Caroline said.

Ben hesitated. Maybe he should let Betty pick it out. What if she didn't like it? "Do ya think Betty would like it?"

Caroline tapped one finger against her temple. "Yes. I think she would. Or this one." She held out another bolt of fabric.

A choice to make. Not what he was hoping for.

"Which one is better?"

Caroline pointed to the second one.

"Great. I'll take it. Can ya wrap it in some brown paper?"

An eyebrow inched its way higher on Caroline's forehead, but she nodded anyway.

Ben held back a chuckle. If he'd overheard the conversation he just had with Caroline, he'd be a bit confused too. He didn't want to give away anything about his plan for tomorrow. He wanted everything to be a surprise.

"You need some help loading that stove in the wagon?" Abraham asked.

"Already asked Paul."

Abraham smiled. "Good choice. Between the two of you, I'm sure you'll get it settled."

Ben paid for all his purchases, almost staggering at the hefty sum. Never in his whole life had he spent that much at the mercantile at one time.

Giddy anticipation sent little flutters to his stomach. Everything was going to be perfect. Betty would be duly surprised, and he was pretty sure she would love every little detail of his plan.

Grabbing the wrapped fabric, he headed to the back of the mercantile where Paul and Snake waited. The three of them, after much jockeying, finally got the heavy iron stove loaded in the wagon. Then Ben began stacking the rest of his purchases around it. Once everything was loaded, he climbed up into the wagon and started it towards home.

Peace settled over him. Home. Not just home to Colter Ranch. Not home to the bunkhouse. But home to his cabin. Even though it was on Colter land, it was his cabin. Every last piece of wood. Every last purchase. Every piece of furniture. It was all his.

Working for the Colters for more than twenty-five years, he saved a rather fair sum of money. Other than making sure he had a few outfits for his job and good shoes; he spent very little of what he earned. He stocked it away in a little box for some day. He stayed away from liquor after he became too dependent on it following Sheila's death. He stayed away from games of chance. Instead, he saved what he didn't need to use at the time. Oh, there were a few times he dipped into the box for something special— like a new saddle or even a new horse. But most of the money he made waited for this day.

He still didn't use it all. Had plenty left in case he needed it.

Once back at the ranch, Will and Snake helped him unload everything from the wagon and into the house.

"Nice place," Will said. "Must feel good to have your own space."

Ben grinned. "Only one finishing touch needed."

"Are you nervous?"

"Some. Bit strange after all this time living with a bunch of rough cowboys to think about settling down."

Will patted him on the shoulder. "Can't think of anyone who deserves it more."

Ben didn't know if he deserved it, but he sure did like it. He thanked Will and Snake as they left. Then he double checked everything before retiring to bed. Tomorrow was going to be one of the biggest days of his life.

———

"Benjamin!" Betty exclaimed when he poked his head into her kitchen. "In town two days in a row?"

"Missed ya so much yesterday. Couldn't bear another day without seeing yer pretty smile."

Heat warmed her face.

"Can I steal ya away fer the day?"

Some of her joy faded a bit. Paul was out at his claim, and she wasn't sure about leaving the Pengs to fend for themselves. "I, uh—"

"Sorry I'm late," Paul said, breathlessly as he bounded into the kitchen.

"Right on time," Ben replied.

Again, Betty felt like something was going on.

"Go on."

"But—"

"Remember what I said yesterday," Paul said, ushering her out the door on Ben's arm. "See you later. Much later."

"Oh, dear," she muttered, now flustered by her son's strange behavior.

"Come on," Ben said as he led her to the waiting wagon. He helped her up into the seat and started the wagon heading out of town towards Colter Ranch.

"What's going on, Benjamin?"

"Got a surprise fer ya."

"I'm already surprised."

He put his arm around her shoulders and squeezed. "Then get ready fer another one."

Silently, she tried to reason through what was going on for several minutes before giving up. He would tell her soon enough.

As they arrived at the top of the hill overlooking the valley where Colter Ranch sat, Ben stopped the wagon. "See that new cabin?"

She followed his extended hand to a spot on the northern edge of the lake.

"Oh. Did someone else move to the ranch?"

"Nope. I moved outta the bunkhouse."

"When?"

"Yesterday."

That must have been what kept him from visiting her.

"It looks like a lovely spot."

Ben straightened on the wagon seat and his face split into a big grin. "Wanna see it?"

"Of course."

He urged the horse forward into the valley. Within a few minutes, he stopped the wagon in front of the quaint little cabin.

Once her feet were on the ground, Betty turned in a circle. The original ranch house, now Adam and Julia Larson's home, sat on the southeastern edge of the lake. The new ranch house where Will and Hannah lived sat on the northeastern edge of the lake. Both places were near enough to walk to quickly from Ben's cabin, but far enough away to afford some privacy.

"Come on in," Ben said, holding the door for her.

"Benjamin! It's wonderful!" she exclaimed, taking in the homey feel of the place.

In one corner sat an iron stove—almost as big as the one in

her new kitchen at the boardinghouse. Near it was a lovely hand-carved and nicely finished table with four chairs. Along the opposite end of the cabin stood a bed, two dressers, a washstand, and a loom.

It was odd that Ben would have two dressers and a loom.

He took her hand in his and led her to the table. She noticed a wrapped item on the table. He motioned for her to sit. Then he handed her the package.

"For you."

She tugged on the string, eager to see what the odd shaped package held. A lovely yellow gingham patterned fabric! "It's beautiful. But what is it for?"

Ben kneeled before her. "I was hopin' ya could sew some new curtains for our home."

"I'd be happy to make you some curtains."

Then his words registered. "Our home?"

"Betty Lancaster, yer the best woman I ever met. Ya got a kind heart and a kind spirit. Ya make me smile just thinking about ya. I was hopin' that ya'd want to be my wife and share this little cabin I built fer ya."

Two dressers. A large stove. A loom. Materials for curtains. It was all starting to make sense. This wasn't Benjamin's home. This was to be their home. Together.

A hint of an objection leaped to the tip of her tongue. Then she remembered Paul's words yesterday. Her son was ready for her to leave. He was ready to take on the challenge of running the boardinghouse alone. He wanted this for her.

"Yes, Benjamin. I would love to be your wife."

Ben slowly stood, bracing one arm on the table. Then he drew her up from her seat and into his arms. His lips found hers and he kissed her with a hint of the passion he held back before. Her heart raced and she eagerly returned the kiss, so thankful that the Lord blessed her with another good man—one she hoped to share the next season of life with.

CHAPTER 36

Prescott

June 18, 1866

Thomas rolled out of bed to the smell of frying bacon, discouraged. He lost the job at the newspaper after a week. His hands were too clumsy to properly set the letters in the trays to produce the newspaper. Mr. Hand gave him a speech that was becoming all too familiar. He hated to let Thomas go, especially with a little one on the way, but perhaps Thomas would find something he was better suited for.

Only he hadn't, yet.

In a month's time he lost the job at the sawmill, newspaper, hotel, and blacksmith shop. It seemed he was good at nothing besides riding. And that was no longer an option.

Dejected, he slowly dressed as Caroline finished preparing breakfast.

"I heard that Barnett and Barth's store is looking for help," Caroline said as she set a plate of food before him.

He started eating. She cleared her throat. When he continued eating, she asked, "Are you going to say grace?"

Biting back a growl, he set his fork down. "Go ahead."

She hesitated for a few seconds before she said a quick prayer. As soon as she finished, Thomas resumed eating.

"So, what do you think?"

"About what?" he grumbled.

"Seeing about the job at Barnett and Barth's."

He clenched his jaw tightly and looked up at her. The intense look in her eyes bothered him, adding fuel to the building fire of his temper.

"I'm not working at a store."

"Why not?"

"Because I'm not."

Caroline parted her lips then snapped them shut.

Good. Maybe she would stop pestering him and let him figure it out on his own. There was no way he was going to work in a stupid store. He did too much of that growing up and hated it.

"I just think you'd be good at it."

Thomas erupted. "Enough! I am not working at Barnett and Barth's. I will find another job. Let it be!" The boiling of his anger overflowed. Shoving the plate from him, he stood. Grabbing his cane, he headed for the door.

"Where are you going?"

He whirled around and leaned over her. "To see what I can find to support you!"

He turned and walked out the door. Slamming it hard, he started down the stairs.

She just didn't understand. He was trying to find something. But with each failure, he felt worse about himself. He was good at nothing. His stupid crippled leg kept him from doing anything physically demanding. His clumsy fingers kept him from doing anything intricate, like typesetting at the newspaper. He was worthless. He should never have married Caroline. She would be so much better off without him.

You're still good at one thing. What? *Gambling.*

His heart picked up pace. He was good at gambling.

Don't do it.

But he had to. It was the only way he had left to provide for Caroline. And he couldn't get fired from it. He would do it just for a while until they had some money saved up for a few months. Then he could stop and get a real job. Surely God wouldn't stop him from doing what he had to do to take care of his family.

He walked to the town square and sat down on a bench where he had a view of Hardy's mercantile. He watched for Caroline to walk down the stairs and into the store. Then he waited for a few more minutes, just to be sure she didn't forget something at home. When she stayed in the store, he walked across the street and into their small room.

Standing in front of his dresser, he bent down to retrieve the small pouch of gold coins from the bottom drawer. He hid the money from Caroline, keeping it in case they were in desperate circumstances. It was the perfect amount to start at the poker tables. He stuffed it into his pocket.

Pushing more clothing aside, he found his revolver. Better to be prepared in case he played with some shady characters. Once his gun was loaded, he tucked it into his pants at the small his back.

He quietly walked back to the door, down the stairs, and onto the street. Scanning the saloons, he tried to decide which one to go to. A few men walked sluggishly from Montgomery's saloon. Thomas moved forward.

Peering inside, he saw a game of poker started in the back corner. He recognized one of the men at the table as Robert Garrett.

His hands shook with nervous anticipation. He needed to calm down, otherwise he would be an easy target for these men. Taking a seat at the bar, he ordered whiskey. Tossing his head back, he chugged the drink, bringing the glass down to the counter with a hard bang. He fidgeted with the glass for a few minutes until he started to relax. Then he ordered another drink.

After taking a few sips, he walked towards the poker table.

"Room for one more?"

Garrett looked up, a flicker of recognition in his eyes. He looked at Thomas from head to toe. "Might be too high stakes for you."

Thomas glanced at the stacks of chips on the table. He could handle it. Tossing his pouch of gold on the table in front of the dealer, he said, "Think that should cover it."

The dealer opened the pouch and counted out the gold coins. He nodded his head then shoved a stack of chips across the table to an open seat. Thomas sat.

When the round finished, Thomas was dealt in. The first few hands he purposely lost, carefully studying each man around the table. By his fourth hand, he had a relatively good idea of how each man played. He won that hand.

"Finally joined the game, eh?" Garrett commented.

Thomas let it go, draining his drink instead.

The next two rounds went to Garrett. Then it seemed the hands bounced back and forth between Thomas and Garrett. As his confidence grew, Thomas placed bolder bets.

On one rather risky hand, he bet over half of his entire pot, certain his hand was better than anyone else's. Garrett took only one card, increasing the size of his bet to a point that would force Thomas to risk almost everything. The other players folded. Thomas studied his opponent, then his cards, then his opponent. There was only one hand that would beat his. Pushing all but a dollar worth of chips to the center of the table, Thomas called Garrett's bet.

"Show your cards," Thomas said.

Garrett nervously played with the edge of one card. Slowly he laid his cards down, acting as if he feared the outcome. When the final card came into view, Thomas's stomach dropped to the floor. It was the one hand that would beat his. As his palms started to sweat, he revealed his losing hand.

Garrett laughed. "Better luck next time." As he gathered the large pot toward him, he tossed two dollars towards Thomas. "Have a few drinks on me. Maybe take a visit upstairs to work off your frustration."

Thomas clamped his jaw shut. Revealing nothing, he pocketed his last dollar and the two remaining charity ones from Garrett. Leaving a chuckling Garrett behind, he headed back to the bar.

Slamming a dollar down on the table, he groused at the bartender. "Keep 'em coming until this is gone."

———

Caroline hurried up the stairs, hoping Thomas hadn't been waiting for her for too long. Abraham had been tied up unloading supplies from a delivery when several customers arrived just a few minutes before closing. One woman seemed intent on taking her time looking over practically every bolt of fabric before making her selection. It was almost an hour after normal closing time before everyone left.

She tentatively opened the door. The room was empty. Maybe he found work.

Looking over the pantry, she tried to figure out what to make for supper. She decided she would make a stew using just one potato and some dried beef. It would be thin but sufficient. She still had to wait a few more days before she was paid next and they were dangerously low on food supplies.

Please let Thomas have found a job today.

Half an hour later, supper was ready. Still Thomas had not returned. Caroline moved the stew to the back of the stove to keep it warm.

Another hour passed. She started to worry as her stomach growled. They hadn't parted company in good circumstances this morning. She hadn't feared that he wouldn't return. He just didn't seem like that sort of man.

What did she know? She barely knew him—even after a month of marriage. He had been moody and quiet most of the time, except for the first few days at any new job. Those were the days she liked the most. He seemed excited about the new job and his confidence returned. Only each time it was cut short. After a matter of days, he lost his job.

Those were the days she liked the least. She could tell his anger boiled below the surface, mixed with self-doubt and fear.

She prayed for him—more than she prayed for anyone ever before. He stopped going to church. He distanced himself. The more time passed without a job, the more morose he got.

Nothing seemed to be getting better.

When her stomach growled again, she looked at the clock. Eight. Standing, she moved to the stove and dished herself a meager bowl. Then she sat at the table.

Lord, keep my husband safe. Bring him home soon. Thank you for this food. Amen.

As she sipped her soup, she tried to figure out where he would be. Maybe he was helping Paul fix up something at the boardinghouse and he lost track of time. No. Betty would have sent him home by now.

What if he was hurt somewhere? Maybe she would stop by Doc Armstrong's and ask if he had seen Thomas.

That probably would not be good. What if Thomas didn't want to come home? Would he get angry if he felt like she was checking up on him?

She finished her meal and washed the dishes. Then she sat in her rocking chair. She picked up a book and tried to read. Only she couldn't. She kept glancing at the clock. Nine. Half past nine.

Finally, at ten, with no sign of her husband, she could stand it no more. She set her book aside and left her small room. Once at the bottom of the stairs, she realized she had no idea where to look for him.

Caroline headed across the street toward Lancaster's. Knocking on the front door, she bit her lip and tried to remain calm. No one came, so she knocked again.

"Dear," Betty said as she opened the door. "What's wrong?"

Paul appeared behind Betty.

"Thomas… He hasn't come home. We fought this morning. He lost his job at the blacksmith, and I suggested he go to Barnett and Barth. He got angry and stormed out. I haven't seen him since."

"Oh, dear!"

Paul scowled and crossed his arms. Odd reaction, Caroline

thought.

"Do you know where he might be?"

"I haven't seen him, dear."

Paul stepped forward. "I'll find him. Go home and wait for us there."

Caroline started to ask Paul if he had an idea where Thomas was, but the shadow on his face stopped her.

"I'll see you home first," he said, offering her his arm.

She walked in silence next to the large broad-shouldered man. He seemed irritated. At the bottom of the stairs going up to her room, he promised her he would return as soon as he could with Thomas.

———

Thomas lost track of time and the number of drinks he consumed and how much money he'd won and then lost. His stomach growled. He looked at the few gold coins he had left. Enough for some food, a few more drinks, and maybe something to start him out at the poker tables again.

He nodded to the bartender and ordered some food and another drink. While he waited for the food to arrive, he sipped the whiskey, appreciating that it added to the heady feeling that had started to slip away. As long as he sat here like this, he didn't have to think about what a miserable failure he was.

The taunting voices mocked him in his head. *Failure. Robber. Gambler. Drunk. Murderer.* Over and over again.

Then his mind remembered a time of freedom. Where had that been? Oh, yes. At Perry's ranch, when Drew visited him. No, that had been a dream. For a time, he felt free—absolved from the things the voices accused him of now.

A scantily clad saloon girl set a plate of food in front of him. Then she slid a hand up his arm and looped it over his shoulders, leaning into his side. "When yer belly's full, I can see to yer other hungers."

Guilt smacked Thomas between the eyes, sobering him.

Caroline waited for him at home. If he could do nothing else right in his life, perhaps he could at least be faithful to his wife.

He nudged the saloon girl away, focusing his attention on his food. He was hungrier than he thought and finished the meal quickly.

He should go home. Only he couldn't bring himself to face the disappointment in those green eyes. When Caroline learned of his deceit and his losses, she would be upset. He grunted and lifted his empty glass, catching the bartender's eye. A full glass of whiskey appeared.

Thomas drank it and requested another.

He couldn't go home. Not yet. He could not face her.

Propping his elbows on the edge of the bar, he rested his head in his hands and closed his eyes. If only he could find an honest job that he both liked and could do well. That would solve all his problems. He wouldn't have to come here to gamble. The lure of this place had been too much today. And he paid dearly for it. At one point, he had been up three hundred dollars. That was one of the largest amounts he had ever won in one day. Then he lost it all. To Garrett. It seemed like that man was trying to leave him penniless.

At one point, he almost put his pistol up as collateral. That would have been foolish. The weapon was for protection, not something he could gamble away. Who knows, he might even need it on his way home tonight if he ran into any trouble.

"Your wife is worried sick." Paul's deep voice rang in Thomas's ears.

He looked up to his friend.

"Time to go."

"I can't."

"Why not?"

"I just can't face her."

Paul placed a hand under his arm and hefted him to his feet. "Time to go anyway."

Thomas stumbled, then let his weight rest heavily against Paul's side. "I lost it all."

The cool night air hit his face. The streets were empty. How late was it?

"What did you lose?"

"All the money I had. I lost it all. I have nothing left."

Paul said nothing.

As they neared Hardy's mercantile, Paul stopped and let Thomas slide to a bench in the town square. Then he stood in front of him, crossing his arms.

"Almost two hours ago your frantic wife knocked on my door asking if I had seen you. It's taken me that long to figure out where you were. I didn't want to believe I would find you in the saloon. What are you doing?"

He swallowed the lump rising in his throat. What *was* he doing? Acting like a fool was what. Throwing away what little money he had. Worrying his wife. Even if he was a huge disappointment to her, he still loved her.

None of the words would form into sentences.

"I know it's hard—what you're going through. You made your living riding for so long. Ain't got no idea what else to do. But going back to your old ways—those ways that God forgave you for—that isn't going to make a single thing in your life better. It will only destroy you and ruin your marriage."

Thomas nodded.

"Decide Thomas. Who will you serve? God or gambling?"

———

Caroline gasped as Paul helped Thomas to bed. The smell of alcohol permeated the room, making it feel confined. After Paul left, she opened the door open and opened all the windows.

Thomas groaned. Then soft snores serenaded her as she struggled to remove his boots.

She yawned and looked at the clock. It was after one in the morning. She quickly undressed and slid into bed beside her sleeping husband.

She closed her eyes, only sleep would not come. Paul's words turned over in her mind. *He gambled away everything. Remember how much you have been forgiven. Forgive him just as much.*

He gambled everything. Caroline didn't even know how much that was. Apparently, he had been hiding money from her. Well, now there was nothing left to hide. They had nothing, save for the few coins she had left from her last pay. Not enough to restock the pantry. She would have to stretch it as long as she could.

A tear slid down the side of her face splashing onto her pillow. Regret mixed with guilt. She should never have let him into her bed. If she hadn't, she would not have had to marry a complete stranger—one prone to drinking and gambling.

What other secrets did he hold?

She turned her head and sobbed into her pillow. She was certain she did not really want to know.

CHAPTER 37

Prescott

July 4, 1866

Caroline put the finishing touches on the spicy venison and beef stew. She glanced over at Thomas as he leaned heavily on his cane, a dark scowl on his face. She looked back to the stew then down at her rather large belly. Maybe she should have made something easier for him to carry to the community celebration and potluck.

"I'll grab one handle and you the other?" she suggested.

Thomas grunted but moved toward the stove and did exactly that.

The awkward trip down the stairs took much longer than she expected. Setting the pot on the last stair, she flexed her fingers before picking it up again. Paul Lancaster hurried toward them and took the pot before either could object. She thanked him.

She looped her hand in the crook of Thomas's arm. "Nice weather for the celebration."

When he didn't say anything, she glanced at him. The earlier scowl remained firmly in place.

She sighed. The past few weeks both remained tense. He hardly said a word to her. She never brought up his gambling and drinking binge. Neither did he bring it up, nor did he repeat it.

Nor did he manage to keep a job. She had lost track now of how many he had quit or been fired from.

"Caroline, dear, come help me with the pies?" Betty asked as they were nearing the back of the dining hall.

She followed Betty inside.

"How are you doing, dear?"

"Fine."

"You look a little sad."

"Hmm?" Caroline pretended not to hear Betty's comment.

Taking a pie in each hand, she waddled to the table outside and set the tasty creations down. Several more trips and the ladies had all the pies set out.

"Caroline!" Julia's voice drew her attention. She hurried to her side. Despite being as round in her seventh month as Caroline was, Julia seemed much lighter on her feet. They hugged each other for several minutes. Caroline needed the closeness of her friend to help soothe her aching heart.

"Linny," Adam greeted her, leaning down to give her a hug. "Thomas."

Thomas nodded his head and extended his hand. The scowl on his face diminished some, though it was not replaced with a smile as she hoped.

"Heard there's a horse race," Thomas commented dryly. "You riding?"

"Naw. Covington represents the Larson Stables. Hawk is riding for Colter Ranch."

"Larson Stables?" Caroline asked.

Adam beamed. "Yep. Will said the place needed a good name. He's still a partner, but he said he didn't feel the need to have his name stuck on everything. Colter Ranch and Colter Meat Company seemed good enough to him."

"Congratulations!" She gave her brother another big hug.

"Have you thought of any baby names yet?" Julia asked as Adam led them to a shady spot in the square. He spread out a blanket and helped Julia take a seat. Thomas helped Caroline before he slowly and clumsily sat next to her.

"If it's a boy, I was thinking of George," Caroline teased.

"As if our family doesn't have enough Georges already," Adam said.

"It will be Andrew if it's a boy," Thomas growled.

Caroline frowned. He ignored her every time she brought up naming their child. Now all the sudden he had a name picked out.

"I suppose you have a girl's name picked out, too. Something you haven't bothered to share with me."

"Don't start."

The tension mounted as Caroline tried to bite her tongue. She failed.

"For weeks I've been asking you if you had a preference for names. And now you've just decided. When were you going to tell me?"

"Before the baby was born. Maybe when it was born!"

Caroline glared at her husband as he glowered back. As their stare down continued, Julia broke the tension.

"Adam and I were seriously thinking of George for our son, but only as a middle name. Maybe Edward George. Though, we're not sold on the name yet."

"Yeah," Adam added. "The sentiment is there, but the name just seems awkward to me."

"But we'd like Catherine for a girl's name."

The significance of the name was not lost on Caroline. She turned attention away from her angry husband to her friend. "After your mother."

"Yes. Even though I barely knew her, I thought it would be nice to honor her—that is if Will doesn't steal the name first."

"Is that a possibility?"

"I'm not certain. He mentioned the name once, but Hannah hasn't said anything about it."

Caroline nodded. "Are they coming today? Isn't she due very soon?"

"She seemed a bit tired this morning, but they were planning on being here soon."

Thomas stood without a word. He shot Caroline a nasty look before heading off in the direction of a game of horseshoes nearby.

"What's gotten into him?" Julia asked.

Caroline sighed.

"Has he found any steady work yet?" Adam asked.

"No."

"Is he any good with horses?"

"He can't ride, remember." Caroline didn't even try to keep the edge from her voice.

"Linny, I was just thinking. Maybe the two of you should move out to the ranch. You could stay with Julia and me. Thomas could work in the stables, mucking stalls, caring for the horses. I mean, he knows his way around them. Maybe he could help repair bridles and saddles and such. Seems to me he'd be good at those things."

She shot back, "Then why don't you ask him?"

"Hey!" Adam put his hands in the air. "Just trying to help out."

She sighed. "I know. It's just... As it gets closer and closer to the baby coming, I'm really worried he's not going to be able to provide for us. We can't live above the mercantile after the baby comes. I won't have a job anymore. And he hasn't been able to hold a steady job, much less come up with a place for us to live."

"All the more reason to consider my offer."

"He won't. It would be too much like charity."

Adam stood and brushed his trousers. "Think I'll ask anyway."

"He means well," Julia said.

"I know."

———

Thomas bit back a curse, insulted that Adam even made the offer. He obviously didn't trust him to provide for his sister. "No thank you. I'm sure I'll find something soon."

"Well, offer still stands."

He started to reply when someone shouted that the horse race was about to start. He should be in that race. If he was, he would win it—especially if he had the chestnut mare—only she died on that mountain side in December, and he was no longer able to ride. It chaffed on his nerves.

The most beautiful horses from the area and the valley below lined up along Montezuma Street. He spotted Covington on a pinto. Hawk's mount was a sleek looking black gelding. Thomas also recognized one of Perry Quinn's men on a palomino mare. Then he spotted the express rider. That should be him.

A gun sounded and the horses lurched forward. The express rider moved to the front, followed by Hawk and Covington. A good distance separated the express rider from the rest of the crowd. As the horses turned a corner from their view, the thundering of their hooves echoed across the town square.

As they moved back into view, coming up Cortez Street, Covington was now in the lead. The head of Hawk's horse inched forward near the flank of Covington's mount. Slowly Hawk gained on Covington as the last few feet of the race came near. Covington leaned forward into his horse's neck and the horse spurted forward, leaving him the clear winner as he crossed the finish line.

A cheer came from the crowd. Hawk crossed the line closely followed by the express rider. Quinn's man was dead last.

Soon, a swarm of cowboys from Colter Ranch, including Will Colter, surrounded Covington and Hawk. Adam left Thomas's side to join them. Thomas moved away from the crowd, still stewing over how incredibly unfair it was that he could no longer ride.

Fingering the change in his pocket, he looked towards the row of saloons. Then he glanced back at his wife. She was engrossed in conversation with Julia. Quickly he darted across the street and into one of the saloons. Maybe a few drinks would improve his mood.

———

Reverend Page was invited to the platform to offer a blessing for the meal. Once he finished, Caroline searched the crowd for Thomas. She didn't see him anywhere.

"Come on," Julia said. "He can eat whenever he's ready."

She hesitated, allowing Adam and Julia to make it to the line. She looked around one more time and made her way there.

"A man like him doesn't change," a man's voice sounded behind her.

She turned and held back a gasp, coming face to face with Robert Garrett.

"Once a drunk, always a drunk. Once a gambler, always a gambler."

How did he know?

Garrett smiled, though the darkness in his eyes froze any warmth. "Had the pleasure of winning hundreds of dollars from your husband. Thank him for me when you see him next."

Now she didn't want to be near this man.

The line surged, pushing Garrett forward into her. A sneer spread across his face.

"I wonder, Mrs. Anderson, just how well you know your hus-band."

"Well enough," she shot back as she dished food onto her plate.

"Shall we put your knowledge to the test then?" he challenged.

She didn't respond.

"What do you know of his various occupations in Cincinnati?"

Caroline took another step forward. Perhaps if she ignored him, he would drop the conversation.

"Thief. Scoundrel. Womanizer. Drunk. Gambler. Has he ever told you he spent time in jail for robbing a bank?"

The air rushed from Caroline's lungs. Thief? Bank robber? Surely not.

"Ah, I see you don't believe me. Perhaps Mrs. Colter can enlighten you. I'm sure she knows firsthand what her brother-in-law was involved in."

Robbery. Again, Garrett reminded her far too much of the stagecoach robber. "I'm sure you know a great deal about robbery yourself, Mr. Garrett. Ever rob a stage by chance?"

The color rushed to Garrett's cheeks. "Don't be coy with me. I'm sure you've heard by now that one of the robbers confessed and he turned in the other. Ah, there's my associate. If you'll excuse me. Have a pleasant day." He turned and started to leave. "Oh, Mrs. Anderson, if you're looking for your husband, you might try the saloon."

The heat rushed to Caroline's cheeks as Garrett stepped from the line. The others nearby started whispering. Obviously, they overheard Mr. Garrett's last remark.

———

Robert Garrett chuckled as he approached his associate. As fortune would have it, his associate found a man that strongly resembled the new Robert Garrett. It was easy to convince Bart to turn himself and the look-a-like in—especially with the promise of rescue. Too bad that rescue would accidentally end Bart's life.

No matter. He had served his purpose. The scapegoat would hang based on Bart's testimony. And no one would be able to trace any of this back to him.

"Is it done?" he asked his associate.

"Yes."

"Good. When can you start the next phase of the plan?"

"Already getting familiar with Colter's patterns. We'll set the whole thing into motion after his men come back from the cattle drive in September."

Garrett smiled. "You're not concerned that there will be too many men there?"

"No."

"Excellent. I'll see that the payment is delivered per your instructions."

"I'll be in touch."

Garrett put on his poker face, though he beamed inwardly. Things were going very smoothly with Owens. No one had been able to prove a connection between him and the missing Colter cattle. He was still supplying reliable information. He wondered if perhaps Owens had done something similar before. He thought he recognized his name as someone he heard of in Texas, but he couldn't remember with certainty.

Choosing him had been a good decision. Little by little he helped eat away at Colter's wealth.

Time was his best ally, and the longer Colter suffered, the better. Soon enough, Colter would regret the day he left Texas and made an enemy of Robert Garrett.

CHAPTER 38

Thomas entered the saloon and headed straight for the bar, his anger still burning. He should have been in that race. He should have won it. Instead, he was a crippled spectator on the sidelines. He hadn't ridden a horse since the night of his injury, and he likely never would again.

God, I thought you took care of those who came to you. Why won't you take care of me?

Not waiting for an answer, he ordered some whiskey and sipped it slowly.

Why was it some people's lives just turned out perfectly and with such little effort? Adam's announcement about Larson Stables—now there was a man who had everything, and it seemed good things just happened to him. Stable, loving family. Good home. Gorgeous and talented wife. Baby on the way. Then he gets his own business handed to him.

Thomas snorted and polished off his whiskey. He nodded to the bartender for more.

Why couldn't his life turn out more like Adam's? He had a terrible life growing up. Suffered tremendous losses. Got in with the wrong crowd and ended up in jail. He lost the last of his family—he was the only Anderson left. The job he loved, he lost. He got a beautiful woman pregnant and now he was saddled with a wife and soon to be with a child.

He kicked himself for that last thought. Caroline, no matter how she entered his life or what led her to become his wife, she was the best thing in his life. She was a good wife when she didn't nag him or tell him how he should go about finding a job.

And she was beautiful, too.

Taking another sip of his drink, he dreamed of what their life together could be like if he could just find that place where he fit in. He would work hard and give her a home. She would make him hearty meals every day. They would have more children and raise a family—one so different from what he grew up with. All of it in this nice town.

"I hoped I had seen wrong," Perry Quinn's voice stirred him from the pleasant images in his mind.

"Perry."

"What are you doing in here, Thomas? Was that change in you while you were on my ranch all just a game?"

The knife of conviction pierced his heart deeply.

"It was one of the most real things in my life."

"Then why are you sitting in here drinking it away, while your wife worries about you out there?"

Caroline was worried?

"I should have been in that race." He raised his glass to his lips and Perry swiped it from him before he could sip. "Give that back."

"No. Self-pity and living in the past are only going to drive you deeper into the bottle. You need to stop. You need to take a good look at your heart with a clear mind, not one clouded in the haze of alcohol."

Thomas reached for the glass again. Perry held it away from him and turned it over, spilling the contents onto the floor of the saloon.

"Hey!"

"Why are you wasting the new life God gave you?"

"I'm not! I've been trying to get a job but everything I try fails. Seems God could expend a little energy to help me out here."

"Hasn't he provided you with each of those jobs?"

Thomas's objection died on his lips. He hadn't really thought about it that way before.

"So many new believers think that once they start trusting God that everything will be perfect. They won't experience pain or loss. They won't struggle with keeping a job. They won't argue with their wives. Whatever it may be, we have somehow decided how *we* think God should act. How *we* think he should show his love to us.

"But it doesn't work that way. Bad things still happen. I still lost my wife. I still had to struggle to get through day after day without her—the ache so deep, so painful, I thought I would die before it ever dimmed.

"You know what I learned through that experience?"

Thomas shook his head.

"God was still right there with me. He never left me. He was there to help me with that pain. He could have brought my wife back, but he didn't. He could have eased the pain quicker, but he didn't. Instead, he stood by my side, working on my heart. I learned to trust him so much more in that time of my life than I had in the easy times."

Perry paused, sighing heavily. "You see, he hasn't left you. He's given you each of those jobs to do the best you could. Trust him to give you the next, and the next, and the next if that is what it takes. He's let you experience the love of a wonderful woman. He's poised ready to shower the next blessing—if you'll do your part. Trust."

Thomas looked down at the bar top. What was he doing here?

He knew. He was doing what he always did. He was trying to solve his problems with his same old bad habits—drinking, gambling. It wasn't working.

Oh, what a fool he was! The change in his heart on that day in Perry's cabin—it was real. He had been set free!

Then he forgot it all. He started looking at all the ways his life wasn't what he had wanted it to be. He forgot he was free.

As Thomas sat up straighter, Perry slapped his shoulder. "Go.

Go find your wife and enjoy the afternoon with her. Then, let tomorrow's problems be handled tomorrow."

He stood and thanked Perry, then left the saloon. He spotted his wife under the same tree as before, this time with a plate of food balanced on the round bump of her belly where his child grew.

Lord, I'm so sorry I keep messing things up. Help me to care for them—my wife, my child—in the way that I should. And help me to trust you for a job.

He made his way to the food tables and dished up a plate of food. Then he found his wife.

———

"Save me a seat?" Thomas asked.

Caroline shaded her eyes as she looked up. A smile lit his face. She patted the spot next to her, confused by his strange change in mood.

Once seated, he leaned toward her and kissed her on the cheek. The smell of alcohol on his breath wiped the smile from her face. That must be it then. He had been at the saloon, just as Garrett said.

"Mmm. The venison and beef stew you made is good."

She nodded her head.

Having finished their meals, Adam and Julia excused themselves from going to watch the miners compete in a rock picking challenge.

If Garrett had been right about where Thomas was most recently, could he also be right about Thomas robbing a bank?

She nervously tapped her finger against her temple as her husband devoured the food on his plate. Should she ask him?

"What's bothering you?"

"What makes you think I'm bothered?" she replied.

"That thing you do with your finger. Usually means something is up."

Her heart softened some towards him. He knew her well

enough to know her nervous habit.

She sighed. "It's just... Someone told me something about you that I... I don't want to believe, but I want to know if it's true."

"What?" He set his empty plate aside.

"Did you spend time in jail?"

The happiness flew from his demeanor. An edge of wariness tinged his voice. "Did Hannah say something?"

"No. Robert Garrett."

The scowl returned. "What were you doing speaking to Robert Garrett?"

"I wasn't speaking to him. He was behind me in line, and he started the conversation. It was very one-sided."

"What exactly did he say?"

Caroline looked away. Maybe she shouldn't tell him. What if he got more upset?

He reached for her hand and ran his thumb across her knuckles. His voice was soft when he spoke. "Tell me what he said."

"He said you robbed a bank. That you spent time in jail. That you're a drunk and a gambler." Her voice caught. She didn't want to believe she married such a complete stranger.

Thomas withdrew his hand. He sat straighter, drawing her gaze to him. He looked away.

"I... When I lived in Cincinnati, I was rebellious, young, and wild. I hung out with some bad men, and I began to act just like them. It was the only place that I felt like I fit in."

He turned to look her in the eye. "I did try to rob a bank." He snorted. "A man was injured, and it was my brother who saved his life. I drank a lot back then. I gambled and very often won. I did spend time in jail, for the bank robbery.

"But by an odd coincidence—or maybe it was God—my sentence was to serve in the army. So I served. I was in the infantry at first. Later, I became a dispatch rider. That's how I ended up here. I was assigned to ride mail between some of the western forts.

"Once the war was over, I was free. I thought my brother settled in La Paz, so I looked for work that would let me search for him. I got a job as an express rider. Then I found out he died and that Hannah lived here."

Thomas dropped his gaze to his misshapen leg.

Caroline's heart moved from anger and betrayal to sympathy. No matter what his secrets were, he was still her husband. She heard the excitement and joy in his voice as he talked about dispatch riding and the express job. He was made to work with horses.

"It's hard—not riding anymore—isn't it?"

Thomas closed his eyes. "I doubt if I will ever find anything so completely suited to me again."

She had to know one more thing. "Did you gamble away hundreds of dollars recently?"

Thomas's eyes flew open. "Something else Garrett said?"

She nodded.

"Yes. I'm sorry, Caroline. I know I have failed you so many times. I've failed myself. It wasn't until even a few minutes ago that I realized I'd gone astray again. I stopped trusting God. I let Him down and I've let you down."

She reached for his hand and held it.

"I don't know what the future holds, but I want to promise you one thing. I am done with the bottle. I'm done with the gambling. The old way doesn't work, and I am not going to do it anymore."

Tears brimmed in his eyes. Caroline's followed suit. She leaned towards him and gave him a kiss on the lips.

Though her heart warned her to be cautious, she ignored it. "I trust you, Thomas, to do what you promise."

She rested her head against his chest. His arms came around her and he held her tight. His voice was thick with emotion when he spoke.

"I want to be a good husband and a good father. I want our child to grow up in a home like you grew up in—not like mine."

"They will."

She just hoped they really would and that someday her heart would believe it too.

CHAPTER 39

Prescott

August 15, 1866

Another long day. But he was almost home. Thomas most loved this last leg of the trip from Mohave to Prescott—because it meant Caroline would be waiting for him.

For the past three weeks, he managed to keep this job. He thought it was odd when Mr. Hardy hired him to drive a freight wagon from Prescott to Mohave and back again. He only wanted Thomas to drive. He had men at both ends to do all the loading and unloading. After an hour resting in Mohave, he headed back to Prescott with a full wagon.

He did not really like the job, but it was one he felt he could do for some time. Though the jostling and jarring of the wagon tested his physical stamina, on this fourth trip his leg hadn't pained him nearly as much as the first. He was getting used to the work.

The town of Prescott appeared before him, the late afternoon sun casting long shadows. In less than an hour he would be seated at the supper table across from Caroline.

He wondered how she was doing. She seemed very tired when he left to head west. She still planned on working at Hardy's mercantile, until he was able to find them a new home. He needed to make that his main priority while he was home for the next few days.

Pulling the wagon to a stop in front of the storage building next to the livery, Thomas set the brake. A group of brawny men started unloading the wagon. He walked around, loosening up his stiff leg, until the men finished. Then he pulled the wagon around behind the livery. He made quick work of unhitching the horses and leading them inside the livery.

"Thomas!" Craig Roundtree greeted him. "I was just asking Mrs. Anderson this morning when she thought you might be home."

"Oh?"

"Will you be around the next few days? I have something I'd like to discuss with you."

"Have supper with us tomorrow evening then."

"Well, I'd like to speak with you alone, first. Don't want to get Mrs. Anderson's hopes up in case you say no."

Thomas was intrigued by the strange conversation. "Then, shall I stop by in the morning?"

"That will be just fine. Go on now. I'll see to the horses."

He thanked Craig and rushed across the street to Hardy's mercantile. Caroline lumbered slowly from the building as he neared. It seemed like she grew bigger every day.

"You're home!"

He placed a soft kiss on her cheek and helped her up the stairs. What an odd sight they must be. Him with his cane taking the stairs slowly, helping his very pregnant wife. He really needed to get a new home—ground level—for them soon. She shouldn't have to manage this in her condition.

Once inside, Caroline sank onto the nearest chair. "Give me a few minutes and I'll start your supper."

An idea sparked. "Let's have supper at Lancaster's."

Round green eyes lit with hope. "Can we afford it?"

Thomas chuckled. "We can this once—if you can get Paul to accept the money."

"Let's go then." She rose to her feet, and he led her back down the stairs and across the street to the boardinghouse.

Having been warned the last time they tried to dine in the dining hall; Thomas led the way to the house. Paul insisted they eat there, with him and a smaller group.

A frazzled Paul greeted them at the door. "Come on in."

"Still haven't hired any help?" Caroline asked as she took a seat at the table.

"No. Mrs. Osborn sends some prepared meals over once a week from her restaurant. It helps, but ever since Ma married Ben and moved out to the ranch, I've been struggling to keep things running as smoothly as she did."

Thomas sat next to Caroline as Paul took a seat at the head of the table.

"The other boarders already ate, so it's just us. I apologize if anything is cold."

"Just not having to cook it is treat enough," Caroline said.

After Paul led them in grace, Thomas shared the news about Craig's strange conversation. "No idea what he wants to see me about."

"Guess you'll just have to find out tomorrow."

———

The next morning, Thomas smiled as he headed across the street to the livery. Craig greeted him and led him into his office.

"Leland Frye and I are looking at pulling up stakes here. Planning on heading out to Verde Valley to take up farming again. Heard its good land and several other folks are looking at growing grain which we'll ship back here."

"Oh. What are you going to do with the livery then?" Thomas asked.

"Well, that's what I wanted to talk to you about. I thought you might be a good man to take over the place."

Thomas blinked in shock. "I can't afford to buy you out."

"I know. That's why I'm proposing you manage the place for me. I'll pay you a salary. You run the place like it is your own. Then, when I come back next spring, we'll talk about how you can buy me out. By then, you should know if it's what you want or not."

"Why me?"

Craig laughed. "Who else would be so perfect to run the place? You're great with horses. I seen the work you did repairing Hardy's harnesses. Quality work. That's what it takes to run a livery."

Thomas didn't move for a minute. He could hardly believe what Craig said. It made perfect sense. He was good with the horses. He already knew how to repair harnesses, saddles, bridles, and more. Those were some of the best skills he picked up in the Army. A dispatcher had to be as self-sufficient as possible.

"I'll take it. Thank you, Craig."

"Don't thank me. Thank the Good Lord. He's the one that brought your name to my mind."

As Thomas shook his hand, he did just that.

"Oh, and there's one more thing. I got a cabin out back. It ain't much. But seeing as you and the missus are needing a home, too, I thought you could take it."

It was all too much. Everything he had been praying for since the Fourth of July. And it was all being answered now, before the baby was born.

"If you want to move in right away, I'd be happy to take a bunk at Lancaster's until I leave."

"Ah… um… That would be just fine."

Thomas thanked Craig at least two more times before he rushed back across the street to Hardy's mercantile. He was out of breath by the time he stood in front of Caroline.

"Craig has offered me the livery and his cabin."

Caroline squealed in delight and threw her arms around him. "See. He does answer our prayers."

"I'm sorry I ever doubted."

Epilogue

Prescott

September 21, 1866

"Thomas!" Caroline shot upright in bed. Air refused to fill her lungs as a sharp contraction hit. "Baby… coming…"

She grabbed his arm as another contraction shot through her body. Her grip brought him fully awake.

"Baby?"

She nodded her head up and down, not that he would be able to see it. The room was pitch black. Then the flicker of a match preceded the soft glow of a lantern.

"Should I go fetch Betty? Doc Armstrong?"

She nodded again. As he reached for the door latch, she moaned with another birthing pain. He started to turn back to her.

"Go."

As he pulled the door shut, she relaxed back into the soft warmth of her bed.

She was so grateful Betty would be here to help. Last week, after Sunday services, Betty and Ben decided to stay at Lancaster's until her baby came. Betty insisted that no first-time mother should be without the support of an older woman.

When Caroline mentioned that Julia would need someone, Betty reminded her that Hannah was there. She told Caroline she could not imagine missing the birth of the Anderson's first baby.

The more she thought about it, she began to understand. After all, Betty had traveled west with Thomas's older brother. Then she seemed to adopt Thomas when he showed up in town. In some ways, this baby would be like another grandchild to Betty.

Another pain hit. When it passed, she panted to catch her breath.

She was glad Ben came to town, too. He already offered to take care of the livery while Thomas spent the first week with Caroline. Thomas didn't think he would need any time away, but Betty firmly told him he would.

A smile played at the corner of her lips. So many things had changed with Thomas since he started managing the livery. His confidence returned. He took to the new role very quickly—almost as if this job was created just for him. He hired a young lad to help muck the stables and with some of the chores that were more difficult with his bad leg.

At first some of the livery's regular customers were leery in dealing with Thomas. Soon, his charming personality won them over. He managed every aspect of the business well. He even began saving away some money, he told her, so he could purchase the livery when Craig returned in the spring.

The sharp pain of another contraction sidetracked her train of thought for a few minutes.

As it eased up, she thought about how much her life changed in the last year and a half. She was so naïve when she left Texas, thinking she was about to embark on a great adventure. Even her plan of being reunited with Adam and Julia hadn't worked out exactly as expected. More than adventure, she experienced so much grace. God had forgiven her foolishness. He protected her in the wake of the stage robbery. He introduced her to Thomas. She made many mistakes with him, but she had been forgiven of those, too. Now she was beginning to see what a good man her husband was, and she thanked God for that blessing.

"Dear!" Betty's voice grew louder as the door opened. "Thomas said it's time."

Another contraction hit. In a breathless whisper, she replied, "Yes."

———

Thomas's heart raced out of control. Caroline had not looked well when he left her. He wished he could run, instead of the fast shuffle-walk his leg required. Betty should be at her side by now, so at least she wouldn't be alone.

He pounded on the door to Doc Armstrong's clinic. A groggy Hank Armstrong answered the door. Thomas's voice failed him.

"Is it Mrs. Anderson's time?"

"Yes."

Doc Armstrong ducked back inside and quickly reappeared with a bag. It was then that Thomas thought he should have fetched the doctor first, with his office being only a few doors down from the livery.

Caroline's piercing scream sent waves of fear over him as he entered their cabin behind the livery.

Doc Armstrong slapped him on his back. "Don't worry. This is normal."

This was *normal*? Thomas prayed that God would help Caroline through this. Then he asked the same for himself.

Several hours later, the baby still had not come. Thomas squinted at the bright sun as he stepped out for some fresh air. Somehow, he missed the sun rising. He paced back and forth in the dirt space between the cabin and the livery. Perhaps he should just go to the livery and start his day.

A rider approached, moving around the side of the livery to the front of the cabin.

"Where's Doc Armstrong?" Matthew Covington asked.

"Inside. My wife is birthing."

"Oh! Mrs. Larson's pains have started. Adam sent me in to fetch the doctor."

Thomas poked his head inside and spotted Doc Armstrong.

He moved to his side and whispered the news.

"Tell the Larsons I'll be along as soon as I can. Mrs. Larson should be in good hands with Hannah there to care for her."

Caroline locked gazes with Thomas. "Julia too?"

He nodded.

She smiled. "Our babies will share the same birthday. Make sure she knows."

He assured her he would. Then he returned to the front of the house to deliver the message to Matthew Covington before returning to his urgent task of wearing a rut in the ground with his pacing.

Another scream, muffled by the cabin walls, reached his ears. This was pure torture—worse than the screams on the battlefield. This was his wife! His child!

He moved to the rocking chair on the front porch, setting it into motion by pushing off with his cane. Trying to calm his anxiety, he thought about how much his life had changed since he met the obnoxious, spunky, beautiful Caroline Larson.

Before meeting her in Wickenburg, his thoughts had been consumed with self-retribution for all the wrongs of his life. At first, she presented him with a nice distraction. Then, rescuing her on the road challenged him. He had to rise to the occasion, something he had not thought he had within him. Then she slowly worked her way into his heart.

One thing was certain, no matter the circumstances that led to them marrying, he loved her more than anything—more than dispatch riding, or riding for the express. She was his life now.

A different cry interrupted his thoughts. He jumped up from the rocking chair and rushed inside.

"Thomas," Betty said. "Come see your son."

Thomas swallowed hard. A son. Another prayer answered. A son to carry on his brother's name, the perfect picture of his life being restored.

He moved to Caroline's side, sitting on the edge of the bed.

"He's so beautiful," she whispered.

Thomas reached out a hand and placed it on his son's head.

"Andrew Paul Anderson. After two of the men who most changed my life." His voice broke as he was overcome with a deep love for this child and his wife.

"Andrew Paul Anderson," Caroline echoed.

Glancing around, he noticed that Betty and Doc Armstrong had left the bedroom. Only his family remained—him, Caroline, and Drew.

"May God always be with you, Drew. Carry your uncle's name well."

Caroline finished the blessing, "And may you have the childhood your father dreamed of. Be well loved, cherished, and always surrounded by parents who love God, each other, and you."

AUTHOR'S NOTE

I hope you enjoyed reading Thomas and Caroline's story. I can identify with them both—wanting to be better, do better, and eventually realizing, I can never hope to do this on my own. I love how each of them comes to that realization.

Like the other books in this series, my goal was to share an interesting and gripping story with some historical facts. One of my favorite facts in this book was the story of how Margaret McCormick met and married her husband, Richard McCormick. You may have recognized Richard from the first book as the first Secretary of Territory for Arizona. He was traveling by steamboat from San Francisco to New York when he met Margaret. He was smitten instantly. Despite her family's protests, Margaret, who previously detested the idea of marriage, became Richard's wife within six months of meeting him. From her journals, we learn that the couple was very much in love. Richard brought her to Prescott in the middle of November of 1865.

Margaret quickly became a member of the community and lived somewhat unconventionally for a society woman. She was known to enjoy a ride in the countryside at a moment's whim. She was well loved by the town, and she bore responsibility for making the Governor's Mansion a home.

For fun, I snuck in a brief appearance of Cowboy Mollie. She was a wild woman whose reputation was pretty much what Caroline described. She was a drunk, a gambler, and tended to be less than faithful to her husband. There're several rumors about which prominent men she had been married to at one time or another. Regardless, she didn't stay tied down. When I needed someone to rescue Thomas after his accident, she came to mind as the only one who might be crazy enough to be out in a blizzard.

The blizzard described in the winter of 1865-66 is true. Many called it the Tobacco Famine because supply freighters were unable to deliver supplies to town because of the snow and subsequent quick warm up. Several historical accounts cited that many residents reused their coffee grounds for four or more months. Sugar supplies dried up. But the most sacred supply was tobacco. It became a commodity that men traded other valuables for.

The stagecoaches used in Arizona during this timeframe were called Celerity stages. Some referred to them as the Butterfield or Overland stage. They were rougher to ride in than the iconic Concord. Most of the time they were pulled by mules and not horses, due to the rough terrain.

I hope you enjoyed the surprise story of Betty and Ben. So many fans have asked for their story that I did not want to disappoint them.

Blessings,

Karen Baney

—

Want More Arizona Territory Romance?

Get a FREE book featuring characters connected to the Pioneers series! Plus exclusive updates on new releases, special offers, and historical insights from the frontier.

Subscribe at: books.karenbaney.com/perry-quinn-story

ABOUT THE AUTHOR

Karen Baney is passionate about writing stories full of flawed characters. She enjoys weaving together stories of second chances, redemption, and overcoming personal trials. As a transplant to Arizona, she loves researching the state's history and finding ways to seamlessly incorporate real history and real settings into her novels. In addition to writing and speaking, Karen works as a Software Development Manager for a Christian ministry.

Her faith plays an important role both in her life and in her writing. Karen and her husband, Jim, make their home in Gilbert, Arizona, with their two dogs, Bella and Daisy. Both Jim and Karen are active at Rock Point Church in Queen Creek, Arizona.

Discover faith-laced stories with characters who feel like life-long friends.

Visit www.karenbaney.com to discover more historical romance series set in the American West. Follow Karen's writing journey and get behind-the-scenes glimpses of her research adventures on social media.

Facebook:	@AuthorKarenBaney
X:	@karen_baney
Instagram:	@AuthorKarenBaney
BookBub:	Follow Karen Baney for new release alerts

BOOKS BY KAREN BANEY

Historical Western Romance

Prescott Pioneers Series:

Step back in time to the wild, untamed Arizona Territory where survival depends on grit, faith, and the courage to start over. Follow three pioneer families—the Andersons, Colters, and Larsons—as they risk everything for the promise of a new life in a land that demands both strength and hope.

A Dream Unfolding
A Heart Renewed
A Life Restored
A Hope Revealed
Hidden Prospects

Desert Manna Series:

Sometimes the most beautiful love stories bloom in the desert. Set in the growing frontier town of Prescott during the early 1870s, these tender romances follow women rebuilding their lives after heartbreak and the unexpected men who help them discover that second chances at love are worth the risk. Set in Prescott, Arizona between 1871 - 1873.

Beauty for Ashes
Joy for Mourning
Oaks of Justice

Colter Sons Series:

Power, legacy, and forbidden love collide in this sweeping family saga set in the Arizona Territory. The Colter ranch empire has weathered decades of frontier life, but now family secrets and buried betrayals threaten to destroy everything. As five brothers—and one resilient sister—navigate the treacherous waters of love, loss, and redemption, they must decide what's worth fighting for.

Set in Prescott and other locations within the Arizona Territory in 1887 - 1906.

The Reluctant Cattleman
The Roaming Adventurer
The Railroad Magnate
The Resourceful Stockman
The Restless Wrangler
The Resilient Bride

Larson Sisters Series
Meet the next generation! These delightful novellas follow the three daughters of Adam and Julia Larson from the *Prescott Pioneers Series* as they navigate love, courtship, and finding their own happily ever afters in territorial Arizona in 1886 – 1894.

In Love at Christmas
In Love with the Rancher
In Love with the Horse Trainer

Contemporary Romance

Vargas Ranch Series:
Love is in the air at the Vargas Guest Ranch & Resort near Wickenburg, Arizona. Meet the Vargas family—five swoon-worthy brothers and their cousins who live by their family motto: "We do not deviate from the Lord's plan." These rugged cowboys run a successful working ranch and luxury resort while navigating the rollercoaster of finding true love.

Falling for a Fake Cowboy
Falling for a Real Cowboy
Honeymoon with a Real Cowboy
Falling for a Shy Cowboy
Falling for a Bossy Cowboy

Falling for a Smart Cowboy
Falling for a Humbug Cowboy
Falling for a Devoted Cowgirl
Falling for a Pregnant Cowgirl
Falling for a Cowboy's Legacy

Steadfast Love Series:

The *Steadfast Love* series follows a close-knit group of friends as they navigate the beautiful mess of modern life in the Phoenix area—workplace drama, complicated families, and love that shows up when they least expect it. These contemporary romances blend emotional depth with authentic faith, reminding us that even when life unravels, God's love never does.

The Heart I Rescue (prequel)
The Air I Breathe

She needed safety. He needed purpose. Hope was the last thing either dared to believe in.

Arizona Territory — October 1866.

Mary Colter's life shatters the day her husband vanishes, leaving her alone with two children and nowhere to turn. With fierce resolve and faith as her compass, she boards a stagecoach bound for Arizona and the uncertain charity of her brother-in-law's ranch. Mary won't let her children see her fear even as the brutal journey tests every ounce of strength she has left.

Warren Cahill never expected to find a widow with a quiet fire at Colter Ranch. As the new foreman juggling missing cattle, volatile cowhands, and mounting pressure from Will Colter, Warren's focus is survival. He never expected the widow's grit—and her children—to stir a loyalty that feels dangerously close to something more.

Just as Mary dares to hope again, a threat from her past resurfaces. Now she must decide if she can trust the gruff foreman who's captured her heart—and if they can fight together for what matters most.

A Hope Revealed continues the Prescott Pioneers series with a stirring tale of grit, grace, and second chances—proof that God's light can reach even the darkest valley.

Will one interview change my life forever?

Mama knew a secret about me...

My name is Sam Colter, and I am the misfit of my family.

Papa wants me to take over the family ranch. I don't think I'm the right son. Will I disappoint him or figure out how to run it successfully?

Then my life turned upside down when a journalist showed up.

The journalist dug into my parents' past. Found a secret about me that rocked me to the core.

Can I get over the shocking family secret and what it means about me?

It was my job to protect the ranch, and I failed. Worse yet, I find myself falling for the woman who betrayed me.

Is she the one? Can I forgive her?

Only the good Lord, and maybe Mama, knows for certain. 1887 is gonna leave a mark.

Set near Prescott, Arizona Territory in 1887.

DESERT LIFE MEDIA

Desert Life Media: *There Is Life in The Desert*

Entertainment–first Christian fiction set in the Southwest, featuring redemption, family, and faith

Publishing clean, wholesome, and uplifting fiction since 2010

If you enjoyed Karen's storytelling and crave more action-packed western adventure, discover R.J. Sloane's *The Rustler Hunter* at desertlifemedia.com